The scene of the crime was just a few yards away, but George didn't look at it; she tried hard not to think about it. She was standing at the bus stop, watching the swallows skim the fields, a week before the upset which would mock her routine without mercy. A car zoomed past: the bus shelter rattled. And another zoomed past, both driven by young men who looked very serious, impatience written into their faces. It made them look ugly, she thought. And it made her feel nervous. She withdrew into the shelter and counted her change, and counted the times she had done this already: three times, since leaving the house.

The bus was late. It was usually late; occasionally very late, like half an hour or so. And once or twice in the last twelve months, it had broken down and failed to show. George blamed the company who had taken over the service: they saw maintenance as a luxury, and they presented you with an urban cast-off as if they were doing you a big favour. And you couldn't blame the drivers for being late, she reasoned; it was a feature of the route.

The bus could be held up by a tractor, a fuel tanker, a queue of cows or a stupid pheasant. And on parts of the route, it could meet a lorry, a camper van, or a hedge cutter coming the opposite way, and one or the other might have to reverse for some time before a suitable passing place was reached.

It was usually just a few minutes late. Which wasn't a problem, because there was always something to watch, and the bus shelter served very nicely as a hide. It was really quite pleasant just to stand there and watch, and George always managed to do this, even when the bus was on time.

Even when the bus was on time, there were moments of

just standing there and watching, because George was always ten minutes early. If the bus was usually late – which it was – then there was a slight chance that it might come early. A slight chance it may be, but this remote possibility had to be taken into account when preparing for the journey, so George was always ten minutes early, just in case.

And she was ten minutes early because she couldn't afford to miss it. There was only one bus a week. It went from Paulsbury to Lydiard Forum every Monday: market day. Then, three hours later, it returned to Paulsbury. A shoppers' bus, for the people of Magnus Chase – or those among them who didn't use cars – to do their weekly shop. Nobody usually got on at Paulsbury, but then, they didn't need to go to Lydiard Forum to go shopping; they had their own shops, plus a rail link. It was more difficult for the people of Magnus Chase, where there was only one shop, in Charlton Minster, and that was really a garage. So every Monday, George caught the bus to Lydiard Forum, and did her weekly shop.

It was usually the same people who caught the bus. Jean Mortimer caught it at Stockwood Melrush; she was bound to be on, rain or shine, sat on the back seat, shouting to those at the front. Then there might be Mr and Mrs Bartlett, Mrs Foss, and Maurice Warnock, the gamekeeper. Maurice Warnock, if he was on, would also sit at the back, at the opposite end to Jean. Then, at Charlton Minster, Mary Holloway was a regular, as were her grandchildren, who helped her carry the shopping when they weren't at school.

Next on was George Tindall, at Quinton Monkton.

George poked her head outside to see the bus turn the corner. It slowed down and pulled in while she was counting her change. The drivers worked to a rota; they were also regulars; they knew most of the passengers.

"Hello," she said. "Isn't it warm?"

She glanced down the bus, looking for the familiar faces. They were all there, but on the right-hand side of the bus, smiling coyly; the left-hand side was empty. She passed the

THE MESSENGER

*T*he *Messenger* is a quixotic tale of science, romance and adventure, with a cast that includes countrified eccentrics, scientists with obsessions, street protesters, Goths, pigeon fanciers, a naked rambler and a VIP (Very Important Pigeon).

Living in an isolated part of the English countryside, George Tindall sits in a room with a view, dreaming of a life cut short, and wishes she had a gardener. Her days follow a pattern: she feeds the birds every morning, goes shopping once a week, and every week she talks to her therapist, every month she meets the ladies of the Lavender Club. But when a racing pigeon turns up at her cottage, with a locket strapped to its leg, her routine is suddenly shattered.

Meanwhile, on a remote island in the Atlantic, scientists are trying to solve the world's economic problems. Profits are falling, economies are facing a global crisis, governments are desperate for explanations, and are willing to fund any project that might provide one. Such as this: the scientists are using technology to simulate the brain of Karl Marx. Their plan is to build a 'thinking' computer – one that will not only analyse economic data, but also produce a new volume of *Capital*, Marx's best known work.

The two worlds collide when George's cottage is invaded by a delegation from the island, apparently in pursuit of that racing pigeon. Why are they so keen to get their hands on it? What's inside that locket? And why are they fighting over it? Whilst George wants answers to her questions, her visitors want to complete their mission, and the household becomes embroiled in a battle of wits as the mystery is unravelled. Meanwhile, on that remote island, the Brain of Marx Project is facing a new problem…

BY THE SAME AUTHOR

NON-FICTION

A Multidisciplinary Study of Fiction Writing

FICTION

The Big Wheel
Larry's Lessons

THE MESSENGER

ANTHONY BLOOR

Simon Siabod Publishing
Shropshire / Y Canolbarth

First published in Great Britain in 2014
by Simon Siabod Publishing

A CIP catalogue record for this book is available
from the British Library
ISBN 978 0 9563544 2 6

Printed in the UK by Imprint Digital
Exeter, Devon, EX5 5HY

Simon Siabod Publishing
6 Street Meadow, Church Stretton
Shropshire SY6 6HY

CONTENTS

THE MESSENGER
PART ONE

MAGNUS CHASE

fare, not sure whether to laugh; it was such a peculiar sight.

"I've had a problem with the front wheel this morning," the driver explained. "I've got a flat tyre, I hope we'll get back all right. It's way down on that side of the bus there, I've been asking everybody to sit on this side. Return to Lydiard is it?"

"Yes please," said George.

"Hello George," Jean shouted.

"Hello Jean," said George.

She found a seat behind Mary Holloway.

"School holidays not started yet then?" said George.

"No, two weeks yet," said Mary.

The next call was a diversion from the main road – along a winding valley to pick up the motley crew from the little village of Top Down. Well, George thought they were pretty motley. Arthur Blagdon always looked as if he'd just crawled out of a hedge. Quite possibly, he had.

There were strange rumours about Arthur Blagdon. It was well known that he collected bits of old things. He wasn't an antique dealer; more of a junk collector. He would return from Lydiard clutching an old piece of drainpipe, or a dustbin lid, or a length of old chain. Nobody ever asked him what he did with these things; it wasn't considered seemly to converse with him. Now, rumour said, he'd bought an old metal turnstile from a football ground about to be demolished, and installed it in the front of his house. Not only that, but was charging people who visited for the amount of time they spent inside. He paid rent, so the rumours said, and had worked out the costs to the nearest hour. Space was money, and it was only right that those who shared his space, albeit fleetingly, should share the costs.

George thought these rumours were just malicious. She'd yet to find anyone who had entered his house, or seen this mythical turnstile. The real reason for these stories, she thought, was simply the fact that Arthur was poor, and didn't go out of his way to disguise the fact. Not only that, but he smelled.

After all, it was Maurice Warnock, the gamekeeper, who had told George these rumours, and he had made it clear that Arthur Blagdon's smell was the reason why he, Maurice, sat at the back of the bus. George didn't like Maurice Warnock. For some reason, he always spoke with a sneer, as if the rest of the world belonged to a lower order. She avoided the back seat.

The smell, though, wasn't a rumour. It wafted in through the door, even though Arthur Blagdon was standing at the back of the queue, keeping aloof from the women. Kate Wimbourne made the usual fuss about finding change: every receptacle must be searched for the correct coins, as if she didn't know by now how much the fare had increased.

"I'm all sixes and sevens this morning," said Kate. "So that means you want another 10p. Just a minute…"

"Hello Kate," Jean shouted.

"Good morning ladies," said Kate, checking the seats for any unfamiliar faces. "Why are you all sat over there? I'm going to sit over here."

Barbara Smiles was more organised with her change; she was generally well organised about everything. She organised the monthly meetings of the Lavender Club, for the ladies of the parish: retired, widowed, or otherwise. These social evenings, with an invited guest, took place in the village hall in Top Down. The next meeting was due this week. She sat next to Mary Holloway and talked about the arrangements.

Tina Weymouth was decidedly strange, George thought. A girl in her 20s, in and out of work ever since George had known her, with glazed eyes that never looked at you. Most definitely overweight, wearing clothes that once might have fitted; the ripples of fat were now falling out of her torn jeans. She was very keen on loud rock music; once, she'd got on the bus wearing a black T-shirt with the words *Iron Maiden* printed on it in silver, gothic style. Kate was always trying to get her to do something about her appearance, but her advice had no effect, it seemed. She walked to the back of the bus, without looking at anyone, and said, "Hello Jean."

When Arthur Blagdon stepped on, Kate Wimbourne turned to Mary Holloway, wrinkled her nose and shook her head. The smell was something like chicken manure, mingled with stale sweat. The chicken manure, George thought, wasn't so objectionable; a sweet smell, which made you think of autumn and ploughed fields. It was the mingling she didn't like; the sour side of the equation.

All in all, it seemed that civilisation had somehow passed Arthur by. His clothes were said to be given to him, from a farmer in return for odd jobs. They were tailored and didn't quite fit, and were always covered in mud. He lived in the woods somewhere, and had a bush of white hair and a beard that made him look goat-like. And when he spoke to the driver, George was reminded that there were other reasons why nobody ever conversed with him.

"Lydiard and first ninety three twenty Lydiard," he said.

"Return is it?" said the driver.

"Thanks please," said Arthur.

It was simply that Arthur could not be understood. George would catch the odd word, and then fill in the gaps with speculation. It might have been the case that he spoke too fast, so fast that the words ran into each other; perhaps because he was very nervous. Arthur himself didn't seem to mind the fact that nobody understood him. He sat in front of Kate Wimbourne, who pulled a face and shook her head. Then, in her sweetest voice, she said, "Hello Arthur."

"Helloh?" he said, turning with surprise.

The bus also turned, and drove back along the valley to the main road.

There was an invisible line between Charlton Minster and Middleton Magna. Those on the Middleton side had their own social networks, to which those on the Charlton side had little access or knowledge. Conversely, those on the Charlton side were much involved in the Lavender Club, which had failed to ignite any enthusiasm among those on the Middleton side.

13

Perhaps, George thought, those on the Middleton side lived so close to Lydiard Forum that they considered themselves to be more like townsfolk, rather than country folk.

What was certain was that the line had little to do with county boundaries. There was a point on Magnus Chase where the three counties of Dorset, Wiltshire and Hampshire all met. It was somewhere on the downs, beyond Stockwood Melrush; George was unsure of its precise location. Paulsbury was definitely in Wiltshire, she knew that much. And Stockwood Melrush was definitely in Dorset. But the people of Magnus Chase looked on Magnus Chase as their county. This was their home, and a world within a world.

And as the bus stopped on the outskirts of Middleton Magna, George thought it very likely that the dividing line was around here, where Hilda Faber and Cynthia Butterwick caught the bus; possibly, the line divided their homes.

Hilda Faber was another local character who was treated as a bit of a pariah by the rest of the locals. The reasons were obvious. Hilda Faber, in her late 70s, never failed to let the entire bus know she was looking for a toy boy. A short, stocky woman, she was reputed to have circa fourteen children and several flocks of grandchildren. She had a voice like a foghorn, and the ladies of the Lavender Club thought she was rather vulgar. Hilda Faber, it seemed, had sex on the brain, and told everyone about it, including the bus drivers. Last winter she'd been full of it, blaming the flu jab; it had made her feel randy, she said. Of course, what she meant was more randy than usual. Now George had heard a rumour that Hilda had been barred from the club at Stanton Parva, apparently for making lewd suggestions to a minor.

Hilda was standing at the bus stop, a few yards away from Cynthia Butterwick. Though they were neighbours, they didn't speak to each other. They'd fallen out some years ago, and hadn't spoken since. George had yet to discover the reason for their falling out; it was one of the mysteries of Magnus Chase. It was probably because of something quite trivial, she thought, and she didn't like to pry. Mention Cynthia to Hilda, and you were likely to get your ears burned. Vice versa too.

Kate Wimbourne turned to Mary Holloway and tut-tutted. "Hilda," she mouthed.

"She must be going in for her hair appointment," said Mary.

Hilda went into Lydiard every four weeks to have her hair cut and styled; her son did most of her shopping. Cynthia was a weekly passenger; she shopped for the whole family. She was short and stocky too, but quiet and refined in comparison to Hilda.

"Thank you, driver," Hilda barked.

"Hello Hilda," Jean shouted.

Hilda declined to acknowledge Jean.

"Hello Arthur," she barked, taking the seat in front of him, while Cynthia sat down almost unnoticed.

Staring at Hilda's bare legs, Kate Wimbourne shook her head. Hilda never wore stockings, tights, or socks of any description, even in the middle of winter. Never have done, she said once, even as a child. George thought she was hot-blooded; she was probably descended from the Vikings and didn't feel the cold. The ladies of the Lavender Club thought it was a feature of her general vulgarity.

Hilda knew she was considered coarse, but she didn't care. "I'm not a lady," she said to George one day; it was a favourite retort. "I've never been a lady, and if people don't like it, that's tough. I'm not going to change my ways. I'm too old to change my ways."

Hilda would speak to George, while snubbing the ladies of the Lavender Club. She didn't consider George to be one of the inner circle; probably because George was a recent recruit. Also, George was Someone Who Had Moved Here From Up North Somewhere, even though she'd been living here for ten years now. But that's how it is, she thought, in rural places. She had no complaints about that; besides, those on the Charlton side of the line treated her like a local now. It was those on the Middleton side who were a bit offish.

Here was a selection, standing by the shelter in the centre of the village: Susan Chard with her daughter, Ruby; that girl whose name George could never remember, with a pushchair and two very young children; plus Mrs Webb and Mrs Norton. The bus was filling up; the driver was worried about the flat tyre. And still two more ports of call: the hamlet of Puddleton St Margaret, where Mrs Drake caught the bus, and Bowldish Farm nearby, where Sally Weymouth normally got on.

But Mrs Drake wasn't there today. Jean began to speculate as usual.

"She was on last week," she shouted. "I wonder if she's all right."

"Do you want me to knock?" said the driver.

"No, she'd be here if she was catching it," said Kate Wimbourne. "Her brother might have given her a lift."

So the driver drove on, stopping by Bowldish Farm, where Sally Weymouth stood by a huge puddle.

George had been living here for years before she realised that Sally Weymouth was in fact the mother of Tina Weymouth. They didn't speak; hadn't spoken for years, as it turned out. So one wouldn't have known. And then, the age of Sally Weymouth was indeterminate. She was quite slim; she looked quite athletic; she looked young. She had long white hair, and you couldn't tell if it was a shade of grey or a shade of blonde. She wore tight trousers and rodeo jackets, and looked rather like a cross between a Hell's Angel and a Country and Western singer. She was certainly no lady, but didn't go round boasting about it as Hilda Faber did. She was a married woman, unlike the widowed Hilda, but the man in her life was cussed and cursed at every opportunity. And Sally had a preference for toy boys, as did Hilda.

George didn't like Sally Weymouth; Sally was truly coarse, she thought, whereas Hilda was really quite a laugh. She found it odd that Sally never spoke to Hilda. You might have thought that the vulgar would stick together. But then, Sally Weymouth didn't consider herself to be coarse; certainly not as coarse as Hilda. Maybe they'd fought over a man. Or a toy boy. Whatever the reason, Sally Weymouth didn't look at Hilda, but swayed down the aisle, speaking only to Mary Holloway. The bus was so full that she was almost obliged to sit with her daughter on the back seat. George was too curious not to turn and see: no, she'd found a seat next to Susan Chard.

Still one more passenger, surprisingly: Mrs Snape, the funny old thing who lived next to the golf course, with the ancient shopping trolley that might have been a family heirloom, and the green plastic mack that she always wore, even on a cloudless day like today.

The bus joined the ring road and headed for the town.

Kate Wimbourne stretched her neck to check for new developments. She was always the first to spot signs of construction, renovation or demolition; then the news was relayed to the back of the bus.

But there was less chance of spotting anything on this occasion. They had just reached the traffic lights at the foot of the hill. As the lights changed to amber, the bus spluttered, stopped, and refused to go any further, or even to make a sound.

"I'm very sorry about this," said the driver. "I'm going to have to phone the depot to send somebody out with a replacement. This is no good at all. I'm very sorry everybody, but you'll have to walk the rest. Up that hill as well! I'm really sorry, but there's nothing I can do. Poor old Mrs Foss, her daughter will be waiting at the top. Will she be all right going up there? I feel awful…"

They all piled out. Jean Mortimer looked after Mrs Foss; Kate Wimbourne fussed over Mrs Snape, but Mrs Snape marched away, pushing her shopping trolley as if it were a tank. Mrs Webb and Mrs Norton ambled to the lights, arm in arm. Hilda Faber wasn't complaining; this was nearer to the hairdressers, she said. Arthur Blagdon stood there looking dazed, as if he'd just landed from the planet Hedge.

George had a few words with Mr and Mrs Bartlett, then decided to go before the urge to throttle Maurice Warnock became uncontrollable. He was talking to Kate Wimbourne with his usual sneer, talking about a march he'd been on at the weekend – a Countryside Alliance march, in London, which no one else on the bus had attended. So, for the benefit of the ladies, Maurice was giving a first-hand account of what life was like on the front line. Field Marshal Warnock tells all, and Kate Wimbourne was all ears!

George strode away in disgust, across the road and into Templetons. She didn't usually shop in Templetons. Templetons was a fairly recent development. A large superstore, on the edge of town; part of a huge chain. There had been many objections to its opening. "Does Lydiard need three supermarkets?" asked the Lydiard Advertiser. George had thought not. For the basics, Pomeroys and Samways were quite sufficient. Nobody who caught the bus shopped there, though Jean Mortimer had confessed to having a peek inside. It wasn't convenient, if you caught the bus. It meant lugging your shopping up the hill.

And it was a shop without a soul. The staff walked around in their tidy yellow uniforms; automatons all. Here, shopping was purely functional: you walked the aisles, loaded your trolley cum basket, paid at the till and left. Not like Samways, where you could easily get caught up in a discussion about the rising cost of a loaf of bread, or the relative merits of Samways mature cheddar. Shopping in Samways was a social event, as well as a shopping event.

On the other hand, there were times when a mechanical exercise was desirable. It could calm you down, quelling those urges to throttle Maurice Warnock. George walked the aisles with a basket, looking for bargains. Not any bargains; to be considered, they must be items on the list. It meant walking the aisles two or three times as she wasn't familiar with the store's geography. After twenty minutes of wandering, she emerged with two Cornish pasties and a large carton of washing powder.

Next: up the hill and into Pomeroys.

Mrs Foss had just made it across the road, aided by Jean Mortimer. At this rate, George said to herself, it'll be time to catch the bus again when she reaches the top.

"Hello George," said Jean. "Have you been in Templetons? I like it in Templetons. It's good value, I think."

"Yes, it's very reasonable," said George.

They ambled a while, talking about the price of meat. Then, looking for an excuse to disengage herself, George walked into Spice & Stuff and examined the Stuff.

Out again, not impressed – the organic loaves felt like house bricks – and through the alley to avoid Jean and Mrs Foss.

She had calmed down now. She could face Pomeroys. Pomeroys was owned by the same company who owned Samways. Yet the same items cost more in Pomeroys. A different clientele too; generally, more hoity-toity. As were the staff, who were renowned for treating their customers with total disdain. But one didn't go to Pomeroys to socialise, or to be treated with respect. One came in search of bargains.

Two for the price of one: jars of Marmite, jars of marmalade. Plus, a six-pack of soft but strong Pomeroys luxury toilet rolls – half-price, this week only.

One had to plan in advance. You couldn't go to Samways expecting to find every essential item, like soft but strong luxury toilet rolls. Sometimes they were out of stock. In fact, usually they were out of stock of at least one essential item on George's list, but you didn't know which until you got there. And then, there would be the trek back along the High Street in the hope that Pomeroys would have the missing item. Otherwise, you might have to go without for the rest of the week.

First though, Popes the newsagents for the Lydiard Advertiser and the Stanford Chronicle.

She didn't look at the cafeteria beyond; she avoided

glancing till she was outside. Yes, sure enough, there was Kate Wimbourne and Mary Holloway, having their private tête-à-tête. Sally Weymouth was there too, sitting at a table with Mrs Snape.

George didn't use the cafe at Popes. The waitress was even ruder than the staff at Pomeroys, she thought. Besides, she had a mere three hours; barely enough time to do the rounds. She would see them later, for an expanded tête-à-tête in the Forum Rooms, which was closer to the bus stop.

Meanwhile, the post office; then the cashpoint machine.

Next, meat. Or should she leave it till later? She was never sure about this. Veg – most definitely left till last, because of the weight. But chilled items were more problematic: if you left it too late, the best meat would have been snapped up.

Stood on the pavement, consulting her list, she met Jean Mortimer coming in the opposite direction.

Another diversion.

Jean had escorted Mrs Foss up the hill to meet her daughter, who'd been worried sick about her. Jean had just taken some old clothes to the Cats Protection League. Jean had had a cat put down just recently – did George know? – Jean was still very upset about it. Did George like cats?

George had decided: sausages from Millers, the best sausages in town. Then, into Market Square to get bread from Helliers, before that went too. After that, she would come back along the High Street for the odd items: toothpaste from Wheeler's Wholefoods; personal items from Youngs the chemists.

She'd just left Helliers when she bumped into Kate Wimbourne, shaking her head.

"I've just seen Mrs Foss's daughter," said Kate. "Mrs Foss has had an accident. She tripped up the kerb and fell over. She's been taken into hospital."

"I saw her not so long ago," said George, astonished.

"It's just happened," said Kate. "I blame the Council, George. Look at this kerb! It's very sharp you know. And it's steep. You could kill yourself tripping up it. The money they've spent on this new pavement!"

"Is she all right?" said George.

"I don't know. Her other daughter's gone with her. Isn't it awful?"

Leaving the chemists, George remembered Wheeler's Wholefoods. Another walk across town. How could she have forgotten the homeopathic potencies of horse chestnut bark, laced with fennel, the taste of aniseed and a hint of bladderwrack? Her teeth were dependent on it; she'd nearly run out.

And how ironic that after buying this item, she should bump into Maurice Warnock, whose breath stank of whisky. Maurice Warnock could have talked the hind legs off a donkey, given the opportunity. He was worse than Jean Mortimer – give him an inch and he'd take a yard. George wasn't giving him an inch, despite his defensive approach. He does look rather sheepish, she thought; perhaps he thinks he's wronged me. Or neglected me.

"I'm off to see my father," he said. "He's very poorly. I won't be coming back on the bus, my daughter's picking me up. It's a nice day, isn't it? How are you keeping?"

"Fine, fine," said George. "I'm a bit rushed today though…"

"I did all my shopping on Saturday. We go to Templetons now. It's got everything we need in there. No problem with parking…"

George glanced at her list.

"Anyway, I'm keeping you," he said. "Look after yourself. I've told the driver I'm not coming back. I've just seen Mrs Foss's daughter. Mrs Foss has had an accident. She's fallen over, she tripped over this new pavement. I blame the Council…"

George had forgotten the soda crystals! And she'd walked past Pickards twice!

Pickards the DIY store, a dark cave full of knick-knacks and old woodwork, where the old man of the shop sat in a corner like somebody out of Charles Dickens…

Now she really was pushed for time; she still had Samways to do yet; plus the veg. There was no time to browse the latest paperbacks in Homer's Books; a quick scan of the window would have to suffice.

It was full of autobiographies. There was a special display of *Born to Conquer* by Butch Gunstone, showing photographs of a snowy mountain peak and a man in dark glasses standing thereon, wielding an ice axe.

George had never heard of Butch Gunstone. She walked into Samways and bumped into Hilda Faber, who would have been quite a match for Butch Gunstone. In fact, Hilda Faber would have placed him over a table and spanked his backside with a crampon for his cheek.

"Hello George," she barked. "Mrs Foss has gone into hospital, have you heard? She fell over the kerb and broke a leg. I blame the Council and this new… bloody pavement. I nearly went over myself. If I see that bloody Lord Mayor I'll give him a piece of my mind, I'll tell him straight, I will. Did you know she's fallen over?"

"Yes, I've heard," said George. "Hello Mary."

Mary Holloway was just coming in; Hilda was on her way out. Mary was followed by Susan Chard and her daughter. Kate Wimbourne was halfway down the aisle already, talking to Cynthia Butterwick.

George studied her list.

The basics. First: tea, coffee, sugar…

Diversion: chat with Cynthia Butterwick.

Followed by another: Mrs Snape blocking the aisle with her shopping trolley.

Next: lamb chops from Mr Pike the butcher, who had his own shop in Samways.

A selection of cheeses. Washing-up liquid and bin liners. Another chat with Jean Mortimer. The price of lamb chops. Things you could get in Paulsbury that you couldn't get in Lydiard Forum. Paulsbury market on Saturdays. Cereals –

don't forget the cereals…

And George noted with great satisfaction that Samways had the luxury soft toilet rolls, but not the soft but strong luxury toilet rolls…

The Samways girls were renowned for dressing up for charity. Today, it was Snow White and the Seven Dwarfs. Or was it Cinderella? Whatever it was, the tills were staffed with ostentatious costumes, massive bustles, powder puffs and very tall wigs. They went to such efforts that only the mean-hearted could deny them a donation.

"Yes, I'll see you in a bit," George said to Mary, who was off to the Forum Rooms for a cup of tea.

George still had the veg and fruit to do. Most of it she bought from Thatchers, not far from Samways. There was the usual banter.

"Spanish navels!" said George. "The first I've seen this summer!"

"Oh, there's been a few about," said Derek the veg. "There was a coach load this morning. With the bare stomachs, you know. Very nice."

"I must have missed them," said George.

A quick walk around the market, looking for bargains. Strawberries from Spain, reduced. They look all right, but the last lot were rather tasteless, she thought. Still, the blackbirds will always eat them.

Bird food from the pet stall; cheese from the cheese stall; more tomatoes; more nuts… and then, half an hour for a sit down.

She saw Hilda's stately waddle. Hilda didn't frequent the Forum Rooms; she had a cup of tea from a stall in the market. Now she was standing by the bus stop, looking for an empty bench.

George stopped for a few words.

"It's a lovely day, isn't it?" she said.

"Yes," said Hilda, "I'll be sunbathing this afternoon if it carries on like this. I've a good mind to go topless. What do you think? It'll give the drivers something to gawp at, won't it?"

"Yes, I'm sure it will," said George. "Your hair looks nice, by the way."

"Thank you, George," Hilda barked. "I try and look my best; you never know who you might meet, do you? I'm still looking for a toy boy. Ooh, I'd like a nice young man, I would. Someone to keep me warm at night. Wouldn't you?"

"I try not to think about it," said George.

"I suppose you still miss him, don't you?" said Hilda.

"Yes," said George, wanting to change the subject. "You don't fancy Arthur, then?"

"Arthur?" Hilda barked. "You must be joking. You are joking, aren't you? Here, I found out this morning that someone on the bus has been spreading stories about me. I don't know who it is, but I've got a pretty good idea and I don't like it. I'd rather they say things to my face, not go behind my back like that…"

George wondered who Hilda was referring to. Kate Wimbourne or Mary Holloway, she was sure. She professed her ignorance of any stories. Which was a lie. But who had told her about the lewd suggestions at Stanford club?

Hilda was still complaining when Sally Weymouth and Cynthia Butterwick walked past, heading for the Forum Rooms. Neither of them spoke, or even looked.

"Are you going for a cup of tea?" said Hilda. "I've had mine. You needn't look so worried George, I know it's not you."

"I'm glad to hear it," said George. "I'll see you in a bit."

The shoppers had taken over two tables in the Forum Rooms. Kate Wimbourne and Mary Holloway sat at one, with a stranger.

"We've saved you a seat," said Kate.

Sally Weymouth and Cynthia Butterwick sat at another.

George sat next to the stranger, who was just about to leave.

"I'll see you again then, Mary," said the stranger.

George was curious. That was Mrs Rawlings, Mary said. She used to be a neighbour. She lives in Stanton Parva now, she said. George was struck by the thought that this sort of meeting must have taken place in the Middle Ages, Monday being market day, which brought the people of Magnus Chase together. The villagers from the surrounding area, coming to the town to buy, to sell and to chat. Catching up on the local gossip…

"Is it true that Hilda's been barred from the club?" she said.

Kate shook her head and muttered, "Hilda!"

"So Mrs Butterwick says," said Mary. "She was drunk…"

"And that's not all!" said Kate.

"She got into a fight," said Mary, laughing.

"What can you do with her!" said George.

"Not a lot," said Kate.

"I couldn't believe it, the last time she got on," said George. "Saying she wanted a baby! At her age! And letting the entire bus know about it! She was serious as well; that's what shook me."

"She wants treatment," said Kate, stubbing a cigarette out and lighting another. "She wants some of that… what do you call it? Bromide, is it?"

"A flu jab!" said George.

They all laughed.

"Oh dear," said Kate, wiping her eyes. "She gives us all a laugh, anyway."

"She's an embarrassment," said Mary. "Can you imagine going on holiday with her?"

"No," said George. "When do you go off with the Lavender Club?"

"Oh, it won't be till next Easter," said Mary. "It's only once a year."

"You're loaded up, George," said Kate.

"Yes, as usual," said George.

"I do most of my shopping in Stanton Parva now," said Kate. "I get that new community bus, you know, Skylarks, on a Thursday. The driver's very good, he takes you right to your door and he helps you with your bags."

"And how do you find Binghams?" said George. "Is it more expensive than Samways?"

The conversation returned to the usual topic – shopping. It was almost time to go. Like George, Mary Holloway believed in being at the stop ten minutes early, just in case. Imagine! Being stranded in Lydiard Forum with umpteen bags of shopping, and having to pay for a taxi! It didn't bear thinking about.

First though, Kate and Mary had to make the usual trip upstairs.

"Watch our bags, won't you?" said Kate.

"Of course," said George.

Just as Kate and Mary were leaving, Sally Weymouth rose from the nearby table. And without saying a word, reached over George's cup and stubbed a cigarette out in the ashtray, very close to George's arm. Then she walked off with Cynthia Butterwick, Cynthia smiling wanly as she reminded George of the time.

Well! That was totally uncalled for, George said to herself. But she didn't need to dig for Sally's reasons. It was simply because George had been talking to Hilda – that was the reason. As if she'd been associating with dirt, and the point had to be made. Underlined even.

The little guttersnipe, she thought. She'd rather talk to Hilda any day than to Sally Weymouth. In fact, she'd never spoken to Sally Weymouth; she was even less inclined to now…

"What's the matter?" said Kate, returning.

"Nothing," said George, gathering the bags.

"We'll have to go down in the lift," said Mary, looking at her watch.

Outside, the bus was just pulling in: a replacement by the look of it. Arthur Blagdon stood there looking dazed, clutching a bicycle wheel, listening to Barbara Smiles. George asked Barbara about the progress of her bees. Barbara reminded George of the next meeting of the Lavender Club, this week. Mrs Whitmarsh will give you a lift, she said. Do come. Stephen Grove will be giving a talk. It's taken us months to persuade him; now he's finally agreed to show us his photos of the Azores.

The chatter continued as they all piled onto the bus.

"Mr Warnock isn't coming back," Kate said to the driver. "He was going to the hospital to see his father. He's very poorly."

"And Mrs Foss isn't coming back," said the driver. "I've just seen her daughter. I suppose you all know she was taken into emergency. I do feel bad about it, I really do. Where did she fall?"

"It's not your fault," said Kate.

"No, it's the bloody Council and that new... bloomin pavement," barked Hilda. "They need a good talking to, they do."

A cackle of laughter from Jean on the back seat, followed by a shout.

"Are you going to give them a good talking to, Hilda?"

"I would, if I saw them," Hilda shouted.

Another cackle, while the driver rose from his seat and stood in the aisle, counting the passengers.

"Where's Mrs Webb?" said Mrs Bartlett.

"She's not coming back," said the driver. "Or that woman who gets on with her, I don't know what her name is."

"Mrs Norton," said Kate. "I've just seen them. They were having lunch in the Forum Rooms."

"And that girl with the pushchair isn't coming back," said the driver.

"Someone wants to get on," said Kate, and a large shape hovered behind the driver.

"Oh, sorry," he said and, edging past the large shape, he sat down to take the fare.

The sight, revealed, was received by one and all with shock

and awe: Bertha Bradstock was catching the bus!

Bertha Bradstock was a bit large, to say the least; in fact, one might have said obese, but George didn't like to – Bertha Bradstock was a bit scary too. She never smiled, and as if to emphasise her largeness she wore tight-fitting trousers and tops. Indeed, her dress sense was... Perplexing. Today, a brown leather jacket and her hair dyed purple, and skin-tight black trousers that made her look like the Michelin Man. She swayed down the aisle and sat on the back seat.

The bus fell silent.

Bertha Bradstock and partner Trevor had taken over the Druids Arms in Plumstone Abbas, the village beyond Charlton Minster. There was a perpetual feud, it seemed, between the Druids Arms in Plumstone Abbas, and the Moon in Quinton Monkton. The cause of the feud was obscure. It was certainly the case that the two pubs competed for the local clientele; but the rest was a subject for rumour. Whatever the reason, Eric Finch and partner Sheila, the landlords of the Moon, were always spreading tales about the Bradstocks, and the Bradstocks were always spreading tales about the Finches.

To hear these tales first-hand, you had to frequent the pubs, of course. Otherwise, you heard the second-hand versions, from someone who had seen so-and-so who had heard from... But thinking about it – which George was – it was the women who spread these stories. They snatched the gossip from the men, who went to the pubs, and the news travelled from one end of the Chase to the other...

"Are we all here then?" said the driver. "It's time. Shall I go now?"

"Yes," said a chorus of voices.

Mrs Snape was first off, together with her ancient trolley. Then Sally Weymouth, cursing her husband for not meeting her with the shopping. Then a honk outside Mrs Drake's house, where Mrs Drake sat in the window, waving. Then the main road and Middleton Magna and a stop for Susan Chard, who now had two daughters with her. Followed by a tricky moment as the bus stopped for Cynthia Butterwick and drove on a few yards to drop off Hilda Faber.

"Thank you driver," she barked.

"You'll be sunbathing, will you Hilda?" he said.

"Yes, I think I'm going topless this afternoon. That might make'm slow down, don't you think? They drive too bloomin fast along this road."

Hoots from the back; snorts and shaking heads at the front. And a "Cheerio Arthur" from Hilda, stepping from the bus in her stately fashion.

Next was the diversion to Top Down. But no, the bus was making an exceptional stop: outside Langley Farm to drop off Bertha Bradstock, who must have been calling on Trevor's father.

"Bye," she said, to no one in particular.

"Bye Bertha," said Mary Holloway.

As the bus drove off, Kate Wimbourne, frowning, turned to Mary and said, "Was that Bertha Bradstock?"

"Yes, that was Bertha," said Mary.

Kate Wimbourne shook her head.

"I didn't recognise her," she said.

She reached over the aisle to whisper, winking at George.

"She looks just like a bag of silage," she said.

Mary snorted, George coughed, and Kate put a hand over her mouth. Arthur Blagdon retrieved his bicycle wheel, which had just taken off and was heading in Jean's direction. The driver was reversing; the bus had met a fuel tanker, coming down the narrow lane from Top Down.

"Right, back to the city centre," said Kate, gathering her bags.

"Just here, please driver," said Barbara Smiles.

But she was so soft-spoken that the driver didn't hear. The bus flew past Orchard Cottage and stopped at the bus shelter by the church; the city centre. Barbara muttered a lament.

"Bye everybody, see you next week, all being well," said Kate. "Oh, I'll be seeing you on Wednesday, won't I Mary, at the Lavender Club? Are you going, George?"

"I think so," said George.

The motley crew said their farewells, Tina Weymouth hurtling down the aisle with a long bag that could knock you flying if you didn't make way, and Arthur Blagdon with an arm through his bicycle wheel, saying, "Hokey cokey!"

The bus turned, drove back along the valley to the main road, where the bags of silage littered the fields, awaiting collection. Black bags, stretched tight, bulging in odd places. George looked at them and smiled.

She gathered her shopping – three bags in one hand, four in the other – and walked down the aisle, saying goodbye to Jean Mortimer, Mr and Mrs Bartlett, Mary Holloway, the driver. There was no one else on the bus.

It stopped at the bottom of the lane, near the pub called the Moon. George stepped off, Jean waving as usual.

Quinton Monkton was a gorge, carved out of the chalk by the Quinton Brook. A line of detached houses and cottages, going up the narrow valley. And on the other side of the main road was Quinton Rushton, another line of houses, following the stream.

For the first fifty yards or so, it was a steep climb. George was panting when she reached the gate of Greenslade Cottage. She paused. Then, down the path to the bottom gate, which was always left open, across the yard and in through the back door, which she'd forgotten to lock in her morning's haste. Straight to the kettle, dumping the bags on the stone floor.

A cup of tea, before the ordeal of unloading. That usually took an hour at least. The best part of Monday was taken up with shopping. The major event of the week, and soon it would be over.

She sat at the wooden table, took a sip of her tea, and, as usual, burst into tears.

2

She took out the scales, unwrapped the cheese, and placed it carefully in the bowl – 175 grammes, said the scales. It wasn't even 200 grammes. Which meant she'd been diddled.

She remembered the sequence of events quite clearly: she had asked for 100 grammes, and Mrs Bellwood had charged her for 200, and George, in the usual rush, hadn't stopped to query it. She'd assumed that Mrs Bellwood must have thought she'd said 200 grammes. Not for the first time, Mrs Bellwood hadn't heard her properly. Or chosen not to. Now she finds out it's not even 200 grammes, which means Mrs Bellwood has diddled her on two counts.

Why, she wondered, do I always end up paying two pounds ninety for a small piece of cheese? One pound forty-five for 100 grammes – scandalous. It was just as well she'd been served with 200, because 100 would have been flattened by Mrs Bellwood's scythe.

Avoirdupois, for God's sake!

Either Mrs Bellwood's hearing was at fault, or George's elocution. But everybody else understood her. It had to be Mrs Bellwood's hearing. Clouded by the vision of a bigger sale.

But perhaps, she thought, she hadn't said 100; perhaps she'd said 200, in error. Or hope.

She opened the fridge and took out a fresh packet of Dibbles, a butter-like spread. 250 grammes, said the wrapper. She placed it on the scales. 225 grammes, said the scales. And it hadn't been opened. Fresh today.

The scales were to blame!

Of course, there was a remote possibility that Mrs Bellwood and Dibbles were both on the fiddle…

But no, the weights and measures lot would have noticed, surely?

Time for another cup of tea.

*

Two hours later, everything had been put away, and George sat at the table, pondering, knowing that it wasn't always... like this.

When Richard was alive, shopping was never an ordeal. They just did it, plus a host of other things in the same day. Shopping was more spontaneous, less planned, more adventurous. Trips to Paulsbury, Stanton Parva, further afield, the coast even. Having a car made the difference.

And Richard...

She wouldn't have the confidence to drive these days. She was never very good when she'd tried it, many years ago. It was pointless thinking about it. And since the accident... But she wouldn't think about that now. It would all be dragged up again on Wednesday no doubt.

Meanwhile, food.

A late lunch. A very late lunch. It would also serve as tea. She wouldn't eat again today. Cheese on toast. No, a cheese sandwich, using that nice loaf from Helliers. Ciabatta. Lovely. And the cheese from Mrs Bellwood. Harlech. Very tasty. She would savour every flake, and forget the cost.

She cut the bread and spread it, cut the cheese and placed it. And tasted...

Meanwhile, the local news.

The front page of the Lydiard Advertiser was still reporting the consequences of Templetons setting up in the town. Fewer people came to the outdoor market in the centre of town, said market traders. There were rumours that Samways might close.

And what a disaster that would be, George thought, turning to the forthcoming events page.

The Lydiard branch of the Right to Smoke Campaign are planning on holding a march in the town centre next Saturday, following reports that the government plans to ban smoking in all public places. Most pubs in the town have already decided to ban smoking...

And underneath, in smaller print, an item on the Lydiard Peace Campaign, who were staging an anti-war demo on the same day...

So, George thought, a crowd of chain smokers will be wheezing their way through the town centre, to cough and pant and gasp out a slogan or two. What a spectacle! She must tell Kate Wimbourne. And where did she hear of a move to ban obese people from all public places? Last week's Stanford Chronicle. There – no, she'd got it wrong. Or had she?

It was in the column written by Andrew Bindon, the local MP. Andrew Bindon's Thought for the Week. Fat people are a drain on the National Health Service, says Andrew. And they take up too much space, compared to the likes of you and me. They should pay twice the fare on public transport. Have you ever been forced to stand on a bus or a train, while a pile of blubber takes up a whole bench? Write to me with your experiences. I am convinced that fat should be used as a way of increasing public revenue, not as a drain on precious resources.

Was he being serious? It was hard to tell these days. His face was rather corpulent. But then, Andrew Bindon didn't use public transport.

And this week, the follow-up: Fat Tax Causes a Stir. Yes, our very own colourful and controversial MP caused a stir last week by proposing that obese people be banned from public places...

So there it was. Anything to sell a newspaper.

Meanwhile, the AGM of the Nettleton Pig Supper Club was disrupted last week by a bomb scare. The Butchers Arms in Stanton Parva was evacuated when the pub received a phone call from a man claiming to represent a militant Islamic group.

Police investigations revealed that the bomb threat was a hoax. The former president of the club, who resigned last year after being found guilty of embezzlement, was helping the police with their enquiries...

No mention of Hilda Faber being barred from the club at Stanton Parva. Some news didn't make it to the local paper. The rest of it was taken up with the usual items: good deeds and sponsored walks, bad deeds and burglaries, local festivals, charity events, a drunken brawl at the Nettleton Young Farmers bash, court cases involving various states of drunkenness, appeals for volunteers, appeals for funds for church maintenance, reports on the decline in church attendance, more news of forthcoming events, concerts, walks and talks.

The Stanford Chronicle had more regional news, plus a page showing the highlights of national and international news. George always looked at this page, because there were items here that weren't reported on the radio.

Like the Naked Rambler.

Doug Allthorpe, also known as the Naked Rambler, had completed his nude walk from Land's End to John O'Groats, despite constant arrests on the way. His nude walk was part of a campaign for human rights and the rights of naturists to go about naked. Now he was walking back, from John O'Groats to his home on the Isle of Wight. He'd be crossing Magnus Chase some time next week. Asked about the possible embarrassment to passengers on the Isle of Wight ferry, he was reported to have said, "If they won't let me on the boat, I'll swim across."

George was quite impressed by the Naked Rambler. She had monitored his progress with mounting excitement; she'd felt a sense of achievement when he finally reached John O'Groats. His protest had touched a childhood nerve, releasing a spirit of benevolent rebellion against all the oppressive and ridiculous things that were happening in the world.

And, she thought, wasn't it oppressive and ridiculous that the establishment should be so upset by a man walking naked from one end of the country to the other? What harm was he doing? Did he have weapons of mass destruction concealed in his beard, up his backside?

She was quite prepared to sit on Magnus Chase and wait for the Naked Rambler. To greet him with a flask of tea. Could she do what he's doing? She doubted it. No, she was so impressed, she wanted to meet him and shake his...

Never mind.

Back to the ridiculous.

More health matters.

According to a leaked report, the government plans to send daily menus to every household in the country, in a bid to redress the poor state of the nation's health. The menus would include suggestions for three well-balanced meals a day, the report says. Responding to accusations that the government was becoming more totalitarian, a spokesman for the Department of Health said, "That's nonsense. The National Health Service is funded by the tax payer. We have a responsibility to make sure that the money is spent wisely. Besides, we don't comment on leaked reports."

Hmm.

It was teatime already.

Ah, these long summer days! She shall sit in the garden, and watch the swallows.

But first, she might as well listen to the radio, and catch the national news too.

An item about a freak wave in South-East Asia, thousands of people are thought to have drowned. Exact figures can't be given, but many are reported as missing. Communication systems have been disrupted in some areas, making it difficult to calculate numbers.

Next item. More war in the Middle East. Now what was that all about?

Enough!

A cup of tea, and a sit in the garden.

*

There was nothing quite like it: sitting outside on her cane chair, on a warm summer's evening, watching the rest of the day drift by. The garden was one of the reasons for buying the place. Long, winding and narrow, with the Quinton Brook flowing at its edge. Which brought the wagtails, tails bobbing, feet hopping, even when the stream dried up to a trickle in the summer.

The stream flowed south from the downs, where the deer used to roam. At the top end of the garden, between two old apple trees, there was a gate that Richard said was intended for their use. A leap gate, he said. Too high for sheep and cattle, but not for the old deer to leap over.

She'd never understood that; it was something to do with the old forest laws.

In days gone by, the chase was part of the royal forest – a hunting forest – where the King would seek enough meat to fill the royal kitchen for the winter. Special rules applied in these areas, Richard said. The deer belonged to the crown. They were free to come and go as they pleased. A farmer had to summon a forester to remove them from his crops. And they were free to come in your garden, and eat as much as they wanted. Not only that, but you had to provide access for them. Hence the leap gate.

George thought it might be nice to have a deer in the garden.

But the leap gate was a part of history now. At some time in the past, the hunting rights were granted by the crown to private landowners, and the forest became a chase, which wasn't subject to the old laws. And in recent times, much of the land had been bought by the National Trust. There were still deer on the chase, but their hunting was a thing of the past. Their movements were confined to the remaining woodlands, and George rarely saw them.

The hunters, meanwhile, had turned to fox hunting. Now there was a kafuffle about banning that. George didn't know what to make of it all. She had no strong opinions, either way. But she was inclined to be against a ban, because she didn't trust the government. Their motives were never straightforward, and their arguments didn't make sense.

Fox hunting is barbaric, said the ban's supporters; we should outlaw cruelty to animals. Yet animals were tortured every day in laboratories, and the government said that was right and proper. Women and children were being slaughtered every day in the Middle East, and no one had suggested that war should be banned; the government was promoting it.

And it wasn't illegal to kill a fox, only to chase it with dogs. That's what the fuss was about, because the thrill was in the chase. Very few foxes were killed as a result of a hunt. The Nettleton Hunt, on its last outing, had failed to find a single fox. That wasn't unusual. Yet it was a day out, and a feature of the English countryside. Which the government wanted to eradicate.

But she didn't want to think about it. The issue had become a bore. Nobody on the bus spoke about it now, unless Maurice Warnock was on. And it seemed that the hunters would just carry on as before. Except that they'd be branded as criminals. Just like the Naked Rambler.

Oh, to be as free as a bird!

But not a pheasant.

A swallow…

She really ought to do something about the garden. The apple trees needed pruning, the flower beds were awash with herb Robert and forget-me-nots, the hedges needed trimming, the lawns needed mowing.

And she ought to do something about the sheds.

The previous owners, she'd been told, had been small farmers. They'd grown their own veg, kept a goat and half a dozen sheep. At some point, they'd bred boxer dogs and sold them, knocking down an old sheep pen in the process, and installing kennels in its place. But the business had failed and the kennels were also knocked down, so one corner of the garden was a carefully concealed pile of rubble. And then they'd decided to keep chickens, for their own use. And now there were no chickens, or goats, or sheep, or dogs, and the sheds were falling apart.

At one side of the house was an old wood shed. Three stone walls and a roof of slate. The walls were solid but several tiles were missing from the roof, the beam supporting it had splintered, and the roof was beginning to collapse.

Adjacent to that was an outhouse that had been used to house the chickens. So she'd been told, though George thought it was intended as a pigsty. Those walls were brick, about four feet high at the front, enclosing an open area, and rising at the back to a tin roof which covered a closed area – sleeping quarters for pigs. Or chickens. And also unstable. The bricks had come loose at the gables, some had fallen out, and the roof had rusted to such an extent that it too threatened to collapse.

At the back of the house, nestled against the slope of the gorge, was an outhouse that was obviously a grain shed as there were still bags of grain stored inside. That had three walls, brick at the bottom and then wooden slats supported a roof of corrugated iron. At the back, where the roof met the gorge, the slats had gone rotten and the beam was gradually sliding down the slope. So the roof was now tilting backwards, at an angle that seemed to grow daily.

And on the other side of the house was an outbuilding where the lawnmower and tools were stored. Three-sided with a roof, all made entirely of corrugated iron, and seemingly more recent as the bolts had only started rusting since Richard…

But she didn't want to think about the sheds now. The tools were fine. And as for the rest, a few holes here and there were useful for the birds to nest in during the summer, and to roost in during the winter. And there were other creatures to consider too. Bats, owls, field mice, and goodness knows what else. They all lived in the sheds and she didn't want to disturb them and every season presented a reason for postponing the work of repair.

So the sheds were never a priority. The priority, she thought, was the garden. And beyond that, the plots where they'd grown their own veg; almost a field in itself.

She wasn't up to it. Richard had always done most of it. Her little patch was the rockery, plus the flower beds, pots and house plants. The rockery was a kind of herb garden. It was her favourite spot to potter about in. As for the rest…

She ought to hire a gardener. Eric Finch would know of a suitable gardener. Eric had been so helpful on the night of the accident.

A worm! Killed by a worm! Even now she couldn't believe it.

She was undecided about Wednesday. Therapy in the afternoon: that was a definite. She would walk over the downs to Stanton Parva, then catch a bus to Lydiard. It meant returning on the school bus, or catching a taxi. She'd be back by five. Then food. The Lavender Club started at 7.30 prompt. Would she feel like going, or would she be too tired? Mrs Whitmarsh will need to know. Stephen Grove, a local farmer, showing his slides of the Azores. It might be quite interesting…

July was a funny old month. The height of summer, yet the land always looked yellow and bare. Shaved by giant razors, the green stuff was now packed away in black bags, leaving fields of parched stubble.

Not here though. Here it was still green, despite the lack of rain. The brook was now a channel of pebbles, with the odd puddle draining away fast. The brook, when it flowed, flowed through Quinton Rushton, then across the lowlands to join the River Chuckle. And George drifted with the stream, along the path that'd take her beyond the river, to the other side of the valley, and the tiny village of Triplecheek St Mary.

Triplecheek St Mary. That scene always sprang to mind whenever she thought about the place:

A gypsy caravan, red and golden; a white parrot in a cage, hanging from the wall of a house; and the rooks above the Scots pines, feeding the squawking rooklings.

Triplecheek St Mary…

They had walked there once, following the stream across the fields.

Once.

In April, when the world was full of colour and the future didn't enter.

Time for another cup of tea. She must ring Mrs Whitmarsh. Then she would bring her book outside, and read.

July was the month when she thought about worms.

*

Dusk: the blackbirds were pinking. And what did it all mean? Swallows – she understood. Sparrows, she understood; the robin, she understood. The wren, more enigmatic; but not as incomprehensible as the blackbirds, pinking.

She used to think they were frightened by the dark. Then, after months of observation, by the little owl. Now she wasn't so sure.

Always at dusk, this pinking. A bit like a bird's Big Ben, telling the bird folk it was time to go to bed.

And as it darkened, the pinking blew up into a wail.

Who were they talking to? She'd changed her mind about this. An alarm call had a double meaning, she thought. First, the obvious: it meant the bird was alarmed, by an intruder or an unseen menace. So the call was impulsive, just as you might yell if your hand happened to touch a naked flame. But second, the call was intended for others. It was meant to alarm others, possibly including the unseen menace.

So what did it all mean? The blackbirds wailed, and still she didn't know.

A blackbird, telling the world:

"I'm going to bed now, and I don't want to be disturbed."

Or a blackbird, telling other birds:

"Right, birds, I'm going to sleep in this hedge, and I don't intend to share it with any redbreasts, okay?"

Or a blackbird, telling the unseen menace:

"Right, menace, I know you're in that hedge, and I'm going to wail until you show yourself. I'll give you two minutes, then I'm coming in. Don't say I didn't warn you."

Then again, maybe they were frightened by the dark.

Ah, these long summer evenings! Bedtime for George too.

July was the month when she tried very hard not to think about worms.

*

The swallows woke her as usual, warbling on the guttering. It was 5am, and she was wide awake. The sky was overcast, full of thunder. Not a morning for sitting in the garden.

She reached for her book – *Night and Day* by Virginia Woolf – and lay in bed, reading for an hour and beyond, waiting for the alarm call that didn't come. The swallows just warbled, and swooped, and warbled. No alarm calls.

Strange, she thought. This was the weather that brought the magpie and the hawk, looking for fledglings. But the timing wasn't right. The first broods had all left the nests, and the swallows had yet to start on the second. Anyway, she'd decided not to respond if the swallows called. She could read in peace for another hour.

Then it was time for a cup of tea.

She went downstairs to the kitchen, thinking about *Night and Day*.

Why, she wondered, is it so soothing to read? There was a homely feel to it; the feel of a return, a homecoming. Why?

Familiarity, she said to herself.

It stirred memories of her childhood. It made her think of

class structure, of the way things used to be.

And it brought to mind an image. A photo of her grandparents, showing a working class terrace, a tiny garden between two brick walls, and they're doing the gardening in their Sunday best. She had shoeboxes full of these old photos, and many were like that: people she didn't know, wearing suits and ties and cloth caps, tending the vegetable plot in their Sunday best. Possibly because that's when the photos were taken: on a Sunday, when the folks had returned from church, and this was the only time of the week for tending the garden.

She couldn't remember where she'd read it, or heard it – the idea that the upper class were seen as a model by the working class, in terms of dress and table manners and the right way to behave. But it wasn't important who said it, because that's how it was, when she was a child Up North Somewhere.

Once upon a time there was the Royal Family – they were at the top of the pile, and their knives and forks were always in the right place. They were really just the highest layer of the aristocracy, or upper class. So if you were looking for models, you couldn't look any higher. Then you had the aristocracy proper, who owned land and property, employed maids and butlers, servants and gardeners. Their houses were large and beautiful, and so were their gardens. They generally had lots of money, because they owned a town house as well as a country house, and they could afford to spend most of their time in the countryside, doing things like shooting game, riding horses and driving Bentleys. And their knives and forks were always in the right place.

Then you had the people who went out to work. They didn't have lots of money. Neither did they own any property – their homes were rented from the local council. They dreamed of winning the football pools, so maybe they wouldn't have to go out to work, and maybe they could do what the aristocracy did. But few of them won the pools, so they had to make do with trips to the cinema, the pub and the fair, and bus rides to look at the countryside, which might include a mansion, garden and fountain, and a glimpse of a country gent. Occasionally times were hard, yet they did more than make do – they laughed, loved, brought up their children with sense and affection, and tended the vegetable plot in their Sunday best. And their knives and forks always had that aspiration: to be in the right place.

As for the middle class – who were they? They were invisible. They were the people who ran the corner shop. And possibly, they were so busy running a business that only on Sundays were their knives and forks ever in the right place.

Yet, she thought, despite the class divide, there were shared values that knitted everyone together; for a start, a morality that was basically Christian.

The way things used to be…

So what had happened to shatter it all into nuclear fragments?

It wasn't the time to think about that now. It was 8am. She must feed the birds.

*

She spent the morning reading. The sky was still overcast, but no thunder. As the hour approached noon, she decided to walk to the pub and ask Eric Finch about gardeners.

It was a bold step, considering. She rarely went to the pub these days. And never on her own. It was usually after a funeral, or to meet Mary Holloway for one of Eric's special lunches. Yet it was only a short walk.

The pub was on the main road, a few yards from the bottom of the lane. She entered the bar and found it wasn't empty. Two men in suits sat by a window, eating meals, and Arthur Blagdon stood at the bar, wearing wellies and an old overcoat.

She wasn't expecting to see him there.

"Helloh?" he said, in that quizzical way of his.

"Hello," said George. "Is Eric about?"

"Hill down in ten door, fork lime," said Arthur, nodding at the lounge.

And Eric walked through from the lounge bar.

"George!" he said. "We haven't seen you for months. How are you keeping?"

"Oh, not too bad, Eric. How are things with you?"

"Hectic today. We've got the Nettleton Brass Band coming for lunch, about thirty of them. Due in… half an hour," he said, looking at his watch. "We'll cope. What can I get for you?"

"Er, I'll have… half a pint of bitter shandy, please."

Eric walked back to the lounge bar.

"Actually, there's something I wanted to ask, Eric," said George.

"I'm a married man," said Eric, returning with a glass of shandy.

George laughed, searching her pockets for a purse.

"It was about gardeners, actually," she said. "Can you recommend any gardeners? You know, ones you can trust."

She was still searching her pockets when Eric, *sotto voce*, said, "Don't worry about that, George, this one's on me." Then he pointed to Arthur and said, "There's your man, George. Arthur's been doing our garden at the back here, haven't you Arthur?"

"Hay why?" said Arthur, his mouth full of beer.

George looked at him.

"I do eeks plot an cum greasy at Lodge Farm, thimbleday," said Arthur.

"Do you?" said George. "Perhaps you could give me your phone number, and I can ring you about it. Are you on the phone?"

Arthur reached inside his overcoat, pulled out a silver-coloured mobile, slapped it on the bar and grinned.

"Double O'Seven," he said, in a mock Irish accent.

"Oh yes," said Eric, "Arthur's got the latest technology,

haven't you Arthur? I'll leave you to sort it out, George. I must get back to the kitchen. Call in again, why don't you? We're always pleased to see you."

"Yes," said George, "I will do, and thanks for the drink."

She sipped the shandy, listening to the scrape of knife against plate. The men in suits were talking quietly about business matters. Arthur took a swig of his beer. She looked at him and smiled, then turned to her glass. Arthur had a different smell about him today. It smelt like damp earth, with a hint of roses. Not unpleasant at all, she thought.

"Do you…?" she said, but Arthur had downed his beer and didn't appear to be listening; his phone was making funny noises.

Arthur grabbed the mobile, reached inside a pocket, and handed her a card.

"Any tighter nine," he said, and moved swiftly to the door. "Right ho! Hokey cokey!"

"Bye," she said, and watched him walk out.

*

The sky had cleared by the afternoon. The wind had changed direction. It was blowing from the south-east, a cool breeze.

Just what I needed, George thought.

She was pottering about in the rock garden, talking to the birds, and sweating as she moved her knee pads, using a trowel to dig up bits of grass.

"There's a big spider for you here, wrenny," she said, but the wren wasn't interested.

George returned to her digging.

"Perhaps it's too big for you," she said to herself.

Then she turned to the robin, hopping about by a bucket.

"What about you?"

The robin cocked its head.

"A spider," she said, pointing with her trowel.

The robin flew to a patch of fresh earth, pulled out a worm

and flew away, the worm swinging from its beak.

She dropped the trowel, raced into the kitchen, sat at the table and wept.

*

When George started walking over the downs the next morning, the events of the previous day slipped noiselessly into her mental filing cabinet. Today was a new day.

Cloudless.

The lane from Greenslade Cottage ended with the trail of scattered houses that made up Quinton Monkton. From this point, a muddy path wound between the trees, following the brook, until it emerged at the edge of a field. The path took you across the field, and then a grass track rose steeply to the head of the narrow valley.

George stood at the top, taking in the view.

On the edge of the downs, a kestrel hovered. From the woods in the distance, the sound of a buzzard, crying.

There were few trees up here. She could look down the gorge and across the valley of the River Chuckle to the hills on the other side. She could see Greenslade Cottage and the long winding garden, the row of trees that bordered Quinton Brook, the roof of the Moon pub. The River Chuckle in the distance. And to the west: the church tower at Lydiard Forum, the keep of the castle.

She couldn't see Stanton Parva, or Paulsbury: both were hidden by folds in the hills.

She walked on.

The grass track followed the downs, fields of crops on either side, hidden by hedgerows. There were many prehistoric sites on the downs – long barrows, and enclosures that no one could explain.

In a way, it felt reassuring that there were these mysteries that no one could explain. Science had explained so much, she thought, and wanted to explain all. And yet these objects, which our own ancestors had created, were inexplicable. As mysterious as modern art. One would have thought, if science could explain anything, it could explain the products of humans. But it couldn't, so there were still limits to its methods. Which meant there was still a place for the imagination…

Suddenly she felt depressed and she didn't know why.

It wasn't the walk; it felt good to be up here.

It was her destination that was niggling; the thought of the therapy session.

But she wasn't there yet, so it was pointless thinking about it. She would think about the problem that was troubling her even more since she'd finished reading *Night and Day*: the way things used to be, and what had happened to shatter it all into fragments.

Yes, she thought, the classless society. Is that really our condition? Or is it just a myth? Is it simply the utopia that successive governments have aimed for, from the Demon Grocer to the Fanatical Banjo Player? Or have they succeeded?

So, two questions. First, what state are we in now? Describe. And second, how did we get here? Analyse.

Starting from the top – the Royal Family. They were now dismissed as a piece of ancient history, as a relic from the past, irrelevant to the needs of Modern Britain. There were noisy republicans who said the Royal Family were too rich and should be done away with, while their defenders said they were good for the tourist trade. Meanwhile, the Royal Family kept their dignity in the face of it all. Their knives and forks were still in the right place, even if nobody bothered to notice anymore.

Next: the aristocracy. They weren't as rich as they used to be. They couldn't be, because many of the old houses had fallen into disrepair. Their gardens were neglected, the greenhouses broken, the houses cold and damp and often empty. Even if they weren't empty, Lord and Lady So-and-So had downsized to the east wing, while dozens of staff had been replaced by a part-time handyman who did everything. Their maids and butlers worked in places like the Little Chef and McDonald's, and their Bentleys were now in museums, replaced by the four-by-four.

It was hard times for the upper class. No longer independent, they'd heard the call to diversify or die. So they were hoping for state subsidy, or rented their land to organisers of music festivals and craft fairs. Forced to sell the family silver, they had downsized their cutlery cabinet to such an extent that their knives and forks had diversified too; now they must be washed and dried before they had a chance of finding the right place.

Next: the middle class.

And here was the crux of the matter, the key to understanding.

The middle class had expanded, exponentially. From being invisible, they were now presented by politicians and billboards as the only class worth belonging to. While the upper class had been forced to downsize, the working class had been encouraged, seduced or bullied into climbing up a rung.

It had started with the Demon Grocer. She had wanted everyone to have a stake in the system, through stocks and shares and home ownership. No matter how humble, the working class was encouraged to buy shares in the privatised transport and utility companies, and to read the Financial Times with growing satisfaction as their one pound share grew in value.

But that wasn't all. Council tenants were encouraged to buy their homes, rather than rent. Home ownership was seen as the key to having a stake in the system. The Grocer's project was to make everyone a property owner, and the idea had taken root and grown.

Meanwhile, what had happened to the working class?

Confronted by the Grocer – that was the flip side to her project. Class war, culminating in the miners' strike. After which, they became a part of our social history. Trade unions became services, offering private health schemes at a discount, mortgages at a discount. The very term became drained of meaning. No one spoke of the working class anymore, because now there was only this one class, the new middle class, to which everyone belonged. Or should belong, even the Royal Family, said the politicians.

The Banjo Player had continued with the Grocer's project. The idea of "democratisation" – what did it mean? It meant sweeping up the remainder of the working class, and raising them to the level of the middle class. They'd all be persuaded to go to university, and encouraged to buy their own homes. More social engineering, using the jargon of equality: it meant dragging some people down, and lifting other people up, so that everyone would be the same. Equal opportunities: the rhetoric was seductive, but opportunities to do what? To have a large debt, and a certificate that showed you were equal. The project remained the same: to eliminate class division by giving everyone a stake in the system. Especially, by giving everyone the chance of a foot on the property ladder, as it was now called.

And what was this thing called The Property Ladder? Where were you meant to climb to? What happened if you fell off? What if you were scared of heights? Or had a fear of ladders?

George thought the idea was a nonsense. A fairy story, like Jack and the Beanstalk.

When they bought Greenslade Cottage, they had no idea they were climbing a property ladder. They bought it because they wanted a home. A place for their retirement. A place in the country; somewhere spacious, with a large garden, nice views. Now the value of the place had increased n-fold, presumably because of this thing called the property ladder.

The property ladder! What did it mean? As if you should spend your entire life buying property, accumulating value on the way! And the politicians encouraged this view. So instead of buying property to live in, people now bought property to speculate, as investments for their offspring, or to rent out in the hope of making easy money. It was the easiest way to make money, it seemed; the government was all for it. As a result of which, homelessness was on the increase. Because there was still this layer of people who couldn't afford to step on the property ladder, and couldn't afford the massive rents of the property speculators, which had also increased n-fold.

Life was so much simpler when your aspiration was to live in a nice home. After all, homes weren't owned by anybody. Homes were what you made. It was only property that was owned.

The property ladder! The whole idea was a con, and the nation had been deluded – deluded into thinking that one's progress in life should be measured by property values. Happiness, presumably, was standing on the top rung, looking down on those below. But there wasn't a top rung, that was the point; the beanstalk offered a glimpse of heaven, but you never quite got there.

And what had happened to moral values, shared values that once upon a time had crossed the class divide? The new middle class had only one value, the value of property. And if property was presented as the highest form of value, it meant that everything else had declined in value. It meant boundary disputes, wars with neighbours, wars within families, a return to tribalism. There were no shared values that knitted everyone together. And the new middle class didn't give a damn about knives and forks. They were never in the right place, and some didn't even bother with cutlery, choosing fast food, plastic spoons and fingers.

The upper class served no longer as a model for the lower orders; the aristocracy were seen as passé. The gap had been filled by celebrities. The celebs were the new aristocracy, who waved with gay abandon from the upper rungs of the property ladder. And they were the model now for the new middle class. And as most of them were thoroughly obnoxious, addicted to cocaine, alcohol, instant gratification, instant success, world rage, the worship of ignorance, a hatred of intellectuals, and various forms of rudeness and aggression, so the behaviour of the new middle class had degenerated into an antisocial free-for-all.

Fast food, fast cars, fast sport, fast sex, fast drink, fast talk, fast fights.

Speed dating and instant bliss.

It was a victory for the media. And a victory for ideology.

The old system has broken down, she thought, in ways that are beyond repair.

*

George stood on a hill, looking down on Stanton Parva. Without being aware of the distance, she had walked six miles. She strode down the slope and joined the road that led into the town. Back to civilisation. She looked at the gardens, and thought of her own, of the work that needed doing in it.

It was strange to think that even Arthur Blagdon had been Modernised. His business card looked quite professional. She could see it in her mind's eye: Arthur Blagdon Dot Com, The Total Garden Service – Hedge Trimming, Tree Pruning, Grass Cutting, Planting, Paving, Licensed Mole Catcher.

She was undecided about Arthur. She wasn't aware that Arthur did garden work. Kate Wimbourne hadn't mentioned it. George thought he did farm work. She would ask Kate tonight at the Lavender Club. The difficulty would be understanding him. Perhaps she could just point. The work was pretty straightforward, after all. She would ask Kate.

The outskirts of Stanton Parva were semi-detached land. Suburbia, without the urbia. She looked at the houses and saw property values. They were all modern, and they all looked the same. Even the gardens looked the same. A lawn, a border, a gravel drive, a garage. Everything trim and tidy.

The rooms, lacking net curtains, invited you to look inside. And what did you see? The same in each house: a three-piece suite, a TV, and not much else. Just a space that said, "Look, we're just like everybody else!" A space devoid of character, which was easier to clean, no doubt.

She was just in time for the bus.

Now she must mentally prepare for the therapy. She preferred not to. If she anticipated, it was impossible not to feel dread. You never knew how these sessions would turn out.

But last week's session wasn't so bad. They had talked about birds. Or rather, George had talked about birds, while Carol McGregor had listened. Carol was always trying to elicit what George felt about everything. Which was hard, because George didn't have feelings about everything. Only about some things. Like birds, which she loved to watch. So Carol had encouraged her passion; she'd wanted her to talk about the swallows and their nests. Three pairs nested at Greenslade Cottage, every year…

But this week, they probably wouldn't talk about birds.

A pity, she thought.

Because she'd just realised that the thing about blackbirds was that they went to bed so late. They left it till it was dark, and the other birds were all tucked up in their hedges. So maybe, the blackbirds weren't frightened of the dark. They wailed because their beds had been taken. They turned up at the hedge, and the hedge was full. There was no room at the hedge. The simplest solution would be to go to bed earlier…

It was a twenty-minute ride to Lydiard Forum and the time had passed too quickly for George to collect her thoughts. The bus had arrived and she must get off.

Her first task was to eat her sandwiches, which she ate on a bench by the River Chuckle. Then she had thirty minutes to stroll along the riverside, up to the castle and into the town.

She'd told no one about her therapy sessions. She was on the look out for familiar faces; she was grateful for not seeing any. Otherwise, she would have to invent a story to explain her being in Lydiard on a Wednesday.

The Forum Centre for Complementary Therapies – she arrived five minutes early. She sat in the foyer, looking at the notices. They offered all sorts, for you and your pets. Psychodynamic Interpersonal Therapy for the Neurotic Dog. Reichian Psychodrama for Cats. Feng Shui for the Horse Box. Everything…

"Ms Tindall? Would you like to come through?"

Carol McGregor's voice! George found it instantly reassuring. It was sort of businesslike, yet warm and friendly.

"And how are we today?" Carol said, holding the door. "Did you walk?"

"Yes, to Stanton," said George.

"It's fine weather for it," said Carol. "Please take a seat. Bear with me one moment while I find my notes."

You never knew how the session would turn out. Carol asked her about the walk. She was trying to find out what sort of mood George had brought with her, it seemed. So George spoke about reading *Night and Day*, and about her subsequent chain of thoughts. Carol was interested in what she felt about the changes she described. It seemed to Carol that George was feeling nostalgic for the way things used to be.

"What do I feel about it? I don't know what I feel," said George. "Yes, I suppose I am a bit nostalgic, because I think there was generally less bad behaviour about in those days. But I know we can't return to the past, so there's no point crying about it. I just wish… I wish there was something that could be done to improve things. For young people, I mean. For a better future. They don't have much to look forward to. And I feel totally helpless to do anything about it. I feel… totally helpless…"

Then she burst into tears.

The session was barely five minutes old.

"I'm sorry," she said, wiping her face.

"There's no need to apologise, George," said Carol.

"Actually, I'm the one who should apologise. I forgot to offer you a cup of tea or coffee. What would you like?"

"A cup of coffee, please," said George.

It was strange, this therapist relationship. Normally, she would be too embarrassed to burst into tears in company, especially with a total stranger. But with Carol, she wasn't. Carol was used to it, and she wasn't really a stranger. In fact, it was quite comforting to burst into tears in Carol's company. She could express herself, and Carol didn't mind. It was part of the therapy.

Carol came in with two cups of coffee.

"Have you had any nightmares since I saw you last, George?" she said. "It's that time of the year, isn't it?"

"Yes," said George. "Something happened yesterday, actually."

"Do go on," said Carol. "Is the coffee all right?"

"Yes, thank you, it's fine," said George. "Well, I was doing a bit in the garden. Pulling up weeds, you know. And talking to the birds as usual. And a robin came down and... ate a worm... I'm sorry..."

A second bout of tears already.

"I know it's silly," said George, "but I just can't help it. I just looked at it and thought... for that robin, that worm's just a bit of food. Of no great significance whatsoever. And yet, and yet... for Richard, the same worm might have cost him his life. I just can't marry the two ideas..."

Another bout. You never knew how the session would turn out.

"Well," said Carol. "I suppose one way of looking at it is that the worm that killed Richard was a very special worm, which you'll never meet again. And all these other worms are very ordinary worms..."

"Yes," said George, "but they wouldn't have been for Richard. He would have said each and every one of them is unique, and to be valued, and the worm that the robin ate would be just as unique, and if it had been wriggling across the road, he would have stopped to pick it up and…"

And splat!

Killed in a hit and run accident. They never did catch the driver. And the driver didn't care. That's what made it so painful. Richard, stopping to escort a worm across the road. And the driver who didn't care about life, his own or anyone else's. It wasn't right; it was perverse. The driver should have been killed, because he didn't care for life. The driver wanted to die, and so he should have done, sparing Richard. If he wanted to die, then let him die, but don't let him take others, not Richard…

So George thought as she wept silently, hiding her face.

Carol would have suggested that Richard hadn't been killed by a worm, but by a car and a reckless driver. She'd tried this before; it seemed an obvious point to make. But it made George very angry, as though the point was so obvious that it didn't need to be made and Carol was treating her like a kid. Her anger was really directed at reckless drivers, Carol thought, and also at her own powerlessness. In a way, it was easier to blame the worm. If Richard hadn't stopped for the worm, he wouldn't have been hit. But then, blaming the worm had led to another string of problems…

She glanced at her notes. Post-traumatic stress disorder. The accident had happened ten years ago. The shock was understandable; they'd spent just fifteen months together in their new home; then the accident. George had tried bereavement counselling for a while; the counsellor had referred her to a specialist. George had tried several specialists. She was a difficult case. It was hard to get her to see things in a different light. She was still in a state of denial: she couldn't come to terms with the fact that their future together had been taken away, ended prematurely.

Last week's notes: the joy of seeing baby swallows leaving their nests, nightmares about worms…

July was the month when George tried very hard not to think about worms.

3

Carol McGregor looked at the tensed body, racked with sobs, and mentally reviewed the ways in which the dead still walk among the living.

It was often the case with bereavement that a particular object or living thing did more than just stir memories of the deceased; it was seen as an embodiment of the deceased. For instance, literally: the urn of ashes kept on the mantelpiece. And then, you have the dead one's possessions. Suitable candidates for embodiment would be an item of clothing or a watch; anything that's become inseparable from the wearer. Or it may be something in the natural world: something that had an emotional significance for the deceased while they were living – or something that was closely involved in the circumstances of their death. As in Richard's case.

Richard and the worm...

They'd spent several sessions talking about Richard. They'd talked about his hobbies and interests, his outlook on life, how they met as teachers many years ago, how they fell in love and got married. They lived in a house in Blackburn or Burnley or Bolton then: or was it Hebden Bridge? Many years later, they decided to take early retirement and move down south, to a rural retreat, where they could pursue their mutual interests in the countryside. They were involved in all sorts, George had said: Wildlife Trusts, the RSPB, the Hedgehog Protection League, the Bat Preservation Society, the Stanton Parva Newt Watchers, the Lydiard Forum Friends of the Dragonfly – all sorts.

Richard wasn't a hunting sort of person, and neither was George. They liked to observe and to study, and they shared a passion for wildlife. But Richard had no special interest in worms, and he had no interest in fishing, so there was no link there. He would have done the same for an earwig, said George, or a beetle; it just happened to be a worm that was crossing the road. And Richard was no Zen Buddhist or Jain, who saw all life as sacred and would have put a carpet of soil across the road for the worm to walk on. Neither was George. No, it was simply the case that George saw worms as sacred because of their involvement in Richard's death.

Some people believe that when a person dies, their soul passes into other things, such as birds or plants...

"When my father died," said Carol, "we had a strange occurrence in the garden. We had these daffodils spring up overnight, all over the lawn. We'd never had any before. It was uncanny. It happened the day after we buried him. When I see daffodils now, I always think of my father. I see my father in the daffodils. It's as though he comes back to life every spring. He comes to visit us."

"That's nice," said George, wiping her face. "I'm sorry. I can't seem to stop today."

"I wonder if it's the same for you," said Carol. "When you see a worm, you think of Richard. Perhaps, when the robin ate the worm, it felt as though he was eating Richard."

"I suppose it did," said George. "I don't like to think about it."

"I know," said Carol, "and I can sympathise, George, because it's very painful. Therapy is a difficult process, and it can be quite upsetting to open our minds to things we'd rather keep buried. But remember, the pain is part of the process of trying to find the roots of the problem. You would like to do that, wouldn't you, George? Find the roots of the problem?"

"Yes," said George. "That's why I'm here."

"Okay," said Carol. "Good. So, let's go back to your nightmares, the ones about worms. I'm interested in how the worms appear to you in these nightmares. Is it the worms themselves that are frightening, or is it something else in the dream?"

Then, leaning forwards with a bright smile, hands clasped and arched beneath her face, Carol said, in a self-parody: "Tell me about your dreams, Ms Tindall."

George laughed, for the first time that day.

*

She could have caught the school bus, but that would have been a nightmare. Not that there was anything wrong with the kids; they were just kids, full of exuberance at the end of the school day. And better behaved than city kids, for sure. City kids would have hijacked the bus, and threatened the driver with a knife if he refused to take them to Alton Towers. Whereas this lot threw bits of paper at each other. Quite sweet really. Like stepping back in time.

But the journey would have been a nightmare: listening to their babble and her head was full already. Besides, she had the Lavender Club at 7.30 and must prepare. Better to return by taxi and never mind the expense, better to sit by the river and recuperate first, because her head was full.

It wasn't as good as last week. More upsetting. Trying to unravel her dreams. Carol forcing her to say what she really felt about worms. Did she love them? Did she hate them? Pushed to declare her feelings. Flustered and shouting, which she rarely did: "I love them! I love worms!"

It was all very confusing, this love-hate stuff. Interesting, but confusing. Interesting when Carol spoke about the virgin and the whore. Or was it the sacred and the profane? No, the virgin and the whore. Well, both actually...

A digression, Carol said, to take George's mind away from the painful. Men's attitudes to women – two contradictory ways of viewing women, which exist, side by side, in a man's mind. One, the virgin: in her purest form, the Virgin Mary, the Madonna, worshipped for her sanctity, her purity – the sacred in human form. Flip her over and she became the whore, the prostitute at the gates of the temple, devoted to Aphrodite, the goddess of love, but not to any man – worshipped by all men, who paid to adore, carnally. And with the flip side came the hatred, the slut who was slapped and abused, for being open to all men, for being a whore. Men loved women. And men hated women.

It was all very interesting but confusing, and what was the connection with George and her worms? A love-hate relationship. George loved worms – because she identified them with Richard, as if his soul had passed into the worm kingdom, a worm being the last thing he ever touched. But then she hated them, because they were linked to the cause of his death. And in her nightmares, the worm juggernaut sped along the roads, devouring everything that crossed its path. A huge creature with jaws of steel, devouring everything, devouring George, till she woke up, sweating and trembling.

So the worm was both sacred, because it was Richard; yet profane, because it had killed Richard.

Yes, it was all very interesting, she thought, but hardly a cure for her troubles. In particular, it couldn't relieve this pit of nothingness in her stomach. A core of nothingness that was totally depressing, and made her wonder about suicide.

Not that she ever would. But she wondered.

It was the latest fad. Everybody was doing it. Farmers for instance; especially in Wales for some reason. Young people generally, especially men. And the way they drove! As if they didn't care whether they lived or died; she knew all about that. The thrill was in the speed. Giving it max, without dying. Perhaps they didn't want to die; perhaps they were just laughing at Death, saying, "Come and take me if you dare," believing that Death wouldn't dare.

But then, they didn't care. If they died, so what? They would rather die at speed, fast and young, than die in a chair, slow and old. Life, the future, must have been so rotten in their eyes that death seemed the better option.

And then there were these group suicides; another fad. It was all the rage in Japan, apparently. People advertised via the Web for companions to die with. The idea was spreading like a virus. Suicide cults in the USA. Not to mention these suicide bombers. But that was rather different. Presumably they did it for a cause, whatever it was. Whereas these others, these cults, did it simply for the pleasure. The pleasure! The pleasure of death! It was like a mass disease, sweeping the globe. Suddenly, death was the place to be, suicide the thing to do. As if God, or the Great Architect of the Universe, had decided to press a switch in the human psyche, so that death not life was the big motivator.

Thanatos. The death instinct had taken over. It meant the end of evolution, as far as men were concerned. Or evolution in reverse, as if men, now aware of the destruction they'd done to the planet, had evolved into self-destruct mode, which might restore a global equilibrium by sending the human race into extinction.

The Gaia hypothesis, as formulated by that biologist, James Lovelock: Mother Earth has her own mechanisms to correct wrongs, to re-stabilise the planet in the face of imbalances. In which case here's the logic: humans have become the greatest threat to global harmony, so Mother Earth gives humans the will to destroy themselves, thereby saving the planet. End of story.

The global virus.

That's how it seemed to George: a global virus. That's why, for years after Richard's death, she had no inclination to go out, apart from the essential shopping trip. If she went out, she thought, she would be infected by the disease, by the suicide bug. Spend too much time with other people and the urge would overcome you. You could catch it anywhere; you didn't know who was infected.

So she didn't go out: not for years, not until she felt safe, protected from the global virus.

She wasn't afraid of catching it now. She was cured.

But still she wondered.

The question that troubled her was whether suicide was a rational act, the result of a rational decision. For those people who advertised for death companions on the Web, it must be, she thought. Some people tried to sell plastic pigs on eBay; others wanted death companions. It didn't seem such a big deal to them, as if it was just an alternative to Internet dating, but more exciting. Let's do death, the magical mystery tour with the one-way ticket!

So they'd thought about it, and decided – let's do it!

George wasn't buying a ticket, no way.

But the worrying thing was the idea that suicide was in most cases not a rational decision; it was the result of a state of mind. That is to say, given a certain state of mind, suicide was a possibility for anybody. It would be done on an impulse, when the opportunity presented itself. It would be the result of a heartbreaking loneliness, or the pits of depression, or the great empty feeling of not being loved, or the terrible feeling of being overwhelmed by physical pain.

In which case, you wouldn't think about it at all. You would just be overwhelmed by one of those moods, and the overwhelming would continue, day after day, week after week, until suddenly you find yourself on a railway platform, and an express train is about to thunder past, and you have the irresistible urge to throw yourself under its wheels, and that would be that, which wasn't a rational decision at all; yet it could overtake anybody, including George…

It was time to find a taxi. The sky had clouded over; there was a light shower, pattering on the trees. How different from the morning!

No, she thought, walking along the riverbank, you could never plan such an event; it would have to be a spur of the moment decision. Can you imagine! Impossible to plan – that express train would never show up on time…

*

Twenty minutes by taxi: it would have taken an hour on the school bus. George had brightened up, enough to comment on the weather to the driver, who – like the bus drivers – knew George as a regular customer.

Now she was sorting out food, awaiting the phone call from Mrs Whitmarsh.

"Seven o'clock, will that be all right?" said Mrs Whitmarsh. "Just a minute, Edward wants to speak. Yes… No, seven thirty… Yes… Yes… Edward says five past seven, George. Will that be all right? It only takes ten minutes, you know how Edward drives. Right, we'll see you shortly."

George found it all rather amusing: this precision of arrangements. Everything had to be just so; otherwise the world would collapse, it seemed. The world of Magnus Chase, that is. Surely it wasn't like that in the city? What was a minute, either way? What if George had said, "Could you make it three minutes past?" It would have entailed another consultation with Edward, another rumination on his part, followed by an outright refusal, a reluctant acceptance, or an attempt at a compromise: "Edward says four minutes past. Will that be all right, George?"

In any case, it would have to be all right, because at this stage there was no alternative. She hated it, this dependency. Far easier to walk, if possible. And Edward was such a misery. A man of few words, with a bushy beard and sad eyes, which always gave George the impression that leaving the house was an unbearable chore for him.

Oh well, she thought, clearing up the dishes, the ride is only ten minutes.

And she remembered the time when she and Richard had arrived ten minutes late for a night of country dancing. The dance, at the village hall in Charlton Minster, was advertised for 7.30. And lo! There they all were, charging across the floor at 7.40. They'd had to wait for an interval before they could join in. That was their first lesson in the etiquette of Magnus

Chase – 7.30 meant 7.30.

So, at 7.02, George was standing by the cottage gate, looking at her watch.

Three minutes later, there was the honk, and there was the car, and there was the sad eyes of Edward Whitmarsh, looking in the mirror as George climbed in, grappling with the back seat.

"Seat belt if you would, please," said Edward.

"Yes," said George, "if I can find it."

He didn't even say hello. And his eyes really did look as though Edward wished his wife hadn't dragged him out of the house.

"Edward likes sitting in the garden on these summer evenings, don't you Edward?" said Mrs Whitmarsh, as if this explained her husband's terseness. "Are you all right there, George?"

"Yes, I've found it…"

"Pull it the other way," said Mrs Whitmarsh. "No, the other way. Have you got it?"

"Yes, I think so…"

"Is she in?" said Edward.

"No, wait a minute. Yes, she's in now."

"Right," said Edward, and the car shot off down the lane.

George cursed the seat belt. Such a performance. It wouldn't have surprised her if they'd burst into a round of applause at her belting up. Edward's eyes seemed to be saying, "Thank God for that!" Why did they treat her as if she was some kind of half-wit? It wasn't her fault; the belt was twisted.

Ten minutes.

George pondered, thinking of possible lines of conversation, items for idle chit-chat. The effort! And was there any point? Edward had no inclination for idle chit-chat. Whereas Mrs Whitmarsh, yes, but her chit-chat was so idle that you might just as well talk to a sparrow. And what was her first name? It was such a struggle to recall… Brenda – it was Brenda. Brenda and Edward. Edward and Brenda. Whitmarsh.

The silence was unbearable.

"I like sitting in the garden when it's like this," said George.

"Yes, it's nice, isn't it?" said Brenda.

"Yes," said George.

"What time will you want fetching?" said Edward.

"We're usually done by 9.30," said Brenda.

"Right, 9.30," said Edward.

"Will that be all right, George?" said Brenda.

"Yes. Fine," said George, who was sorely tempted to suggest 9.35.

"We're usually in bed by ten," said Brenda. "Are you an early bird, George? Going to bed, I mean."

"No, not that early," said George. "Usually by eleven; then I read."

"Oh, that's late," said Brenda. "That would be a late night for us, wouldn't it, Edward?"

"Hmm," said Edward, turning the car with a squeak.

"Oh, I hate that noise," said Brenda. "I do wish you'd get it fixed, Edward. Not so fast! Look, there's a tractor!"

They were now on the single-track road that led to Top Down. George could almost see the steam coming out of Edward's nostrils as he slowed down to a crawl.

"Carrying silage, by the look of it," said Brenda. "Oh, good, he's turning off."

Edward put his foot down. Two minutes later, they were in the car park at the village hall. Brenda had opened the door and climbed out while George was still trying to extricate herself. And Edward was turning the car already...

George fell out and swung the door. Then she shouted.

"The seat belt!"

There was a shower of little white sparks as the metal clip dragged across the concrete. Edward heard the noise and slowed. He leant across the back seat, opened the door, did the business and squeaked away, glaring at George as he drove off.

Ten minutes, and she was shaking. Not helped by Brenda's chatter as they entered the building.

"He's such an impatient driver," said Brenda. "Are you all right, George? You've gone very pale. It shakes you up, doesn't it, driving fast. I can feel my bones rattle when he drives like that, but that's how he is, he'll never be told. The doctor said he ought to slow down at his age, it's better for his heart. Let's have a cup of tea and a quiet sit."

The hall was sprinkled with the ladies of the Lavender Club, milling about at the front, at the back, and some were sitting already. Barbara Smiles stood at a table at the front, talking to Stephen Grove, the guest speaker. Kate Wimbourne stood at a table at the back, just inside the door, serving tea.

George and Brenda joined the queue.

The table was spread with cups and saucers, plates and serviettes, a selection of cakes, and small neat sandwiches cut into squares, which George stared at. They looked so tidy. Carefully arranged on clean white napkins. Spread sparingly with marge. Spread thinly with salmon and cucumber as usual; she could tell by the smell.

"Barbara's been busy again," said Brenda. "She makes lovely cakes. Have you tried one of her cakes, George? Can I get you a piece?"

"They're very nice, I have tried them, but I'll have a piece later perhaps. I think a cup of tea will be just fine for now."

"I suppose they'll have to close the curtains if he's showing slides," said Brenda, casting glances around the hall. "It'll seem funny, won't it? Sitting in the dark while it's still daylight outside."

The daylight was pouring in through the large windows, lighting the summer frocks that showed all manner of floral patterns. Flowers in the windows too. And outside: the serene light of a summer's evening.

"Hello George," said Kate Wimbourne, pouring the tea. "I'm so glad you could make it. Mary's not coming. She's feeling very tired, poor thing."

"Oh, I think this weather is very tiring," said Brenda. "Hasn't it been warm today? You sit down, George. I'll just have a word with Barbara."

George found Brenda very tiring.

So did Kate, who shook her head as Brenda wandered off. "I'll see you in a minute," Kate said to George.

George sat down and marvelled at the strangeness of life. Edward and Brenda. Brenda and Edward. Edward the Bear and Brenda the Mouse. Better: Edward the Crow and Brenda the Sparrow. Such a peculiar match. How did they ever get married? Two grown-up children as well. The idea of them making love! Crow's beak and Sparrow's feathers – it made her feel ill, thinking about it...

"Barbara's in a bit of a tizzy," said Kate Wimbourne, sitting beside her. She nodded her head in Barbara's direction. "That Stephen Grove, can you believe it? Apparently, he's not going to show us his slides after all. And he's kept us waiting all this time! When did he come back from the Azores? Last year, wasn't it?"

"It was last summer, I think," said George.

"Last summer, and Barbara's been on to him ever since. And now, he finally agrees to give us a talk and he's not going to show us his slides. I think it's a very poor show. And he may not even talk about the Azores."

"What's he going to talk about then?" said George.

"I don't know," said Kate. "Farming, I think. Barbara's very worried he's going to bore us rigid."

And indeed, Barbara Smiles was listening to Stephen with a look of horror. Brenda Whitmarsh had been dismissed with a wave; Brenda had joined a group of ladies who were now drifting towards their seats. The meeting was about to begin.

Brenda and Edward. Edward and Brenda. And here, George thought, was another odd match, centre stage: the diminutive Barbara with her bob of grey hair and summer frock; Stephen the giant with his head of dark curls and open-necked shirt, sleeves rolled up, as if he was preparing for milking. His brown, thickset arms made Barbara's thin white ones look like cocktail sticks.

She suddenly remembered she'd meant to bring her glasses.

"Thank you all for coming," said Barbara, and the room fell into a hush.

Kate cupped an ear and leant forwards, frowning, making it obvious to Barbara that her usual soft-spoken manner was not sufficient when addressing a room full of ladies. Barbara cleared her throat.

"I think we're ready to start," she said, raising her voice a decibel or two. "I'd like to welcome Stephen Grove, our guest speaker this evening. Stephen has been a farmer for many years, and those of you who live in Rhomboid Minster will know him well. He has recently started a new career as a journalist…"

Stephen laughed at the suggestion.

"He's very modest about it," Barbara continued, turning to smile at him. "But we all read your piece with great interest, Stephen. Those of you who read the Stanton Chronicle will know that Stephen writes a weekly column on country matters. Last year, Stephen went on a trip to the Azores, and tonight he's going to tell us about his experiences. He was part of a team who were, er, doing research on farming, is that right, Stephen? No? Oh! Let's hear what Stephen has to say about it then. Ladies, will you please give a warm welcome to our guest this evening, Stephen Grove."

A round of polite applause as Barbara sat down.

"Thank you ladies," said Stephen. "Thank you all for inviting me. Yes, last year I went to the Azores, as most of you know. It's a beautiful place, and I appreciate you were expecting to see some pictures this evening. Now I'm sorry to disappoint you, but I haven't brought any. The reason is simple. All of us who took part in the project were sworn to secrecy. Let me explain."

He reached to the floor, picked up a carrier bag, placed it

on the table. Then he proceeded to rummage before turning to the audience.

"These are difficult times for farmers," he said. "There are few small farmers left now on Magnus Chase. Some have sold up and gone to Australia or Canada, and those who have stayed here have tried to break out into other fields. Diversification – the key word. Meanwhile, the big boys have taken over. We've all been suffering – poor returns, more regulations, higher costs, and the hours we put in don't get any less. Some farmers have committed suicide because their troubles were too much to bear. And many of us suffer from depression."

Some of the ladies bowed their heads at this elegy, as if they were in church and ought to feel the agony. Which some of them did, as their husbands were farmers.

Stephen laughed.

"I've suffered from depression myself, but I didn't mean to depress you, ladies," he said. "Anyway, last year – no, it was two years ago now – I saw an advert in a national daily. It was addressed to us farmers, especially those of us who were prone to depression or suicidal thoughts. It was offering us a three-month holiday in the Azores, all expenses paid, and a wage on top, in return for taking part in an experiment. Of course, it wasn't a real holiday as such, but it felt like a holiday to me. I jumped at the chance. I replied to the ad and I was very pleased to have an interview in London, with these science boffins. They explained what it was all about. The experiment was simple enough – it was a trial for a new antidepressant drug. They were looking for people to test it on, people who were suffering, like. And I was suffering, so I said I was all for it. I had to sit a test for sums and words, and then they said they'd let me know. They had hundreds of applicants, so I felt very lucky when I was selected. And let me tell you, ladies, I've never felt better."

At this point Stephen took a deep breath, flexed his muscles, stretched his neck and stared at the ceiling.

"Yes," he said, turning to the audience. "I'm a new man. A new man. You see, taking the drug was simple enough, but that wasn't the half of it. Oh no. We were there for three months, and what did we do? We read books, ladies, books. Oh yes. My eyes have been opened – to the wonderful world of words."

Moving to the front of the table, he then sat on the edge of it.

"We had a reading group, with a wonderful tutor. That was part of the test, to check up on our reading skills, like. And we read a book by a man called Marx. Some of you may have heard of him, but I knew little about him, except that he was connected with communism. So it was a big surprise to me when I learnt to read him. It opened my eyes, yes indeed. And that's why I'm not going to talk about the Azores tonight. I'm going to talk about land reform."

Kate Wimbourne, perched on the edge of her seat, leant back and gave George a wink.

"You see," said Stephen, "we complain about being depressed and feeling miserable, but, at the end of the day, it's our own stupid fault. Oh yes. Us farmers."

Stephen looked for the carrier bag, reached inside and pulled out a newspaper, which he held up for the audience to see. George, sitting on the back row, cursed her memory for not bringing her glasses.

But Kate could see it plain enough. The front page showed a picture of that brutal dictator, whose name she whispered in George's ear: "Robert Mugabe!"

"Yes," said Stephen, "Robert Mugabe. We all hate him, don't we? And why do we hate him? Because he's ruined the country? No – much of Africa has been plundered and ruined in the past, and none of us kicked up a fuss then, because we in the West were getting the benefits. Because of his brutal methods? No – think of all the brutal dictators in the world, who get by thank you very much without a word of criticism from the likes of us. No – we hate him because he's black, and because he's dared to take land away from the white farmers."

George looked around the room. Barbara Smiles was sitting with her head bowed, a hand over her face. She really did look as though she were in church. Kate Wimbourne shook her head.

"I know what you're thinking," said Stephen. "We taught them everything they know. There were no farms over there before we showed them how to farm. And that's why he's ruining the country, because the people with the know-how are being thrown off the farms, and the blacks who are taking over know nothing. Now I'm sorry, but you're wrong. If anyone cares to study history, they'll find that farming came from the East, from Africa, from Asia, many, many years ago. The knowledge wasn't planted by God in the white man's skull, from day one – it was them who learnt it, and then they showed us. And who owned the land before we went over and stole it from them? They did, of course – the blacks. And now they want it back, and we're kicking up a big fuss. Well, good luck to them, I say. Let them have it, and good luck to them."

Someone coughed. It was the cue for a round of splutters and sneezes. George could feel a dozen vocal cords aching to speak. Or to scream.

"Yes, I know you don't agree with me, but my eyes have been opened," said Stephen. "And now I'll probably shock you all again when I say a similar expulsion has happened over here. Not recently but two, three hundred years ago. We forget, but it wasn't so long ago when everybody worked on the land. We didn't have cities then, only small market towns, where people gathered to buy and sell. We didn't have factories, only farms, and mills, and arts and crafts. So what happened when the factories came? I'll tell you what happened. People were thrown off the land. Yes, just like Mugabe. Thrown off the land to work in the cities. Kicked out by brute force, by the likes of us and our henchmen. Oh yes, it happened here. It's part of our history. And it's all our fault, the fault of us farmers, the fault of our ancestors. We are the brutes…"

This was just too much for Mrs Bartlett from Stockwood Melrush. George recognised her as one of the bus regulars as she stood to her feet, muttered an Excuse Me, and walked promptly to the back of the room. Kate's head was shaking very slowly, a sure sign of troubled waters.

"Er, perhaps we should have a tea break, Mrs Smiles," Stephen said.

"Yes," said Barbara, leaping to her feet. "We'll have the break now, and then see if, if… there's any questions."

"To arms!" said Kate, leaping to her feet. Then she leant towards George and whispered: "Do you think he's been brainwashed?"

"I don't know," said George. "I wasn't expecting this."

"I don't think any of us were," said Kate, and rushed towards the water urn. Then she turned and said, "George, would you mind washing some cups? I think we've run out."

*

George stood by the sink, listening to the echoes of the ladies' voices, now drowned by the swishing of the hot water. Cups, cups, and more cups, which Kate brought in on a tray.

"Are you okay for a minute?" said Kate. "I think that's about it. It's bedlam in there – Mrs Chilcott has fainted."

"Oh dear," said George, and Kate rushed out.

The echoes grew louder as Mrs Chilcott was escorted to the door. It's the heat, said one. Get a glass of water, said another. She'll be all right outside, sit her by the door, said another.

And then a man's voice said, "I'll help you dry."

It was Stephen Grove, who had entered the kitchen unnoticed.

"I seem to have caused a bit of a stir," he said, reaching for a cloth.

George stifled a laugh.

"Yes," she said, "I think you have. Never mind, it makes a change from the usual flower arranging."

Stephen laughed; it sounded like a cough.

"I didn't mean to," he said. "I think I ought to apologise."

"I'm sure that would go down very well," she said.

The water swished as she washed; the cups squeaked as he rubbed. I'll wash if you dry – how many times, she wondered, have those words been said? A countless number. An infinite number. She glanced at his arms. Then he said: "I'm sorry, I don't think I know you, do I? Are you new round here?"

"No, I've been here ten years," she said. "I've only just started going to these meetings."

"Ten years," he said. "There's a lot of new folk here now, people I don't recognise. That's what I was going to say next, in my talk. I suppose that might offend some people."

"It might," she said. "It depends on what you're going to say about us. Are you saying we should all leave?"

"No, no, I'm not saying that," he said, "and I didn't mean you, honestly I didn't. I didn't mean to upset anybody."

"You didn't upset me," she said.

"I didn't? Oh, you surprise me."

"I used to be a history teacher," she said. "What you were saying about farming coming from the East and that..."

"How are we doing?" said Kate, rushing in. "Oh! I'm not intruding, am I? I'm after clean cups."

"We're just about done now," said George.

"Right," said Kate. "Stephen, you'd better have a word with Barbara. She's very upset."

"Right ho," said Stephen, and walked out.

"You two seem to be getting on fine and dandy," said Kate, piling the tray.

"We were just talking," said George, and felt herself blushing.

In the hall, Barbara was trying to gauge opinion. Some of the ladies had left already, whisked away by their husbands, who had been summoned by the call of the mobile. The rest were stranded.

Stephen said he had more to say; Barbara asked if he might talk about the Azores. But Stephen said he really wanted to talk about land reform.

"There are these new laws about access to the countryside," he said. "It affects us all, not just farmers. No, I'm sorry, Mrs Smiles, I won't mention Robert Mugabe. Yes, I will apologise."

Barbara tried to draw the room's attention with a wave and a decibel.

"I think," she said, "we're going to start again. Stephen would like to say a few words."

And the meeting continued.

"I'm very sorry," Stephen said, "for causing an upset, ladies, I really am. I didn't mean to, I was just expressing my opinions, like. Now, what I was going to talk about was land reform, and I hope I don't upset anyone this time by what I'm about to say."

Even without her glasses, George knew he was looking at her. Kate followed his gaze and frowned.

"The countryside has changed," said Stephen. "We all know that, and though we don't agree on a lot of matters, you may all agree with me on this point – in my opinion, the changes have been for the worst."

The ladies murmured their consent. Kate took a deep breath. "Absolutely," she sighed. Stephen, smiling at the response, continued.

"Apart from the problems we farmers have suffered, we have a serious housing problem in the countryside. We have a desperate shortage of affordable housing. In the last few years, as you know, house prices have rocketed. And what we have in the countryside are these second-home owners, buying places to visit for their country weekends, or buying property to rent as holiday homes, or to rent out to local people at extravagant prices. In any case, what they're doing is pricing the locals out of a home. Yes, everybody wants to live in the countryside – or buy property in the countryside,

I should say – and yet local people can't afford to buy a home. It's even worse if you're a first-time buyer. Young people can't get a place of their own…"

George listened with mounting anxiety. She was safe, she thought, because she wasn't a second-home owner. But what was he advocating?

"… and they're forced to live with their parents till their parents are sick of them, because they can't afford to move out. Of course, that's less of a problem for us farmers. We've always had our children at home, so as we can teach them how to farm while we're able, and then, when we're old and sickly, we've got our kids there to make sure we're looked after. Yes, we're very lucky in that way – there's no care home for us. We are, as Marx might say, a privileged aristocracy. Oh yes, because we pass on our land to our children, for them to own and farm, and for them to pass on to their children and their children; that's our tradition. Now that's all very well for us, but what about the locals who don't inherit a farm? And what about the children who don't want to carry on farming? They see how we suffer, and they say, No Thank You, Not For Me. So what happens to our farms then?"

Kate, perched on the edge of her seat, turned to George.

"He'll be running for parliament," she whispered, and nodded sagely.

"These are big problems," said Stephen. "Not just for us farmers, but for all the locals who live on Magnus Chase, and for country people everywhere – and the policies of this government aren't helping matters."

Kate gave George a knowing wink.

"Nor of the previous government I might add – oh no. We've had the Thatcher Revolution, and now we're a nation of home owners, so we're told. She was the one who brainwashed us all into thinking ownership is good, renting is bad. Yes, she was the one who taught us the ethos of ownership. And now, people want to buy not rent, and the kids look on those who rent as the poor sods who can't afford a home – pardon my language, Mrs Smiles, but that's what they think, it really is. And what does this government do? They and their cronies build expensive city apartments so as they can rent them out and make a large profit. Oh yes, we've all heard it on the news – this government is corrupt, it's rotten to the core."

"He's right, you know," said Kate, sweeping the room with her nods.

"So," said Stephen, "what can be done about the housing problem? Very little while this government is in power – they're making money out of other people's misfortunes, thank you very much. But what should be done about it? The answer is simple when you think about it. Private property is the cause of all these problems, and the simple answer is – we do away with private property. Yes – nationalise the land, I say. Public ownership of the land is the answer. Get rid of birthrights and aristocracies, because when we're dead and buried, it doesn't matter a fff… flipping penny, except to those who stand to inherit. I think it's all wrong. It's unfair, it's unjust, and it's wrecking our country…"

Barbara Smiles had shrunk once more into her seat, holding her head.

"He has been brainwashed," said Kate.

"And just think about it for a while," said Stephen. "Let me ask you this – who really owns the land? I mean, really and genuinely owns the land? The Queen, you might say, because all land truly belongs to the Crown. And I'm sorry but I don't agree; I say no, because even she will be dead and buried one day, bless her. No, I believe we're here on this earth just a short time. We share it with our fellow creatures, and it's our duty to look after it as best as we can, and not leave it in a mess for our descendants to clear up, because who really owns the land is not us but God."

Another buzz of consent: some of the ladies were ardent churchgoers.

"We should never forget that," said Stephen. "And yet we

do because of this ethos of private ownership which rules our culture to the ruin of us all. Now this may shock you, but I'm beginning to think there's something in this Moslem business..."

A frown from Kate; a cough from the lady on the door, who was keeping an eye on Mrs Chilcott.

"Yes," said Stephen, "I think they're onto something. Somebody told me the Moslems don't believe in private property, and the profits of their banks are donated to good causes, and relieving the distresses of the poor. Now I ask you, is that a bad thing? Speaking for myself, I don't think it is, and I don't mind telling you I've a good mind to find out more about this Moslem business. Maybe they're right and we're wrong. Maybe we in the West have lost the plot – we've been corrupted by money and greed and the lust for property, and we've forgotten our time here is but a wink of God's eye..."

George saw the creases in Kate's forehead, more brazen now as the daylight waned. And suddenly there was a frantic honking from the car park, which, under the circumstances, led some ladies to believe they were hearing God's trumpet. The honk sounded again: three short honks and a longer one, as if the driver was engaged in a Morse code. George stared at the window; then jumped when she felt a tug on her sleeve. Brenda Whitmarsh was standing there, out of breath – "It's Edward!" she said.

*

The thing about blackbirds was that the day just wasn't long enough for them, even in the summer. The idea of going to bed early was alien to them. And this one had eyes in the back of his head.

George sat in the kitchen, listening to the song. The blackbird stood on a telephone pole, singing his heart out. He was singing when George fell out of the car, and singing now as the dusk darkened.

Life is so simple if you're a bird, she thought. You spend the day eating; you spend the night sleeping. You go to bed when it's dark; you get up when it's light. Unless you're an owl, in which case the reverse is true. But then you might be a little owl, in which case your habits could be rather erratic…

And there he was – on the wire as usual, screaming like a monkey, and sending the blackbird into pinking mode.

Simple nonetheless, she thought, even if there are enemies to deal with. Every spring, you make love and breed. Maybe twice. Or thrice, if you're a house martin. Or a swallow. And then, when you feel like it, you sing. And if you're a blackbird, sing for two or three hours at a stretch. Till it's bedtime.

She wanted to talk to Stephen Grove. She wanted to tell him about *Night and Day*, about the changes that she had seen. She wanted to see him again, alone.

Interesting and provocative, she thought, and slightly mad.

But she may not see him, if it's left to chance.

Wednesday.

And her next outing will be Monday, no doubt.

The shopping trip.

Tomorrow, she will do some tidying.

4

George's favourite room. A large room with a high ceiling. And a picture window, which took up an entire wall and filled the room with light. A room with a view – a panorama, stretching east and west, along the wide valley of the River Chuckle; over the valley to Triplecheek St Mary, along the river to Lydiard Forum. How could you want a TV with a view like this? A kaleidoscopic wallpaper, she thought; always changing. And another prime reason for buying the place. So they could sit up here and watch. Richard's favourite room.

She sat there with her binoculars, scanning the valley. She was looking for traces of that scene, which her mind's eye saw clearly:

A gypsy caravan, red and golden; a white parrot in a cage, hanging from the wall of a house; and the rooks above the Scots pines, feeding the squawking rooklings...

Triplecheek St Mary.

They had walked there once, following the stream across the fields.

She could see the trees now, the top of the church tower. But no rooks...

And up on the hill, behind Triplecheek St Mary, was the village of Rhomboid Minster, where Stephen Grove lived. Precisely where, she didn't know. She could see one or two farms there, the houses in the village. And a tractor, cutting the grass for silage...

And the cars in Quinton, zooming along the main road.

She returned to the pile of notes. Still that fusty smell. But the pages had warmed in the sun.

Richard's notes. Their wildlife diaries.

Of course, you couldn't dwell on the past; she knew that. But Richard was very sharp in his observations, sharper than George. It was good to look back on that first year. Besides, the notes needed airing.

The words were swimming. She turned to the window.

The swallows were skimming the mown fields at great speed, jumping the overgrown hedgerows, feasting. And now she could smell the gorse, blown by a draught through the open skylight.

She sipped her rosemary tea and started to read.

Then the wren called.

Slowly she rose, placing her cup on the notes, so that the draught wouldn't blow them about. Along the corridor, turning on a light, down the stairs she walked, through the living room and out through the open door, looking for the owl.

Past the wood shed, where the babies would emerge at dusk. All quiet in there now. Past the old chicken shed, scanning the tin roof. No owl there; just a pigeon on the yard, pecking at the stone flags.

The pigeon didn't fly away as she walked past. It stood and watched as she walked past the bottom gate, heading for the grain shed, scanning that roof, then the roof of the house.

The wren was hopping about the bags of grain, tutting still.

"What is it, little wren? Is it the owl? Where is he? I can't see him."

Still the wren scolded, its head bobbing up and down as it tutted, its tail jutting up into the air.

"What's the matter, little wren? I can't see the owl. Where is he?"

The pigeon had followed her through the open gate. Now it walked towards the grain shed, cocking its head; listening to her chatter, it seemed.

"Is he in here? He's not in the usual places. Is he snoozing? Has he fallen asleep?"

She stood a while, listening for the familiar snore. And the pigeon stood there too, cocking its head as if listening, while the wren flew out of the grain shed to perch on a barrel of compost.

She heard the sparrows on the roof, chirruping; then the wren, bursting into song. It was her cue to walk away.

"He's not in here. Are you okay now?" she said.

The wren tutted, then flew onto the roof of the grain shed.

She looked again at the guttering, at the telephone poles, at the cables, at the oak tree covered in ivy, at the roofs of the sheds: the little owl's favourite perches.

"Oh, you are skittish today!" she said, walking away. "Well, I can't see the owl, so I'm going. All right?"

She walked past the pigeon, who stood there cocking its head. She walked past the chicken shed, past the wood shed, across the yard and into the house, feeling vexed.

If it wasn't the owl, she thought, then who? Or what? Possibly squirrels, who were just as troublesome as the owl.

Up the stairs she walked, along the corridor, past the open skylights, her face brushed by the draught of warm air.

She sat down again by the picture window, watching the swallows swooping over the fields. She picked up a page from the pile of notes, put it down again, and sank into a state of reverie.

July – and the birds were busy with nesting.

She remembered a summer when the owl had eaten a swallow's eggs; the swallows upset, whirling about the yard, wailing. It didn't happen very often, as far as she could tell; but then, she couldn't be on guard for the entire day, every day. And the smaller birds didn't trust the owl; that was obvious. Whenever they spotted it on one of its perches, the sparrows screeched; the chaffinches chimed; the blackbirds hopped around it with their pinking, tinkling cry; the swallows dive-bombed it with their droppings; the house martins coughed their disapproval; and the wren, tiny thing, stuttered in dismay.

And George would go out and shoo it away.

Usually he was easy to spot, because the swallows made such a racket, and told everyone else about him, including George. One summer, the swallows had led her around the garden, calling her to follow while the owl fled from perch to perch. So there was George, in pursuit of the swallows, who were seeing off the owl!

But the owl was quite a comical chap, and George was really quite fond of him, as Richard had been. In the winter, the sparrows, the blackbirds and the finches still made a rumpus about him, but George chose not to interfere, because he was actually looking for voles, his main source of food. On those cold and frosty mornings, she would watch him through the binoculars, sat on one of his perches, looking at the grass below, unruffled by the din of the finches. There he would watch and wait, till a vole's movements made him fly to the ground.

And this year, he had been nesting in the wood shed, with his partner of course. George hadn't known about it till, one day, looking from a skylight at dusk, she saw two balls of fluff, with legs like twigs, standing on the edge of the wood shed – owl twins! The twins had spotted her and scampered inside. They weren't ready to fly yet; they came out at dusk and stood there, waiting to be fed.

It was all very exciting. They nested every year, usually in a tree, but she'd never known them have babies before.

And it was a result, she thought, of their new relationship – trust. There was an unspoken agreement now – if the owl left the swallows alone, then George wouldn't go out and shoo him away. That was the deal, and the owl seemed to understand. Which was perfect, in George's eyes, for maintaining a sort of harmony between all the creatures who lived at Greenslade Cottage. Live and let live. One big happy family, with George as a sort of godmother. After all, there was room for them all to nest, side by side, as long as they got on – the swallows in one shed, the owl family in another, the wren in another, the sparrows, the house martins in the eaves, and so on.

But whenever there was a rumpus, it was usually the owl who was causing it. And then, in the summer, sometimes it was the sparrow hawk, an invader, who would fly across the downs, looking for young birds. He would hide in the hedgerow while the swallows would circle above, keeping their distance as they screamed. Then George would go out to see him off. But sometimes the swallows didn't spot him; sometimes he hid in the holly, to swoop on a young house martin on the stone flags, and then it was too late to do anything about it; the baby had been devoured.

Now she sat there feeling irritated, and trying to work out why she was so irritated. This was Carol McGregor's doing: getting her to analyse her feelings. She was feeling annoyed, she thought, because of a wasted journey. Nothing had been found; it was a false alarm; the wren was just being skittish. And she was feeling disappointed because she hadn't been useful, because her instincts had been wrong, because the owl was nowhere to be seen. But then there should have been something there, because birds don't make alarm calls without a reason.

She looked at the armchair where Richard used to sit, knowing that he would have had an answer. The yellow dye was fading away, scorched by the sun...

There was a loud clatter, outside but very close.

Turning her head, she looked out of the door and out of the skylight to the grain shed. A pigeon had landed on the metal roof and was standing there, looking at her.

Stupid creature, she thought. She had little time for pigeons. Slow, clumsy things, who were always bumping into you. The number of times she and Richard had walked the streets of London, trying to avoid the damned things! It had been one of their great discoveries when they came here and made friends with the swallows. A bird with intelligence! To return to the same nesting site, year after year, following a journey of God knows how many miles. And their sense of fun!

82

According to Richard, theirs was a life of play:

"The secret of happiness, taking the swallow as our model, is to know your enemy, know your friends, and do everything, and I mean absolutely everything, with passion. Feel the pulse of life, whatever it is you are doing!"

So said Richard, and George had made a note of it.

It was the swallows that kept her spirits up.

Every year, she looked forward to the day of their arrival; every year, she shed a tear when they departed.

And she helped them when they were nesting, knowing that Richard would have done the same.

One summer, she realised that the same three pairs had been nesting there for the last four years: one in the chicken shed, one in the grain shed, and one in the outbuilding where the tools were stored. By which time, a sense of trust had been set up between them, and one pair decided to build a new nest right above the front door. And what a summer that was!

An unforgettable summer, she thought.

At dusk, mother would perch on the nest, sorting out the bedding; father would perch on the porch light, keeping watch, and staying there unflinching while George ducked her head to step outside.

And what a struggle that summer, fighting off the magpie! Stones at every window; a hammock by the door; and a can to rattle at dawn!

And they had won. The babies had left the nest, and George could sit outside once more.

So George had put out a deckchair and sat there, thinking how the summer was almost over. And the swallows! Three families, six broods, thirty-three birds in all – one by one they had gathered on the washing line and then sang, the whole lot, singing their thanks to George.

Which had brought tears to her eyes, knowing how Richard would have loved it, a moment to be cherished.

The nest hadn't been used since.

It was still there, in the porch, but they'd chosen not to use it.

Three pairs had continued to come, every year, but this year had seen a great reversal – two pairs of swallows arriving early, claiming the tool shed and the chicken shed, and frightening off the usual pairs when they arrived two weeks later. Not only that, but diving at George whenever she went out of the door, and she couldn't work out why.

She put it down to squirrels. She had caught one once, heading for the chicken shed when the swallows had been screaming. She had chased it around the yard, while the swallows had chased her, as if she was the enemy.

And the two pairs of invaders had failed to raise a brood, for reasons unknown, while one of the usual pairs had nested in the summerhouse without a fuss, and the babies were now flying over the fields.

Things had settled down a little since the divings, but the swallows were about to start on their second brood, and George wasn't looking forward to it. It was heartbreaking to think that now she was seen as the enemy.

After all my efforts to help them over the years, she thought. This lot aren't aware of that, ungrateful and stupid things. How different from that summer, when the swallows gathered on the washing line, singing their thanks!

It seemed so long ago now.

These were different times, different birds. Invaders, who didn't understand.

Now she had decided not to go out when the swallows called. She would answer the calls of the other birds: the sparrows, the blackbirds, the wren. They didn't see George as the enemy. The wren had been singing every morning since she'd fed it with cheese last winter; and the blackbird sat on top of the telephone pole in the evening, singing for two hours at a stretch, and didn't raise the alarm when George went out to listen.

She was pulled from her reverie by a loud bang.

The pigeon! Now it was standing on the open skylight, on

84

the edge of the skylight, with its feet on the wooden casing, looking at her through the glass.

And George thought: what does he want?

She sat with her head turned, looking through the doorway, looking at the window, at the gap between the window and the wall, at the pigeon with his feet on the casing. And the pigeon looked at her.

Her neck began to stiffen and she looked away.

Then she heard a thud.

She leapt up, fearful that the bird was coming inside.

And there he was, underneath the skylight, standing on the window frame, poking his head through the gap.

"Shoo!" she said.

And she grabbed the window lever with one hand, and waved at the pigeon with the other.

Slowly she pulled down the skylight, leaving just a small gap, while the pigeon, hissing as it withdrew its head, leapt back onto the casing.

"What do you want, piggy? Is it food you're after?"

The pigeon stared at her through the skylight, cocking its head as if listening.

"What is it, piggy? What do you want?"

Their faces were just inches apart. And the pigeon appeared to be smiling! There was a twinkle in its eyes, and tiny wrinkles besides. It was like the smile of an old granny.

"Do you want some food? Are you hungry? There's plenty of grain outside. What is it you're after?"

The pigeon winked at her. Then it wagged its beak as she spoke, opening it then shutting it.

"You're hungry, aren't you? Is that what you're trying to tell me? Why don't you have some grain?"

She looked at its feet, a ring on one leg, a dark growth on the other, an inch long at least. It looked revolting.

So it's a domestic pigeon, she thought. A racing pigeon, I guess. Like the one that the hawk devoured.

"What do you want, piggy? Is it bread you're after? I'll see if I can find some bread, shall I?"

Along the corridor she walked, pulling down the skylights, leaving just a small gap. Down the stairs she walked, into the kitchen, taking a slice of wholemeal. Back up the stairs, along the corridor, past the pigeon, who stood there on the window, staring at her through the glass.

She walked into the bathroom. That skylight was still wide open. She tore the bread into chunks and threw them onto the roof; then she closed that window. The pigeon stayed put.

Back along the corridor.

They stared at each other through the glass.

"There's bread there!" she said, pointing.

The pigeon didn't move. It stood there cocking its head and winking, and it seemed to George that the bird was smiling.

"I give up then. I don't know what you want, you funny old thing."

At least it's not afraid of me, she thought. And if it's not afraid, it won't leave droppings all over the place.

It was difficult to reach the outside of the skylights. From the inside, anyway. And George cleaned the windows from the inside.

She returned to the picture window, to the pile of notes on the table.

Her rosemary tea had gone cold.

*

The pigeon was still there at dusk. George had decided to ignore it. It had stood there watching as she walked to and fro, into the bathroom, down the stairs, up the stairs, into the room with the picture window; the upstairs lounge, as they called it.

What did he want? She didn't want him in the house. It was bad enough with the wren last winter. Having feasted on her cheese, the wren had decided that George was a true friend, and wouldn't mind if she, the wren, slipped inside the house when the north wind blew. And George didn't mind, really – it was icy cold out there. So the wren had followed her about the house. The wren had sat on the teapot, watching George cook sausages, quite content just to sit and watch. But then, come bedtime, George didn't know what to do. The wren didn't want to leave, and George didn't want to go to bed with a wren in the house. The wren would have woken up in a strange place, she thought, and would have been frightened because she couldn't get out. And George didn't want to leave a window open as the wind was blowing with fury. On balance, she thought it better if the wren was shown the way out. So she opened a skylight and eventually – after much coaxing – the wren – with great reluctance, George thought – flew out into the dark night.

But a wren was one thing; a pigeon was another. There was no telling what a pigeon might do. Mess, for a start.

What did he want?

Watching her movements with great interest, his eyes blinking, and it really did look as though he were smiling.

Now it was dusk and the owl was whooping, a noise she'd yet to fathom. Possibly intended to frighten the voles into sudden movement, thereby exposing themselves to the owl's roving eye. The whoop started off like a cat's mewing; then exploded into a screech as the owl got very excited about something or other.

The pigeon didn't seem put out; the pigeon wasn't moving from his chosen spot, perched on the skylight. He was settling down to sleep now, with his head buried under his wings; rather like a tortoise, she thought. For safety no doubt, as a pigeon's head was a vulnerable thing. A favourite target for the falcon, for a start. And the owl might take an interest.

She turned out the light in the corridor. Now the pigeon was in semi-darkness. And outside, the owl whooped, whooped, and exploded into a screech.

A second owl screeched, from the other side of the house.

Then a third, and a fourth…

George walked down the stairs, through the living room, out into the yard.

"Quiet!" she said. "You noisy things! What a racket! We'll have the neighbours complaining if you carry on like that!"

She stood a while, pondering: who were the neighbours? There was no one else down the lane; the nearest house was the Moon pub. And up the lane, there was Rose Cottage, just over the brow, and that was currently unoccupied. Still, she thought, the owls don't know that.

They were silent now.

She walked inside, up the stairs, past the pigeon, who didn't seem put out at all. There he stood, his head buried under his wings.

Then the owl screamed.

And another.

And a third, and a fourth...

The screams were surrounding the house – one hell of a racket.

"Oh God!" said George, to herself this time. "How am I going to get to sleep if they carry on like this all night?"

Down the stairs she walked, asking herself, Why the racket? Perhaps it's the pigeon, she thought, standing on the window like that. He's drawing a crowd; four of them. Something's got them worked up. But they won't be told, not when they're in this state.

She walked into the kitchen, filled the kettle, still pondering. And outside, the owls whooped and screamed.

Then she realised.

The owl twins! There were four owls out there, all flying – the babies were flying! Their first flight – no wonder the excitement!

She made a cup of tea, took it upstairs, wondering what Richard would have made of it all.

And on the skylight the pigeon still perched, sleeping, it seemed, despite the racket.

A long line of mothers, heading for the school. Crawling along like a caterpillar. Held up by a tractor, no doubt. Yes, there it was, leading the queue – she could just see the bags of silage, flitting between the trees. She watched the train go past – ten, twenty cars in all – while the babble on the radio continued.

The morning's news. The war against poverty. American planes in bombing raids in the Middle East. It was all very confusing, especially when you weren't paying attention. Someone had got it wrong, surely? Eliminating poverty by bombing the poor – whose idea was that? Surely, even the American President wasn't as devilish as that? Perhaps they'd misunderstood his instructions.

Perhaps not.

The age of uncertainty, as someone said.

Next item: legal wrangles.

You can kill foxes, but you can't chase them with foxhounds. Or can you? No, that wasn't right, you can chase foxes, but your dogs mustn't kill them. No, that wasn't right either – it was illegal to hunt wild animals with dogs. So then, Eric Finch at the Moon, taking out his spaniel to look for rats, was actually breaking the law. Or was he?

It was all very confusing. Now you could be breaking the law by doing something you've always done. You could be a criminal, and you wouldn't know.

The age of uncertainty: more work for lawyers.

Next item. A scientist doubts global warming. No, that wasn't right. Global warming exists, he says; no doubt there – but he doubts whether it's the fault of us humans. Could be the result of circumstances beyond our control, natural processes that we don't quite understand. After all, we're still recovering from the last Ice Age…

Perhaps he has a point, she thought, remembering an item about the sun – solar explosions on the sun's surface; the equivalent of God knows how many atomic bombs going off.

Surely, she thought, we would feel the heat? Why doesn't anybody make the connection? Maybe the sun itself is getting warmer. Hotter and hotter, till it explodes, and ends up burnt out; then we're all done for. The doomsday scenario. The big bang. Going out as we entered, if you believe the theories...

Enough!

Just a quick blast of the local news – then it would be time to feed the birds.

The progress of the Naked Rambler. Arrested, yet again. Undeterred, he expects to be walking over Nettleton Common next Monday...

Monday! Shopping day! She could go out in the afternoon, walk up to the downs with her binoculars. Nettleton Common wasn't far away. Imagine, if he came through Quinton! And stopped at the Moon for a quick half! She could offer him lunch. Or tea...

It was time to feed the birds.

*

The pigeon had perched on a telephone pole, watching her. She knew it was the same one because of the way it sat there, cocking its head. And it had a sort of blue-green patch on its neck; a sheen that was catching the sun. As she moved about with her bags of feed, chattering away to the birds, the patch seemed to change colour, till at one point it shone like a rainbow.

It was an odd bird, she thought. Too familiar, in the way it had tried to climb inside, the day before. A little bit frightening. And its expression! Smiling at her with those twinkling eyes, a bit too human-like. And too bold, the way it's flown down to the yard now, pecking at the stone flags, approaching her without a hint of fear.

She scattered a few seeds.

Now she noticed that the pigeon walked with a slight limp, as if its foot was injured. It must be that horrible growth, she thought, staring at it. And now she saw that the growth was symmetrical, shaped like an ellipse, with thin yellow lines curling around it, and thin wires, which curled around the bird's leg. It wasn't a growth at all: it looked like a metal locket, attached to its leg. And weighing the poor bird down, she thought.

The pigeon pecked at the seeds.

George walked past, heading towards the house. The feeding over, she sat down by the front door, on an old wooden bench, watching the finches at the feeders. The pigeon walked towards her, cocking its head.

"Now what do you want, piggy?" she said. "I've given you some seed. And you don't like bread."

The bird seemed to be listening, wagging its head as she spoke.

Then it suddenly flew at her – she raised her arms and covered her face – and landed on her shoulder with a flap and a flutter.

She was too frightened to move; her hands still covered her face.

"Now what do you want?" she said, an eye peeping between her fingers. "You really are an odd thing, aren't you?"

She felt the bird's warmth against her hand. Soft and warm, brushing against her. Yet she was on the verge of panicking: what if it took a fancy to her ears? Bit off a lobe? She edged a thumb in that direction, wishing that her hair was longer, wishing that she hadn't had it bobbed in the spring – and the bird, with a flap that sent George to her feet, flew to the ground and walked away.

George sat down again, feeling her shoulder, feeling her face. There was blood on her fingers.

"You funny old thing," she said. "Look what you've done! You frightened me then. What on earth do you want?"

Not food, she thought; there's plenty of food about. Love and affection, maybe. But how do you give a bird love and affection? By feeding them, for a start. By talking to them. By protecting them from potential enemies, especially when they're nesting. One could do no more.

But that wasn't enough for this bird. This bird was just too human-like, standing there watching her with an expression that reminded George of an old aunt.

The bird was trying to tell her something.

She looked at the metal thing, attached to its leg.

"What do you want to tell me?" she said. "Come on then, show me your foot."

The pigeon pecked at the flags.

"Oh, now you're being coy," said George. "All right, I'm going inside then."

She stood at the threshold, wondering whether to close the door. It was good to have a current of air blowing through the house. She left it ajar, pushing a jamb underneath. She glanced at the pigeon: it had returned to the trail of seed. Then she saw, just by the bench, a small black object.

She walked to the bench and picked it up. Tiny black screws in a plastic case, with a clip on one side. No controls, no display, no phone number, no address; just a serial number. It meant nothing to her. An unidentifiable flying object, which had fallen from the pigeon, she thought, in its mad encounter with her shoulder. Some kind of ID, perhaps.

She walked into the utility room, placed it on a shelf, and looked in the mirror. Nothing missing; it was her hand that was cut.

Pigeon racing has become too sophisticated, she thought, washing her hands and face. Whatever happened to the old metal tag? And why that locket thing, strapped to its leg? Curious…

Back upstairs to her favourite room, where the pile of notes waited on the table. She picked up a page.

"Apart from breeding, and warding off the enemy, all they do is chase each other, make love and feast, and when they do stop for a rest, they watch everything with that panoramic 360 degree vision of theirs. They certainly enjoy life to the full.

Why can't we?"

That was Richard on the swallows…

And now: a thud. The pigeon had landed on the skylight.

"Oh God!" she said. "This bird!"

She stared at it. It wasn't going to leave her alone, it seemed.

A stalker! Imagine – being stalked by a bird!

Yet the bird was harmless, she reasoned. It was just… overly friendly. And obsessed with George, for some reason.

The bird was trying to tell her something; that seemed obvious. The bird was carrying something. The bird was carrying a message, intended for George. But no, she thought, that's absurd. Why should someone send me a pigeon? And who?

No, the bird was on a mission – most likely a race. But then, why stop here? Why hang about the place, and stare smilingly at you, as if it wanted a home? Maybe, because the bird was homeless. Maybe, the bird had been held in captivity; the bird was an escaped prisoner. Inside that metal thing was a message, saying, "Please help me. I am being tortured by a cruel pigeon merchant."

The bird wanted a home…

The house was big enough. Four rooms upstairs, plus the bathroom. There was the lounge at this end, with the picture window; then two small bedrooms, and a large bedroom at the other end, on the other side of the stairs. They used to joke about it, calling it The Master Bedroom. George didn't use it now, hadn't used it since The Master was no more. Now she slept in the small bedroom, next to the lounge, and closer to the bathroom.

Then there was downstairs. The large lounge, underneath the master bedroom, with the big bay window, overlooking the garden; a lounge that George didn't use, it being so dark in there. And the living room, which was also dark. She didn't use that either. If she was downstairs, it was either the kitchen or the utility room. Or the toilet. And upstairs, the lounge or the bedroom. Or the bathroom.

There was plenty of room for a lodger; that was certain. And a pigeon wouldn't take up too much space. Leave a window open, and it could come and go as it pleased...

"What am I thinking of!" she said, turning away with a stiff neck. "Pigeons live outside, they don't live indoors!"

And the pigeon started to coo, a quiet coo, more like a purr.

George stood up now and looked at it.

So why, she wondered, does this one want to come indoors? But perhaps it doesn't want to come indoors, perhaps it just likes company.

"What do you want, piggy?" she said. "Why won't you let me look at your foot?"

She walked out of the room, passing the pigeon without speaking, along the corridor, down the stairs, through the living room and out through the open door.

She sat on the bench.

I'll give him five minutes, she decided.

The pigeon didn't show.

She returned to the lounge: the pigeon had flown. Not far though. It was on the roof of the grain shed, pecking at the moss.

He knew, she said to herself. He wasn't put out because he knew I'd come back; he knew it was just a game, and he couldn't be bothered to play.

In the afternoon, she decided to go for a walk. Just a short walk, up to the downs and back. It was really because she wanted to see what the pigeon would do. Would it follow, or would it stay put?

And sure enough, the pigeon decided to follow. She walked up the lane, and the bird flew from tree to tree, following the brook. She left the lane and walked up the muddy path between the trees, listening to the flap of his wings. As she crossed the field, the bird raced ahead and settled in a tree. She walked up the green track, and the bird stayed put. It was the last tree before the ground rose sharply to the downs.

When George reached the top, she looked through her

binoculars. The pigeon was still there, on the uppermost branches.

Now, she mused, what if I walked on? What if I walked to Stanton Parva? Would he follow me then?

But she didn't want to walk on; she'd reached the downs and that was that.

And the bird had followed, thus far.

She scanned the landscape, looking for naked ramblers. No sign. Too early yet.

She turned back. So did the pigeon.

Then it struck her again that the bird knew – the bird had made its own observations, and concluded there was no point flying any further because George had reached her limit. George would be coming back.

Most uncanny, she thought – it was as if the bird could detect her motives, as if the bird was testing her; and the bird knew better than she did that she wouldn't want to go any further.

She walked down the lane, perplexed, while the pigeon flew from treetop to treetop.

The nagging question: what did he want?

The pigeon was pecking at the stone flags when she returned. She sat on the wooden bench.

The secret's in that locket, attached to its leg, she thought. He's been sent with a message, and he's decided to give it to me – there's no other explanation.

"Come on, piggy," she said. "Come and show me your foot."

The pigeon cocked its head, but there was no mad flight this time. She coaxed and coaxed, and the pigeon pecked and pecked, yet listened.

"Oh, blow you then!" she said, and went inside.

*

That was another thing about blackbirds – they could see

through net curtains. There was George, sat in the downstairs toilet, the only room in the house with a net curtain, and there was the blackbird, pinking outside. Because of George, behind the curtain – he could sense her shape, peering at him. And he always did this. He had a thing about net curtains. If he spotted you inside, in a room without a curtain, he wasn't worried. But stick up a net curtain and it bothered him. He couldn't see what you were up to, that was the thing. Yet the power of his vision! He could see inside, more clearly than George could see outside. Which rather defeated the purpose of a net curtain. Now the entire neighbourhood would know that George was sitting on the toilet.

If there were any neighbours to hear, she thought.

The house was really too big for her to manage. But she couldn't bear the thought of moving. They had settled here. And there was always the possibility that her brother might want to visit, with the three kids. Their last visit was five years ago, when his wife was expecting. These days, they rarely spoke from one month to the next. The kids were so time-consuming. And it was a long journey, from Yorkshire; the kids would be bored. Still, they might want to visit. She couldn't remember her last visitor. She couldn't remember anyone, apart from the postman, crossing the threshold for years. It just wasn't done in these parts. One normally went to fêtes and village halls to see people.

Unless you happened to be a bird, such as a pigeon.

She had decided.

She would leave the window open, in the big bedroom. Then the bird could sleep there, if it wanted to. And George could creep in and inspect its foot. If he didn't mind. He obviously liked the place. And he was intelligent, more so than the normal pigeon. It would be a shame to see him go, in fact. His face was so comical, with those twinkling eyes and that smile-like expression. And the way he wagged his beak! As if he was trying to speak. Imitating her mouth movements, his beak opening and closing.

Perhaps she could teach him to speak. Hilda Faber had a pet budgie who, according to Hilda, could speak. It was company, she said. God knows what the bird said. Knowing Hilda, the bird might be quite vulgar. Imagine! A young man at the door, and the budgie saying, "Toy boy! Toy boy! Give us a kiss, toy boy!" And possibly worse. Much, much worse.

Possibly, the net curtain was the wrong way round...

*

Now that George had opened the window, she was having second thoughts. What if, the message delivered, the bird decided to leave? Well, she thought, and what if? The bird must belong to somebody. The bird doesn't belong to me. He'll go when he's ready, and that'll be that. Besides, the owner might be worried about him. It's probably got a contact number on its foot. If I can find it, I can ring the owner.

She remembered the last time. A headless pigeon, lying by the leap gate at the top of the garden. A metal tag on its leg, with a phone number. Burnley of all places! They were on the phone for an hour, talking about her old haunts, lamenting the loss of the cinemas, the ballrooms, the corner shops. Chatting to a complete stranger, on the phone, about pigeons and hawks and falcons and the state of her garden.

The plastic object is probably a speedometer, she thought. Or a mileage counter. God knows how it works. I must ring the owner and tell him it's fallen off.

That night, the bird ignored the open window. It found a place in the grain shed, tucked between the beam at the front and the roof. The owls were screaming. George worried about him. Pointlessly – the owls were looking for voles.

The next day, his obsession seemed to be on the wane. She pottered about in the garden, and the bird kept his distance. Often she would look up and see him on the top of a telephone pole, observing. But he wasn't looking at her; he was looking at the downs. It was as if he was preparing to take off.

Then, at dusk, the pigeon landed on the open window. She heard a thud, then the sound of his feet, scratching the glass. The skylight, fully open, was horizontal. She could hear him sliding about on the glass; then another thud, inside.

She waited for him to settle. Later, she heard a cooing, coming from the bedroom. She waited till all was quiet.

Then the owls started whooping.

It was never quiet in the countryside, even at night.

She'd jammed the door ajar; it had an irritating squeak. She was about to step inside when she was struck by a memory – the date! She'd forgotten the date! It was the anniversary! Richard's death! Why hadn't she thought of it before?

She felt sick. Yet she must go in; it was too late now. Her hands were shaking, her stomach churning.

Moonlight on the quilt. And on Richard...

No, not Richard. On the bird, lying in the centre of it, his head erect, listening.

George listened.

Snoring.

Richard, snoring...

No, not Richard. And not the pigeon. That sound was coming from the owl, from the grain shed outside.

She sat on the bed.

The pigeon hopped away, onto a pillow. She coaxed, using baby talk.

"Come on, piggy, come to me. Who's a good boy then. Show me your foot..."

Soft words, cooing words, enticing. The bird walked towards her. And then, flopped into the quilt.

Her hands, flat on the bed. It wasn't going to work, she thought; she ought to be behind it – now the bird would fly at her, if she reached.

But the bird didn't flinch as she moved her hands. She slid them across the quilt, and the bird didn't flinch. Didn't flinch as she reached up to cup the body.

Then the bird jumped. She should have warmed her hands.

She waited a while, feeling the soft warmth.

Richard, warming her hands…

She picked him up, placed him on her lap. She studied his leg, studied the locket. She saw a silver clasp, catching the moonlight. She stretched her little finger and pressed hard, till the clasp pierced her skin. She heard a bump.

The locket was open, and empty inside. She closed it, released the bird. Still it didn't move, looking up at her as if surprised. She placed him on the quilt.

And on the carpet, what? An object about an inch long. White, it seemed; but that might have been the moonlight.

She picked it up. It felt like a tooth; she couldn't quite see…

She stepped outside, into the light – it was a tooth! An old tooth, with brown stains, yellow stains, green mould, strands of moss, dirt and grit – a dog's tooth. No – human! A fang but human, complete with root and crown. A canine tooth. And quite disgusting. Totally disgusting.

Today, of all days!

She tossed it to the floor, raced along the corridor, into the bathroom, and puked.

Outside, the owls whooped and screamed.

*

A sleepless night. Those owls! And that tooth! Sleep, finally, at 4am, followed by nightmares. The usual ones and more – worms devouring corpses, death masks, fangs with dripping blood, horrible little green men dancing about in the garden, and all sorts.

She didn't wake up until noon. Noon! And she hadn't fed the birds! The tooth – she picked it up and took it outside, planted it by the little animal cemetery, which they'd always called the mound. Then she fed the birds.

It was her own fault, she thought. She should have left it alone. Pandora's box. A can of worms. The cat, let out of the bag. What did it mean? A sick joke. But who could do such a thing?

She blamed Carol McGregor, for reasons that were inexplicable. She just knew that somehow Carol was involved. Carol was laughing at her, at her foolishness. Now she had sunk into a pit of depression, and must turn to Carol for help. Which Carol knew, of course. Carol was in control. Weeks of therapy could be undone, just like that, by Carol's idea of a sick joke.

Meanwhile, the pigeon pecked at the stone flags, totally oblivious to the devastation it had caused.

She looked at it.

She could hardly blame the pigeon, poor thing. Still limping, despite its loss. And the locket wasn't heavy; so it must be limping because of an injury.

And what will he do, she wondered, when I go out for the day?

Which would be… tomorrow. It was Sunday already.

Sunday! She must prepare for Monday!

The shopping list…

5

George stood at the bus stop, watching the swallows, the fields, the lane; scanning the trees. She was still shaking from the morning's trauma. She didn't want him to follow her, and she didn't want him to leave. But would she recognise him? There were so many pigeons about – wood pigeons, collared doves, hybrids; flocks in the distance…

A car zoomed past: the bus shelter rattled. She withdrew into the shelter and counted her change.

This week, the bus was almost on time.

A different driver. Fewer people.

"Hello," she said. "Isn't it warm?"

"Return, is it?" said the driver.

"Yes please."

No Maurice Warnock, no Mrs Foss. Two college girls from Stockwood Melrush, a lad from Plumstone Abbas. Plus Mr and Mrs Bartlett, Mary Holloway, and…

"Hello George," Jean shouted.

"Hello Jean," said George.

She found a seat behind Mary Holloway.

"School holidays not started yet then?" said George.

"No, next week," said Mary.

George stared out of the window, feeling thoroughly antisocial.

Mary turned with a wry smile and said, "I hear you had a lecture on Wednesday."

"A lecture?" said George. "Oh, the Lavender Club. Yes, Stephen Grove. He caused a bit of a stir."

"So I gather," said Mary. "I don't know what's come over him."

"No, it was a bit of a shock. He sounds quite normal when

you read his column in the paper. Still, it made a change, I suppose."

"A change!" Mary said, and laughed.

A pause, then she said: "Mrs Foss is still in hospital."

"Oh dear," said George. "And how are you feeling yourself? You didn't make it on Wednesday."

"No, I had a bad cold last week. I felt worn out. I haven't been out the house."

"Strange time for a cold."

"I know, but there's one or two who've gone down with it. There's something going round, I doubt."

George stared out of the window, feeling thoroughly antisocial.

That bird!

The morning's trauma – another attempt to land on her shoulders. She, sat on the bench, and in a rush to finish the chores. And what if? Her greatest fear – that the bird would land on her head and she wouldn't be able to shake it off. Ten minutes to catch the bus, and she'd arrive at the bus stop with a pigeon on her head. Or her shoulders. She'd have to take it on the bus.

Showing off her new friend.

"And how much is it for the bird?"

"Return is it?"

"Yes please."

A curse and a blessing. Blighted by a stalker, yet flattered by his attention.

No, not blighted. She loved him.

Which was a curse, she thought. Because she cared more for animals than she did for people. She didn't care for people, and it just wasn't natural. Besides, love was binding; any love. It tied you down…

But someone had to care more, to redress the balance. And she had been blessed by having a rapport. Blessed by the capacity for love. And they trusted her, which was a great honour, not to be snubbed or flouted. It came with responsibilities. Not to let them down.

Yet she wouldn't want them to become tame. That meant dependency. And dependency tied you down.

Blessed by love. Which was a curse…

Damn Carol McGregor! It was all her fault. She knew this would happen.

Top Down already. No Arthur Blagdon today.

Arthur Blagdon! She'd meant to ask Kate Wimbourne about him.

"Hello Kate," Jean shouted.

"Good morning ladies," said Kate, checking the seats for any unfamiliar faces.

The usual fuss about finding change: as if she didn't know by now how much the fare had increased.

"I'm all sixes and sevens this morning," said Kate. "So that means you want another 5p. Just a minute…"

No Tina Weymouth today. Just Kate and Barbara Smiles.

"Now then, ladies," said Kate, sitting opposite George. "What did you think of that Stephen Groves? Wasn't he awful? Is his name Grove or Groves?"

"Oh, I am sorry," said Barbara, sitting opposite Mary. "I didn't know he was going to go on like that."

"I didn't think he was that bad," said George.

"You didn't?" said Kate. "Poor old Mrs Chilcott – she fainted."

"I hope it hasn't put you off," said Barbara.

"No, not at all," said George.

"Who's coming next, Barbara?" Mary asked.

"We've got Emily Quiddington talking about snails," said Barbara.

"Oh, that sounds… interesting," said George.

"Let's hope she doesn't upset Mrs Chilcott," said Kate.

"I think snails are fairly safe," said George.

"She might show us some slides," Kate said, and put a hand over her mouth, as if she'd said something very naughty.

"Stephen's slides," Barbara muttered.

"It was right what he said about the government though," said Kate, frowning. "Don't you think so, George?"

"Yes, they can't be trusted," said George.

She stared out of the window, feeling thoroughly antisocial.

Yesterday's trauma – thinking about today. Leaving the bird, and what would he do. Filled with panic and doing her list.

The last time she'd felt like this was the summer of the magpie. The swallows, nesting in the porch, and the psychopath who turned up every day, waiting for the right moment. The defenceless moment. And not only every day, but several times during the day. Morning, noon and night. Dawn watch, dusk watch, and George not wanting to tear herself away. Racing back from the day's shopping, expecting a disaster. Which didn't happen.

Baby killer: two now, flying across the fields.

"No Hilda today," said Kate.

"She doesn't come every week," said Mary. "It's every four weeks, when she has her hair done."

The outskirts of Middleton Magna. Cynthia Butterwick.

"Hello, hello, hello Jean," said Cynthia, sitting down in a fluster. "Oh, I had some goings on last night. We had to call the police. There was a man in the garden, I thought he was trying to break in to our shed. He was running over the backs of the houses, shouting and swearing and what not. They didn't catch him."

"Oh!" said Mary.

"What did he want?" said Kate.

"I don't know what he was after," said Cynthia. "The police said he'd stolen a car. I think he must have been drunk. He wasn't wearing a shirt, I thought he didn't have any clothes on…"

"The Naked Rambler!" said George.

"Pardon?" said Cynthia.

"You know – that man who's walking to the Isle of Wight, naked," said George.

"Oh, him," said Cynthia. "No, it wasn't him. I think it was someone who'd had one too many."

"I think that Naked Rambler's had one too many," said Kate.

Middleton Magna. Mrs Webb and Mrs Norton. Susan Chard with two daughters. That girl whose name George could never remember, with a pushchair and two tots.

"Are you all right?" Susan Chard said to Cynthia. Then, turning to Kate Wimbourne, "We had a maniac in the village last night."

"So we've been hearing," said Kate.

"They've found the car," said Susan.

"Have they caught him?" said Cynthia.

"No, they're still looking for him," said Susan.

"I was frightened to death," said Cynthia. "My son was out, and you know how it is when you're on your own. There's nobody you can call on, is there? And when you see a man half-naked in the garden…"

"Did Hilda see him?" said Kate.

"I think she was in bed," said Cynthia.

"That was fortunate," said Kate. "She'd have invited him in, knowing her."

"Oh, Hilda!" said Cynthia. "She's embarrassing…"

George's conclusion – there was something in the newly hatched bird that made it particularly tasty to the magpie. One day, two day, three, four days old – after a week his interest fades. She had willed them to grow, to grow fast, beyond his reach. And her prayer, if it was a prayer, had been answered: that moment when they left the nest!

His timing had been uncanny. He seemed to know just when the eggs were about to hatch. He was there, waiting, charging at the porch at first light. The swallows screaming, calling George. George, leaning out of the window, just in time…

Puddleton St Margaret. Mrs Drake, clutching a stick.

No one told her about the madman. Mrs Drake was old and

frail and lived on her own. Why give her cause to worry?

Bowldish Farm. Sally Weymouth standing by a huge puddle.

"Have they caught him yet?" she said, to Susan Chard.

"No, he's still on the loose," said Susan. Then, throwing caution aside, she turned to Mrs Drake and said, "We had a drunken driver in the village last night."

"Oh," said Mrs Drake. "Did he do any damage?"

"He made a mess of our fence," said Cynthia.

"He ran across our flowerbeds," said Susan.

"He drove through your garden?" said Mrs Drake.

"No, he left the car. The police were chasing him…"

The pigeon was a different matter. He'd slept indoors again last night; George had left the window open for him. She'd heard the sound of his feet, scratching the glass, the thud as he hopped to the floor. She crept inside later, to find him on the quilt again. And this time, he had hopped into her lap without any coaxing. Softly cooing as she stroked his feathers…

George couldn't make him out. His foot was sore; he may have been injured by something or other, and wanted rest and recuperation. Some of that – what was it? – TLC, the ads called it. Tender loving care. If he wanted a home, she would offer him a home…

The golf course. Mrs Snape with her ancient shopping trolley.

"She's on again," said Mary.

"She's becoming a regular," said Kate.

The traffic lights. No Templetons today. George would make do with Pomeroys and Samways.

The High Street. They all piled off.

Kick-off time.

Mrs Snape, marching up the road with her trolley. Susan Chard, strolling down the road with her daughters. Mrs Webb and Mrs Norton, arm in arm, ambling to the nearest shop window. That girl whose name George could never

106

remember, arranging her pushchair and two tots. Barbara Smiles, merging seamlessly with the flow of the tourists – seconds pass, and she's out of sight in the stream.

Meanwhile, the chatterers, hanging about. Kate Wimbourne and Mary Holloway, talking to Mr and Mrs Bartlett. Sally Weymouth talking to Cynthia Butterwick. Jean Mortimer talking to Mrs Drake.

George was in no mood for a dawdle.

Go directly to Pomeroys: pass the can shakers, the flag wavers, and look for bargains.

Aber Valley extra mature cheddar – half-price, this week only. Pomeroys sunflower spread, reduced by 30p. Pomeroys luxury cornflakes, family size – two for the price of one.

Midway to the till, she decided to take them back. This week was potato week, she recalled, and she couldn't carry the cornflakes, family size, two packs, plus a large sack of potatoes.

These were the moments when she wished she could drive, or had a neighbour she could call on at short notice. And how would she cope in the future? When a small bag of sugar would feel like a leaden weight?

She didn't like to think about it.

Next, Popes the newsagents for the Lydiard Advertiser and the Stanford Chronicle. She didn't look at the cafeteria beyond; she avoided glancing till she was outside. Yes, sure enough, there was Kate Wimbourne and Mary Holloway, having their private tête-à-tête. Mrs Drake was there too, sitting alone with a pot of tea. Waiting for her brother, no doubt. The last time, he didn't show. Sad.

Meanwhile, the post office; then the cashpoint machine.

Next, meat. Or should she leave it till later?

Stood on the pavement, consulting her list, she met Jean Mortimer coming in the opposite direction.

A diversion.

Jean had just taken some old bric-a-brac to the Cats Protection League. Jean was still very upset about her cat.

She'd had it put down, the vet recommended it. There was nothing else she could do. His kidneys had gone. Didn't George like cats? George ought to have a cat. They're company...

Next: eggs, bacon and sausages from Millers the butchers. Then the bread – into Market Square to Helliers the bakers. Followed by the trek backwards, along the High Street for the odd items: water filters from Wheeler's Wholefoods; personal items from Youngs the chemists...

Damn! And a birthday card for her nephew – it must be bought, written and posted to arrive on time. The card shop – another trek across town. And she had Samways to do yet; plus the veg. There was no time to browse the latest paperbacks in Homer's Books, and no time to scan the window.

Samways: Mrs Snape, blocking the aisle with her shopping trolley. Cynthia Butterwick, telling Jean Mortimer about the madman in the garden. Susan Chard, talking to Kate Wimbourne about the maniac in her garden. Her daughters, inspecting the chocolate. Mary Holloway, scanning the shelves.

George studied her list.

The basics: cocoa, Horlicks, honey...

Diversion: chat with Mary Holloway.

Next: a meat pie from Mr Pike the butcher.

A selection of cheeses. Brown sauce and tomato ketchup. Another chat with Jean Mortimer. The price of meat pies. Things you could get in Paulsbury that you couldn't get in Lydiard Forum. Paulsbury market on Saturdays. Mayonnaise and sandwich spread – moved to a different shelf. And the chutney – don't forget the chutney...

"Yes, I'll see you in a bit," George said, to Kate Wimbourne.

First: fruit and veg from Thatchers. Derek away today, his son serving.

A quick walk around the market, looking for bargains. More strawberries from Spain, reduced. For the blackbirds. Plus, bird food from the pet stall; cheese from the cheese stall;

more tomatoes; more nuts…

She sat on a bench and scribbled a card. The postbox – the other side of town. She would post it when she got off the bus, using the local stump.

Finally, half an hour for a sit down.

In the Forum Rooms, Kate Wimbourne was telling Cynthia Butterwick about Stephen Grove. George sat down with a cup of tea.

"It was dreadful," said Kate. "Mrs Chilcott fainted. Wasn't it dreadful, George?"

"I didn't think it was that bad," said George.

"George is a fan of Robert Mugabe," said Kate, winking at George.

"Stephen Grove made some interesting points, I thought," said George, blushing. "I agree with him on the government…"

"Yes, he was right there," said Kate.

"They're corrupt," said George. "And as for Blair, he's ruining the country. I think he needs a good slap on the face…"

"With a wet kipper!" said Kate.

"Where's Sally?" said Mary Holloway, joining the table.

"She's not coming," said Cynthia. "She was still doing her shopping when I saw her."

"Oh!" said Mary.

"We were just talking about Robert Mugabe," said Kate, winking at George. "George thinks he'd make a good Prime Minister."

"Oh?" said Mary.

"She's joking," said George.

George wished that Kate wouldn't do this. George knew that Kate had never seen a black man in her entire life. They were aliens, as far as she was concerned, and a suitable butt for jokes.

On this issue, they were worlds apart.

And George wished that Kate wouldn't do this because, if pushed too far, she would be forced to say so, and a rift would open up between them. Or rather, the rift would be made obvious. Best not to say anything, she thought.

But then, because she didn't say anything, they wondered what she really thought. And egged her on, provoking her to speak her mind...

"I'm no fan of Mugabe," she said, "but it's true what Stephen said about farming coming from the East. I think people forget that."

"Do you miss teaching, George?" said Kate.

"I wouldn't like to be a teacher now," said George. "The education system's falling apart..."

"And look at the way they dress!" said Kate, nodding at a nearby table.

George wished that Kate wouldn't do this either. Three heads had now turned to the nearby table, with disapproving stares and frowns. And four heads at the nearby table, noting the fact, were reddening as they ate.

College kids: their lunch break. Wearing jeans that looked like they were about to fall down but were actually designed that way – lots of air space around the backside. And jeans that looked like cast-offs from a burnt-out rodeo star, but were actually designed that way too...

"And look at the way they eat!" said Kate. "Ooh, it makes me feel sick!"

Kate, pulling a face, looked as though she were about to vomit into her tea.

George threw a sideways glance: plates full of chips, burger baps, and a hint of lettuce.

Kate didn't eat chips. Not only that, but Kate didn't believe in the very concept. The concept of chips came with attachments, like grease and fat and the smell of vinegar, chip shops and mushy peas, kids hanging around street corners, and goodness knows what else. It just wasn't ladylike.

"Look at the time!" said Mary. "I'd better take a trip upstairs."

"Is it time already?" said Kate.

George breathed a mental sigh, grateful they were now

leaving. Kate was quite eccentric, she thought. Chips weren't ladylike; yet she smoked like the proverbial chimney. Manners were everything; yet she stared at people just feet away to the point where it became embarrassing. Had nobody told her it was rude to stare?

But then, this was her weekly outing. George's weekly outing. The chance to look at things other than cows and pheasants and bags of silage. Like, people. College kids. How they dressed and what they ate. Even so, to stare like that...

No Bertha Bradstock today. Just the regulars, and less of them.

The driver, doing the tally.

"Mrs Webb and Mrs Norton aren't coming back," said Kate.

"And Mrs Drake isn't coming back," said the driver. "She's got a lift with her brother, she said."

"Sally isn't coming back," said Cynthia. "She's got a lift with a neighbour."

"She bought a return," said the driver. "Are you sure?"

"That's what she said," said Cynthia. "She must have met somebody, I suppose. She said, don't bother waiting for her."

"I wonder who that was then," said Mary Holloway.

"I don't know," said Cynthia.

Another mystery of Magnus Chase. Bowldish Farm was an isolated place, harassed by the winds that blew across the golf course. The nearest houses were in Puddleton St Margaret. Who was Sally Weymouth's neighbour?

First off was Mrs Snape and her ancient trolley. There was no Sally to drop off, and no Mrs Drake. Several faces stared out of the windows at the large prairie fields, as if they were all looking for a trace of Sally's neighbour.

"I can't think who that would be," said Mary Holloway.

Mary Holloway had lived on Magnus Chase for decades. She knew every house and most of the occupants, by name at least. Except for the new arrivals in Middleton Magna, who had bought the latest plots.

Susan Chard wasn't one of them. Her daughters helped her

with the shopping as they all stepped off with a round of cheerios. Followed by that girl with the tots and the pushchair, whose name…

"What is her name?" George whispered to Mary.

"I don't know," said Mary.

Next off was Cynthia Butterwick.

"Ooh, look at Hilda!" said Kate Wimbourne.

Hilda was sitting on a bench, sunning herself by the side of her house.

"Thank God she's got her clothes on," said Kate.

"Bye everybody," said Cynthia.

George missed seeing Hilda today. She'd meant to tell her about the Naked Rambler. Hilda was the one person on Magnus Chase who would have sympathised. Apart from George, of course. Too old to be a naked rambler though; Hilda's arthritis was very bad.

The narrow road to Top Down.

"Right, back to the city centre," said Kate, gathering her bags.

"Just here, please driver," said Barbara Smiles.

But she was so soft-spoken that the driver didn't hear. The bus flew past Orchard Cottage and stopped at the bus shelter by the church. Barbara muttered a lament.

"Bye everybody, see you next week, all being well," said Kate. "Bye Mary, bye Jean."

And a nod to George, which prompted the question: now what have I done?

The bus turned, drove back along the valley to the main road. Most of the silage had been gathered now. Yet still there were one or two bags, scattered here and there. Huge black bulging things…

George wondered whether Kate could read her mind.

She gathered her shopping – three bags in one hand, three in the other – and walked down the aisle, saying goodbye to Jean Mortimer, Mr and Mrs Bartlett, Mary Holloway, the driver.

It stopped at the bottom of the lane.

She stepped off, Jean waving as usual, then remembered the postbox. It was by the bus shelter, which meant crossing the road.

She delved into a bag and posted the card.

Down the road, at the Moon, Eric Finch was in the car park, bending over the bonnet of his van. He saw her and waved. She waved back. A car zoomed past. The bus shelter rattled.

She crossed the road, walked up the lane, the steep climb to Greenslade Cottage. She was panting when she reached the gate.

A pause.

Then, down the path to the yard, looking for signs. He wasn't on the telephone pole; the thought had crossed her mind that he might be at the bus stop, waiting for her. Not in the grain shed either.

Past the bottom gate, which was always left open, and in through the back door, which she'd forgotten to lock in her morning's haste. Straight to the kettle, dumping the bags on the stone floor.

A cup of tea, before the ordeal of unloading…

But no, she must have a look around first.

Another look in the grain shed.

"Where are you, piggy?" she said.

Back through the open gate, searching the yard, the chicken shed, the wood shed. Walking across the terrace, searching that side of the house. Then the outhouse where the tools were stored – there were two wood pigeons on the roof, clapping wings. Foreplay. Reminding her that it was summer.

But no sign of that bird.

She stepped through the undergrowth, heading for the summerhouse. They called it the summerhouse. It was really a greenhouse, with bits missing. The swallows loved it – warm and dry, and they could come and go as they pleased. An ideal place for nesting. They were in there now, twittering merrily – the four newborns.

113

She envied them. Their freedom from bricks and mortar, and the pile that we call home. They would be gone in three months, leaving for a warmer clime. Travelling the globe, and returning to the same place, the same nest. Yet no attachments to bricks and mortar. If home is where the nests are, an alternative home might be found, which would do just as well. The invaders had shown that.

But this lot were the regulars, who had come here for years.

Why was their leaving so painful? And why did she feel so wistful? If the pigeon had gone, so what?

She walked back to the house, looking again at the tool shed, the yard, the wood shed, the chicken shed, the grain shed. She walked into the kitchen and picked up her binoculars.

Outside again.

She walked to the top of the garden, to the gate between the apple trees, disturbing the owl. Leaning against the gate, she looked through the binoculars.

She followed the line of the brook, down through Quinton Rushton. And her gaze continued, beyond the River Chuckle, crossing the valley to Triplecheek St Mary.

Triplecheek St Mary! They had walked there once, following the stream across the fields.

Once…

The second time, they didn't make it.

She turned and looked at the treetops. Through the binoculars, she followed the line of the trees, reaching to the foot of the downs. Wood pigeons, collared doves, hybrids; and on the downs, a man…

She dropped the binoculars, fingers shaking. The man was looking at her, through a pair of binoculars. And it wasn't the Naked Rambler; that was certain. The man was wearing clothes. And not any old clothes, but Richard's clothes. The man was wearing Richard's clothes. And not only that, but his face! Richard's face!

But it couldn't be Richard. Richard was dead.

She looked again. Still looking at her, and the man was Richard's twin – the same mop of grey hair, that cagoule that he used to wear, those overtrousers…

But he couldn't be Richard. And Richard didn't have any brothers.

She lowered her binoculars.

Who was he, and why was he looking at her?

She looked again. The man had gone.

It must have been a delusion, she thought. Like looking into a mirror, and seeing your partner's face. Richard's ghost! Surely not?

She was tempted to phone Carol McGregor. Carol McGregor had told her to ring if there was anything disturbing her, anything she wanted to discuss of a confidential nature. She hadn't rung so far. But maybe this was the occasion…

She looked again.

No, it wasn't a delusion. The man was there again, striding down the path now; blocked before by a dip in the slope. Who was he, and what did he want?

Oh, this is madness, she thought. He's probably a hiker, walking over the downs, and now he's heading for the Moon for a drink.

The shopping to unload; things to put in the fridge; things to put in the freezer; six bags to sort out. It usually took an hour, at least. And she must have that cup of tea.

She walked back to the house.

"Where are you, piggy?" she said.

She looked again at the tool shed, the yard, the wood shed, the chicken shed, the grain shed – the complete cycle, again.

A sense of loss, which might have overwhelmed her had she not been struck by two thoughts.

The first was that the pigeon was probably in the bedroom, upstairs, having a snooze. The window was still open, and he'd spent the last two nights in there, she reasoned.

The second was about that man up there. It was niggling,

and more disturbing – *Squiggles*.

Into the kitchen and straight to the kettle. She stared at the bags. The best part of Monday was taken up with shopping. The major event of the week, and soon it would be over.

But not yet.

She sat at the wooden table, took a sip of her tea, and thought of *Squiggles*.

A cagoule and a pair of overtrousers: regular wear for walkers, and the colours weren't unusual – a yellow cagoule, green overtrousers. That man up there – the clothes could have been a common coincidence.

But the label! Now she wished she'd checked – she could have sworn it said *Squiggles*. A red design on a yellow background, with a curly *S*, top and bottom both serpentine, and a *quiggles* that ended in another curly *s*, winding around itself – Richard's cagoule. And it must be Richard's, she thought, because the firm had gone out of business six years ago. These days, you didn't see anybody wearing a Squiggles cagoule. They used to be a local firm, based in Lydiard. Making products for walkers. They'd only lasted two years.

And where was the damned thing? Hanging up in the utility room, where it's always been.

She opened the door and felt sick. The clothes peg, empty. Someone had walked into the house and taken Richard's clothes. Someone who looked like Richard. Taken his clothes, and more – his binoculars were missing!

Then she heard a knock on the door. The back door, close to the kitchen. She nearly died. She never had visitors; only delivery men called at this time of the day, and she wasn't expecting anything.

"Who…?"

She had to clear her throat, cursing the fact that she still hadn't finished that cup of tea.

"Who is it?"

"Excuse me," said a man's voice.

She looked for a suitable weapon. Plastic knives – useless.

Nothing better than a trowel. She walked into the kitchen, clutching the trowel with a trembling hand. Another knock on the door. The man hadn't heard her.

"Excuse me," he said.

The man had an accent: he sounded Spanish.

"Who is it?" she said, searching for a knife.

Too late: the man appeared in the doorway.

"I am so sorry, madame. However, the doors have been opened."

"I quite often leave them open," she said. "But I don't expect to see strangers walking about and taking things."

So polite, she thought. And definitely Mediterranean. Dark hair, bronze face. And a youngish look about him.

"I can explain," he said. "You see, we arrive, and the doors is open."

"The doors were open."

"Excuse me?"

"Were open, not is open. The doors were open."

"Sorry, madame, I am not understanding."

Suddenly a crash, coming from the living room.

"Oh my God! What was that?" said George.

She peeped around the living-room door and saw nothing. Whoever it was – whatever it was – had disappeared into the toilet, or the utility room, or gone up the stairs, or through the door into the corridor that led to the…

She turned and nearly died – again!

Whoever-it-was had gone into the utility room, and now he'd entered the kitchen – a man dishevelled and bloody. Tall and thin, dishevelled and bloody, with cuts across his face, a gash above his eye where the blood had congealed, eyes red and swollen, dark hair streaked with mud, shirt hanging in strips, trousers covered in mud. And in his hand – a crowbar, hanging by his side.

George remembered a monster from a 3D movie: the creature from the black lagoon…

"I'll handle this, Miguel," said the creature. Then, to

George: "Where's the bird?"

Another accent; this one sounded French. She was surrounded – Miguel at one end of the kitchen, blocking an escape via the back door; the creature at the other, blocking the door into the utility room. And behind her, the door into the living room; ajar. She edged towards it.

"I thunk, think," she said, "I'm due for an explosion, explanation."

Miguel reached for a pocket. The creature lifted the crowbar.

"Don't try anything, Miguel," he said.

George was beginning to swoon. The creature wanted the bird, and the creature wasn't a bird lover. That was obvious. An ardent twitcher didn't carry a crowbar in his gadget bag. He didn't look like a nice man. He was decidedly angry. If she didn't get away soon, she would collapse…

The creature stepped forwards, pushed the door to with the crowbar.

Trapped!

"Please," he said. "Where's the bird?"

George didn't answer. Wouldn't answer, couldn't answer. Taboo to give info that would put a life in danger.

She edged towards the door.

"Please don't do that," said the creature, moving towards her.

She backed away, glanced at the window.

And saw – Richard! Yes, Richard! Standing there with that mop of grey hair, the glasses with the gold frame, and still wearing his old cagoule, the yellow one – *Squiggles*!

The excitement proved too much for George. She fainted.

THE MESSENGER
PART TWO

THE BRAIN OF MARX PROJECT

1

Many years before that last event, Bob Rheingold stood at a porthole, staring at a sea of ice. His thoughts were interrupted by a tap on the shoulder, followed by the usual quip.

"Don't stare at the sun – you'll go blind! Are you coming for a coffee?"

This was his supervisor, Dan Kramer, whose suggestions were rarely declined by his research team. Bob Rheingold forced a chuckle.

"I was just thinking about the Eskimos," he said. "Apparently, they have several words to describe white. We have one."

"I've developed a few more since I've been here, I can tell you," said Dan, rubbing his hands. "Come on, let's get a drink."

Bob Rheingold smiled to himself as he thought of that expression: a white lie.

A white lie, because he'd really been thinking of Mary Shelley's *Frankenstein* and the fate of the monster. Pursued by his creator, the monster sought refuge in the icy wastes of the North, and wasn't seen again until the movies brought him back to life.

And here I am, he thought, not far from the North Pole, working on a project that my girlfriend says is Frankenstein stuff. Bringing the monster back to life.

He hadn't seen Suzy for six months now. Standing at that window, he remembered their parting, the arguments, the falling out.

"Why the fuck do you have to go to the North Pole?" she screamed. "And what's all this about squids? I thought you were an engineer, not a marine biologist!"

Trying to explain; it was tough. He, fresh from Harvard with a PhD in physics; she, a law student in her final year, struggling with her own jargon.

"A SQUID is a superconducting quantum interference device. They're used for measuring things, small changes in magnetic fields basically. They rely on Josephson Junctions, which is what my PhD's all about, and that's why I was offered this post. I can't turn it down, Suzy, it's a great opportunity. I'll be working with Dan Kramer, one of the world's experts in the field."

His first post: working on a research project funded by the US Navy, designing SQUIDS. Being hypersensitive to small changes in magnetic fields, the SQUIDS would be used to measure movements in the magnetic poles. Used also – it being the 1970s and the Cold War still in vogue – for submarine detection.

More explanation: the problems associated with SQUIDS. These measuring machines depend on materials that have the property of becoming superconductors only when cooled to very low temperatures, so low that they need massive structures to house them. An icebox, kind of, made out of liquid helium.

"We're not talking kitchen freezers, Suzy. We're talking temperatures that are way below minus two hundred and sixty-eight degrees Celsius – the temperature of Outer Space. Is that cold or what? This has got to be an adventure. And I'll be able to design a supercomputer, the fastest yet…"

A look of horror.

"Bob, this is Frankenstein stuff," she said.

Frankenstein stuff!

Tedium actually.

Stuck in a research lab, surrounded by snow and ice, with one word for white and nowhere to go for light relief. Long dark days and a fleeting sun. And the evening's entertainment – a light show.

The Northern Lights. The only pleasure in being there. The

highlight of being there. Standing at that porthole, watching the show.

Silvery white, streamers of light, with tints of green, a burning red, and sometimes yellow's there too. Dancing in the night sky, appearing and disappearing like fluorescent snakes behind a torn curtain. Or hanging down like jewelled daggers. Or spread in the shape of a fan. In the evenings he would stand at that porthole, waiting for the lights.

As for the project…

His enthusiasm had waned while the days had lightened; the sun was feeding his yearnings. Three months into the project and he wanted to be somewhere else, doing something else.

His expectations had been thwarted, right from day one. His PhD work was about using Josephson Junctions in logic circuits. He'd been led to believe his expertise would be instrumental in designing the latest breed of supercomputers: ultra-fast computers, using superconductors and faster logic circuits. That work was going on, but as an adjunct to the main project.

"At this moment in time, they're simply not practical for mass application," said Dan Kramer on his induction day. "The logic is fine, okay? It's the materials that are the problem. Think about it: computers that'll function only when the temperature's close to absolute zero – they're unlikely to catch on, Bob. The Navy don't see it as a priority. You can't fit a SQUID in a backpack."

Bob Rheingold was then in his 20s.

He stuck the post for two years, then returned to the States to join a medical research team in southern California. This team was designing a SQUID to monitor brain activity: the SQUID would record the magnetic fields created by neurological currents. Suzy was now a memory – married and living in Florida, a world apart. But Bob was getting a tan.

Meanwhile, two scientists in another part of the globe had

made a breakthrough in superconductor research. Their discovery was that certain ceramic materials can be made to superconduct at much higher temperatures, compared to the absolute zero temperatures of the stuff then used in SQUID manufacture. The implications were enormous – SQUIDS could now be built and operated without the need for bulky and costly cooling apparatus.

More discoveries follow, bringing down manufacturing costs. And also, increasing the range of potential applications. SQUIDS are on the march, but expertise is needed to design the new logic circuits.

Bob Rheingold joins a team at the University of Cincinnati, working on these high temperature SQUIDS.

Conferences, conference papers, books, promotions.

Another change of post, a professorship, consultancies.

And a romance, a proposal, a marriage, two kids.

Then the arguments.

His wife, complaining about his work addiction.

Her sordid affairs, her running off with the kids; his filing for a divorce.

Yet somehow managing the workload, and being promoted to head of department.

And twenty years or so after staring through a porthole at a sea of ice, Bob Rheingold realises his dream. He's on a flight to a remote island in the Azores, head of a new research project, closeted from the eyes and ears of the world. Their mission is to design a new kind of supercomputer. An international collaboration, dedicated to economic forecasting: the World Economy and Enterprise Project.

*

Liz Kendal was still a student at the London School of Economics when Bob Rheingold donned a white coat on his first day in the Arctic. While Bob was staring out of a porthole, Liz Kendal was sat in a snack bar, discussing the tactics of the current sit-in, and getting embroiled in a debate about the role of the revolutionary party.

"The working class needs leadership," she said, her hand slapping the table. "These strikes are all very well, but going on strike isn't sufficient to bring about a revolution. That's why agitation and propaganda are necessary, and that's the role of the party. We have to locate the vanguard, and show them how reforms aren't feasible under the capitalist system. Why don't you buy a paper?"

"Red Weekly? You must be joking! I ain't buying the Red Weekly. Here, why don't you buy ours?"

Liz Kendal peered at the title, thrust under her nose: Libertarian Struggle.

"No thanks, I've read it."

Bloody anarchists, she thought. I might have known.

"What I think is this," said the anarchist. "I think you lot don't have any respect for the working class. You tell them what you believe, and what you think they ought to do. You're like bloody teachers. We've had enough of that shit. We can organise our own struggles. We don't need no party. It'll end up like Russia, and you lot'll be the new Stalinists, locking everybody up who don't agree with you."

"Yeah, the dictatorship of the proletariat!"

Liz turned to this second speaker.

"The dictatorship of the proletariat is a temporary phase in the revolution," she explained. "And it's essential if the working class is to hold on to power. It'll come to an end when the property of the bourgeoisie, the factories, banks etc, are totally under the control of the working class…"

"Yeah, and what happens to the revolutionary party?"

"And what happened to you lot when the police arrived the other day?" said a new voice. "Notable for your absence, I'd say. If you guys had been running the show, we wouldn't be having a sit-in. Hello, Liz, how are you? Have you sold these guys a paper?"

More bodies leapt into the fray. The snack bar was buzzing,

and no one was talking about exams. There were discussions at every table, people circulating. Some were handing out leaflets, and others were milling around, selling newspapers: Socialist Worker, Red Weekly, Workers Vanguard, Workers Fight, Workers Muscle, Womens Voice, Gay News, Libertarian Struggle, Workers Fist, Anarchist News, The Morning Star, plus the Maoist lot – the Communist Party of Great Britain (Marxist-Leninist), not to be confused with the Communist Party of England (Marxist-Leninist), who were handing out leaflets, declaring, "LSE Students' Union are the Running Dogs of British Imperialism! Victory to the Glorious Proletarian Revolution!"

Rhetorical crap, Liz thought. Just as absurd as the Workers Revolutionary Party with that newspaper headline, demanding, "General Strike Now! Organise Workers Councils!" Silly buggers had no concept of Trotsky's transitional programme and the steps to a socialist state. Unlike the International Marxist Group, of which Liz was a supporter.

But there were so many groups and factions, all of whom stuck tenaciously to their point of view, that Liz had her time cut out arguing with them all. It was a constant source of wonder to her boyfriend how she managed to get any work done. But she did, in between reading snatches of Lenin's pamphlet on *Left-Wing Communism – An Infantile Disorder*, important ammunition for smashing the arguments of the Workers Revolutionary Party.

And still she found time for a night's headbanging at the Marquee Club in Soho, the heart of London, where she got into an argument with Phil, her boyfriend, about her lifestyle.

"What you've got to understand, Phil, is that I'm not just an academic. We're living in revolutionary times, if only you'd care to notice. You – you just want to get stoned and have a good time. Okay, fine, but I can't do that; I've got my PhD thesis to finish for a start. And how can you see what's going on in the world and not want to be involved? Vietnam,

Portugal, Chile – it's happening all over the world, the working class is organising globally to smash the system. I draw inspiration from that, as many of us do, but you just want to bury your head in the sand. Oh shit, I've just kicked your pint over, I'll get you another one, sorry."

Liz shouting as a crowd of hairies chanted "Out, demons out!" and "More!" while the Edgar Broughton Band drifted back on stage for a second encore. The old anthem of the underground was sounding rather jaded, she thought; Phil was stuck in a post-Woodstock time capsule. And back in her flat in Camden Town, she tried to explain how her PhD work was bound up with the agitation and propaganda.

The title of her thesis: Using Marx's *Capital* to Model the UK Economy.

"What I'm trying to show," she said, sucking at a joint, "is that the usual ways of making predictions about the economy are doomed to fail, because they're all based on a total misunderstanding of how the capitalist system works. Basically, what it comes down to is this: Marx's analysis is still as relevant today as it was over a hundred years ago. The system is basically the same; companies exist to make a profit. And where does profit come from? From the exploitation of the working class, as Marx explained. And the essential feature of the capitalist system is the tendency for the rate of profit to fall. What do we see happening now?" (puff, puff) "Workers are being asked to work for longer hours for the same wage or less – more exploitation" (puff, puff) "to increase profit. And the rise in consumer credit" (puff, puff, puff) "to boost spending. All of which, as Marx clearly pointed out, are short-term measures which can only postpone the inevitable crisis. What's endemic is the cycle of upturn and downturn, with recessions occurring more frequently, and each one worse than the previous. Ultimately, the state's only solution is fascism or dictatorship, as a way of keeping the working class at slave wages, or war, as a way of bolstering the economy. Basically, the choice we're faced with is socialism or barbarism, as Marx predicted. Oh come on, let's go to bed, I'm fucked. This has gone out, sorry."

"Man, you're so uptight," said Phil, taking the joint. "Your enthusiasm is freaking me out. Let's loosen up, babe. Come on, let's have a hug."

Phil, always hopeful. But shagging was not on the agenda. Having consumed several pints of beer, Phil couldn't produce a stiff one, despite the naked body beside him, and Liz had no desire to assist him.

So the exposition continued.

"It's not inevitable that the system will collapse of its own accord. It'll just become more barbaric, unless we fight back. That's how my thesis is tied up with my political work. Theory and practice, do you follow me? My understanding of how the system works makes me want to change it. And if we don't act to change it… Are you listening?"

"Yeah, I'm listening, but give us a break, Liz, it's Friday night. Why don't we listen to some sounds? Put some Hawkwind on."

"Oh, you shit-head! All right, I'll put some Grateful Dead on, but I've got to get up in the morning – we're selling papers tomorrow."

Twelve months later, Liz Kendal left the LSE with a PhD in economics. While Phil was about to resit his first-year exams for the third year running, Liz was about to start her first research post: working at the Centre for Economic Forecasting at the Greater London Business School.

Phil said she'd sold out.

"Greater London Business School! Oh man, and you call yourself a Marxist! Do Marxists wear *suits*?"

"Phil, one has to live in the real world. This is a great opportunity for me. I'll be working with Adam Meccano, a leading expert on alternative models of the economy. He was my external examiner; he's an okay guy. He's well into Marx."

Phil sat there shaking his head, his hair sweeping his knees.

"Business School! And what's happened to the

revolutionary party?"

"Theory and practice, Phil. You may not believe it, but this research could change the world. We're gathering company data and treating it to a Marxist analysis. Theories of surplus value, etc. This could be the material for a new volume of *Capital*, updated for the twentieth century."

Liz was about to enter a long period of data gathering.

Statistics: loads of it.

Fed into computers to test theories, alternative models of the economy.

Three years later and Liz was still gathering the data, while Phil had buggered off to India for an indefinite period – doing the obligatory hippy backpack trippy trek shit, Liz said. Losing his brain cells while I'm trying to change the world.

Meanwhile, the data. The project had guaranteed finance for five years, with possible renewal for another five years, subject to adequate progress. But progress was far from adequate, and the five-year review was looming.

Adam Meccano explained the problems to Liz one day.

"For this project to be successful, first, we need to show how our model gives a satisfactory explanation of the past. That is to say, given input X, which we know, our model should be able to produce output Y, which we also know. Second, we need to compare our findings with the results using other models, and demonstrate that our model gives the superior explanation. And then, we use our model to predict the future. The problem, Liz, is the amount of time we're having to spend on collecting the stats before we can test the models, plus the processing time. Our computers are so damned slow. If we can persuade our sponsors that the results are going to be worth it, we could possibly get the finance to buy a faster supercomputer. But we need one now, to produce the material that'll persuade them. And apart from all that, we have a problem now with the models we're proposing to use. Some of our sponsors are a little uneasy about your, er, enthusiasm about the relevance of Marx..."

"Oh shit! I suspected as much when I chaired the Futures conference. I wasn't very diplomatic, I'm afraid."

"Yes, I'm sorry to say we've had several complaints..."

Damn! Liz thought. This was a consequence of her being promoted as the public face of the project. Tall and leggy, with long dark hair, she'd attracted the attention of her fellow researchers and a couple of professors in the department. Adam Meccano had gone further, inviting her to dine out one night. While she'd accepted the invitation, she hadn't anticipated his amorous suggestions at the dinner table, which had been prefaced by the seemingly innocent one, namely, to chair a semi-public meeting on the prospects for the UK economy. Which she'd also accepted.

So there she was, sat at the top table in a large conference room, a banqueting suite in a plush hotel in London's West End, paid for by one of their sponsors, Yinyang Motors. She'd put on a long red dress for the occasion, and the plunging neckline had drawn a few stares. The Chancellor himself had spoken, painting a rosy picture for the benefit of his audience, most of whom were potential investors in the UK economy.

And none of whom had any awareness that their sponsorship was being used to plan another volume of Marx's *Capital*.

Until Liz opened her mouth, that is.

Angered by the Chancellor's speech, she'd added a footnote, saying what this really meant was more exploitation for the working class, and that the way forward was for a deeper understanding of the system, based on a Marxist analysis of the economy, which, pending further funding, would be forthcoming very shortly.

The Chancellor was not impressed.

"It's partly my fault, Liz," said Adam Meccano, who was desperately trying to hide his embarrassment. "I should have given you a proper briefing beforehand. You see, we're not yet at the stage where we can test the models; we've yet to recruit the programmers we need to carry out a full computer simulation; and given the timescale, we're being pressurised to use more conventional methods of forecasting. All in all, I think we'll just have to put Marx on the back seat for the time being..."

And Liz thought: thunder and damnation!

Still, it wasn't as though Marx had ever reached the front seat. Or even the back seat for that matter. It was more the case that he was squashed in the boot, being transported on a very long journey, and wanting desperately to come out for air.

And Liz was determined that he should come out for air, guns blazing, metaphorically speaking.

She wasn't alone in this enthusiasm; she knew that for a fact. For a start, she'd acquired a new set of comrades, having changed her allegiance from the International Marxist Group to the Revolutionary Communist Group.

The seeds of disenchantment had been sown on Saturdays, standing on street corners in the pouring rain, trying to sell copies of the Red Weekly to bored shoppers. Until she decided that enough was enough.

The crunch came at election time, with a newspaper headline that was telling people to "Vote Labour with No Illusions!" This she refused to sell, arguing that the group's orientation was in fact doing the reverse – encouraging illusions in the Labour Party, in the naive belief that its left wing, organised around the charismatic figure of Tony Benn, could bring about socialism while the capitalist state was still intact. After a heated argument at a supporters' meeting, she'd stormed out, claiming that the group had now degenerated into opportunism and populism.

A few weeks later, she became a supporter of the Revolutionary Communist Group, who, she decided, had a clearer programme for the emancipation of the working class. They saw the need for an educated cadre of supporters, grounded in an understanding of Marx, who would spread this understanding among the militants in the trade union movement and elsewhere. Setting up reading groups to study Marx's *Capital* was seen as a priority.

And there was always this fact to consider: that despite the internecine warfare between the Trotskyite and Maoist groups of the far left, they were all agreed on one thing – namely, that *Capital*, as a scientific analysis of the capitalist economy, was still relevant to the 1970s.

The need for theory: so sadly lacking in the weekly rush to increase paper sales. Now she could combine her work as a researcher with an evening in Camden library, leading a reading group which included factory workers, cleaners and bus drivers. True proletarians, she thought.

But meanwhile, the data. It was driving her to despair. There it all was, awaiting analysis.

Marx spent years in the British Library looking at this kind of stuff, she thought. And now it's back to the laws of supply and demand. Shit! What am I going to do? Pass the info onto the comrades, I suppose. It really needs someone with Marx's genius to make sense of it all. A modern Marx, someone who can *think* like Marx. Someone with the *brain* of Marx.

*

While Liz Kendal was sat in her office, pondering the need for a modern Marx, Nicolai Perepenko, a research professor at the Moscow Brain Institute, was showing a student how to use a new kind of microscope. Underneath the microscope was a slice of Lenin's brain.

The Moscow Brain Institute had been set up by Stalin in 1926. Its mission: to study the brains of great Russians.

Lenin, who'd died in 1924, was in no position to deny this vital organ being donated to scientific research. Nor could he have any say in what happened to the rest of his body. Following a decision of the Immortalisation Commission, his body was embalmed, much like the Pharaohs of old, and still lies, according to rumour, by the Kremlin wall. As for his other organs, their location is the stuff of Western legend.

Lenin's brain was followed by those of other great Russians. According to Western rumour, these included Sergei Eisenstein, the poet Mayakovsy, and Stalin himself. And the rumours were plenty, because for several decades the doors of the Moscow Brain Institute were permanently closed to Western observers. Its proceedings were a total mystery, as was the fate of Lenin's brain. One report says that Lenin's brain was sliced into 7,500 slices; another says over 30,000 slices.

Suffice it to say, that the work went on.

The study of genius, the shape of genius, the physical matter that produces genius – what made Lenin so exceptional? The results of this research would soon be announced to the Western world.

Meanwhile, Nicolai Perepenko had begun a collaborative project with Boris Vladimov, a psycholinguist at the Moscow Linguistics Institute. His work was concerned with textual analysis: in this case, analysing the texts and speeches of great Russians. He'd shown how verbs, phrases, the use of tense, the use of person, etc, all reveal a trace of the author's underlying personality and intentions. The writer Pushkin, for example, was diagnosed as a manic-depressive, and Vladimov's research showed how his stories reflected this – plotted like a sine curve, with a sharp rise towards delirium followed by a rapid slide into gloom. Boris Vladimov was developing a computer program that would analyse a text and give an indication of this underlying personality, looking at aspects such as determination, optimism, certainty and realism.

The collaboration was centred on Lenin.

The object of the exercise was to sketch, using samples of Lenin's writings, a map of the mind beneath the text. More than this: to look for correlations between Lenin's mind, as revealed by textual analysis, and the structure of Lenin's brain.

Meanwhile, great changes were taking place in the world

outside.

The Soviet system was under threat – not from Western aggression, but from forces within.

In Poland, shipyard workers go on strike. The workers organise an illegal trade union, Solidarity, whose leader looks like a movie star. He's presented in the Western media as a hero. Some on the left say he's a pawn of Western imperialism; some argue he's part of a Papal conspiracy.

And in Russia itself, a change of leadership brings to the fore another hero – Mikhail Gorbachev. The President introduces two policies: one, known as glasnost, lifts taboos on freedom of the press and is designed to make the Soviet state a more liberal society. The second, known as perestroika, is a process of restructuring, whereby the Soviet economy will be open to Western influence, collaboration and investment. The market arrives in Russia.

To the non-aligned observer, the process looks very odd. The market arrives in Russia, not because of Western imperialism, but because its own leaders have lost confidence in the Soviet system.

To compound the process, the USSR, as a union of republics, is in the process of being dismantled. A number of states in the federation demand independence, while the Eastern bloc is falling apart from bloodless revolutions. In Poland, Hungary, Bulgaria, Czechoslovakia, mass protests result in democratic elections. In Romania, President Ceaucescu, the mad dictator, ends up running for his life. Like the proverbial deck of cards, the communist states are collapsing.

And the culmination: the tearing down of the Berlin Wall, the symbolic barrier between the capitalist West and the communist East. Communism is no more, and the whole process has taken less than a decade.

But inside the research laboratories, the work has proceeded regardless.

Then, after seventy years of research, the Moscow Brain

Institute opens its doors to Western observers for the first time.

There is a press conference, at which Oleg Adrianov, the director of the Institute, delivers the long-awaited verdict on Lenin's brain.

"The brain of Vladimir Ilich," he says, "was undoubtedly the brain of a talented man. But the area of the right hemisphere's outer surface was only just bigger than average. And the weight of the brain was less than two-thirds of that of the nineteenth-century novelist Ivan Turgenev's. In summary, gentlemen, Lenin's brain was not exceptional."

Standing behind the press photographers, Nicolai Perepenko is smirking.

*

Back in the UK, the collapse of communism had a strange effect on the Trotskyite far left. They sat and watched, open-mouthed, as the drama unfolded. Having defended the Soviet Union against Western imperialism for so long, while at the same time criticising its Stalinist degeneration, they now faced the prospect of having little to defend and nothing to criticise. When communists turn to capitalism for their salvation, what arguments could the left muster to present communism as a viable alternative to capitalism?

There was no alternative. Almost overnight, to call yourself a communist was to invoke bouts of laughter, much finger-poking, and possibly an invitation to join the funny farm. The spectre of communism was no longer haunting Europe, as Marx once said, but was about to run for cover, finding sanctuary inside the broad church of the Labour Party, where calling yourself a socialist was still acceptable.

Liz Kendal, meanwhile, had moved to Cambridge.

The project at the Business School had managed to secure another five years of funding, and she had continued to gather the data while lamenting the fact that Marx was still riding in the boot. Her political activities were limited to the *Capital* reading group on Tuesday evenings, competing with the local bell-ringers just around the corner, plus social evenings with the comrades, discussing the latest developments on the world stage.

The first of which was the change of government in the UK: the Thatcher years had started. While Gorby was making plans to fraternise with the West, the Iron Lady had sent gunboats to recapture a large flock of sheep from Argentina; then, flushed with her success, had set out to deal with the enemy within. Of which there were millions, it seemed.

The mission: the organisations of the working class were to be demolished; rendered ineffective at least; and any talk of socialism would be banished for ever from this treasured isle. Teams of lawyers were recruited to this ambitious project, drafting various laws to make strikes more or less illegal, to make trade union democracy more cumbersome and costly to administer, and to threaten sequestration of assets if the laws weren't obeyed.

All of this came to a climax with the decision to settle scores with that last bastion of working class militancy: the National Union of Mineworkers.

The miners went on strike just before Liz Kendal took up her new post in Cambridge. The strike went on for twelve months. It ended in a precarious stalemate, with Thatcher declaring victory and the miners declaring the absence of defeat. But the purpose of the strike was to prevent a pit closure programme, and the closures went ahead.

Liz Kendal blamed the left. Having sown illusions in the Labour Party, the left was in no fit state to defend the working class. She went to London occasionally and ended up on street corners, collecting for the strikers' families. There was much sympathy, much generosity. But as the strike proceeded with no end in sight, the whole thing began to feel more like a symbolic act. The working class, as an organised, collective force with a historical role to play in the overthrow of capitalism, was in the process of being transformed. The traditional working class was almost disappearing as more people were now employed in services than in manufacturing. And when the strike was over, it seemed that the old working class was now a spent force.

That, and the communist drama then unravelling, led to a sort of political numbness on Liz's part. The *Capital* reading group was no more; her former comrades she rarely saw. She had the impression they were no longer active: disengaged from politics like the rest of the left; those who hadn't disappeared into the Labour Party, that is. And one or two, it was rumoured, had become ardent Christians. Which made Liz question her own zeal.

Perhaps zeal is the thing, she thought. Having zeal, whatever one's cause. If someone is instinctively zealous, then it might be just a matter of chance that they take up this cause, as opposed to that cause. But then, political economy is a matter of science. Marx's *Capital* is a work of science; it's not a cause. And it's still relevant now. More relevant than ever, because capitalism has gone global. What's needed is an update for the current period. A new volume of *Capital*, written to explain the peculiar times we're going through. But who is going to write it?

Meanwhile, Liz had settled into her new post: assistant director of a new research centre, affiliated to Cambridge University. Its label – the Centre for Research into Enterprise, Entrepreneurship and Prosperity; otherwise known as CREEP. This, after all, was the era of the upwardly mobile, and Liz, like everyone else, had to earn a living doing something.

And suddenly there was plenty of scope. Still going through a process of transformation, the new Russia wanted advice from economic experts. Companies, government officials, educationalists, were all crying out for help in how to implement this thing called capitalism.

The British Council was asked to send a team of experts

over to Moscow, and Liz was contacted as a matter of course. Thus she found herself on a plane full of academics, leading a small delegation from CREEP. She sat with her eyes closed, dwelling on life's ironies.

Like, how the far left used to draw inspiration from the Bolshevik revolution: a model for the overthrow of capitalism. And now she's going over there not to seek enlightenment on the Soviet economy, but to offer her advice on the running of capitalism.

But the visit proved to be enlightening nonetheless. For a start, that's when she heard the rumours about Lenin's brain.

*

Nicolai Perepenko was getting used to entertaining Western visitors. It was inevitable that, once the doors were open, the brains of famous Russians would be something like a tourist attraction for the Institute. He and Boris Vladimov ushered the latest set into a coffee lounge, where the delegates were keen to continue the discussions.

The latest set was a team from the University of London, who were all engaged in research on the brain. Nigel Price was telling Boris about the new SQUIDS, which had revolutionised brain-scanning equipment. They'd just installed a new generation of brain scanners in their cognitive neuroscience lab back in London.

"In a typical experiment," he said, "our subjects are asked to perform a range of tasks, and the brain scanners monitor which area of the brain is active as they perform each task in turn. We now have a pretty good picture as regards areas of activity – linguistic, visual, and so on. The new machines should enable us to add more detail. What we're looking at are things like literacy and numeracy, and what parts of the brain are active in reading, writing, and doing simple arithmetic. We're hoping to find out what separates experts from novices, whether experts use parts of the brain that are not used by learners. I understand your main interest is language, is that right?"

"Yes, that is correct," said Boris. "We do similar things, I think. We are also mapping the brain in this way, but, as you have seen, our machines are very old. We have been using other techniques also, as my colleague explained I believe… But I am very interested in these new brain scanners. Tell me, from where do they become available?"

Nigel was hoping for this response, having seen the trip partly as a chance to do a spot of business before the Cambridge lot flew over and clinched a deal. The trip was proving to be productive on all fronts: an exchange of information about the latest research in neuroscience; arrangements for future collaborations; plus earning a few bob from a sales deal.

Yet the Russians were very cagey about some things, he thought. Like, what had they really found out about Lenin's brain? And then, the question of techniques. The Russians had been pioneers in brain research, going back to the 1930s. It was rumoured that they'd used open brain surgery in their experiments, taking as their subjects people who were known to have suffered brain damage. Probing the brain led to the discovery that certain areas were implicated in various disabilities: thus began the process of brain mapping. The results were of great significance for the development of science, but the means?

They didn't want to talk about it, it seemed. A bit like, don't mention the war. Which it was, in a way. The subjects would have been prisoners in the Gulags, victims of Stalin's war against political opponents. As with the Nazis, prisoners of war provided suitable subjects for daring experiments, which would be impossible to carry out in peace time. War provided the ruse for secrecy, while the subjects could hardly refuse to take part. And despite their public distaste about methods, the USA and the UK were very keen to know the results of such tests – deals had been struck with the Nazis.

Returning to his hotel to collect his belongings, Nigel Price shuddered as he thought about these things. But all in all, the visit had been a great success. And on his return flight he found himself sat next to a rather attractive brunette, whose skirt was a bit on the short side for a plane ride, and whose legs were so long that they brushed his own from time to time, sending a pleasant thrill to his cerebellum.

It turned out that she too was an academic, returning to the UK from a similar kind of visit. A scientist, she said. From Cambridge.

"Oh? You're, let me guess… a psychologist?"

Do I look like a psychologist? Liz wondered.

She dreamed of spinning a yarn, of her being an engineer or such like, but decided it was wise to come clean.

"No, an economist. A social scientist."

Such an intense look, she thought. So she smiled and said, "Though some scientists wouldn't agree that economics is a science. Personally, I think it depends on how one approaches the subject. And you? You are…?"

"Er, Nigel Price, from Imperial," he said, offering a hand, which Liz shook. "Neuroscience is my subject. I've been visiting the Moscow Brain Institute with my colleagues. Fascinating, absolutely fascinating. Was it your first trip?"

"To Russia? Yes it was – what about you?"

"My sixth, but the first to the Institute. What always strikes me is how the Russians are so advanced in some things, yet completely backward in others. What were your impressions?"

"I, er… I found it difficult to adjust to their social customs; that's what struck me most I think – like, meeting you with a big kiss, everywhere we went. Total strangers too. But they were very respectful. They went out of their way to make us feel welcome. I was giving advice on running the economy, as it happens. As far as that goes, running a market economy is such a recent thing for them, they're obviously way behind us on that one. I'm afraid I don't know much about their scientific advances. Tell me more."

"I can only speak with authority about brain research, obviously, but what's striking is that they found out several decades ago things that we've learnt only recently. One of my areas is memory research, for instance. We've just found out that memory capabilities are dependent on the size of the hippocampus, which is a part of the brain that deals with spatial tasks. Basically, the bigger the hippocampus, the better the memory. Now, we've only found that out because of more effective ways of monitoring brain activity. The extraordinary thing about the Russians is that they came to similar conclusions in the 1930s, without such techniques... Am I boring you?"

Liz stifled a yawn.

"No, not at all, it's very interesting. So what do they do at the Moscow Brain Institute?"

"Er, it's similar sort of work to what we do. It's... Did you know they have a collection of famous brains in there? I mean, dead brains – such as Lenin's and Stalin's? Extraordinary."

Liz smiled. With his untidy mop of grey hair, his worn spectacles and threadbare suit, Nigel Price had the appearance of the eccentric scientist.

"And what do they do with these brains?" she queried.

"They study them. Have been for years. They're fascinated by the idea of genius. But I'm not sure what they've discovered exactly. They were quite cagey when it came to specific details, apart from obvious things, like size and weight..."

"Size?"

"Yes, size. Take Lenin's brain, for instance. The most remarkable thing about it, as far as I can make out, is that it was actually quite small. For someone of his undoubted intellect, I mean. Which shows that the size of a brain is no measure of intelligence."

"Hmm, interesting!"

"Isn't it? But it's a fact that is now generally known, I think. Take birds, for instance. Calling someone a birdbrain used to

141

be an insult, but their intelligence is quite exceptional, given the size of their brains. Did you know… Obviously, you know that parrots can be taught to speak, but did you know that they can be taught the use of language? Human language, I mean. It's now been shown that they have the ability to *learn* human language, in the sense of being able to converse, rather than just imitate what they hear…"

"Which suggests that they have a good memory and, from what you were saying before, a bigger hippocampus. Wasn't that what you said? The larger the hippocampus, the better the memory. So the size of a brain is an indicator of intelligence after all. Unless I've misunderstood you."

This woman is sharp, Nigel thought. And smiling rather mischievously. Trying to catch me out. Bitch!

"No, you're right, of course," he said. "But I was talking in general terms. Overall, Lenin's brain was on the small size. But relatively speaking, his hippocampus was… larger than the average… You're laughing! Why are you laughing?"

"I'm sorry," said Liz, wiping away a splutter. "It's just that… Do you really think that intelligence can be measured by the size of the brain? Surely, it's what you do with it that's important."

"Yes, absolutely! I agree with you! Didn't I say that the size of a brain is no measure of intelligence? I did say that, didn't I? You're confusing me!"

"Yes, you did say that. But the hippocampus…"

"As an indicator of memory! My point is that there's more to intelligence than memory. You could remember everything that ever happened to you, for instance, but would you really want to? In minute detail? Better to be selective, surely. Which I'd say is another measure of intelligence, do you not think?"

"But there may be times when you want to remember every minute detail…"

So the conversation continued, descending at times into banter, rising at others into frank debate, and settling after a while into a seeking after something. This, when Nigel

142

decided that Liz wasn't trying to catch him out, and Liz decided that Nigel wasn't trying to impress her with his knowledge. But what they were seeking remained elusive.

They were still deep in conversation when the plane landed at Heathrow, arguing at this point about that old chestnut: social factors versus heredity in the development of intelligence. Nigel was talking about the Human Genome Project – the DNA factor, and its influence on diseases such as Parkinson's and Alzheimer's. Liz, sceptical of the idea that intelligence is transmitted from parent to offspring, conceded that social factors didn't explain everything either.

As they walked towards the car parks, they found themselves reaching a compromise. Not surprising, perhaps, as neither wanted to disperse on a sour note. They swapped addresses, best wishes, the hopes of meeting again soon.

Two years were to pass before that happened.

*

Liz Kendal didn't know what to make of the world. Change was so rapid; it was hard to keep your balance. Once upon a time, she recalled, the communists suffered a crisis of their own making. Party leaders, seemingly overnight, lost confidence in the Soviet system and, lacking the will to govern, decided to hand over responsibility for running the economy to market forces. Philosophers declared that history itself had come to an end. Capitalism was here to stay. For ever and ever. Amen.

But cracks had appeared in this seamless future.

In the West, now it seemed that people had lost confidence in capitalism.

Western economies were stagnating, or going through a recession. In some countries, manufacturing and productivity were at an all-time low. The gap between rich and poor was increasing. Personal and corporate debt was at an all-time high. People had lost fortunes through bad investments and the misuse of pension funds. Corrupt financiers had become commonplace. And as it was now official – the absence of an alternative, that is – the future looked bleak for those who had lost out in the ups and downs of the market.

Governments denied there was a crisis. But the loss of faith in Western economies was felt most by those who were directly involved – the more experienced City traders, investors and such like. Economic experts and government think tanks were raising doubts about the ability of capitalism to expand ad infinitum. And the American economy was seriously in the red. In more ways than one, as its survival was now dependent on loans from China of all places, whose economy was one of the few to be growing. Exponentially, it seemed – like Russia, China had now embraced the market. Yet in Russia, some former communists were now questioning the wisdom of embracing a system that appeared to be bankrupt. Drugs, crime and corruption were the only obvious changes, while people still queued for a loaf of bread.

Liz Kendal viewed these developments with mixed feelings. On the one hand, she like her colleagues was afflicted with a sense of gloom about the future. But on the other hand, she felt a strange sense of elation about it all. The finger of understanding pointed once more to Marx. The prospects for the global economy, she thought, provided ample evidence that his predictions were sound.

Strangely, others were beginning to think so too.

One day she had a phone call from Adam Meccano, her former boss at the Greater London Business School, who told her of the latest rumour. There was now a Nobel prize up for grabs, he said, for anyone who had the intellectual clout to produce the next volume of Marx's *Capital*.

"Stick with it, Liz," he said. "Some day, who knows? How are things at CREEP?"

"Very busy, as you can imagine. We've got fingers all over the place. Lots of collaborations with European partners. We're very much in demand at the moment. But to be honest,

I feel a bit of a fraud sometimes. People turn to us for solutions to their particular crisis, when really I feel like saying… Well, you know."

"I do indeed. We miss you here. I know it's a bit late, but I don't think I congratulated you on getting the directorship. So, congratulations!"

"Thanks, thanks for the thought. I'll have to call in some time."

"Yes, please do, you'd be most welcome. By the way, I've suggested you for a new think tank the government's setting up. Alternative models of the economy, would you believe; now the government's involved. I hope I wasn't too presumptuous, but I wasn't the only one to propose you, I must say."

"Oh, fame! Thank you for that. It'll make a nice change from the usual jabber."

"No problem. They'll contact you in due course. Er, how's the love life? No, don't answer that, I shouldn't have asked. Anyway, I must go. Bye."

"Bye… and thanks."

As Liz replaced the phone, she was struck by the thought that Adam Meccano now looked on her as an equal. A sign of her new status maybe, but the directorship had happened by chance.

Charles Bingley, CREEP's previous director, had been asked to resign after a disciplinary procedure found him guilty of serious misconduct. The news emerged that over a period of years, he'd built up a large expense account while spending weekends abroad with his secretary, supposedly on company business. Liz had kept her suspicions private, but the whistle had been blown by the secretary herself. Her cue came when Charles ended the affair, and then tried to fire her. The disciplinary board was outraged – Charles was charged with misusing company funds and bringing CREEP's name into disrepute. In short, the director of CREEP was a creep.

It was all very sordid, Liz thought. And quite in keeping

with the flavour of the times.

The directorship had its downside: more administration. Charles Bingley had left the company accounts in a total mess, and Liz was faced with the task of sorting them out. A weekend job – weekdays were chock-a-block these days.

Weekends were getting that way too. A few days after Adam's phone call, Liz received an information pack on Atlas, the latest government think tank. A letter was enclosed, inviting her to its first meeting. It sounded like fun, she thought: a weekend in the Cotswolds, at a private mansion, debating with academics. The theme, as Adam said, was alternative models of the economy.

*

Brainstorming: that was the general plan for the weekend. Liz looked at the men sat around the table and thought, What's going to come out of *their* brains?

It was such an odd collection of people. For Liz, their oddities seemed to be heightened by the fact that, outside, the English countryside rolled away in a sort of November normality – golden trees and green fields; a breeze, stirring the leaves on the verandah; a robin, singing by the window.

And inside, a group of academics, led by the most flamboyant among them: Jerry Mendoza.

Liz looked at him and saw Groucho Marx: a short chap with dark curly hair, bushy eyebrows, a moustache, a yellow shirt, a red suit and tie, and a habit of smoking cigars, tearing the ends with a relish, much like… Groucho Marx?

It had started with a round of introductions – so-and-so from such-and-such – with Liz feeling self-conscious as she was the only woman from the UK; the other one came from New York.

Then Jerry Mendoza's preamble. Unlike many think tanks, he said, the composition of this one was a deliberate mix of different viewpoints, the idea being to transcend those traditional designations of left and right, centre-left or centre-right. Feel free to say what you like, he said; that's why you're here. We don't want restraint.

And the first to speak: the corpulent Humphrey Dillinger, a man who said at the outset that he put American interests first.

Let's be blunt, he said. We are the only nation in the world that has a global plan. This talk of economic crisis is bullshit. There are global opportunities for expanding the market. There are countries, whole continents, where people are starving. All of us have an interest in eliminating poverty, because that's the first step in the creation of a new market. We must help to build these countries for our own sakes, for the continuation of growth, and for our future prosperity. Take China, a good example of what I'm talking about. Not so long ago, China was a land of peasants, toiling from dawn to dusk in the paddy fields. Now what do we see? An expanding economy, the fastest in the world. Factories, manufacturing of all kinds, a flexible labour market, people leaving the fields to work in the towns. Take Korea, another good example. Taiwan – likewise. South-East Asia is now the home of the leading economies of the world. The Middle East will be the next; then Africa. The major problem, as I'm sure you'll all agree, is stabilisation. For the market to expand, we need stable societies. That's why we all have an interest in getting rid of tinpot dictatorships and installing democratic systems. If that requires force, dammit, we'll use force. Democracy is essential for a free and open market. To expand the market, we need to export democracy…

Liz looked at her watch: 10.30. It was Saturday morning, and the event wasn't due to finish until 3pm, Sunday.

Alternative models of the economy? This is US imperialism, she thought, pure and simple.

Jerry Mendoza caught her eye, a faint smile crossing his face.

Two more speakers before the coffee break.

Liz, hackles raised, listened with one ear. Someone talking about a biological model of the economy; how it evolved, on Darwinian lines. Someone else talking about mixed economies; a balance of state intervention plus a free market – old stuff that she'd heard many times before.

Then the coffee break.

She queued for a cup; then looked for Jerry Mendoza, who stood in a corner and seemed to be waiting for her arrival.

"I know what you're going to say," he said, lowered voice. "Dillinger's views may not be to your liking, but you'd be surprised how many people think along those lines. You may think he's an extremist, but in the States it's not the case."

"I take it you know of my work then," said Liz, who was visibly steaming.

"Yes, of course, I read your PhD thesis many years ago. I was impressed."

"Oh! But this think tank…"

"On alternative models of the economy. Yes, you may not like them, but Dillinger's views are quite rational. And from a certain standpoint, they make perfect logic. His model of the economy is US-centred, but so what? It's a model for global expansion, and I think it's important we hear a range of views before we thrash out strategies."

"Strategies? You're not going to get a consensus with this lot!"

Jerry Mendoza was unmoved. He took out a cigar and said, "Oh, I don't know. You may not believe it, but Humphrey Dillinger used to be a Marxist."

Liz excused herself, and walked to the biscuit tray.

*

Two days after this event, Liz was still asking herself how it came about that some sort of consensus did emerge by the end of it. She put it down to Jerry Mendoza, and his ability to see connections where others saw empty spaces. Herself included.

She'd delivered her talk in the afternoon. It was on her favourite theme: the falling rate of profit. Explaining what Marx meant by it; showing how it still applied; looking at the fortunes of a couple of UK companies, once leaders in their field, now shadows.

She'd expected Humphrey Dillinger to throw a tantrum. But no! He sat there absorbed, chin in hand, taking notes from time to time. And in the afternoon break, he approached her with a proffered hand.

"Excellent talk!" he said.

"Oh! Thank you," she said. "I hear you were once a Marxist."

"That's right. In a way, I still am. As far as understanding the economy goes. Marx had his finger on the pulse, yes indeed."

"But I don't see how…"

"There's no contradiction. Okay, so you and me know how the economy works. The question is, what are we going to do about it? Communism is finished. Once you accept that, then the only way forward is to apply the measures that Marx himself describes – increasing credit, extending the working day, exporting work abroad where the labour comes cheaper, and so forth."

"But those are only short-term measures to postpone the crisis! In the long-term, the rate of profit will still fall… and there are limits to extending the working day – people will just keel over!"

A loud laugh from Humphrey Dillinger.

"You bet!" he said. "The question is, how short is short-term? Listen lady, I take the Marxist analysis on board. Everything we see happening now bears it out. What was that expression? The law of uneven and combined development, or something similar. So, okay, you've got Britain, the oldest industrial power in the world, which has now become the most senile capitalist power. Yes? Do you agree? Come on, where have all the manufacturers gone? Abroad, right? Right!"

Liz nodded, while in her mind's eye she saw a kitchen knife and an engraving: *Stainless Steel, Made in Sheffield*. Whatever happened to British Steel? She should have mentioned that in her talk. Pick up a knife these days, and the word is Korea.

Meanwhile, Dillinger.

"Then you've got the most recent industrial powers – like Taiwan, Korea, China, etc. They're now at a stage that the UK was in, say, a hundred and fifty, two hundred years ago, right? So they've got at least two hundred years of expansion before the rot sets in. But then you've also got the Middle East and Africa – I tell you, it's going to be a while before the possibilities are exhausted."

"So you do agree there are limits to...?"

"Absolutely! Of course there are limits – the world is a finite place, for God's sake, and I don't think there's any chance of finding markets on the moon. But the point is lady, why the hell should I worry about it? I'm not going to be around when an industrialised Africa starts going senile, am I?"

"I guess not, but..."

"But what? Communism is finished. Don't tell me you still believe in that revolution crap. The working classes are not going to rise up and take over, and I'll tell you why – because they're so goddam stupid, that's why! So what's the alternative? We raise the quality of life, is what we do, so that they live contented lives, from cradle to grave. What's wrong with that?"

"Nothing, as far as we in the West are concerned. But what if you were born with a curse, like living in Baghdad? Or Gaza?"

"Right, okay, I see where you're coming from. That may possibly be a curse, I'll grant you that. But try and see things from our point of view. The worst threat to democracy, and to an expanding economy, comes from these goddam terrorists, who don't give a shit about anything or anybody, not even themselves. Somebody's got to stop them, don't you agree?"

"Something has to be done, yes, but do you have to be so gung-ho about it?"

Another loud laugh from Humphrey Dillinger.

"It's Marx again, lady! The laws of the market – they also apply to war, you know. The fireworks just keep getting louder. And there's nothing you or I can do about it. We're dealing with people who are beyond reason. If they'll only respond to force, we'll give'm force."

As Jerry Mendoza had said, his position did have a certain logic. Though Liz didn't agree with him. A finite world means finite resources, not just limits to market expansion. And, she thought, American foreign policy makes no distinction between collateral damage and the people it was supposedly helping. She avoided further debate with him, knowing they would never agree.

So what was the consensus that emerged? Liz struggled to remember. Jerry Mendoza had made it seem so easy. It centred on Marx, she thought. No one had a word to say against Marx.

More than that, Jerry Mendoza was an enthusiast.

He too had given a talk. This was on the Sunday; the topic was computational tools for economic modelling, hardware and software. He spoke about statistical analysis and the need for speed, about supercomputers and parallel processing, about a supercomputer designed by Bob Rheingold which was dedicated to economic forecasting. Then he spoke about the latest fad – DNA computing.

"I'll try and keep things simple," he said, "for the non-technical among us. Conventional computers use microchips made from silicon. Supercomputers use other materials, based on their physical properties as superconductors. DNA computers use biological materials – enzymes and proteins. They're also known as molecular computers, okay? They're radically different from conventional computers in that they don't rely on electricity. The materials, enzymes and proteins, react to light and heat. The molecules combine as a result of this stimulus, so you get a change of state, okay? Now, for computing purposes, we take this change of state and see it as the solution to some problem, which is encoded in the original set of molecules..."

Liz's understanding stumbled at this point. The solution to some problem – what was the problem? The explanation continued, without becoming any clearer.

"A DNA computer uses a collection of DNA strands, specially selected so that, when combined, they give us the solution to a particular problem. It's programmed in a similar way to a digital computer, taking base pairs of DNA as bits of data – the programmer's task is to get the DNA molecules to follow instructions."

He looked around at the blank faces.

"Okay, that's enough on how they function. Now, what's the point of these computers? First and foremost, the advantage over traditional computing is massive parallelism. By that, I mean a DNA computer can carry out any number of calculations simultaneously. This is where it has great potential for economic forecasting..."

DNA computing was Jerry Mendoza's pet subject, it seemed.

He spoke about the work at his research centre in San Diego, California: a collaboration between biologists, computer scientists, and economists. Economics provided the problems, which the hardware teams set out to solve. Our work is focused on simulations, he said. We take various models, translate them into computational form, and test them for robustness before we use them in making predictions.

This was familiar stuff to Liz; she'd been doing this sort of thing at the Business School. When the day was over, she spoke to Jerry about her work. She spoke about the external pressures, about the postponed plans for a fresh volume of Marx's *Capital*. And jokingly she added, "With all this technology at your disposal, perhaps you should think about using it to simulate Marx's brain."

Jerry Mendoza didn't raise an eyebrow.

"I'm already working on it," he said. "We've been using your PhD work in our research, in fact. That's why I was keen to have you here."

Then, taking her arm, he startled her with an appeal.

"Listen," he said, "I'd very much like you to come over to San Diego and see what we're up to. We're hosting a conference on consciousness in a few months' time. It'll be an international event with some of the leading thinkers in the field. Why don't you come over? We'd send you a formal invite as a visiting lecturer, a fee plus travel expenses paid. What do you say?"

"Consciousness? It's not really my thing. I wouldn't have anything to say about it."

"That doesn't matter. It's a good excuse for inviting guests. You can see what we're up to and we can thrash out a few ideas. And then, if you get bored, you can take a nap at one of the forums. How does that sound?"

She laughed.

"That sounds fine," she said. "Yes, I'd like to come over, thanks for the invite. I've always wanted to go to California. When's the conference?"

"It's some time in May," he said. "I need to check the dates and then get back to you. Will you excuse me? I must have a word with Humphrey Dillinger before he goes."

He rushed away. Liz joined the rest of the party, who were saying their farewells.

Six months later, she was on a flight to San Diego.

2

Jerry Mendoza sat in his office on the eighteenth floor, looking through a file of cuttings, taken from various journals.

"Scientific advances in DNA research," he read.

"In 1984, following a study of Egyptian mummies, scientists discover that it's possible to extract DNA fragments from soft body tissue. The mummies were approximately 3,000 years old…"

"In 1988, another first. In the archaeology department at Oxford University, a researcher manages to extract DNA fragments from ancient bones. Her work proves useful in solving age-old mysteries, such as unsolved murder cases. Her expertise is sought not only by archaeologists but also by the police; her current projects include a collaborative effort which is trying to identify the Pacific Islanders' country of origin…"

"Inspired by her work, archaeologists have set up the Old Bones Centre at Oxford, dedicated to the study of ancient DNA. One of its first ventures is the Oxford Dodo Project, which is analysing genetic material taken from the bones of a dodo. They believe the pigeon to be the dodo's closest relative, and are comparing the DNA of both types of bird. Scientists believe that studying the dodo will throw light on evolution, and hopefully help save other creatures from extinction…"

Putting the cuttings aside, Mendoza returned to his computer. He scanned his list of email addresses, till he found Karen Sparks at the Oxford Dodo Project. Then he started to write: "Karen: re your query on automation techniques for multiplying DNA fragments…"

*

Waiting at Heathrow, Liz Kendal had nearly missed the plane. It turned out that the San Diego flight went via Frankfurt; it was all so confusing. And at Frankfurt, the connection was delayed. There were rumours of bombs, intensive baggage checks. Eventually, the passengers were asked to board. That's when she bumped into Nigel Price, the neuroscientist, last seen two years ago on a flight from Moscow.

When Nigel Price sat down beside her, Liz was trying hard not to feel wholly frustrated by the business of travelling.

A series of errors, starting with the booking process: she thought she'd booked a cheap flight, found out there was more to pay in airport tax plus a weekend surcharge, then realised it was her fault for not reading the small print. That point still rankled. And now she remembered she hadn't responded to Nigel's last email, which he'd sent three months ago. They'd never got round to meeting, despite their words of intent, and email had been their only line of communication.

"How extraordinary!" he said. "And what a pleasant surprise! You're bound for San Diego then, I take it?"

"Hopefully," she said. "At least I'm on the right plane now – you wouldn't believe the problems I've had…"

The cue for a round of travellers' tales: Nigel had been visiting Moscow again. Now he was flying to San Diego with two colleagues, bound for a conference on consciousness. And you? he asked.

"I'm visiting colleagues," she said. "At the university."

"Really? In San Diego? Now there's a coincidence! Perhaps, if you've got a spare hour or so, we could go sightseeing. There's a zoo that's worth seeing, so I've been told."

"Sounds interesting," she said. "I'll have to check my timetable."

"And how's work? Has anything exciting happened since we last spoke? Ah, refreshments!"

The hostess was doing her rounds.

They talked about the latest government initiatives sweeping the universities, until Liz suddenly felt very tired. She suggested a video; then, five minutes into *Terminator Thirteen*, dozed off, her head slowly tilting till it found a resting place on Nigel's shoulder.

He sat there rigid, not wanting to move, and suffered a terrible cramp when she finally stirred.

*

San Diego in May – blue sky, blue sea, and already there were surfers about. It was so much warmer than the UK. Sat in Jerry Mendoza's office, a noon sun blazing through the windows, Liz Kendal was beginning to sweat. The ventilation system had broken down, and now she was facing a barrage of questions from Jerry and two of his colleagues. It felt like a job interview.

That morning, she'd had a tour of the labs, where the latest DNA computer could only be viewed through glass screens. The problem with DNA, she was told, is that it gets everywhere; cleanliness is paramount. The technical explanations were plentiful, but outside of her realm of understanding, and the equipment looked like a series of bath tubs; like a sauna suite, she thought, without the steam.

Then her interest had soared when Jerry led her into the terminal room, where a printer was churning out sheet after sheet of mathematical calculations. Constant capital, variable capital, surplus value, the symbols and the formulae were all there!

"What… what is this?" she said.

"This is just a test run," Jerry said. "We're showing how the collapse of the Balsam Corporation was inevitable, given their failure to find new investors. It's more evidence for the falling rate of profit. And it's all thanks to you, Liz."

She'd stood there bewildered, thinking how she'd dreamt of producing this kind of stuff and had been warned off, so many years before.

Then he'd taken her arm and said, "Liz, we wouldn't have started this work if it hadn't been for your thesis on modelling the economy. We've now got some of the world's experts working on our project, and we'd like you to join us. We need your expertise, Liz. Let's go up to my office."

Liz, blushing, followed Jerry into the lift, his two colleagues stepping swiftly behind her. Then into Jerry's office, where he'd started by giving a brief history of the international collaboration, known as the Brain of Marx Project.

"I'll explain more tonight," he said. "As I said, Stage One is already in progress. Stage Two is about to start, and we're recruiting right now. Liz, how do you feel about working on the Azores?"

"The Azores? I've never thought about it, why do you ask? I'm not even sure where they are. Why the Azores?"

"Why the Azores," Jerry repeated. "Let me answer that by asking you a few questions, if I may. Please stop me if you feel unable to carry on."

Then the interrogation had started. How did she feel about secrecy? Working on a top secret project? Could she be trusted? Did she have any outside affiliations, political affiliations, and if so, to whom? Had she ever been in a position where she'd betrayed the trust invested in her?

It felt like a job interview. And it was a job interview; unsolicited and totally unexpected.

Liz answered, feeling flattered yet perplexed by it all, and not entirely confident about her performance.

Finally, Jerry turned to his colleagues in turn, sat on either side. No words were spoken. Then he opened a drawer, produced a sheaf of paper, and passed it to Liz.

"This is a contract of employment," he said. "Have a look at it; I'm sure you'll find the terms are very favourable. Liz, we'd like to offer you a post on the project. Take the afternoon to think about it. If you accept, which I sincerely hope you will, you'll be able to meet some of your fellow workers tonight. I'll explain more then."

*

A large room on the eighteenth floor, with a wall of windows, no curtains, looking out at a fluorescent skyline. A circular table, matt black, with Jerry Mendoza's guests sat around it, one chair empty. The presentation and discussion, led by Mendoza.

Liz Kendal would remember this event in detail. It was the first meeting of the team that Jerry had gathered from various parts of the globe, with one end in mind. He'd persuaded them all to work for him, on Stage Two of the Brain of Marx Project.

The presentation had started with an apocalyptic introduction.

The world was going through a crisis, Jerry said; a global recession no less. Our planet has grown smaller; the global village has become a reality. Economies are so tied up with each other – more than ever since the collapse of communism – that falls in the Tokyo stock market have reverberations in America and elsewhere, and the converse is also true.

But the point is, he continued, nobody has any real understanding of why the global economy is the way it is. It cannot be put down to a single factor, such as the price of a barrel of oil. Some time ago, the US government offered funding to projects that might explain the crisis and, hopefully, provide long-term solutions. Short-term solutions will not suffice, they said.

And we have a duty and a responsibility here, said the government. The former communist states are looking to the West for inspiration. If capitalism can't deliver, we're all doomed. Already there are people who hanker after the former system, and there's a danger that these countries will slide into anarchy and civil war. What's required is a comprehensive analysis of the current situation, and one that

158

will point the way to long-term stability. However long it takes, by whatever means, the government will fund it, without interference.

So I decided to take up the challenge, said Jerry.

Initially, when I mentioned Marx, there were raised eyebrows. Then I said that capitalist production cannot be understood merely as a way of making things, as a way of producing use values: its driving force is to create value and surplus value, to be realised in the form of profit. Marx was the first who understood this. Capital is not a thing but a social relation, between the creator of value, and the means of production. What's required today is someone with the brain of Marx; only he would have the ability to make sense of today's complexity.

And I managed to persuade them. The funding is secure. However, there is a proviso. There is no public knowledge of this project. The project will run in secret, until the results are known.

Another proviso: I was asked to find a suitable location, as remote and as isolated as possible, where the project could operate without fear of public perception. That's why we located it on a remote island in the Azores. We have the full cooperation of the Portuguese government, on the pretext that it's part of our military installations there.

So, why all this secrecy? You've all asked me, and you're all due an explanation. And the simple answer is Marx.

Mendoza sighed, reached for a cigar; then, glancing at the command on the wall, put it back in his pocket.

It's a sad fact, he said, that few people in the world have actually read the three volumes of *Capital*; fewer still have understood it. What we have are rumours, second-hand reports, ill-judged opinions, bias and prejudice. For many, his name is inseparable from Engels and the Communist Manifesto. Hence the association with Lenin, Stalin and everything bad, while his economic and social analysis is ignored, reduced to the status of a Penguin Classic.

My friends, it's time to rectify the situation.

*

The presentation had already started when Nigel Price entered the room. He whispered his apologies and sat in the remaining seat, reddening as he did so. Liz Kendal froze, avoiding his eye by staring into her lap. Jerry Mendoza had moved on to the technical aspects of the project.

"Okay," he said, "to simulate Marx's brain, what do we need to do? Let's work through the logic. First, we make this assumption. The brain is basically a processing mechanism, much like a computer. So, we can use computational methods to simulate a brain; that's our assumption. Next, there's the question, what do brains have in common? Practically all the work that's been done in artificial intelligence, cybernetics, etc, has been concerned with the workings of the brain in general – a sort of universal mind, as it were. So, we have systems designed to simulate basic processes such as attention, perception, vision and language understanding. There's a whole body of work here, which has a long history. We have work done under the umbrella of artificial intelligence. What this involves is designing a system that simulates human vision, for instance…"

The gaze of Nigel Price, scanning the faces around the table, had stopped at Liz Kendal, who was staring into her lap.

"… Then we have the more specialised brain, which is also no one's in particular. This involves designing a knowledge base, or a number of knowledge bases, using the rules of logic to represent reasoning in a particular domain. Thus you have expert systems, okay? Say, in medical science, botany, or whatever. Think of it as a kind of encyclopaedia, with reasoning powers. Take, for example, a medical system. A client consults the system with a few symptoms, wants to know what's wrong. The expert asks a few questions, gets a clearer picture, makes a diagnosis, okay?"

This was nothing new to Nigel Price. But the project brought together academics from different disciplines, he reasoned, so maybe Jerry thought an explanation was necessary for their benefit. For the others, like Liz Kendal...

"Now," Jerry continued, "some of this work is going to be useful to us. Marx was an expert in economics, right? So we need a knowledge base containing knowledge of Adam Smith, Ricardo, their methods and assumptions, etc. That's not a problem – we've been working on that, and I can show you the latest version tomorrow."

He paused at this point to glance at the notes spread in front of him. One or two took the opportunity to clear their throats, sniff, or rub their eyes. The ventilation system was supposedly working again, yet the room felt suffocatingly warm.

"Yeah," Jerry said, "I should say that there's also a body of work done under the umbrella of cybernetics or robotics. Here we're dealing with physical objects that move about and do things, within a very limited domain – say, a team of robots that play baseball. That's of no great interest to us; what we're concerned with is the mechanics of thinking, okay?"

Nigel Price was the first to interrupt.

"Pardon me," he said, his glance taking in Liz, "But please remind me, what's the purpose of this project? What are we trying to achieve? I'm totally in the dark here. Help me out."

Jerry Mendoza stepped back, cracking his knuckles.

"Okay," he said, "Let's recap on the global picture. The aim of the project – the ultimate aim – is to produce a new volume of Marx's *Capital*. Why? As an aid to understanding the current state of the world. The world is facing a global economic meltdown; that's why the US government is funding the project..."

"Yes," said Nigel Price, frowning, "I'm sorry I missed your précis, but if that's the goal, don't we need someone who's going to sit down and write it?"

"We have been working on the writing," said Boris Vladimov. "Our text analysis software has been adapted for

161

text production. We are testing it now on personality states…"

"Yes," said Jerry, raising a hand, "Sorry to interrupt, but we'll be talking about that later. Obviously, another sad feature of Marx's great work is the fact that much of it is unreadable; incomprehensible even. Thus we have the depressing picture of generations of academics, all claiming to reveal what Marx really meant. Boris, for those of you who don't know, has been producing a more readable version of the existing volumes of *Capital*. Returning to Nigel's point, it's a question of method. If we had the substance, there'd be no problem in producing a lookalike text; that is, a text that could have been written by Marx, if he were alive and writing in the current period. But first we need to produce the substance, and to produce the substance, we need to think about structure and method. *Capital* wasn't produced in a day, and consider Marx's method – moving from the abstract to the concrete. In other words, we have an intermediary goal here – we need to *think* like Marx, okay?"

He looked at Liz, who smiled, briefly.

"Look," he continued, "We've got all the statistics we need – we have company data from around the world – and theoretically we're in a much better position than Marx – better informed, at any rate – to produce an analysis on a global scale. The question is, what would Marx make of it all? Going back to the aims of the project, we need a computer that can handle vast amounts of data, too vast for any one of us to handle. And to process it, we need to simulate Marx's way of thinking; we need to simulate his brain."

Another pause.

Liz Kendal remembered a movie about a mad scientist, with a brain gurgling away in a glass bottle. Then she pictured the tubs of enzymes that she'd seen that morning. She had an urge to laugh, and suppressed it with a cough.

"Let's suppose we had such a thing," Jerry continued. "Let's suppose we had the brain of Marx. Then, in crude terms, we'd test it by feeding the input data, the knowledge known to Marx, and jiggle about with the processing mechanisms until we produce the output, *Capital* volumes one, two, three. Then we feed the brain a new knowledge input, and the brain produces a new output, *Capital* volumes four, five, six, etc. Which takes us back to procedure: what do we need to simulate his way of thinking? For starters, we need a number of expert systems, a number of knowledge bases; some of which will be general, shared with the likes of us, and some of which will be particular, peculiar to Marx. The first will deal with things such as reasoning, scientific method, the laws of logic, etc. The second will deal with the body of knowledge that was unique to Marx: the books that he studied, the social history of the time, his personal experiences, etc. Much of this work has been done, by one or two who are sat around this table, but there's a large proportion still remaining. Which includes, I should say, the major task of updating the body of historical knowledge. What I propose is a multidisciplinary approach, using a range of methods – conventional computing, neural networks, DNA computing…"

There was more technical talk: an explanation of neural networks, where the input is known, the output is known, but the process that produces the output from the input is not known. So what do we do? asked Jerry. We manipulate the process, or rather the structure, until it produces the result we want. Then we test it on other inputs…

He decided it was time to wind up. He then introduced everyone; a team of twenty-four, Liz counted. There were chemists, biologists, physicists, geneticists, linguists, mathematicians, economists, psychologists, neuroscientists, cognitive scientists, computer scientists, and a couple of philosophers even.

Presumably, Liz thought, to give moral guidance.

She strangled another laugh, while Jerry said there was now time for discussion.

A pause, until someone asked about the advantages of

DNA computing. This prompted a repeat of what Liz had heard at the Atlas think tank.

The man who put the question was Daniel Rousseau. He wasn't impressed by Jerry's gloss.

"You say a DNA computer is basically a programmed chemical reaction, which doesn't rely on electricity. But if we're aiming to simulate a brain, surely we need electricity? The brain is an integrated electrochemical device; it needs both properties to function. To simulate its processing, we cannot rely on chemistry alone."

"I take your point," said Jerry, "and I don't rule anything out, let me make that clear. Biocomputing has many possibilities. I was talking simply from the point of view of parallel processing and speed when we're dealing with mathematical calculations. Any more questions?"

A long pause.

No one had anything to say.

"If there's no more questions," he said, "can I suggest that we retire next door, where you'll find a range of refreshments."

They all trooped out, exchanging smiles, and sauntered into the next room, where a table was spread with wine, fruit juice and water, a selection of biscuits, slices of cake, canapés and various hors d'oeuvres.

Liz, standing there with a glass of wine, found herself talking to a man with smooth dark hair and a blue suit, who introduced himself as Carl Meyer from MIT, the Massachusetts Institute of Technology.

"I do language," he said. "Language as a biological organism. This is big Chomsky idea. We – all of us – are born with capacity for language – *every* language. Every language is here," he said, tapping his head, "waiting for the switch to turn on. English, Dutch, Swahili, Chinese, plop! And you? Language, yes?"

"No, economics," she said, shuffling aside, where Nigel Price stood a few feet away. "Excuse me," she said. Then, turning to Nigel, "Hello, how was the consciousness

164

conference?"

Nigel saw a mischievous smile.

"I'm surprised to see you here," he said abruptly.

She shrugged her shoulders.

"Well, here I am," she said.

Nigel was looking at her as though she'd deceived him; yet he was the one who said he was attending the conference. Strange man, she thought, stiffening.

"And what's your role in the project?" she said.

His face lightened.

"My field is mapping the brain, as you know," he said. "Think of the brain as a processing mechanism, as Jerry said. I shall be looking after the overall design, on the assumption that parts of the brain will correspond to certain features of this... proposed computer. And what about you?"

"I'll be looking after the modelling aspects," she said. "The economic theory."

"Hmm. Fascinating... I'm, I was planning a trip to the zoo tomorrow. Would you like to come along?"

"I think we'll only have a couple of hours to spare. In the morning, I think. Is that enough time?"

Nigel looked doubtful.

"Possibly not," he said. "I've a better idea. We could take a look at the Sea World Adventure Park. It's closer, and we could make it a short visit."

"Sounds good," she said. "And what about the conference?"

"I've been to a couple of sessions," he said. "To be perfectly frank, I fell asleep. Still suffering from jet lag."

They both laughed.

*

Jerry Mendoza spent the rest of the evening sat in his office, clearing away the day's tasks. The first of which was reading his emails. Top of the queue, a message from Karen Sparks at the Oxford Dodo Project.

Hi Jerry

Thanks for the info on automation techniques. I take it your proposal was intended as a joke. We have enough problems at the moment in piecing together a genome from a jigsaw of DNA fragments. Supposing we succeed, there would be more difficulties using a sequence to make viable chromosomes and cells. And then we would need to find a suitable surrogate mother in which to grow an embryo.

I have been informed by the director of our project that we have no plans to clone the dodo. I have to say he thinks your ideas are science fiction. He asked me if you'd seen Jurassic Park.

Best wishes
Karen

Next: news from Simon West at the Human Genome Project, on the discovery of a literacy gene...

*

The next morning, Liz Kendal sat by the swimming pool at her hotel, sipping a glass of orange juice. Then she remembered she had an engagement. She rushed away.

Sea World: there was plenty to do and plenty to see, and not enough time for either. They could have done the interactive killer whale thing, the shark thing, the wild Arctic thing – a simulated journey to the North Pole. But they did none of these things, apart from shake the hands of a simulated octopus. Instead, they wandered about, looking at the smaller tanks, pointing to this and that, until Nigel turned to Liz and said, "How long have you known Jerry Mendoza?"

"About six months," said Liz. "I was invited to sit on a think tank, which he chairs. Why do you ask?"

"Oh, no reason. Just curious."

"Have you known him for long?"

"Yes, several years. He's an international expert on computer architectures. Neural networks used to be his field;

166

that's how I came to meet him. Now it's this DNA computing. What next, I wonder."

"For someone who's just joined the project, you don't sound very enthusiastic."

"No, seriously, I am. It's just that – don't you find him rather fanatical?"

"You have to be a fanatic to get a project like this off the ground. Thank goodness there are people like him in the world. I would have loved to have pioneered something myself, but I don't have the contacts. Or the confidence I guess."

"Liz, what do you know about DNA?"

Nigel looked alarmingly serious.

"Very little," she laughed. "I know it's in the body, and it leaves traces, and it's unique to every individual. It's a daily feature of forensic science now, it's used a lot in crime detection. And the Human Genome Project – that's something to do with DNA, isn't it? Or genes at least. What's the difference?"

"DNA is basically a chemical – dio-something-or-other acid. It combines to form enzymes and proteins. A gene is made up of a DNA sequence. It's a bit like the difference between words and sentences. A DNA string contains three-letter words, which are grouped together to form sentences; the sentences are the genes."

"So you need to be a bit of a linguist then, to understand it all?"

"Yes, you could say that. And a mathematician, because there are only four letters in a human's DNA alphabet, but there are three billion letters in one cell. It's the permutations and combinations that make for variety."

"And what's the reason for your interest?"

"What?"

"You asked me, what do I know about DNA?"

"Oh, yes. Well, don't you find it odd that there are few among us who fully understand the nature of the project we're all working on?"

"No, not really. That's bound to be the case on a big project like this. Do you fully understand it?"

"No, I don't. And there's only one person who does, it seems."

Liz looked at him.

"Jerry Mendoza," he said.

She was still looking at him.

"It's just an observation," he added. "That's all."

Just an observation, but to Liz it sounded like a warning.

"We'd better make a move," he said, glancing at his watch.

*

Jerry Mendoza was attending the consciousness conference that morning. Daniel Rousseau was giving a presentation on biocomputing. The title of his talk: The Cloning of Consciousness.

"What I want to talk about," he said, "are the ways in which biology and computer science can come together to help us understand the very roots of consciousness. First, let's look at how the brain functions."

He gave a brief review of the current state of knowledge, dealing with brain chemistry, the nervous system, the sending of signals around the body, and speaking of the thalamus as the "bouncer on the door of consciousness."

Jerry Mendoza made a note of that.

Then he talked about neural networks.

"These are computational systems," he said, "which consist of artificial neurons, interconnected, and transmitting data via logic junctions that mimic the synaptic functions of the brain."

The main problem, said Daniel, is that there are billions of connections in the brain; in fact, more connections than there are base pairs in a human genome. We want to know what biological processes enable us to store knowledge, to retrieve memories, to respond to stimuli. *Eh bien*, we may never answer these questions, because the processes may be infinite.

Recent discoveries make the task more complex, he said, yet at the same time show the way forward. The current estimate is a hundred billion neurons in the human brain, and possibly five thousand billion supporting cells, known as glia. These glia fall into two main subgroups: one has an influence on the velocity of data transmission; the other plays a role in integrating sensory data input. At this moment in time, we don't have the full picture.

And we need the full picture if we are to understand consciousness, he said. Therefore, for future work, I recommend that we study all the relationships of neural and non-neural cellular interconnections, not just those between neurons.

Finally, a word on DNA computing. This may prove significant for finding molecular algorithms, for understanding cellular mechanisms, but can it go beyond essentially biochemical problems and simulate consciousness? I think not, said Daniel. A true biocomputer will transmit data electrochemically as in a synapse. The way forward is the multidisciplinary approach, bringing together biology, chemistry, physics, computer science and neuroscience. Then we may begin to tackle the problem of consciousness through a rigorous programme of scientific research.

Applause.

From all but Jerry Mendoza, who sat there taking notes while comparing the young Rousseau with the older Nigel Price. Rousseau had been a recent find; Price he'd known for years – intelligent of course, and an international expert on brain structure; yet lacking the dynamism of the younger man.

Though age can be useful, he thought. Nigel's influence was crucial in persuading Bob Rheingold to become more involved. I must send Bob an email; he must know the current state of affairs.

*

Liz Kendal glanced at the clock on the wall; she was flagging a little. More tours of the research labs, that was the plan. The new team had divided into groups of five. Mendoza wasn't around; his colleagues had organised the day: chaperoning them to the refreshments, and demonstrating their latest work in expert systems.

Liz stood by Carl Meyer, the man from MIT, as a sequence of formulae and figures filled the screen.

"Basically," said the demonstrator, "you present the system with a problem, and the system answers according to its methodology. So, for instance, you've got the Ricardo method; or you've got the Marx method, which is what you're looking at right now…"

Carl Meyer was frowning.

"You don't use the Venus Three Zero Plasma Plus terminals? Is a much better display, yes? More resolution, bigger screens. Just like TV."

"Yeah, we have those, but they're in the graphics lab. We find these adequate for statistical work. The state of the art stuff is next door. What I'd like to show you is a version of this system which has embedded design rules. What it does basically is analyse other systems and then offers a critique, from a Marxian point of view. Then, if you want, it can reconfigure the system; it can also design a whole system for you from scratch. It's a system that reproduces itself, basically."

"Like a virus?" said Carl Meyer.

The demonstrator laughed.

"It could be," he said. "It depends on what you want to do with it. We had a trainee once who was shit hot. He got it to attack every spreadsheet program on the campus network, and all the balance sheets mutated. It was asking the user for things like number of employees, so it could work out the rate of exploitation and stuff. Let's go next door, and I'll show you what it can do."

As they followed him out, Carl Meyer turned to Liz and said, "The phoenix rises, yes?"

"Hopefully," she said.

*

On the Azores, there were rumours that Pico mountain was going to erupt. There'd been a slight earth tremor on the island, and one of its cones was puffing out black smoke. Bob Rheingold listened to a local news broadcast, which was telling people not to panic: a group of explorers had lit a camp fire. In the two years he'd spent on the islands, he'd learnt a smattering of Portuguese, enough to understand weather talk – here, as elsewhere, a useful topic for idle chat. Essential rather than idle, in fact, because apart from the threat of earthquakes and volcanic eruptions, there were rainstorms that filled the sky.

Given the potential for a natural disaster, it was a strange place to locate a research establishment, he thought. Vast amounts of money had been invested in the equipment alone; plus the housing of it, custom-built, and an entire village to house the staff. All paid for by the Global Economy Initiative, and indirectly by the US government. Presumably, he thought, they'd checked out the insurance premiums before choosing the location. He must ask Mendoza about that.

Yet, he asked himself, was the danger any worse than in Florida, say? Earth tremors were nothing compared to a hurricane. Besides, Pico was about five hundred kilometres away. It was the islands in the central zone that were most at risk; and even then, the most recent eruptions had been at sea. Torre de Columba was fairly safe: no eruptions for five hundred years, and the craters were thought to be extinct. And from the scenic point of view, the location was a humdinger – a chain of mountains rising from the sea, the tops often covered in mist; the white cliffs on either side; the lush pasture down below, crossed by lines of hydrangea, herds of dairy cattle, and a farmer with a horse and cart. From the windows of his house he could see orange trees, the remains of a plantation, and the Atlantic beyond. The winters were mild, there was no snow.

And the work was progressing at speed; the project was ahead of schedule. The supercomputer was already functioning; more tests were needed. The work force had been terrific, releasing time so that he could explore his surroundings.

That was before the recent developments, when Mendoza floated the idea that he might design a new SQUID for brain-monitoring purposes. There was no mention of that in the contract. Initially he'd balked at the idea, but the challenge was too tempting: to design a brain-scanning device that was truly portable, sufficiently light not to be a handicap.

The main problem was getting parts at short notice. There was no problem getting hold of them, as such; US jets were to-ing and fro-ing every day, between the States and the Middle East. They stopped here for fuel. But freight wasn't their prime reason for flying. You had to go through the proper channels, and be diplomatic about it. Which took time.

Meanwhile, the emails.

First, one from Mendoza, alerting him to another visit from Nigel Price. Nigel Price will be arriving with further specifications for the new headset. No cause for alarm, said Jerry. The plans are still the same, we just need to discuss the finer details.

*

Liz Kendal had a week in California; all of it in San Diego, and most of that at the university. She'd planned to hire a car and drive along the coast to San Francisco, but distance was a problem, plus time.

The distance was awesome. On the map, a thumbnail; then she finds it's around five hundred miles to San Francisco and the trip's not feasible; it would have been like driving from Cambridge to the far north of Scotland.

And time: the week was fairly packed. More tours of the research labs; more talks and presentations – all members of the team were asked to give one for the benefit of the rest. Plus a seminar for the economics department, on CREEP's work in exporting capitalism to Eastern Europe. That proved to be the most difficult task, because already her heart wasn't in the job.

Then there were meals out. One, for the whole research team. Restrained, but pleasant enough. And one with Nigel Price – embarrassing. He wasn't the greatest entertainer; his obsession with parts of the brain was a bit much even for the waiters. She felt relieved when he said he was flying to New York, as it meant she would be flying back alone. Time to relax.

Then the return. Her house in Cambridge. Valuables that would have to go into store. She didn't want to sell; she would rent it out through a reputable agency. Her contract was for ten years; big earnings tax free, plus free accommodation, and travel expenses that allowed for two home visits a year. The package was too good to refuse. Yet even so, ten years on the Azores…

She stood in the bathroom, looking in the mirror, with that question beginning to gnaw: how did I get here? Her hair, now cut short, slight traces of grey. The curse of having black hair: so soon does it change colour. In ten years' time, what would it look like? She was now in her forties, unmarried, no children, but these things didn't feature in her vision: not of the past; not of the future. She was committed to the project, and that was that.

Six months later, she was flying to the Azores.

*

Liz had her own bungalow, built recently in the local style –

whitewashed walls and a roof of red tile. Warm, bright and spacious, with views of the island, meadows and mountains, the blue shades of the Atlantic. No complaints there. But if she ever wanted to leave...

This was an island that was closed to tourists, it seemed. No mention in the guidebooks, and Liz couldn't find it on the map.

After flying across the Atlantic from Lisbon to Sao Miguel, she was met by a Portuguese guide and escorted onto a private jet which took her to Terceira, an island further west. Her fellow passengers were two US military personnel, one of whom said "Howdy!" when she got on, while the other said "Have a nice day!" when she got off.

Island hopping: that was stage one.

At the airport at Lajes, a helicopter took her on the next stage, to an airfield on the island of Flores, north-west of Terceira. The pilot climbed down and told her to wait. She looked out of the window as he shouted at the fuel men, arms waving and pointing to another helicopter, with a pilot on board. An argument about who was meant to be driving, it seemed. Or the lack of fuel. There was a smell of gas, and then she was back in the air, taken further west to the little airfield at Lindoso, on Torre de Columba. There she was met by another guide, who carried her baggage, grinning whenever she looked at him. The bungalow was a short walk away. There weren't many cars on Torre de Columba. Or roads for that matter.

The transport arrangements had been explained in the briefing documents, sent shortly before her departure. They contained a few surprises.

For a start, the map. The Azores were bigger than she'd thought. Or rather, longer. On her tourist map, the archipelago stretched about four hundred miles, with a hundred-mile gap between the south-east group – Sao Miguel and Pico were the main tourist destinations – and the north-west group of Flores and Corvo. What it didn't show was the islands to the north-west of Flores, stretching another hundred miles into the Atlantic. Most were just bare rock, uninhabited by humans, nesting places for cormorants. But at the end of this stretch, Torre de Columba was a little oasis, with green fields, a couple of farms, a village at both tips.

And an international research centre.

The briefing documents had also explained that there were a large number of military bases dotted around the islands, air and naval, and that security was currently a matter of some concern. There were consequences for the research team. All air and sea traffic must be authorised, said the briefing. Please observe the enclosed code of practice; we ask you to bear in mind that these arrangements are for your own safety.

The day after her arrival, Jerry Mendoza said it was just a formality. Jerry, it seemed, had the powers to authorise.

"The official line is that all traffic is subject to clearance from the military," he said. "This includes any departure from the island, even if it's just a shopping trip. What it means is that I have to fill in a form, send it to them for clearance, and wait for the thumbs up. Unofficially, I just send the form, full stop. If it comes from me, they'll give it the OK."

Liz was forming a picture: of the island as a boarding school, with Jerry as the headmaster. He saw her look of concern.

"It's not a major problem," he said. "Life goes on just the same. All the scheduled air and ferry services are in the clear, so they're operating as normal. It affects us though, because the only scheduled service to this place is the air bus, which brings the mail. That runs daily, but they're not licensed to carry passengers. Then there's the supply boat, which comes once a week to deliver food and stuff. They do have a licence to carry passengers, but that's a recent development. The island was uninhabited till a few years ago. The population had either died out or emigrated. Can you blame them? This is as remote as you can get."

"So… What if I want to go shopping?"

175

Jerry produced a cigar, pausing to light it.

"There are shops in the village," he said. "The next shop is a hundred and sixty kilometres away, on Flores. For that you'd need clearance. You could take the supply boat, but then you'd be away for a week. Or the air bus, in which case you'd need an overnight, and I'd still have to get clearance. If you wanted a day trip, we'd have to see what machines are available. It's no problem, seriously. I just have to fill out a form."

The next surprise came when Jerry gave her a guided tour. The research centre was on the edge of the village; everywhere was within walking distance here. From the outside it looked like the village school, with whitewashed walls and red tiles. Except that the buildings formed a large complex, far bigger than the village. And inside, away from the foyer, the walls were lined with metal. She was introduced to Bob Rheingold, who'd been living out here for three years, designing a computer. Then she was shown the labs, where the parts were being assembled for a new electronic device. The workers were Chinese.

Jerry saw her quizzical look.

"We had to use imported labour," he explained. "The locals are excellent at fishing and farming, but when it comes to IT… These workers know their stuff, and they're fast. They've had a lot of experience."

Liz wondered what the locals thought of the place. But where were the locals? She took a walk around the village at lunchtime. The workers in the shops were all Chinese. Then, in the square, she saw the man who'd carried her baggage. A local – the local? A peasant at any rate, and definitely Mediterranean, if not Portuguese. He stood in a doorway, grinning at her, several teeth missing.

Meanwhile, sat in his office, Jerry Mendoza picked up his list of unfinished business. First item: a report for the UK government on the deliberations of the Atlas think tank…

A sigh, and he turns his mind to Stage Two once more. The

176

Brain of Marx Project. With Liz's arrival, the new recruits are all in place.

*

About a year after being introduced to the new members of the team, Bob Rheingold opens a door and ushers Jerry Mendoza into a room full of video monitors. Colours flash across the screens. Bob stands there admiring his work; his own version of the Northern Lights. He knows he's not making the lights; he's just the facilitator. Yet even so, the results are impressive, and it's all due to him.

The colours are coming from the portable brain-monitoring machines, which incorporate the very latest in SQUID design. And not even from them, but from the subjects wearing them, who are now approaching the end of their two-week trial.

He glances at the far wall, where a giant map of the brain is pinned. It reminds him of the old navigators' maps of the world, charting the unexplored waters, the unknown territories.

Technology!

He turns to Jerry.

"Have you ever read Hakluyt's *Voyages and Discoveries of the English Nation*?" he says.

Jerry looks puzzled.

"I can't say that I have," he says.

"I read it when I was in the Arctic, many years ago," says Bob. "The old explorers – they'd embark on a voyage and be away for two, three years or longer. Then they'd return – God willing – very often starving, diseased, and with little to show for their efforts. Now look at us, four hundred years later. The explorers are exploring themselves. And mapping the brain at a far greater speed than it took to map the world. Thanks to technology."

"Thanks to you, Bob," says Jerry. "You've done an excellent job. I can't thank you enough."

"Don't embarrass me," says Bob. "But… thanks for saying that."

Bob turns to the giant map, looking for gaps, and not finding any.

Jerry looks at the screens, hypnotised by the lights. He's still waiting for two of his research team. They know he's there, but they were in the middle of doing something. Now they approach in their white coats, and Bob turns to Jerry.

"I'll leave you to it, then," he says. "Let me know if you need anything."

"Sure," says Jerry. "I'll speak to you later. And thanks again, Bob."

Bob leaves them to it.

*

Daniel Rousseau and Nicolai Perepenko were leading this experiment, one of many on the workings of the brain. It was Daniel who'd sprung the idea. A bit like one of those TV shows, where a number of people are stuck in a house together, unable to escape until time is called.

This one was the pilot, the result of a brainstorming session.

"Okay, so we have expert systems," Jerry had said. "They're all in place and they all work, up to a point. The problem is, we need to study thinking in action, experts at work."

They discussed objectives, experimental techniques. There would be a series of experiments, designed to answer questions such as: How do experts think? How do scientists think? How do Marxists think? How would Marx think? The programme needs a structure, said Jerry.

"So," said Nicolai, "we ask a famous scientist to take part. Perhaps a Nobel prize-winner. We monitor the brain in action as he attempts to solve a complex problem."

"Yes," said Jerry, "but first things first. We need to test the helmets in action. We need to see what they're capable of measuring."

"It would be a disaster," said Nigel Price, "if we invited a Nobel prize-winner to take part, and then found out the helmets weren't up to much."

"Always the optimist, Nigel," said Jerry. "But you're right in this case. We should start with a simple exercise. Maybe using students."

Carl Meyer turned to Liz, smiling.

"Perhaps Liz would like to volunteer," he said. "Then we can do our test on a Marxist, yes?"

Liz coloured.

"I don't think I'd qualify as a model Marxist," she said.

"It wouldn't be a good idea to involve ourselves in this," said Jerry.

"I have it!" said Daniel. "Why don't we assemble a group of young academics and monitor their brain activities as they go about the process of writing academic papers? I know this has been done before, but never with such advanced measuring equipment as we now have. And the helmets are portable. The subjects can set about their tasks with minimal interference."

And so it was decided, the idea being to monitor the scientific brain at work.

The procedure was discussed at length.

First, it was decided that scientists from the UK would be invited to take part, as they were used to working under the pressures of the UK's Research Assessment Exercise.

Next: method.

Young aspiring scholars were chosen; their careers had barely started. They were all told to produce four papers in two weeks, on matters of their own choosing. Before they arrived on site, they were divided into four groups. They were all given the same instructions, but each group was given a different context for their task.

One, the control group, was told simply that they were taking part in a brain-monitoring experiment, and to go about their activities in their normal way. The second group was told that their universities were going through a financial crisis, and their jobs were dependent on the results of the experiment – if they failed to complete the papers in the allocated time, they wouldn't have a job to return to. The third group was given a financial incentive to complete the work, with a bonus on completing the fourth paper. And the fourth group was given the promise of a raunchy night with a famous pop idol, who had been bribed into giving a video address in person to these young hopefuls.

The academics were all male.

"A mixed group would be a disaster," said Jerry. "These people are going to be sleeping in the same houses for two weeks, do you follow me?"

The organisation of the experiment had proved to be a nightmare, in terms of time and expense. Extra planes had to be hired, and the subjects blindfolded to keep the location a secret. Plus the materials they needed to write the papers. Access to library materials was provided via the Internet, but every academic had a personal library that was also essential if the work was to be seen as part of their normal activities.

Next: results.

Twenty-four hours into the experiment, and Jerry Mendoza was rubbing his hands with glee, thinking it well worth the months they'd spent organising the event.

"Look at this!" said Daniel, pointing to a monitor. "Was it Freud who said we think about sex at least once a minute?"

"I don't know," said Jerry. "Is he thinking about sex? He's meant to be writing a scientific paper."

"This one is horny! Every thirty seconds, he has a sex thought. See how this hormone activator lights up!"

"Christ!" said Jerry. "Which group is this?"

"He's in the control group. But incredibly the other groups show similar results. Apart from the fear group; their sex drive is way down."

"Hmm, a pity we can't monitor their sleep. I wonder what

that would tell us."

"Ah! The answer is on this one," said Daniel, pointing to another monitor. "He's in the fear group. He didn't sleep at all last night; he worked throughout at the keyboard. Now he's dropped off, and look at that hormone activator! It's like he's making up for lost time."

"Hmm, any other observations? What about productivity?"

"It's too early to say," said Daniel. "At this stage, the fear group is in the lead, and the control group is last. There's no difference between the sex group and the money group."

"Incredible! So fear is the great motivator?"

"It seems so. Of course, their work may be total garbage. Boris is analysing the texts now."

"Excellent!" said Jerry. "I'll call back in a couple of hours."

The beauty of the experiment was that everything was being monitored – not only the brain activity. The actions of the subjects were recorded via video cameras; their computer input recorded via hidden software. Thus it was possible to match a pause at the keyboard with lights on the brain screen, showing what parts of the brain were active, or inactive, and to compare the results with the text in production.

Two weeks later, and the experiment had produced a mountain of data.

"It's going to take months to process this," said Jerry.

When the helmets were finally removed, he visited each house in turn.

First, the fear group.

"I'm pleased to say that nobody has lost their job as a result of this exercise," he said, producing a bottle of champagne.

A round of applause from the four contestants, who had completed their quota in the two weeks. The other groups were less successful, though some contestants did manage to complete four papers. The control group was the least productive: no one in the group managed to complete.

There was now an awkward situation with the sex group, two of whom were expecting the reward of a night out with

Candy Tuft. Free concert tickets weren't quite the same thing. Jerry decided to delegate the job of informing them to Nigel Price, who muttered his disapproval of unscrupulous methods, yet was as eager as the rest to know the results.

*

Liz Kendal had been on the island barely a month when she reached that monumental decision: she liked the place. Monumental, because it wasn't quite what she had in mind when she'd thought about it, months before in California. Asked to consider the post, she'd gone straight to the library and sought out info. The Azores had its own university so she'd assumed, without asking, that the project would have some links with it – on Sao Miguel, where most of the population were situated.

But this island's isolation was a positive feature, as far as work was concerned. Here was solitude and space for thought. No distractions, no students, few cars. No pubs, drunken brawls, street fights. Hardly any noise at all in fact, apart from the jets, a regular stream, which followed the chain of islands to and from Terceira.

And on the island, there was a constant stream of visitors, most of whom were taking part in some experiment or other. Everybody was occupied with their own bit of business; the Chinese kept a closed circle. Occasionally she would see a farmer with a cart, moving cattle. More often, the helicopter, bringing post, and boats bringing supplies, which seemed to show up every day.

Every day too, Bob Rheingold.

The nature of the project meant that she and Bob were working together on the supercomputer. Bob had designed it, the Chinese had built it, and now Bob was testing it, with data and software supplied by Liz.

And indirectly by Adam Meccano.

She'd called to see him before her departure, almost twelve

months ago. She was picking up the pieces, several years on, and the material was essential, she said. And he'd said that, strictly speaking, the material was copyright.

"But most of it's in the public domain," said Liz. "Why should it be copyright? Anyone can go to Companies House and get this information, for a small fee."

"Some of it," he said. "But only the most general figures. If you recall, the large part came when we asked for it, and we had to sign a waiver concerning its use. The software was written by the programmers here, and we own the copyright."

"But the software is based on my thesis, which you don't own. Without the theory, the software wouldn't exist."

Adam glanced at the door.

"Yes," he said, "you may have a point. I'll have to look into this. Sorry, Liz, but I've got a student waiting to see me. What are you doing tonight? Why don't you come round for dinner, and we can discuss this at our leisure. It may be our last meeting for... er, some time I guess."

It took a night's indiscretion before he gave the project his blessing. A blessing plus an oath of secrecy. On her side too, as it happened. Adam was a married man.

Meanwhile, back to the data.

Statistics. Post-war facts and figures. The global economy. The national picture. Data from the UK, USA, France, Germany, Japan, South-East Asia, etc. Multinationals, company details, balance sheets.

The falling rate of profit.

After several months of this, Liz was provoked by an idea that threatened to send her into fits of laughter. It started with a childhood memory, of a game she used to play called mums and dads. With dolls, she recalled.

Now it took an adult form. This work was in fact a game. She was mum, feeding the computer. Bob was dad, patting it on the back. Their baby.

And when she saw him, the urge to laugh was overpowering. He, in his white coat, could have been wearing a pinafore. Should have been wearing a pinafore.

On the third day of the game, he decided to say something about it.

"Is everything okay?" he said.

"Yes thanks, fine," she said.

"You've been working very hard," he said.

She didn't know what to say to that. So she shrugged her shoulders and smiled.

"I enjoy my work," she said.

"What are you doing tomorrow?" he said.

"Tomorrow? Feeding... Er, working on this data I guess; there's loads to do. Why?"

"It's Saturday. Would you care to go for a walk?"

"A walk? Where?"

The village, the harbour, the airfield, the meadows. Liz had seen it all, several times over.

"We could explore the island a little," he said. "It's not very big. You can walk to the end and back in a day."

"Oh," she said. "Yes, I'd like that. I think I need to get out. A change of scenery. Yes, I'd like that."

"Right," he said. "Tomorrow."

*

Mist over the mountains, sunlight down below. On the cliffs to their left, a colony of rock doves, two cooing as Liz and Bob walk over a heather moor, following an old cart track.

"It reminds me of Wales," said Liz. "Except for the black rocks. What are they? Do you know?"

"They're lava rocks," said Bob. "Basalt. These mountains are volcanoes."

Liz looked up. The mist was creeping down the slope, where the heather gave way to a litter of black boulders.

"They're not active, haven't been for five hundred years," he said.

"It's very atmospheric here. I like it."

"It's the first time I've been up here since... Let's think... I think the last time was before you arrived. Have you settled in now? How's... Miguel! *Bom dia!*"

Out of the mist, a man wearing a dark brown jacket, and a dove perched on his shoulder.

"*Bom dia senhor, senhora,*" he said.

There followed a few words in Portuguese, which Liz didn't understand. She looked at the dove; the dove sat there blinking. Then Miguel bowed towards her, taking his leave with a large smile.

"He tames doves," said Bob. "Trains them, I should say. That one had a bad foot."

"You speak Portuguese?"

He laughed.

"What you heard just now was stretching my limit," he said. "I taught myself a couple of years ago. Enough to understand the weather forecast."

"I wish I knew a few words. So, you've been here... is it three years now?"

"It'll soon be four years. It's wonderful. It's a good place to work, don't you think?"

"It's an excellent place to work. Though I guess you need to be dedicated."

Bob looked at her.

"You're not dedicated?" he said.

"Yes, I am. I meant – I know some people who would get very bored here."

"The lure of the big lights."

"Yes. Not for me I have to say. I've been working on this project for too long not to see it through."

"You have a mission then, I take it."

"Yes, I suppose I do."

Beads of mist on his steel-grey crew cut. He swept them off.

"Liz," he said, "I don't mind telling you this is the strangest project I've ever worked on. The Brain of Marx Project! When

185

I started working on it, it was known as WEEP – the World Economy and Enterprise Project. Funded by the Global Economy Initiative, with a focus on economic forecasting. I had a ten-year contract to design and build a computer. It's up and operational in record time, and then I'm asked to design a portable brain scanner. All fine and dandy, and I enjoy the work, but... Liz, what do you know about UK farmers?"

"Oh! Not a lot. I know they've been having a bad time with BSE. Why do you ask?"

"A group arrived on the island the other day. For tests. Experiments. Jerry asked me to show them the helmets. They're taking part in a literacy experiment, he said. Now maybe I'm stupid, but I just don't see the connection with economic forecasting. Or the brain of Marx. Do you?"

"No. It wasn't mentioned when we talked about the programme. Is this economic literacy?"

"He didn't specify. Look!"

Higher up, a gap in the mist, giving glimpses of the sea beyond. The track was stonier here, black boulders on both sides. They stood a while, uncertain of the path.

"Do you think it'll clear?" she said. "I haven't seen the tops for weeks."

"It's like that sometimes. It might stay for a morning, might stay for weeks. It's totally unpredictable. There's an old whaling post up there. They must have had fun."

"Whaling?"

"Yeah, a lookout post. It used to be very big round here. Someone would keep watch and give the shout when whales were about."

"What happened here? I mean, why did everyone leave?"

"It's so isolated, that was a big reason. Apart from cattle and fishing, the only thing that kept the island going was oranges. There were plantations on the *fajas*, that's the flat lands where we are, and at the far end. Some years back there was a disease that ravaged the whole crop. There was nothing else for them. So they left. Migrated to the States. The families that are here now are a new generation of settlers. They came about ten years ago, as far as I can make out. They were here when I came, I know that. Shall we go back?"

Liz looked at the path.

"It's about seven kilometres to the end, but the path gets very boggy and I don't think the mist'll clear. We can come again."

"Yeah, another day. Tell me, where does the name come from? The island I mean."

He laughed.

"There's a few tales about the name, and I'm not sure that any are true. Torre de Columba – I think it means the tower of Columbus. Christopher Columbus. The first European to sail to America, apparently, though I think the Vikings beat him by centuries. Anyway, there's various legends that link him with the Azores. Some say this was where he first landed on his return journey. Apparently, he stood on the top of the volcano, looking for the rest of his fleet – hence the tower. The old whaling shelter is meant to mark the spot. Another story says that the volcano erupted just after he left the island, so the volcano took his name…"

Liz was frowning.

"What happened to the farmers?" she said. "I didn't see them land, and I've seen no sign of them since."

Bob stopped and looked at her.

"That's another strange thing," he said. "They're staying in Sebo, at the other end of the island. It's an old fishing village. We'll walk there one day, when the weather clears. On days like these, it's easier by boat. So they're sightseeing, it seems. Meeting the local farmers. It's like a holiday for them."

Liz laughed.

"So Jerry's turning the place into a holiday resort," she said.

"I don't know what he has in mind," said Bob.

They carried on walking, passing the cliffs without

speaking.

Through the mist, the sound of the rock doves, cooing.

3

Nicolai Perepenko and Boris Vladimov sat side by side, comparing and analysing. Nicolai held the time sheets of the brain's activity; Boris held a pile of notes produced by the brain's owner. Nigel Price stood behind them, waiting for the results.

"It is as I thought," said Nicolai. "Lenin had a well-developed spatula."

"Spatula?" said Nigel.

"It is a little-known area of the brain, here," said Nicolai, pointing to the map on the wall. "It is generally inactive in most people, more used with creative people, creative thinkers and writers. It corresponds to the moment when the thinker has a flash of inspiration. I call it a Eureka moment. See, this spike here."

"Ye–es," said Nigel, drawing out the vowel. "Yes, I see. But it's so brief."

"A matter of nanoseconds," said Nicolai. "This is a large-scale time sheet. The detail would not be picked up on an older scanner. Brief, but in that short space of time the writer developed a plan of his entire paper. He made all the connections."

"Incredible!" said Nigel. "And these flashes occur... how often?"

"For this writer, once in each paper, towards the beginning. His four papers show similar tendencies. However, it varies. Another one has a flash in the middle of his papers, and goes on to make significant alterations. We are now picking up similar spikes with our Nobel prize-winners, but more frequently."

"The former Marxist, not so frequent," said Boris, laughing.

"Oh," said Nigel. "Jerry won't be pleased to hear that. You mean he's not very inspired?"

"He's no Marx," said Boris. "His writing is very dull…"

"I've heard that said about Marx," Nigel muttered.

"… It lacks the emotive factor," said Boris.

"His spatula is a disappointment, it's true," said Nicolai. "But what is interesting about the others is the velocity of the glial activity. The spatula lights up, then we see a rapid firing of neuronal chains, left and right."

"Ah!" said Nigel. "Harmony then. A flashbulb moment."

"Yes," said Nicolai. "A flashbulb moment. We've noted this feature also: there are not so many chains firing in these younger academics, compared to our Nobel prize-winners."

"Their flashbulbs are of lower wattage, I suppose," said Nigel.

"Excuse me?" said Nicolai.

"Jerry will be very interested to see this," said Nigel, turning away. "I'll go and see if he's available."

*

Jerry Mendoza was sitting at his desk, holding his head and assessing the current state of progress. The location was now a handicap, he thought. There was no secure way of shipping the DNA computer to the Azores; it was too unstable. And even if there were, the university in San Diego wouldn't allow it. Fair enough: it was their property; not tied to the project. So he'd started the process of building a fresh one, using the California one as a model. In the meantime, he was flying across the Atlantic twice a month to supervise operations on both sides, and getting exhausted in the process.

He needed reassurance that the problem was simply a practical one, of shipping materials. Rumours of war didn't help; if that were to happen, the problem wouldn't be so simple.

And so tired was he, that he had to remind himself of the

reasons for building two computers in the first place.

Why?

One, because the DNA technology was untested, whereas the supercomputer was more reliable. The idea was to feed the same input into both devices, using the output of the latter to test the precision of the former. Play about with the processing mechanisms till it came out right.

And two, because of the possibilities of biocomputing. After all, the idea was not just to produce statistics, but to simulate a brain. Marx's brain. And to do that, he said to himself, we need an electrochemical device, as Daniel Rousseau pointed out.

Plus a design plan. A map of the proposed brain. Its architecture. Which we have, almost, thanks to the programme of experiments. We have the basic structure, we know which bits are responsible for what, and new details are emerging every day, thanks to our measuring techniques. Plus, we have the genetic data that's flooding out of Sebo, which will help us to tweak the chemistry of the new machine.

Machine! No, not a machine. A brain. Artificial maybe, but with all the processing capabilities of a real brain. And maybe not so artificial, not so much tweak as build from scratch, using human enzymes…

"Eureka!"

The shout made Jerry jump out of his chair. He turned to see Nigel Price standing there.

"Sorry," said Nigel. "But the door was open."

"What's happened?" said Jerry.

"Developments, developments," said Nigel. "Have you heard the news about Lenin's spatula?"

*

It seemed to Liz that all members of the team were now busy with second jobs of some sort or other. In her case, it was back to the days of Camden library and the *Capital* reading group.

It took a mental pinch and a glance at the window to be sure that history wasn't repeating itself. She wasn't in Camden, and she wasn't working with cleaners or bus drivers. And they weren't meant to be discussing revolutionary politics. At least, Jerry had said not; and she couldn't imagine a group of British farmers forming the vanguard of a revolutionary party. Although, she thought, Farmer SG54 showed great potential. She was stunned by his admiration for Robert Mugabe: had she been duped – by the BBC no less – into thinking that Mugabe was a brutal dictator? Farmer SG54 seemed to think so, and now she wondered.

When Jerry had told her about the farmers, she had struggled to grasp the reason for the experiments.

"We're testing their literacy," he said. "I thought a reading group would be a good way to measure their progress. Using Marx would be even better. And as you've done this sort of thing before…"

"Yes, but I don't understand the relation to the project. Why should we carry out literacy tests? Isn't this what colleges are for?"

"Not exactly," he said. "I may as well be straight with you, Liz. These are genetic implant trials."

"Genetic implant trials? Implants of what?"

Jerry's face was taut. Explanations, it seemed, tried his patience.

"I'm in regular contact with the Human Genome Project," he said. "This has come about as a result of their discoveries, not mine. They've identified genes for literacy and numeracy. We've given the farmers injections, based on their findings."

"So they're all on drugs?"

"Yes. These are trials."

"I still don't see the relation to the project."

"Liz, we're designing a brain. The brain will be an electrochemical device, using materials that simulate the human equivalent. It's going to be a monumental feat that requires genetic engineering to be successful. Literacy and numeracy are fundamental. If this works, we'll have the basic infrastructure. Do you follow me?"

"Yes, I see the connection. But these drugs… They haven't been tested, presumably?"

"No. Not on humans. They've had the usual rat trials, tests for side effects. Nothing came up. Nigel's agreed to lead the numeracy group, and I have to say their progress is excellent. They're working on logarithms already. So will you do it? It should take a couple of hours each day. Then you can leave them to work on their assignments."

So Liz agreed to do it.

And the results so far seemed to confirm that materialist law of the progress of nations: history as a march of uneven and combined development. Was that Marx? Or Lenin? She couldn't remember; but she remembered the last time she'd heard it – Humphrey Dillinger!

Anyway, she thought – advances and setbacks.

Setbacks, like Farmer FA22, who, while Liz was talking about abstraction, was struggling with a more fundamental problem. Namely, the urge to count the number of words on a page before he could contemplate reading them. Jerry thought he'd been given the wrong implant by mistake. He's suffering from some sort of hyper-numeracy, he said; he's developed the urge to count everything. Give him a week and we'll review the situation. Maybe we can stick him in Nigel's group.

But the situation had worsened. Before the week was over, Farmer FA22 insisted on wearing his ID badge clipped to his ear, and counting the same page endlessly to check that no words had gone missing. Next: mooing noises at night, coming from the walls of his cottage.

I think he's going senile, said Jerry. This is terrible. It must be a side effect. I don't know what we can do to stop it.

Isn't there an antidote, said Liz.

Antidote? said Jerry. This isn't Alice in Wonderland, Liz. We haven't got a magic potion labelled, "Shrink Me!"

Farmer FA22 had returned to Sebo for further tests.

Meanwhile, Farmer WB47 was now halfway through *Capital, Volume One*, and feeling jubilant about his progress.

"This is a piece of social history. I never knew this," he said. "Our ancestors are guilty of terrible crimes. The peasantry must never know. We could be faced with large claims for compensation."

"No, that's where you're wrong," said Farmer SG54. "The peasantry must be informed at once. Public ownership of the land is the only answer."

"Nationalisation?" said Farmer TY33. "Never! You sound like Mugabe. It was a bloody good job clearing the peasants off the land. There's not enough work in the country. Somebody's got to run the machines."

"There are no machines in the towns," said Farmer SG54. "And what do we have in the countryside? Second-home owners, pricing the locals out of a home. Nationalise the land, I say."

Liz talked to Bob about these developments. They were walking over the heather moor, blessed by a pale blue sky for once.

"It really is extraordinary," she said. "This group has advanced more in two weeks than my old lot did in two months."

"Yes," said Bob, "But they're doing it as a day job and getting paid for it. Handsomely, I gather. I was talking to Nigel about it."

Nigel's group had sprouted Farmer 58PL who was now a master of calculus, said Bob. Farmer 58PL was trying to find a loophole in a recent proof of Fermat's Last Theorem. Plus, trying to rouse the group to a collaborative enterprise: proving Goldbach's prime number conjecture, an unsolved piece of mathematics. "We could all win a prize," said Farmer 58PL. "Loadza money!"

"So much for the idea of miserable farmers," said Liz.

"They were pretty miserable when they arrived," said Bob.

"The older ones especially. Why do they always shout? It was like a goddam rodeo."

"I suppose they're hard of hearing," said Liz. "They've spent their lives working with tractors. And they're used to shouting at animals."

"Whatever, they've calmed down now," said Bob. "I think the noisy ones have returned to Sebo. Jerry will be giving them a voice implant, I guess."

"Is there such a thing?"

"I don't know."

"You don't sound very enthusiastic about these trials."

"The results are impressive, I don't deny, but I do think they should have been tested. We've got four casualties doing rehab. The news could cause a scandal."

"Yes," said Liz, ruminating. "Still, overall, a success story, don't you think?"

"Undoubtedly," said Bob. "But can we be sure the results are due to the drugs?"

"What do you mean?" said Liz.

"We're not running a control group, for a start. Jerry said it wasn't necessary. They were given basic tests before they came over; they're all starting from square one, he said. So how do we know if basic schooling wouldn't have achieved the same result?"

"In two weeks? Impossible."

"You underestimate farmers," said Bob. "The idea that they lack basic literacy and numeracy is a myth. I spent my boyhood on a ranch, so I got to know a fair few. They may not read books, but they can read a daily newspaper from cover to cover. And some of them think about cash as often as the rest of us think about sex. At least once a minute, Daniel said. And they're always counting. Counting costs, counting dollars, counting cattle. They've got economies to manage. Spend as little as possible, sell for what you can get. They are businessmen. Why shouldn't they be interested in *Capital*, with a little bit of coaxing?"

"So you think it's my coaxing that's brought about this miracle?"

"Maybe," said Bob.

"I underestimate myself, obviously," said Liz. "As much as I underestimate farmers. I always thought they were illiterate. Not to mention miserable."

Bob saw the traces of a smile.

"Creep!" he said.

*

Jerry pulled up a chair as Nicolai unrolled the chart; it was his third visit that morning.

The news about Lenin's spatula was intriguing. Nigel had professed his total ignorance of this little-known part of the brain, yet Boris and Nicolai were more than familiar. When quizzed, Nigel had shrugged, claiming he was a cognitive neuroscientist, not a clinical neuroscientist. Besides, the Russians have the advantage of hands-on experience, he said. Jerry had brushed the quip aside. Clearly they were onto something.

"See, this spike here, and this one here," said Nicolai. "We are now finding something remarkable. The brain temperature is consistent in all cases. Exactly the same, and unique."

"So what are you saying?" said Jerry. "I don't quite follow."

"The Eureka moment, we are talking about," said Nicolai.

"Yes, go on," said Jerry.

"It occurs when the brain temperature is at a certain level. At this level we have a Eureka moment. And the temperature is consistently the same at these points."

"I'm sorry, I still don't follow," said Jerry. "What do you mean by unique?"

"It is unique for each writer," said Boris. "They have their moments at different brain temperatures. One will have a Eureka moment at temperature X, say, and it is always at X.

Another will have his moment at Y."

"I see," said Jerry. "Bear with me one moment, I just need to think about this."

Jerry stared into space, looking for sense.

And it made sense, he thought, because who could think straight at sub-zero temperatures? Or write a masterpiece if you were sweating rivers? You needed a certain ambience for the mind to function creatively. Warmth helped. To a point. Too much heat, and your brain would just go to sleep. But then, wouldn't the required ambience vary according to your usual habitat? If Sibelius had moved to the Congo, would he have written a symphony? But then, we're talking about brain temperature, not the body. Possibly, the optimum for the brain is more or less a constant. Neuro-chemicals, when all's said and done. Like the enzymes in a DNA computer, which require a critical temperature to interact the way you want them to…

"The subjects in these experiments," he said. "Can you remind me – they were all from the UK, yes?"

"Yes, that is the case," said Nicolai.

"And how much do these temperatures vary? At these critical moments, I mean. The difference between X and Y."

"Very minute amounts. We are talking many decimal places. But the situation is complex when we look at temperature variations across the brain."

"Across the brain? I'm not following you again, sorry."

"We are dealing with averages. When I say brain temperature, I mean the overall temperature of the brain. However, certain parts will be warmer than others, depending on how many neurons are active. The variation in the temperature of the spatula is more significant than the difference between the averages. A surprising discovery, we believe."

"Really?" said Jerry. "Why so surprising?"

"The temperature of the brain is regulated," said Nicolai. "Like a thermostat, you might say. So it is fairly constant. Yet within the constancy, we see these wide variations between parts of the brain. A spatula that generates little heat itself, yet much heat elsewhere. And conversely, one that generates a lot of heat, but little heat elsewhere. Yet in both cases, we have a Eureka moment. The spatula is generally inactive the rest of the time."

"This is fascinating," said Jerry, patting the chart. "I just wish I knew what it all means. Tell me, do we have DNA samples for these guys?"

"I don't know," said Nicolai. "Nigel was looking after that."

"I'll ask Nigel," said Jerry. "And I'll see you guys later."

He rushed away.

So much to do; so little time.

Back to the office, reminding himself that he must speak to Liz about economic cycles.

Talk to Liz.

Economic cycles.

The Chancellor wants his data.

The project was now attracting international funding, from government departments as well as private corporations. Good news, but sometimes there were strings. Like the latest request from the UK, whose Chancellor was renowned for his esoteric prognostics. His figures always showed that the economy had grown during the "last economic cycle." But his jargon was mystifying, and no one had an inkling of how these cycles were measured. The Chancellor decided when the cycles would start, and when they would end. Now it seemed that he wanted advance information of possible economic downturns, so as to plan his prognostics accordingly. Creative accounting, as it were. Nobody could accuse him of fiddling the figures.

First though, he must finish the morning's tasks. A clutter of emails. Top of the list, a message from Karen Sparks at the Oxford Dodo Project:

Jerry

Speak to Donald Rutherford re the Tasmanian Tiger Project.
Karen

Next: a press release from Mark Appleton, on the discovery
of a new enzyme…

*

The private language of lovers! Liz had never been involved
in that sort of thing. Or so she thought, till it struck her that
she and Bob were now on the verge of it.

It was his doing, she thought. His declaration, after their
third night together, that their affair was a marriage of weep
and creep: she, creeping into his bed; he, weeping after a night
of passion. A joke of course, the labels pointing to their
erstwhile projects. But the labels had stuck, to be bandied
about at moments of tenderness or dispute.

And the most embarrassing thing about love affairs, she
thought, are those pet names like honeybunch or lovebunny
or pussywillow or squidgy, which really ought not to be
repeated outside of the bedroom, and certainly not in the
presence of strangers.

Still, the names had remained private. As was the nature
of their relationship. To the outside world, they were
colleagues who had struck up a friendship. The intimacy was
between themselves.

And they carried on working as though nothing had
changed.

Potentially claustrophobic, she thought: working under the
same roof every day, then sleeping in the same bed. But then,
it wasn't every night. Besides, they took nothing for granted.
They were lovers with their own lives. Mature adults, in
quotes, who weren't aching to tear the pants off each other.
That side of things they could take slowly, with the added
advantage of time and space. After all, they were stuck in the
middle of the Atlantic, and would be for some years. Why

rush?

The first night seemed a natural consequence. They'd spent several evenings together, wining and dining. On the island of Torre de Columba, there was no alternative to home entertainment. Bob had thrown the first invite; Liz had reciprocated. And so it went on, till Liz found herself with sleepless nights, counting sheep and thinking of farmers, and thinking of Bob, alone in bed. So on the next occasion, she suggested that perhaps she could stay. "Sure," said Bob, without a hint of surprise, "If that's what you want." Which was rather ambiguous, she thought. But no problem. It was a night of just lying close. Why rush?

Their walks over the mountains were marked by a similar feature. Mist, bogs, landslip and floods had disappointed their efforts to walk to the other side. Still, the island was only ten miles long. Why rush?

She'd been on the island two years when, finally, there came a day when they didn't turn back halfway.

The cart track was more or less a straight line between the volcanoes on either side, reaching its highest point in the middle of the island. The land there was more bog than heather moor, with dense forest that obscured the view. The track became a path, winding through rushes. Then, descending, the ground was stonier, littered with the familiar black boulders, and the track reappeared. Then hedgerows, scattered with hydrangea, and fields, some cattle. And finally a view: cliffs on either side, and a steep path descending to the *fajas*, the flat lands down below.

And on the *fajas*, the village of Sebo…

Boats in the harbour, bobbing in the wind. Whitewashed cottages, creeping to the water's edge. And away from the centre, a large industrial complex, including a tall chimney that towered over the surrounding buildings and was blowing out steam.

"What is that?" said Liz. "It looks like a business park."

"It used to be a chemical plant," said Bob. "Owned by an

Italian company during the last war. Then it was abandoned. Jerry's taken it over. They're processing the stuff for the DNA computer. Shall we walk down?"

"It looks rather steep. Is it safe?"

"I don't know. I haven't been beyond this point."

"Perhaps we could take a boat round there."

"That's always an option."

"So this is where the farmers went? For tests?"

Suddenly a cry. A wailing sound, like a soul in torment.

"What the hell was that?" said Liz.

"A seagull," said Bob, pointing. "Don't panic. It wasn't a farmer. Unless it's the one who disappeared. Maybe he's turned into a gull."

Liz had sat on a tussock. Bob sat beside her.

"The rest have all gone back, I gather," he said. "Apart from Colin Edwards, of course. Yeah, this is where they came for tests."

"The problem would be," said Liz, "walking back up again."

"We'll take a boat one day," said Bob. "I'll speak to Miguel."

"So Jerry's not shown you round that place?"

"No."

"Strange."

"Why strange? It's of no real concern to my work. He tends to slot people into compartments, for all his talk of collaboration. He has no cause to show me the place."

He reached inside a back pocket, pulling out a slip of paper.

"Anyway," he said, "I'm not sure I want to know what goes on in there."

"Tanks full of enzymes, I suppose. It's probably not very exciting."

Bob was staring at the slip of paper. He passed it to Liz.

"I found this lying in the corridor today," he said. "I was going to give it to Jerry, but I couldn't find him."

Liz took the slip, glanced at it and gasped.

"Oh!" she said. "Humphrey Dillinger!"

"You know him?"

201

"Yes, we met two or three times at a think tank. But what's this? This is a receipt…"

"A receipt for twenty million dollars, concerning a payment from Humphrey Dillinger to the New Development Corporation."

"The New Development Corporation? What's that?"

"I haven't a clue. Another one of Jerry's enterprises, I guess."

"You'd better give it to Jerry," said Liz, passing the slip.

"I shall," said Bob.

"You think it's suspicious?" said Liz.

"I don't know," said Bob. "This project is receiving funds from private companies and benefactors, so what? It may be totally innocuous. It may be just a trading name, a bank account. I was more startled by the amount. But who am I to judge? I know that Jerry's received funds from the EC for regeneration projects, which includes house building and harbour refurbishment."

He shook his head, waving a hand at Sebo.

"What you see is what you get," he said, "so I don't understand it. There's little scope for expansion. That strip of land is full already. So is Lindoso. As for the rest of the island, you could terrace the mountains maybe and plant vines, but you'd need soil. Where's that gonna come from? You'd have to import it. Is this guy a philanthropist, this Humphrey Dillinger?"

"No," said Liz. "He's no philanthropist. Let me put it this way. I can't imagine him investing that amount of money in a house-building project on a remote island in the Atlantic, unless he was guaranteed something in return."

A pause. Then she said, "Of course, there is a simple explanation for this."

"Which is?" said Bob.

"It may be a donation to the project, and quite above board. It may be just a trading name, as you say, and Humphrey Dillinger may be very rich. It wouldn't surprise me."

"Yes," said Bob, pocketing the slip. "And you may be right.

Shall we make a move?"

They walked back. Mist was descending over the peaks. They could just see the old whaling lookout before it vanished: stone walls and a sheet of corrugated iron, flapping in the wind – rusting iron, the wind making a whistling noise through the holes.

"Maybe Humphrey Dillinger is planning to resurrect the whaling industry," said Liz.

Bob's reply – a noise, more like a grunt than a laugh.

She reached for his hand.

He took the reaching hand, kissed it and let it fall, saying, "We ought to walk faster. The mist is falling."

They walked in silence, their steps punctuated by the sound of the rock doves, cooing.

*

Six months later, they were discussing the results of the genetic implant trials: an interim report, as the results were incomplete. Jerry was undecided about the event, its success or failure. On the whole, he thought, a success. However, there were mitigations. Like, casualties and rumours.

The casualties were the older farmers, who were now in care homes back in the UK. Jerry had offered to pay the costs, averting claims for compensation and the glare of publicity. What had happened to them was beyond reckoning; the implants had accelerated the process of ageing, it seemed. Still, he thought, they were due for retirement in any case.

But then there was David Morris, formerly known as Farmer DM72, who had simply vanished without a trace. On a night, according to the islanders, when a strange light had appeared about Pico de Columba. Not the sign of a *caldeira*, erupting, but a white glow. The ghost of Christopher Columbus, said one report. Then came the news that David Morris had vanished, followed promptly by the rumours, which spread from Sebo to Lindoso. David Morris has been abducted by aliens, the harbour men said, crossing themselves.

And then there was Colin Edwards, formerly known as Farmer CE60. Success or failure? Difficult to say. It was just that he had decided to stay on the island. He'd had enough of his family, he said, and was using his newborn literacy skills to learn Portuguese.

As for the rest...

"DH Lawrence wrote about this, you know," said Nigel, tapping a sheet of paper. "In my view, these results provide evidence for the essential brutality of the Celtic mind."

"What are you talking about, Nigel?" said Jerry. "These are English farmers, from the UK. What has the Celtic mind got to do with it?"

"Well..." said Nigel. "Where did they come from, Daniel?"

"Cornwall, Dorset, Cumbria, Herefordshire, Shropshire..." said Daniel.

"Borders," said Nigel. "There you are then. Celts, as good as. It's in their genes. Give them a literacy implant and their systems reject it like a poison."

"I think what Nigel means is that reading skills do not instantaneously translate into writing skills," said Daniel, looking at Jerry, whose eyes were bulging at Nigel's retort.

"Nothing of the sort," said Nigel, shaking his papers. "I was referring to the content of their essays. They were asked to write a précis of the first section of *Capital*, and this is what they come up with. One of them wrote a piece about land reform. Not what was asked at all."

"Their spatulas are non-existent," said Boris.

"Dead," said Nicolai.

"But we hear news of Farmer SG54 that he has now started a new career as a journalist, working on his local paper," said Carl Meyer. "Isn't that right, Liz?"

"Yes, that's what I heard," said Liz.

"And several reports from the numeracy group, all good," said Bob. "Four accountants, one draughtsman, plus someone who's out to win a Nobel prize for proving Goldbach's theorem."

"Even so, no Eureka moments, no sign of any spatula activity," said Nicolai.

"No," said Jerry. "Obviously something extra is needed. I wasn't expecting them to turn into literary geniuses, I must say. The results are more than I'd hoped for."

A consensus emerged, steered by Jerry. The implants were a limited success. Potentially hazardous in certain circumstances. Not to be tried at home, and not to be tried on the elderly. Best to genetically screen your subjects first.

Jerry withdrew to his office. The next set of subjects were due to arrive. A group of businessmen, discussing the advantages of horizontal integration over vertical integration. Or vice versa. A brain-monitoring experiment, looking for that Eureka moment. No implants this time.

First: check the emails.

A press cutting, sent from Donald Rutherford at the Australian Museum in Sydney, re the Tasmanian Tiger Project.

Jerry reads the caption: "Can we clone an extinct beast?"

"The Tasmanian tiger," he reads, "which resembles a dog, was slaughtered to the point of extinction. The last one died in captivity in Hobart Zoo in 1936. Now the Australian Museum has begun a controversial project to clone the tiger from DNA fragments taken from the bones and teeth of a preserved pup in its collection."

At a press conference, a spokesperson for the project said, "The annihilation of the Tasmanian tiger was an appalling crime against the indigenous species here. It was the last of a family of marsupials that had existed for twenty-four million years. It was the largest land carnivore in Australia, and we just blew it away without a thought. Australia has the highest number of extinctions of any continent. Do we not have a moral obligation to redress this, to reinstate the tiger and give it a fresh opportunity? Its environment is still in place, and we believe that the hunting instinct is embedded in the tiger's genes. While there's no guarantee of success, we feel we have a responsibility to make the attempt."

Jerry scans the rest.

A total waste of money, say the critics. The problems of fitting together a genome, making living cells, not to mention breeding the tiger…

So, Jerry says to himself, what's new?

The spokesperson responds: "Recent developments in DNA amplifying and analysing techniques and in cloning have made the project achievable. Sequences are being amplified and copied, but our resources would need a substantial increase to sequence the genome."

Another scan.

Technical details, sums required…

Then, words that catch his eye. A geneticist, quoted as saying, "Cloning with dead cells is not currently feasible, but it may be eventually."

Jerry sits back, pondering.

Possibilities, possibilities…

*

A neuroscientist dressed as Santa Claus, handing out presents with a simulated chuckle. Liz was finding it all sad and dull: weren't they a bit old for this sort of thing? Showing not the slightest trace of enthusiasm, she agreed to pull a cracker with Carl Meyer.

Pop!

"Please, the hat," said Carl, holding a flaccid piece of red paper.

"I'm not wearing a hat," she said.

"You want?"

"No, please take it. I'm not wearing a hat, no way."

"Thanks," he said, sidling away.

The party had been Jerry's idea. Most of the team were used to going away for Christmas. But this year, there were transport difficulties. At the airports on Terceira and Sao

Miguel, the baggage handlers had gone on strike, and all passenger flights had been cancelled. They were stranded on Torre de Columba, and would have to make do.

It hadn't felt such a chore the day before. Two helicopters had taken them to Sao Miguel, and they spent Christmas Eve shopping and sightseeing, followed by an evening meal in Ponta Delgada. Whereupon Nigel announced his willingness to play the grand old man. "It was always a childhood aspiration of mine," he said.

And there he was, in full regalia.

They'd all drunk a drop too much, it seemed; unsurprisingly, as they weren't used to it. Liz propped herself against a chair, listening to the conversation a few steps away: Daniel and Jerry, talking about…

Now this is novel, she thought. Christmas Day, and they're standing by a drooping Christmas tree, talking about Marx! And why not?

"So you think the whole of *Capital* was conceived in a single moment?" said Daniel.

"I believe that, yes," said Jerry. "It's not as strange as it sounds. Many of the world's greatest thinkers have said how they had a moment of inspiration, and then spent the rest of their lives drawing out the consequences. I think Marx's *Capital* was conceived in such a moment."

"I have read somewhere that writing is one percent inspiration, ninety-nine percent perspiration," said Daniel.

"Yes, exactly," said Jerry. "I think Marx had his Eureka moment, in which he visualised the entire structure of *Capital*. Then all he had to do was write it."

"All!" said Daniel.

"I don't mean he had it all worked out," said Jerry. "What he saw was the framework in which he could work things out. The things that he hadn't worked out before, that is."

"Yes, I understand," said Daniel. "What we must recapture is that Eureka moment."

"Precisely," said Jerry.

Liz glanced at Bob, standing on the other side of the tree. He strolled to her side.

"Merry Christmas," he said, raising his glass.

She laughed as she clinked it.

"Merry Christmas to you," she said.

"And do you still consider yourself a Marxist, Miss Kendal?" he said.

"Yes, I do," she said. "Who wants to know?"

"I do, because it struck me back there that I've been making love to a red revolutionary these last few months," he said.

"A red revolutionary? I don't know about that," she said.

"As a Marxist," he said, "don't you believe in revolution, in communism and the overthrow of capitalism?"

"I believe that capitalism creates waste, poverty and alienation," she said, "and is using up the world's resources to the point of exhaustion. In my opinion, it's long past its sell-by date. As for the rest, I don't know. Revolution, yes, we need one, but the idea of the revolutionary party died some time ago, as did the idea of communism."

"So doesn't that make Marx redundant?"

"No, not at all. You know as well as the rest of us that Marx is still relevant, and you wouldn't be working on this project if you thought otherwise. Marx the theorist and political scientist, that is. He had little to say about practical politics; it was Lenin who wrote about the revolutionary party. I don't think the Communist Manifesto even mentions it. We've talked about this before. Are you trying to wind me up, Mister Rheingold?"

"No, I'm just curious as to what motivates people. Take Jerry, for instance. He was brought up in Mexico. His family had little money. They were involved in a communist group in Mexico way back in the 60s. I can understand where's he coming from. Whereas I was fortunate, my family never lacked money. And I've never been political, myself. Whereas you, you I can't quite fathom…"

"I used to be political, but having money or the lack of it

had nothing to do with it. It was more the case that here was an analysis of the world that I could agree with. And I still agree with it. As for practical politics, there's nothing to be involved in anymore. There is no alternative voice."

"There are terrorist movements…"

"Terrorism! The voice of despair There is no articulate alternative. Terrorist groups may use Marxist rhetoric, but it's only rhetoric. They might just as well use the language of Holy War, or whatever comes to hand. Marx wasn't an advocate of terrorism, whatever people may say. He saw the overthrow of capitalism coming from a mass movement, emerging out of class conflict. I can't see that happening now, there's no basis for it. People in the West have become totally middle class in their outlook on everything…"

"Liz, there's a brilliant moon outside. Shall we take a stroll?"

"Oh yes, let's," she said. "I need to escape."

The party was breaking up. Jerry had drifted back to his office, Nigel was clearing up the mess, and Daniel was now talking to Nicolai about the latest world news: rumours of another war in the Middle East. More jet activity across the Atlantic.

"The strike does not affect them?" said Nicolai.

"The baggage strike? No, I think not," said Daniel. "They load their baggage before they come. Then they drop it soon after," he added, chuckling.

"Drop?" said Nicolai. "Ah! Drop!"

He barked a laugh and stared gloomily into his glass. Nigel, still dressed as Santa Claus, left the room with a bag of rubbish. Walking along a corridor, he saw a light in Jerry's office. The door was open. He planted the bag and stepped inside. Jerry was sat at the computer.

"I know your private life is no concern of mine, but why are you looking at a pair of sprout nets?" said Nigel, peering at the screen. "And on eBay of all places. If you're desperate for a pair of underpants, I would suggest that you don't buy second-hand."

Jerry laughed.

"Sprout nets? I like that," he said.

"It was my grandmother's term," said Nigel, removing his beard. "She had the largest pair of bloomers I've ever seen. Underwear has generally been shrinking since her day. Now they wear those, what do you call them, thong things."

"I wouldn't know," said Jerry. "And these are not for me. They're reputed to have belonged to Engels, Marx's ally."

"Really? I hope they've been washed. Too large for you, are they? Were you looking for something smaller?"

"I had no intention of wearing them," said Jerry, closing the screen. "I was curious to see if there was any Marx memorabilia for sale."

"Marx memorabilia," said Nigel, looking at the walls. "It would make a change from potted plants, I suppose."

Jerry turned, chuckling.

"Nigel, you're fishing as usual. If you really want to know why I happen to be looking at a pair of oversized underpants, reputed to have belonged to Engels, why don't you just ask? In fact, I posted an ad, offering large sums, just to see what would materialise."

"And this is the result? A pair of underpants?"

"Plus one or two books, reputed to have passed through his hands. A lock of hair, taken from his beard. Pens and pencils. Quite a collection. Of course, there's no way one can verify their authenticity."

"No, I suppose not. Is that important?"

"It depends… I was thinking, Nigel, it may be a way of locating a DNA sample."

"Oh, for God's sake, Jerry. Why don't you contact his descendants? Or the British Museum? They must have items that have passed through his hands."

"I'm working on that. Nothing's come up yet. We shall see…"

"Right. Well, I must return to my sack. Merry Christmas and all that."

"Merry Christmas, Nigel. And don't forget your beard."

"No, you're right, it wouldn't do to step out naked. See you later."

Nigel stood by the sack of rubbish, pausing to fit the beard. Jerry listened to the echo of his steps, fading; then he turned to the computer.

*

Stage Three of the Brain of Marx Project: it came without a fanfare. There were no grand declarations, no announcements from Jerry that the project had entered this new phase. Just a statement one morning, saying that he'd recruited some new members to the team: Karen Sparks, from the Oxford Dodo Project; Donald Rutherford, from the Tasmanian Tiger Project; and Titus Cranfield, formerly of Advanced Membrane Technology.

The new members will be based in Sebo, Jerry said. They'll be working on the DNA side of things; they're due to start tomorrow.

The three arrived as scheduled and were introduced to the rest of the team; then they were whisked away to the other end of the island.

Meanwhile, in Lindoso, the work went on as before.

The supercomputer was fully operational. Liz now faced the task of coordinating the Volume One test. Bob, who was spending most of his time supervising the brain-monitoring machines, was a phone call away if there were any technical problems.

The materials were all in place. Every scrap of knowledge known to Marx had been fed into the machine, slotted into various compartments. The Chinese data handlers had sweated buckets to complete the job. The current problem was sorting out the processing mechanisms that would output a replica of *Capital, Volume One*.

The initial results fell depressingly short of the target.

211

"It just comes out with lists of facts," said Liz, talking to Jerry one day. "There's no problem replicating the facts, but we lack the inspirational element, the magical something that will restructure the facts and present them in a different way."

"From the abstract to the concrete," said Jerry. "And you've tried that new software?"

"The package called Aristotle? Yes, and it's precisely that – Aristotelian. So it gives us structured lists, like an encyclopaedia. Hardly Marx. We need something like... Dialectical Materialism."

"I thought Boris was producing that."

"It's not finished. He's still busy analysing the results of the experiments."

"Hmm. I'll have a word with him. We might need more help."

"How are things at the other end?"

"Fine, but slow progress. DNA work is like that."

"I don't really understand what they're doing, to be honest."

"I thought you did. It's not that hard to grasp, surely? They're designing a DNA computer."

"Yes, I realise that, but... these new members. I gather that Karen's speciality is archaeology. Collecting DNA from the dead."

"That's right, and she's very good at it. We're trying to locate suitable DNA samples of the great man. It should help the engineering aspects."

"Hmm," said Liz. "But the processing mechanisms will be based on this machine, yes? So if we can't get this to work, it's not very likely that the other one's going to work. Or am I missing something?"

"No, that's right, but we're meant to be working together on this, Liz. We can't stop the DNA work till you produce the goods, can we? Besides, the DNA work may throw some light on that missing ingredient."

Liz conceded the point. Jerry had to rush away to the next appointment. He had the idea that Liz was jealous of Karen

Sparks for some reason. Her looks? Her youth? Her glamour? Hardly the traditional archaeologist, with her short skirts and subtle make-up. But she knew her subject inside out and that, he thought, was what mattered.

Meanwhile, Liz felt that the focus of the project had shifted to Sebo. Jerry had lost interest in the supercomputer. Yet it was fundamental to the whole project. And everything was all in place, barring that essential ingredient. Somehow, it had fallen on her shoulders to sort it out.

*

It was obvious that Jerry was feeling the strain. His face was noticeably thinner, his eyes bloodshot – deep shadows underneath – and his hair was strikingly Afro. He was spending more time away from Lindoso, staying over in Sebo, where there were now regular meetings of the Northern Group, as Liz called it, and still flying to California, only to discover that he was meant to be in three places at the same time.

Liz walked into his office one day to find him staring into space with bulging eyes. She reminded him to talk to Boris about the software problems.

"I'll do that now," he said. "We've been overspending, Liz. I've just been going through the accounts. Unbelievable! I shall have to ask for more money from the government. Let's hope they're agreeable. There must be limits, even to America's borrowing. We'll have to work out what we can show them, in the way of results. I'll go and talk to Boris."

Boris was sat at a large table, decked out with an array of charts, time sheets, statistical calculations. Nicolai stood at his side, pointing to a chart.

"Boris," said Jerry, "about the Dialectical Materialism software…"

"We have it!" said Boris, leaping to his feet. "Concrete evidence! The critical temperature is encoded in the DNA!"

"What?" said Jerry, reaching for a chair.

"It is as you suspected," said Boris. "The temperature of the spatula is a unique feature, genetically determined. It is encoded in a person's genes. We have examined the codes of several specimens, and the clue to the critical temperature is given by the subject's DNA code."

Jerry, white-faced, seemed on the verge of fainting.

"Remind me," he said, clutching the table, "the critical temperature is what, exactly?"

"The critical temperature is the temperature of the spatula when the brain has a Eureka moment. It is unique to each individual. Now we have the confirmation that the information is genetically encoded."

"Incredible," said Jerry. "I think I'm about to have a Eureka moment. But before I forget, about this Dialectical Materialism software…"

*

Three days after this last revelation, Liz entered the computer room as usual and sat at a terminal to log on. She was greeted with an error message: *Invalid password. Please try again.*

She tried again, with the same result. And again: the same. Cursing, she rang Bob's mobile.

"This has never happened before," she said.

"You've not changed the password?" said Bob.

"No."

"And who knows the password, apart from me, you and Jerry?"

"No one else. Just us three."

"I haven't changed it. I haven't logged on for weeks. Jerry must have changed it."

"Without telling me? That's just… infantile."

"These things happen. As I recall, it's timed to ask for a new password every four weeks. That's automatic. And if you don't change the password, it won't allow you to log on."

"I know that, and it's a pain. I have to think of a fresh password every month."

"Was it due for a change?"

"I don't know. I don't keep a record."

"I should think Jerry was asked to change it, and he didn't have the time to tell you; he's very rushed at the moment. Can't think of any other explanation. Leave it an hour and try again. I'll drop by at lunch."

Liz was cursing all morning. After several attempts, she was still unable to log on. Jerry's mobile wasn't responding. At the back of her mind, she had this dark suspicion that he was cutting her out. He was plotting something, and she wasn't involved. The Northern Group now formed a sort of inner circle, which included Jerry, Nigel, Daniel, Karen Sparks, Donald Rutherford and Titus Cranfield. Everyone else had only a small inkling of what was happening.

Then she told herself that she was just being paranoid, that it was simply a case of Jerry's current tendency towards amnesia. Bob thought so too. He couldn't do anything to rectify the situation without taking the machine apart; best to wait for Jerry, he said.

Taking the machine apart? she said. How come?

Security, Liz, he said. It was designed that way. Basically, it means you can't hack into the machine simply by tampering with the software, but I won't bore you with the technical details. We'll sort it out, no worries, just wait for Jerry.

Jerry rushed into the room, mid-afternoon.

"Sorry, Liz, I've been in Sebo," he said. "Bob tells me there's a problem."

"I can't log on," she said. "I've been locked out all morning. Have you changed the password?"

She had a sinking feeling as she asked the question. It was as though only now, with Jerry in the room, could she be rational about the event, struck by the thought that Jerry, like Bob, hadn't logged on for weeks – it was only Liz who'd been working on the supercomputer.

"No," he said, sitting at the terminal. "Can't remember what the password is, actually. You'll have to tell me."

They sat at the keyboard, to no avail.

Jerry turned and stared at her; his face was white.

"Someone's broken into the system," he said.

Just at that moment, Boris came rushing into the room, waving a CD and grinning.

"Your wish is my command!" he said. "Dialectical Materialism, at your service!"

Liz and Jerry turned with a cold stare.

"I'm very sorry," said Boris. "This is very late, I know."

"Your timing is perfect," said Jerry.

*

Given the weighty influence of Catholicism, Liz had been surprised to find a display of naughty lingerie, tucked away in a department store in Ponta Delgada. Still, she thought, the islands do have the tourists to cater for. And then, those nuns have a saucy reputation…

She'd been out on a day's shopping expedition, looking for clothes. Tops, trousers and skirts, in particular. Which she bought, together with a range of black stockings, bras and suspenders in pink and white lace, gauging them in degrees of skimpiness, and thinking that it might add a bit of spice to her love life. Which it did.

The occasion was Bob's birthday. She'd struggled to find a suitable present. In the end, she bought an old map of the Portuguese explorers, and offered herself for the evening, suitably attired.

In the weeks following Bob's birthday treat, it was always Liz who chose the occasion.

She found it addictive. Dressing up and generally being sexy: it sort of kept her in trim. But then, it didn't take much to arouse a man. In her black stockings and white lace, Bob found her irresistible, and they could and often did spend the entire evening rolling around by the fire. Bob had a sheepskin rug in front of the hearth, which they now referred to as their sex mat.

Two days after the password lockout, they were on the sex mat engaged in their physical exercises when, unusually, she suddenly felt bored with it all. She wished she hadn't worn the lingerie that night. She couldn't concentrate. She wanted to talk about the latest developments.

She was sitting on top of him, bouncing slowly, feeling him expand till he exploded inside her. She waited a while, squeezing his shoulders. Then she moved her legs, while he slid out with a plop.

"Jerry's thinking of asking us all for fingerprints, or even DNA samples," she said. "He wants to check the computer for forensic evidence, but he doesn't want any outsiders to be involved."

"Hmm? Oh, that! Hmmm, come here, creep," he said.

She flopped beside him, curling an arm around his stomach.

"It couldn't have been a hacker," she said, "because the supercomputer's not connected to the Web. So it must have been one of us. But who?"

"I don't know, and why would anyone want unauthorised access?"

"Possibly to destroy the data. One of us may be a saboteur."

"Or possibly to remove the data. One of us may be thinking of that Nobel prize."

"What Nobel prize?"

"For the person who writes the next volume of *Capital*."

"Oh yes, I'd forgotten about that. You don't think Jerry's decided to go it alone?"

"No way. The idea's absurd. I did wonder some time ago whether he was shifting all the data to California, for his own personal use. But no, look at the guy, he's wrapped up in the project, heart and soul. It must be someone else."

"And when am I going to be able to get into the system again?"

217

"I don't know. It'll take a few days for me to fix it."

"Computers! I detest them. Did you ever ask Jerry about that Humphrey Dillinger donation?"

"Yes, he wasn't very forthcoming. Actually, it was as you said. A donation to the project, using a trading name. And Humphrey Dillinger is a millionaire. In which case, why is Jerry so concerned about a funding shortfall? It doesn't make sense. So – I've been doing a bit of research myself on this Humphrey Dillinger. I'll let you have the results in due course."

"God, you're so formal," she said, pinching his stomach.

"It's my upbringing," he said.

"Oh, and I thought it was genetic," she said.

It was his turn to pinch.

*

Ten miles away, Jerry was having a conversation on the same topic with Karen Sparks, though the circumstances weren't as athletic. Jerry, sat on a hard chair, a glass of port at his feet, was feeling quite immobile. Karen, in black tights and a short red skirt that clung to her slim torso, was standing by an empty bookcase, resting an arm on the wooden shelf.

"Jerry darling," she said, "surely you don't think it was one of us? We haven't set foot in the place since we arrived."

"I can't be sure who is responsible, though I have my suspicions," he said. "I know it wasn't you."

"Thank you," she said. "It would be impossible to work under a cloud of suspicion."

"The problem is… broader than that though," he said. "To put it bluntly, Karen, the project is facing a crisis. We're desperately overspent. If we can't find new backers, we could be facing bankruptcy."

"Jerry, that's awful."

"Yes, and we're so damned close to a breakthrough. If only we had… How much time do you think you'd need? On the fragments?"

"I think we're talking years, not months, Jerry. And to be perfectly honest with you, we may not succeed. That pencil I'm working on – it's probably passed through fifty pairs of hands since Marx handled it. And he may not have handled it in the first place. Even if we could piece together a code, which I very much doubt, we couldn't be sure it was Marx's code. I'm sorry Jerry, but the situation is hopeless. When I agreed to work on the project, I was expecting something a bit more solid to work on. At least, something more than a bag of pencils and a large pair of underpants, which Engels may have lent to Marx. Or may not, as the case may be."

"Sprout nets."

"What?"

"Never mind. I'm sorry too. I fed you false hopes."

She picked up her glass, walked to his chair, placed the glass on the floor and sat on his lap. Jerry had no inclination to push her away.

"Jerry darling," she said, stroking his face, "don't be so despondent. There must be an alternative course of action."

"I suppose you're used to working with... old bones," he said.

"Hmm," she said, and wriggled her bottom. "Old bones. Hard bones. Dry bones."

"There's no chance of that," he said, "unless we dig up Marx's grave."

She giggled.

"What an idea!" she said. "And would that be such a wicked thing, do you think?"

"Come on, Karen," he said. "The idea's ghastly. And who's going to volunteer to dig up a grave? It's positively Victorian. Can you imagine? Wanted: two gravediggers, all expenses paid. It's probably a criminal act. Desecration."

"Jerry," she said, shifting her position, "I have some very weird friends. You wouldn't need to advertise."

"Go on," he said.

219

"There are some pretty weird people in this world," she said. "I've heard there are people who break into graveyards at night, and literally make love to the dead."

"And these are your friends," he said, wrinkling his face. "I don't think I want to know any more."

"No, those aren't my friends. I'm citing it as an example of weirdness. There are also people who think they're vampires, and go to bed at night in a coffin."

"Yes, I think I've heard about that sort of thing. Someone was so convinced that he tore people's necks apart. He's now serving a jail sentence."

"Yes, I heard about that too."

"So what do your friends do?"

"Nothing quite as ghastly. They're Goths, basically. They like spending their evenings in graveyards, with a bottle of wine and a tape of Black Sabbath."

"Black Sabbath? Are they Satanists?"

"No! Black Sabbath is the name of a group. They play heavy metal, with a sort of gothic feel. I don't think they exist now. They were around in the 60s, and let's face it, anybody who's still into Black Sabbath after thirty-plus years must be pretty weird."

"Hmm. They don't break into graves then."

"Not yet, but I'm sure they could be persuaded, for a small fee. They like sitting on gravestones."

He groaned and said, "Sounds like a recipe for piles."

"Oh, Jerry," she said, "you'd be amazed how many people there are out there who do this sort of thing. They have a sort of fascination with the dead."

"And tell me, Karen, are you a Goth?"

"I used to be," she said. "It's a phase one goes through. Only some don't quite grow out of it. Like Beelzebub and Salomé."

"Beelzebub and Salomé?"

"My friends. The Goths."

"Beelzebub and Salomé! Karen, I think I'm going to have

to sleep on this. I'll take the couch."

"Oh," she said, wriggling her bottom. "Do you not want to…?"

Jerry raised his arms and hugged her close.

"I think I should… take the couch," he said.

But Karen felt a paralysis seeping through his grip – Jerry appeared to be frozen.

*

He had stared into the abyss and seen a candle: the light of science: his only guide. The logic of the project pointed in one direction. There was no alternative, and he must pursue it; too much at stake to brush it away with a besom of morality.

Karen's advice he trusted. A tooth, two teeth, would suffice, she said. She had already done this: extracted the DNA code from one old bone.

It had seemed an age, hugging her close. Then he said, "Karen, do you think… you could speak to your friends?"

She had gone away, with a plan to seduce Beelzebub and Salomé. The back catalogue of Black Sabbath plus a crate of wine should do the job, she said. I can't guarantee they'll agree to the idea, but I'll do my very best.

Days passed, Jerry wandering around like a ghost.

Then, good news finally from Bob. The system's up and running again, he said, and nothing's been tampered with. Checked it for bugs, viruses, worms, ants, beetles, etc, and it's clean. The data's all there and intact. Liz says no problems. We've checked the file inventory and it seems the entire corpus was copied on the day in question. No clues as to who was responsible.

So that was the plan, Jerry said to himself. A data thief! But who? And why? For personal gain, or for corporate intelligence?

More days passed, Jerry a bundle of nerves. Then, an email from Karen:

Jerry
B and S are agreeable. I await further instructions.
Karen

Action at last! Practicalities, practicalities! A map of Highgate Cemetery, for a start. Should have done it before, but did I really think it would come to this?

A week passed, and they spoke over the phone.

B and S were now totally committed to the idea, Karen said. Everything had been planned. They'd checked out the grave, made sure it was the right one, decided on tools for the job, and arranged the date. B and S had entered the spirit of the occasion and had fixed a date for the next full moon.

Jerry groaned, hoping to hell there wasn't going to be any hanky panky.

"Just two teeth, Karen, okay?" he said. "And no weird rituals, for heaven sake!"

Then he felt pangs of guilt for not being there. He was allowing her to do it on her own. Surely it needed someone to supervise the operation, in case of any mishaps. The whole project could be sunk by the reckless behaviour of a couple of graveyard ghoulies.

But he hadn't spoken to anyone about the scheme. Who could he talk to? Who could he send?

He juggled ideas through nights of insomnia.

Then, two days after speaking to Karen, he heard the bad news.

From Boris, who came into his office, saying, "The world goes mad."

More war plans, said Boris, have you heard?

The US was stepping up its operations in the Middle East. Blanket bombing, targets unknown. The jets wanted a freeway across the Atlantic. They'd effectively declared a no-fly zone over the Azores, because they couldn't guarantee the safety of non-military air traffic. As a result of this warning, all passenger flights to and from the Azores had been cancelled for an indefinite period, as from June 27.

"Shit!" said Jerry.

More words from Karen.

"What shall I do? I won't be able to get back."

"Can you bring the date forward?"

"I doubt it… In fact it's impossible. B and S are away at Glastonbury and they're not responding to my mobile. And they wouldn't want to come back anyway – Black Sabbath are doing a revival gig. They won't be back till June 30. And they've set their sights on the night of the full moon."

"Shit!"

He told her not to worry, he'd think of something, he'd get back to her.

He listened to the news: the war could go on for months. Months! Supplies would not be affected, said the report, but may take longer than normal. There's no reason to panic.

Panic!

He couldn't face another night of insomnia. He must talk to somebody, somebody he can trust. He shall talk to Bob.

*

It was a kind of love-hate relationship, which had dominated her life for God knows how many years. Technology! Computers were wonderful when they worked, she thought, and thoroughly depressing when they didn't. Most of the time she took them for granted, till the next incomprehensible error message popped up; then she detested them for their inability to communicate.

"They rule our lives!" she said to Bob.

"Yes, and there's no escape now," he said.

Mood swings caused by machines – absurd but true.

Tonight she was on a high, and all because she'd spent the day working on the system, testing the Dialectical Materialism software. And though she didn't like the idea of the technological knight, helping the distressed damsel in her struggle with the machine, she had to admit that it was all thanks to Bob's handiwork. She wanted to celebrate, and she wanted to thank him, in the way he liked best.

It was a night for naughty lingerie.

"I'll cook you a meal," she said. "*Porco à alentejana*."

"Great," he said. "*Casa Liz* or *Casa Bob*?"

"*Casa Bob*," she said.

Red peppers and garlic, clams and pork and olive oil: they ate Portuguese style, with plenty of wine. After which, they slid down to the rug, in front of the fire.

Her dress was flung over a chair; his shirt and trousers likewise; their bodies were lying together in a state of intimacy when they heard a frantic banging on the front door.

"Shit!" said Bob. "Who the hell can this be?"

"It's me, Jerry," said Jerry.

"Hang on a minute!" Bob shouted.

Liz grabbed her dress and raced into the kitchen. Bob slid into his shirt and trousers.

He unlocked the door.

"I know it's late," said Jerry, "but I need to talk. I'm in a dilemma, Bob. I need... your advice."

"You'd better come in," said Bob.

Jerry flopped into a chair and held his head. He looked wilder than ever. Out came a string of words, whose meaning Bob failed to grasp.

"Now let me get this straight," he said. "You've arranged for a team of gravediggers to dig up Marx's grave, right?"

"Yes," said Jerry, staring at the floor.

"And they're doing what? Dentistry?"

"Removing two teeth," said Jerry.

"In the hope you can extract a DNA sample, yes?"

"Yes."

Bob was looking at Jerry in a different light. Jerry, staring at the rug and seeing a black stocking, was beginning to wonder about Bob.

Then Bob began to laugh.

"Jerry," he said. "You are totally off your rocker! Man, you are nuts! Clean off! Up the pole!"

And another round of laughter.

Jerry raised his head.

"There's more," he said.

"Oh Christ!" said Bob. "Go on, tell me."

"The no-fly zone, you must have heard about it. Karen can't get back. We'll have the information, everything we need, and we won't be able to do anything with it. Maybe not for months."

More laughter. Bob was holding his stomach.

"A war zone! Now you know what we used to do in war zones, Jerry. If you want my advice, I suggest you use a homing pigeon. Fix a tooth to the pigeon, and he'll carry it all the way home…"

More laughter, demented laughter. Followed by the sound of another laugh, coming from the kitchen: a woman's laugh.

Jerry turned his head. There was Liz, in a dress that was half-buttoned, holding her sides and shaking with mirth.

Jerry looked at the stocking; then at Bob, laughing without restraint.

"How long has this been going on?" he said.

"Three years," said Bob.

"Three years?" said Jerry.

And he too began to laugh.

*

Dirty grey clouds, blowing from the west; sheets of rain in the distance. Liz and Bob, walking by the whaling post, and the wind was getting personal – blasting the most intimate parts.

They decide to head back.

"I thought you were joking," said Liz.

"No," said Bob. "I've spoken to Miguel, and he reckons he has a suitable bird."

"Could they find their way back, from London?"

"If it had to, it would, but it won't need to. There's no restrictions on flying from the UK to Lisbon. So he'll bring it back to the mainland, and release it from there. He's let them off from France before, and they've found their way back, he says, no problem. They follow the coastline. They have a way of knowing the points of the compass. No one knows how, but they do."

Liz glanced towards the cliffs, where the rock doves were now breeding.

"These are wild birds," she said. "I don't see how…"

"The rock dove is your original racing pigeon," he said. "The homers, the racers, are basically domesticated rock doves. Miguel trains them. He's used them to send messages from Portugal, says it was quicker than the mail."

"Oh," she said, pondering. Then: "I always thought pigeons were rather stupid birds, myself."

"Don't you believe it!" he said. "These birds can cover four hundred and eighty kilometres in a day; their average speed can reach eighty kilometres an hour. They can fly a long distance too – I bet you could release one in Scotland, and it would still find its way here."

"Oh," she said. "Not so stupid then. So what's the plan?"

"I fly over with Miguel tomorrow, with the bird."

"Tomorrow! That means… this will be our last night together. I may not see you for months."

"Yes you will. I'll come back on the supply ship. I'll probably be away for a month, at the most."

Liz looked at him. He was smiling.

"So what's the point of the pigeon?" she said. "Why can't you just bring the… booty with you?"

Bob was laughing now.

"Because Jerry's got deadlines, and he reckons that the pigeon'll be faster, given the travel restrictions. And if anything happens to the pigeon, there's me with the backup. The booty is two teeth, remember? Liz, the project is becoming a farce. I've every respect for the abilities of Miguel's birds, but I suggested the idea as a joke and Jerry's taken the whole thing seriously. So let's go with the flow. The bird flies with one tooth, and I sail with the other; possibly arrive before the bird, possibly not. It's a game. It's a race, between me and the pigeon."

Liz sighed.

"A game," she said.

"It's a holiday, Liz!" he said. "I need a break! That guy has been driving me nuts!"

"He's driving everyone nuts, including himself," she said.

"Yes, and there are limits," he said. "I'm not into body snatching, Liz. If I didn't have my suspicions that Karen suggested the idea in the first place, I'd be tempted to persuade her to an alternative, though God knows where we could find two suitable teeth… Liz, I'm thinking of resigning. After the race."

"You're leaving?"

"I'm seriously considering my options."

"And do they… include me?" she said.

"Yes, of course," he said. "Assuming… you want to be included?"

"Yes," she said.

"I'll think about the possibilities, while I'm away. I just need a break, Liz. I need to clear the head."

"Yes," she said. "Don't we all."

He slid an arm around her.

That night was a night of passion, even without the naughty lingerie.

Moans and groans on the sex mat: Liz, thinking she might never see him again; Bob, not knowing what he might decide.

Doing it doggy style, both of them frantic: Liz, wanting to hear that he loved her; and Bob, having the best night of his life.

She was so open, so wild, he thought; so open, so wild…

And he was on the verge of saying it, she thought; on the

227

verge of saying it...

"Oh Liz! Oh Liz!"

"Oh yes! Oh yes! Come on!"

Just three words, and he was almost saying it, when the totally unexpected occurred. She heard a crack, then a moan of a different sort as Bob stopped, just like that...

"Oh no! Oh, please, no! Please, please, no!"

"What's happened?"

"It's my back! My back's gone!"

Then it struck her that Bob was approaching his 60s, and that such a thing was possibly bound to happen, given the rigour of their physical exercises.

He was still rigid inside her, unable to move either way. She glanced over her shoulder. His face was in agony.

She crawled forwards – with difficulty, as his weight was pressing on her back. Bob fell sideways, still in a crouched position, and sighed with relief from both ends.

*

Another crisis for Jerry: Liz, the bringer of bad news.

"He's done what!" he said.

"It's his back. He's stuck. Go round and see him."

"I shall! Right now!"

Liz had thrown a blanket over him. Bob, unable to stand, was lying on his side, full of apologies.

"Somebody else will have to go," he said.

"We're running out of time," said Jerry. "What do you suggest?"

Bob raised himself on all fours.

"Call a meeting," he said. "Tell everyone, ask for a volunteer. Just come clean. Explain your motives. They'll understand."

"Yes, you're right," said Jerry, and Bob thudded back to the foetal position.

"I'd be grateful if you didn't mention, you know..." said

228

Bob.

"Mention what?" said Jerry. "That Bob's burst a bloody blood vessel through too much shagging and sends his apologies! No, don't mention it."

"Sorry, Jerry," said Bob, but Jerry was closing the door already.

*

It was one of the most difficult decisions he had ever made: where to hold the bloody meeting? There was no obvious choice. They couldn't all squeeze into his office, and the canteen was a ramshackle affair, hardly the place that would set the tone for the words he was about to deliver.

A night of insomnia, and he still hadn't decided. Then he walked into the room full of monitors, where Boris, Nicolai and Daniel had gathered around a table, looking at charts, while Nigel sat at a desk, going through the morning's mail.

So, the decision was made: four members of the team were here; he just had to summon the rest.

"I'd like a group discussion this morning," he said, in the most authoritative voice he could muster. "About the future of the project. Let's see… we'll need a few more chairs…"

It took an hour to find everybody; then another moment of agony as he decided whether to call Donald Rutherford and Titus Cranfield, who would have to fly by helicopter from Sebo.

He made the call.

Now there was time to gather his thoughts, until he heard the chug descending from the mountains. They were already there when he walked into the room. There was only Liz who had an inkling of what was coming.

"My friends and colleagues," he said, "excuse this interruption, but we have an urgent decision to make. The project faces an uncertain future. We are now at a crucial stage, and you've all worked very hard for us to get this far.

We've travelled a long distance together, we've made many achievements on the way, and the final one is just around the corner. Now I'm asking for your indulgence, in taking the project that one step further. A critical step, my friends, because there is every reason to believe that our goal is within our grasp."

He paused for a sip of water.

"As you know," he said, "the supercomputer is fully operational. The software is currently being tested, and we're well on the way to producing a replica of *Capital, Volume One*."

Liz stared at the floor.

"The DNA computer is also operational, and we're currently testing it for consistency. This is, of course, the brain of our project, the brain that will produce the new edition of *Capital* – *Capital* for the twenty-first century. All the data from the supercomputer will be transferred to the other machine, the brain of our project. The brain will then be in a state of preparation, assimilating the material that will enable it to achieve our goal."

Another sip.

"However," he said, "there is one thing missing, one essential ingredient. We've all heard of the superb achievements of Boris and Nicolai, and Nigel, in showing us in great detail how the brain operates; its chemistry, its biology, its physics. They have shown us how the laws of science underline those moments of inspiration, which great thinkers such as Marx experience only rarely, perhaps once in a lifetime. They have shown us how the brain, in those moments of inspiration, functions at a critical temperature, unique to the individual. They have shown us all that and more: how this information is encoded in the genetic code of the individual concerned."

Another pause; another sip.

"Now imagine, my friends, if we had the genetic code of Marx. We would have a source of vital information; in particular, we would have the information that would determine the physical conditions of our simulated brain, the conditions that would enable our brain to say, Eureka! Regrettably, we do not have this crucial information, but a simple act will obtain it for us."

He lowered his voice.

"Consider, my friends, the terrible deeds that have been done in the name of science. Only consider vivisection, and the medical pioneers who cut up animals alive, simply to find out how their insides are structured. Now, I ask you my friends, if Marx the materialist would complain if we took away a tooth or two from a body that was no longer of use to the world? Yes, I know that digging up a grave is a criminal act, but it bears no comparison with the deeds I've just mentioned. Hardly vandalism or sacrilege, when we remember that our goal is the development of Marx's own work. Would he not thank us for developing his work?"

He looked around the room, noting a few frowns.

"I think he would, my friends. That is why I've taken the unprecedented step of condoning a ghoulish act, for the purpose of scientific advance. And when I tell you that no more's involved than a couple of teeth, you may laugh for its triviality and my prudishness in consulting you all in this way. But the point is, we need an extra pair of hands. As you know, the flight restrictions begin on…"

"Excuse me," said Nigel. "Am I hearing you correctly? Am I right in thinking that you've hatched a scheme to exhume Marx's body and remove two of his teeth?"

Jerry looked at Nigel, and noted that at least two people had crossed themselves. He couldn't make out who: they were too quick.

"That's correct," he said.

"I see," said Nigel.

"Look," said Jerry, "I didn't ask you all here because I wanted your approval; that wasn't my intention. But perhaps I should. Perhaps I should ask for a vote of confidence. So, in the light of what I have said, in the light of what you all know, about my motives, about the project, about the current state of our progress, let me ask if anyone has any objections to the scheme. Please speak."

"I think there's a slight problem with your proposal," said Nigel. "I've seen Marx's grave. My great-grandfather's buried at Highgate. If I remember correctly, it's an extremely large block of concrete, upon which sits the huge head of Karl. It would take a JCB to shift the whole thing. Are you planning a smash and grab raid?"

"You're referring to the Marx memorial," said Jerry. "That's for tourists. His original grave is in the western half of the cemetery, which is now closed. That's where his remains are; don't be fooled by the tourist attraction. Marx's grave is a private place, hidden away, but easily accessible if you know where to look…"

"I have the plot number!" said Nicolai.

"Thank you," said Jerry. "Fortunately, we've managed to sort that out. There shouldn't be any problems finding it, or getting into it. Is there anything else?"

"I've never been a gardener," said Nigel. "I'm absolutely useless with a shovel."

"No digging is involved," said Jerry. "That's taken care of. The job is merely one of transport. Basically, I'm looking for a courier. Any other questions?"

There was no response.

"In that case, can I ask for a volunteer?"

He was stunned by the show of hands. All, apart from Liz.

"I think we'll have to draw straws," said Jerry.

There was a break in the proceedings; a hubbub of voices as Jerry cut up a sheet of paper into squares, marked one with an X, and placed them all in a bucket. He passed it around, avoiding Liz.

"So," said Jerry, "who…?"

Cut short by Daniel, raising a hand, showing an X.

"Daniel it is then," said Jerry. "I should have said that it means flying today, by the way. And given the flight restrictions, there'll be some delay, we don't know how long, before you can return."

He looked quizzically at Daniel.

"No problem," said Daniel, smiling. "It is for science."

"Yes," said Jerry. "Of course. Er... perhaps two people would be best. Nigel, would you be willing to accompany?"

"Yes, I'm game," said Nigel. "But no digging."

"There's no digging," said Jerry.

*

Liz walked up the path, wanting to tell Bob the news. She'd come away thinking that maybe Jerry had a point, that maybe it wasn't such a mad idea after all. In theory, at least. In practice though...

She was startled to see the door of Bob's cottage opening and a young Chinese woman stepping out, dressed in a white medical coat. They approached, the woman looking down at the ground. As they passed, the woman looked up swiftly with a mysterious smile; then her gaze returned to the path.

The door wasn't locked. Liz walked in to see Bob in bed, lying on his back with his legs still bent in the all-fours position.

"Someone's been having fun," she said.

"That was Dr Lee," he said. "She thinks something's slipped. A disk or a bone."

"How did you get up here?" she said, sitting on the bed.

"I crawled. This is the most relaxing position, I find."

She reached under the sheets.

"You're obviously pleased to see me," she said.

"Dr Lee tells me..."

She squeezed.

"What? What did she tell you?"

"That Torre de Columba – oh! – that the meaning has nothing to do with Christopher Columbus..."

She squeezed harder.

"And what else?" she said. "What else did she tell you?"

"She says it means – oh! – the tower of the dove…"

"Does she?" she said, squeezing harder.

"Or in your case," he said, "I guess it would be – oh! – the tower of the pigeon…"

"Creep!" she said, and swung her legs onto the bed, holding his lever.

THE MESSENGER
PART THREE

FLIGHT

1

Memories of that night were to haunt Nigel's dreams in the days that followed. And was it all a dream? It had that quality, he thought. Throughout the proceedings he walked in a daze, as if his body was being moved by an external force.

Seeking the grass with their soft shoes, avoiding the crunch of the gravel…

It was just like a scene from a movie he'd seen: the only thing missing was a bat or two. No, not quite the only thing – they should have been carrying stakes and a crucifix. And that dog should have been howling, not barking.

It was a night of drizzle, rain dripping from the trees, the smell of damp leaves, the smell of wet stone. Karen was leading the procession, followed by Beelzebub and Salomé; then Daniel and Nigel.

No one had spoken for some time; not since they had entered the hallowed grounds.

Nigel had checked out the grounds in the daylight, paying two pounds for a tourist tour, simply to get a feel of the place. His bearings were lost now. The tour hadn't ventured this way.

Tombstones, tombstones, everywhere, and spiders' threads that tickled his face. And a smell of honeysuckle. Or was it Salomé's perfume?

Whatever it was, it blocked out the memory of what they were here for. It made him feel… light-headed.

The full moon had yet to show itself, but the grey night was a better disguise. They were walking in darkness, torches at the ready, and all dressed in black from top to toe: Karen in a trouser suit, Beelzebub and Salomé in long black cloaks and fedoras, he and Daniel in cast-off suits from a charity shop. Beelzebub and Salomé were a bit weird, he thought; but he had been warned.

Nosferatu, *Night of the Vampire*, *Phantom of the Opera* – he couldn't quite place them. They lacked the white face paint of *The Phantom*. Karen had told them to take it off; it wouldn't do; it must be black. But the red eyeliner they refused to remove. Holding hands and walking close – only by their hats would you know there were two.

But there were three gasps when he bumped into Salomé, who'd stopped. Then he felt a hand on his genitalia.

"Slow down, big boy," she said.

The husky tone went straight to his bloodstream.

"This is where we turn off," Karen whispered. "There's a grass path, between these rows of trees. Follow me."

Karen had briefed them all. They were looking for a mausoleum. Or a catacomb. Or a crypt. Or simply a tomb. It varied, depending on the interruptions of Beelzebub and Salomé. But basically a box, she'd said, with a door in it, covered in moss – that's the entrance to the mausoleum, she said. You mean catacomb, said Beelzebub. No, it's a crypt, said Salomé. Oh bloody hell, said Nigel, what does it look like?

"This is it," Karen whispered. "Behind this rhododendron. We have to walk through the hedge."

"Are you sure it's the right one?" Nigel whispered.

"Ttssssssk!" said Beelzebub, turning abruptly and brandishing a pencil-sized torch as if it were a sword. "The Professor lacks faith! Look, the sign!"

He swung his pencil to the bark of a tree, turning it on to reveal a fluorescent glow. Nigel, thinking of Zorro, looked for a Z till his eyes got used to the light. Then he could just make it out: the outline of a hammer and sickle.

"Ultraviolet," said Beelzebub. "We marked the tree."

"Good man," Nigel whispered.

Beelzebub bowed, removed his hat, and head-butted the

rhododendron. Daniel followed while Karen swept the branches aside. Nigel turned to Salomé, and was alarmed to see what she was wearing under her cloak: black stockings and a black skirt, which barely covered the tops of her suspenders

"After you, big boy," she said, smiling.

Through the hedge he went, speeded on by a hand feeling his backside. And there it was: a shed. Or a box. Covered in moss. He felt it. It was hard stone. Granite. And an old wooden door with a padlock and chain, which Beelzebub was in the process of unlocking.

"How did he find a key?" Nigel whispered.

"Kevin used to be a locksmith, if you know what I mean," Karen replied.

"Kevin?" whispered Nigel.

Karen bit her lip.

"Sorry," she whispered. "I mean, Beelzebub."

The door creaked open and Beelzebub turned, waving to Salomé. They stood at the threshold in a noisy embrace, ignoring Nigel's loud whisper.

"That dog's still barking," he said. "Do you mind? This is hardly the time for a snog!"

The slurping continued; it sounded like a dog lapping water. Then, suitably refreshed, Beelzebub turned to Karen and said, "Farewell, Queen of the Night. We must descend, before the hour of dawn strikes." Then, swirling his cloak with a flourish, he grabbed Salomé's hand and pulled her inside.

Nigel looked at his watch. No problems so far, he thought. He offered to hold the camera, which Daniel was about to place on the tomb. It was part of the ruse, should they be stopped by police or security. They were a film crew – that was the story – shooting stuff for a pop video.

"There's five tombs down there," said Beelzebub, his face poking round the door.

"Five?" Karen whispered. "There should only be four."

She looked at Nigel, who shrugged.

"Perhaps he had another mistress," he said, remembering the briefing. Karen had said his wife and daughter were buried with the great man, plus his mistress. Now what?

"Which chest holds the treasure?" said Beelzebub.

"I would say... the biggest," said Nigel.

"Do you have a tape measure?" said Beelzebub.

"I have a measure," said Daniel.

"Oh, this is hopeless!" said Nigel.

"You'd better go down," said Karen. "Both of you. I'll stay on guard. I'll hoot three times if there's any danger."

Nigel looked at her, thinking of the Famous Five.

"Go on," she said. "You can't expect the two of them to lift a bloody concrete lid on their own!"

"Workers of the World, Unite!" Nigel muttered, and crept through the door, shining his torch.

Squeaking rats and a stench of mildew, but the cobwebs had been pushed aside already. Down the hallowed steps to the slabs at the bottom.

"What I suggest we do," said Nigel, "is take one coffin each and search for inscriptions."

Beelzebub was already searching.

"There's five tombs," he said.

"Four," said Nigel. "We can tick this one off the list... too small."

"Your quest is at an end, master," said Beelzebub. "Workers of the World, Unite... 1818 to 1883."

"Excellent," said Nigel. "Now, the lid... one at each corner..."

"Here, look," said Beelzebub. "There's a window."

And there it was: green and dusty, but a window nevertheless, which, once upon a time, would have permitted a glance at the face of the great man. But now...

"The Pearls of Wisdom!" said Beelzebub, wiping the glass.

Nigel looked and felt his heart jump. Not with joy but fright. And not at seeing the skull, but at Beelzebub's reflection: his black hair, long and lank, his two-tone face, thin and gaunt, and those red eyes.

"Let's move the lid," Nigel said.

"Wait!" said Beelzebub, producing a candle.

He placed it in a niche, lit it, and returned to the lid.

"After three…" said Nigel, and they heaved.

An effort because it was made of stone, but they did it; just enough to let a pair of hands slip inside and…

"What are you doing?" said Nigel.

Beelzebub and Salomé had joined hands and were now waving them towards the gap and snogging, noisily.

"Don't forget these! And aim for the target!"

A pause, while Nigel passed surgical gloves to them both. Then another snog, which didn't stop till the act was done.

Beelzebub reaching inside, guiding Salomé's hand while glancing askew at the treasure. A snap, and another, and the hands, still joined, withdrawing…

Then, to Nigel's horror, Salomé reached inside her cleavage.

"Christ!" he muttered. Could a lifetime's work be ruined by the thoughtless act of a buxom Goth? He buried the thought with a loud whisper: "The lid!"

And the job was done.

Quickly up those hallowed steps, now defiled, and out into the grey night.

"Is everything…?" Karen whispered.

"The Pearl of Wisdom," said Beelzebub, showing a palm.

"The Key to the Universe," said Salomé, showing hers.

"Excellent!" Karen whispered.

"I'll take that," Nigel said to Beelzebub, who was offering his palm to Daniel. "The, er, samples go in here."

Placing a surgical bag beneath Beelzebub's hand, Nigel was trying to remember his instructions. The samples go in one bag, the gloves in another. Jerry.

"He's so greedy," said Salomé, when Nigel held a bag beneath her hand. "One's not enough for him. He must have two."

"Thank you," said Nigel. "And the glove?"

Beelzebub, items disposed, had returned to the padlock and chain. Salomé sidled up to Nigel, slid her glove off, tossed it into the receptacle, and cupped a hand about his scrotum.

"Are you satisfied, big boy?" she whispered.

Nigel, smelling her perfume, felt her hot thigh pressing against him. And was speechless.

"It'll be daylight soon, we'd best be out of here," he whispered, but stood there feeling hypnotised: would a cock crow, and Salomé return to her coffin?

Then Karen said, "Okay, let's go!" and Nigel remembered that they were trespassers who had broken into a grave.

Salomé patted his privates.

"Come on, big boy," she said. "You're coming back with us."

*

Twenty-four hours were to pass before Nigel was able to sit down once more at Mrs O'Sullivan's, with breakfast spread out on the table. So pleasant to return to formalities, he thought.

He poured a third cup of tea; his colleagues had declined his offer to fill theirs. Miguel was still on the toast and marmalade, Daniel on the cornflakes. The place was hardly five-star, but a bed and breakfast in Wembley was the best they could muster under the circumstances.

Their absence the previous morning had been noted by Mrs O'Sullivan, who had spoken to Miguel at the breakfast table.

"They go to see a film last night," he'd said, following Nigel's instructions. "Then they go to a casino."

Nigel wished he'd thought of a better ruse. Mrs O'Sullivan now had the impression they were all loaded, with fingers in everything from casinos to pigeon racing. When he and Daniel had staggered in yesterday evening, looking haggard after the ordeal of the night, and the ordeal of the day, she had taken some persuading to rise before dawn, to cook breakfast for them all. Her gamble turned out to be lucrative, thanks to

Nigel's wallet. And recompensed for the early start, she'd been perkier than usual this morning, talking to Miguel about pigeon fanciers' clubs – Nigel reaching for the cornflakes, Daniel yet to appear.

"You'll be wanting the best of the daylight," she said, "I'm sure. So, I hope you win and good luck to you. It's a bright morning and he knows it, doesn't he? They say it'll rain later, so he'll be wanting to get moving. Yes, on a morning like this, he wants to be flying, don't you my pretty..."

Nigel was intrigued by the bird's prospects: a flight of two and a half thousand miles, roughly, including a thousand miles of ocean. Possibly longer, according to Miguel. It depended on the bird's route.

"To be perfectly frank," said Nigel, "I don't see how it's feasible. I can appreciate their following the coastline, but I don't see how they can negotiate the Atlantic."

Miguel wagged a knife, smiling.

"*Senhor*," he said, "never underestimate the determination of a rock dove. It is a mystery to me too, yet they do it. Those I release from Lagos, sometimes they fly west, sometimes south. South is longer, but they can rest and eat – they fly the coast to Africa, then the sea to Madeira, which is seven hundred kilometres. Madeira to Açores is another nine hundred kilometres. One bird, she do it in one day, Madeira to Açores."

Nigel was mentally doing the conversions: 900 multiplied by 5 divided by 8, giving 550 miles approx. And at... what? 60mph, these birds, according to a previous conversation. Giving approx 9 hours flying time. Nine hours without a break? Impossible, he thought.

Miguel saw the scepticism, written in Nigel's face. He wiped his mouth, reached inside a waistcoat pocket, and produced a device that looked like a mobile phone. A tracking device, he said, passing it to Nigel.

"Oh!" said Nigel. "It's not such a mystery then."

"How they do it is a mystery, *senhor*; their routes is not. The bolder ones fly west from Lagos. Sometimes they wait for a boat and steal a ride; sometimes they rest on rocks. They are rock doves, *senhor*; they know how to find rocks. They see long distance, their sight is very good. With blue sky, they see forty kilometre."

"Forty kilometre? That's…"

"Twenty-six miles. On a clear day."

Nigel was astonished. Bird intelligence he was aware of; such as the ability of parrots to learn human language. But pigeons, he used to think, were rather dumb. He studied the tracking device.

Miguel, spreading a piece of toast, saw that Nigel was impressed.

In the old days, said Miguel, the birds were befriended by sailors, who used them for navigation. The birds knew the uncharted waters; they knew where the rocks were. There are tales of near disasters, only avoided because of the doves. The doves would fly to the rocks, which the sailors couldn't see in times of mist. They were useful birds to have on board, and so the sailors fed them. It is an old custom, going back to the days of the great explorers, the days of Christopher Columbus, who took his name, some said, from the bird…

Christopher Pigeon, the great explorer! Not a dumb bird at all, Nigel thought.

Listening to Miguel, he had one of those rare moments when his expertise felt somewhat deficient in the face of a more primitive kind of wisdom – stories handed down by word of mouth from generation to generation; stories with a purpose. How to avoid earthquakes, volcanic eruptions; that sort of thing. Taking cues from Mother Nature, because she knew better than we how to survive.

Jerry had touched on this before their departure. Not exactly a briefing, because there wasn't time. More like words of reassurance, along the lines of, "Trust me, Miguel knows what's what." Provoked by Nigel, who'd been shaking his head at the folly of it all; the pinnacle being Jerry's belief that a wild pigeon could be released on Wimbledon Common and find its way to the Azores.

We're talking about birds, Jerry said, and some birds fly amazingly long distances. These birds, in particular, are quite extraordinary.

Pigeon racing is now the second largest sport in Portugal, Jerry said, and Miguel's family are all involved – Jerry had spoken at length to Bob Rheingold, who'd got the information from Miguel. And Miguel has won prizes, he said, thanks to the speed of his birds. His rock doves are not fully domesticated; they fly much faster than the usual racers; speeds of 110kph have been recorded. Miguel is very proud of his achievements, and very keen to show off his birds' capabilities. It's a challenge for him, as they haven't flown so far before. He's released them from France, no problem, and this won't be that much further; a short trip across the Channel. I have every confidence in him; so should you.

But, Nigel had said, why not release him from the mainland? Trust me, said Jerry. It's better this way. Safer. The alternative would be two plane flights for the bird, outward and return, with him cooped up in a cage for the duration, which'll make him totally sick, or a long, long wait on the mainland, also cooped up in a cage, waiting with Miguel till you arrive with the samples. Either way, not good. They like being free, they like being at home. Release the bird ASAP, and it'll race home ASAP. Wimbledon Common, okay?

Nigel passed the tracker to Miguel, who waved a hand.

"I have two," he said. "You take it, till we return."

"Right," said Nigel, "thanks. You'll have to show me how to use it."

"No problem," said Miguel. "Later."

Nigel looked down at Miguel's feet, where the pigeon appeared to be dozing in his cage. Miguel was devoted to the bird; he hadn't let it out of his sight the whole trip. And he wouldn't wake it up last night, so the kit had been fitted this morning, Miguel insisting that only he should handle the bird.

Miguel knew that the bird was carrying the tooth of a great man. But he didn't know how the tooth had been acquired. Nigel had agonised over this with Karen. What shall we tell him? he said. What does he need to know? she replied. He's a devout Catholic, he said; if we tell him we're robbing a grave, he'll think we're all cursed and won't cooperate. What does he know about the project? she said. There's a rumour on the island, he said, that we're studying the DNA of pigeons and rock doves. Which isn't far from the truth, she said. Yes, he said, but the rumours say for breeding purposes. The mysterious research lab is about to launch a new breed of racing pigeon, the fastest yet. Oh, she said.

So, she said, tell him it's the tooth of a great man. We're expanding our research. We're looking at old bones in the British Museum, and it can only be done at night. Old bones need to be protected from daylight. Tell him it's the tooth of a pharaoh. Or an ancient emperor. An old king of Britain. Like King Arthur. And our work is top secret. Strictly hush-hush.

Nigel thought Karen had taken something.

Now he couldn't remember what he had told Miguel. Except that it was the tooth of a great man.

Miguel had been curious, but not that curious. He was more concerned about the bird, his precious Gabriel.

Gabriel! The bringer of good news! A tooth in a locket, fixed to his leg!

And an electronic tag on his wing…

Well, Nigel thought, they may be intelligent, but I would call them freakish birds. Sea birds, more or less, who live on cliffs and make nests of dry seaweed. Yet they don't eat fish and can't swim. Ocean birds who eat seeds and grain. An odd link in the evolutionary chain.

But there it was, by his side: this strange bond between man and bird. It was totally alien to Nigel. On certain things, he decided, Miguel knows more than I. Including how to track a pigeon. Jerry hadn't told him about that; it was clearly Miguel's department.

He picked up yesterday's paper, waiting for the others to finish breakfast. An item caught his eye straightaway.

"Heavens," he said. "They're proposing a mass cull of pigeons in Trafalgar Square. Let's hope he doesn't fly north."

He looked at Miguel.

Miguel carried on eating while casting a brief glance of disdain in Nigel's direction.

"Sorry," said Nigel. "Shouldn't have mentioned it."

He remembered his last quip to Jerry, shortly before leaving. "And what's wrong with Hampstead Heath? Next door to Highgate!"

North side of the city, Jerry said. Wimbledon's south.

Everything, it seemed, had been taken into account.

Except the wind.

The dust was eye-stinging as they left the house, and Miguel was staring at the clouds. Not a good sign; it was blowing from the south-east, he said.

"There's not a lot we can do about it," said Nigel, holding the car door, while Miguel, clutching the cage, still hesitated.

Miguel climbed in, sitting in the back with the cage. Daniel sat in the front, his hair dishevelled and eyes like slits.

"I take it you didn't sleep well," said Nigel, starting the engine.

"No," said Daniel. "The settee was very lumpy. I had bad dreams."

"Dreaming of vampires, I suppose," said Nigel, thinking of Salomé and the day before.

And what a day! Trying to sleep with them two moaning, groaning, humping and bumping. Right above their heads! No wonder Daniel looked shattered. He'd refused the offer of a tot of whisky, so Nigel, pissed off with the noise, had drunk the whole bottle and slept through the rest of the day, dreaming of vampires, or one in particular, and only waking when Karen walked in to open the curtains for the evening.

Karen's parents owned the place; a house in Finchley, converted into flats. A spacious flat, with high ceilings and a large guest room. Only one though, so Karen had taken that, and he and Daniel had shared the lounge, but not the couch. Nigel had slept on the floor. And snored, according to Daniel, who hadn't slept much at all. Who had in fact – this from Karen, when Daniel was out of earshot – who'd been wandering about the house. In her room too; she'd woken up and was dead scared, she said, knowing it wasn't Beelzebub.

"He was probably looking for the toilet," said Nigel. "Sleep walking perhaps."

"I don't think so," said Karen. "He was kneeling on the floor, looking inside my bag. He frightened me to death. He just said sorry and walked out."

"What was he looking for?"

"I don't know. Unless…"

Nigel glanced at Daniel. Had he really been looking for the teeth, as Karen had suspected? The tools, the bags – everything had been stashed in the guest room under Karen's supervision, apart from personal items. Which, possibly, Daniel had mislaid, or had been stored with the rest of the stuff, by mistake.

Nigel threw another glance.

"Were you dreaming of vampires?" he said.

But Daniel, caressed by the warm air, by the relentless drone of the engine, had nodded off.

Hammersmith: they crossed the river. Daydreaming, Nigel saw the beauty of having wings. Even at this early hour, the roads were crammed.

Wimbledon Common: now here's a place of legend, Nigel thought. Possibly the only place in London where you could still find a windmill. Something of a tourist attraction; there was a cafe and a car park there. And beneath the respectable veneer of joggers, dog walkers, golfers, model aeroplane enthusiasts and people just out for a stroll, there were stories of flashers, rapists, drunken tramps, pickpockets on skateboards, noisy motorbikes, furtive men who hung around toilets, drug users with syringes, secret meetings, rude awakenings, moments of madness, UFOs, pets stolen by aliens, kites stolen by aliens, pagans at midnight, clandestine whippet racing, rumours of bear baiting, dog fighting, gatherings of pigeons and their fanciers...

The road to the windmill: he drove past the car park and stopped some distance away, on the gravel.

Gabriel's moment – time to fly!

"Everybody out," he said.

Miguel had also nodded off, draping himself over the cage. They stirred and climbed out while Nigel sat in the car.

"Are you getting out?" said Daniel.

Seconds passed before Nigel answered.

"I might as well," he said, and opened the door.

They walked a few yards. Then Miguel stopped, checking the wind, looking for the higher ground. He was about to place the cage on the grass when Daniel grabbed it, turned, and made a dash for the car. Tried and failed because his foot slipped in his haste, and the cage, flung by his outstretched hand, hit a tree and fell to the gravel.

The bird limped out.

Miguel muttered something in Portuguese.

"Shit!" said Nigel.

Daniel lay spreadeagled on the grass. They left him there and walked towards the pigeon. It hopped away, flapping its wings.

"He's hurt his wing," said Miguel.

"Shit!" said Nigel, and his body came to a standstill.

Miguel followed the bird as it limped away, flew a few yards, then limped again, pecking at the ground.

"He's hurt his foot," he said, and muttered in Portuguese.

Nigel watched. Miguel seemed on the point of catching it; then it took off, and settled in a tree.

"He's upset," said Miguel.

"I'm not surprised," said Nigel.

Then he heard the motor and turned to see the car, Daniel at the wheel, crunching the gravel.

"Shit!" said Nigel.

A cry from Miguel, who was more interested in the bird. The bird, startled by the squeak of the brakes, had taken off, heading south. Miguel looked at Nigel, a pained expression on his face, and shook his head, slowly. Then he too saw the car, screeching down the drive. He turned to Nigel; a quizzical look this time.

Nigel shrugged.

"He won't be going far," he said.

"Gabriel?" said Miguel.

"I don't know about Gabriel," said Nigel. "You'll know more than me on that one. I'm talking about Daniel. The car's due back at Heathrow tomorrow. I'll report it as stolen. In fact, I'll do it now."

He reached inside his jacket.

"Blast!" he said. "My mobile…"

*

Daniel's moment of madness. This had happened before. As a child, he had been diagnosed as having Compulsive Celebrity Disorder, after repeatedly stealing Elvis gear and Beatle wigs from his competitors in the school's fancy dress. Compulsive Celebrity Disorder – this was the urge, the impulse to do spur-of-the-moment crazy things, whenever there was the lure of a big prize, and the possibility of winning it, by fair means or foul. Such as a Nobel.

And now, his secret was out, and nothing had been gained.

He drove around London, following cars at random, trying to understand the impulse, his act of desperation – fighting over a tooth!

Was it so important? Yes, of course it was; he had seen the evidence himself. The missing ingredient: the DNA link.

He had never planned it this way; he hadn't really made a plan. It was a series of coincidences, which had all worked in his favour. Such as drawing the X in the lucky dip; a sign, surely, that he had been chosen. Such as being there to catch the password that day, Liz sat at the terminal, unaware of his presence. Even then, he wouldn't have acted but for the timing: the news of that link, which had inspired him to copy the data.

He hadn't even been thinking of the Nobel prize; not consciously; not then. It was simply that he could produce the goods faster if only he were to control the show. He knew that right at the start, when Jerry was parading his DNA computer like a kid's toy. Jerry's chemistry set as the answer to everything. It was he, Daniel, who had shown him that things weren't so simple; he, Daniel, who was showing him the way forward.

But there was no way of controlling the show with Jerry in charge. Impossible to imagine that he'd ever give up. And it was useless working in teams, unless you were the one in charge.

Things took so much longer. Organising experiments, waiting for the results. It was the way of science; a necessary pain. Worse when you were following someone else's whims. He'd seen it before: students working on experiments designed to prove their supervisors' idiotic theories. Academe wasn't the place if you had ideas; it could take decades to put them into practice. If ever.

He could produce the goods faster if he worked alone. But you couldn't work alone on a project like this. You needed teams. So he would produce the teams. New teams, working under his directorship. He had his contacts. He had the data, he knew what to do, he could work fast; a Nobel prize was waiting.

And what if his sources were questioned? He would have to make them up. A minor problem. What mattered was the result. Data crimes, knowledge crimes; they were happening all the time. A theorist changes his views; no explanation given. And all because he's studied the work of a colleague, a name he doesn't want to acknowledge; the work of an underling. Academic empires were founded on such crimes. Student plagiarism was the tip of the iceberg; ignored by many because they too had been guilty.

The right place at the right time: the data was now at his fingertips. The next stage was… The next stage had been bungled!

Again, an opportunity presents itself. But this time, he messes it up. So now what? He couldn't return to the project; he was in disgrace. He had the data, but not the clue to designing the device that would make something of it. The clue was vital, and he had bungled the event. Could he do without it?

His thoughts were interrupted at this point by a jingle, coming from the glove compartment. The sound was familiar, as was the tune: *God rest ye merry gentlemen…*

Nigel's bloody mobile!

He reached inside the glove compartment but couldn't find the phone. The tune was annoying; the same line repeated. He would have to pull over. Where? He was now on the North Circular; there were signs to Brent Shopping Centre. He drove into the car park, the jingle still jingling.

He opened the glove compartment. It was full of all sorts – chocolate wrappers, crisp bags, cigarette packets, lighters, torches, maps, papers, documents – a pair of gloves even. Plus, two mobile phones.

But one of them wasn't a mobile. It was a tracking device.

Daniel examined it.

Another piece of microchip technology, with an enormous amount of detail compressed therein. Maps, at various scales. A blinking light, indicating the position of the bird. It hadn't got very far. It was still on Wimbledon Common.

He left the car park and headed south.

*

It was just another day in the life of a cognitive neuroscientist,

Nigel thought. Yesterday, raiding the tomb of the founder of Marxism. Today, running circles around Wimbledon Common, trying to catch a bloody pigeon.

Except that Miguel was doing the running; Nigel was watching.

The bird appeared to have no sense of direction whatsoever. It had flown south, but only as far as the woods on the common, where it settled in a tree. Then it returned, almost to Miguel's feet, where it started pecking, angrily, at the ground. Its aim, it seemed, was to stay in their company without being caught.

Miguel wanted to inspect it for damage. He doubted whether it could carry out the voyage. If that was the case, they would have to take it back with them, he said.

Nigel was hoping it would fly to the Oval, so that he could watch the Test Match. A fanciful vision: the pigeon strutting by the boundary, as they do, while the Radio Four commentators described its unusual markings, as they do.

No chance – Gabriel didn't want to leave the common, it seemed.

It was a curious game of flirtation: Gabriel allowing Miguel to approach him; then, just as he was about to grasp him, flying away a few yards.

Leading him on. And walking in circles.

"He doesn't trust you," said Nigel, who'd decided to sit down at this point, propping himself against a tree. "He's avoiding the cage, I suppose."

"He's very upset," said Miguel.

"Perhaps if you sit down, he'll come to you," said Nigel.

Miguel didn't want to sit down.

Nigel closed his eyes.

It was still fairly early; the sun was warm. Today was meant to be a day of rest; they were meant to be flying to Lisbon tomorrow, staying at Mrs O'Sullivan's for one more night.

When Nigel opened his eyes, he saw the blue Mondeo at the end of the drive. Now what? He checked his pockets:

Daniel had his tracker. Nigel stood to his feet. The Mondeo did a U-turn and drove away. Nigel returned to his seat.

The game of flirtation continued.

Nigel dozed.

Mid-morning: Nigel was getting hungry; people were getting curious. Two old men had been chatting to Miguel about pigeons; now they were chatting about windmills – there were quite a few on the Azores, it seemed.

Time passed, till Nigel decided to hunt down a sandwich bar and a phone box, preferably one that took cards. He must speak to Jerry about developments; he must tell the police about the Mondeo. He spoke to the old men, who told him the cafe was closed for refurbishing. They gave him directions to Wimbledon High Street, and he walked away, advising Miguel, somewhat flippantly, not to wander off.

When he returned, the spectators had grown to five old men, two greyhounds and a young lad, who should have been in school, Nigel thought. Still, this wasn't the occasion to play the truant inspector. It may have been his lunch hour; besides, Nigel was more put out by the old men, who had taken his seat by the tree.

They ate the sandwiches, Miguel opting to sit down at last.

Gabriel was the centre of attention; he seemed to like it. Then, as if he was bored with it all, he flew to a tree. Two minutes later, it started to rain, just as Mrs O'Sullivan had predicted. The old men decided it was time to go, taking the greyhounds and the lad with them. Miguel went off in the bird's direction.

"We've got a plane to catch tomorrow, you know," said Nigel.

Miguel's response was a shrug.

Nigel thought about making plans. Jerry had told him to stick with Miguel at all costs; the item must be retrieved, he said, and don't let Daniel gets his hands on it. So, there was no alternative but to pop over to Imperial and see his former colleagues, with the aim of borrowing a car.

He told Miguel his plan. Less flippantly this time, he told him to stay on the common, around the windmill area.

"I may be gone some time," he said. "I should be back around teatime, say sixish."

He'd been determined to stay incognito on this visit, as far as friends and family were concerned. It was no longer feasible; he must invent a pretext for being here. Like, a sudden death in the family…

Four hours later, he was driving to Wimbledon with his head full of the latest gossip: "Apparently, Ms So-and-So of the Royal Society (you know: renowned for her short skirts and violent lipstick) has landed a windfall from the US government – she's receiving funds to set up experiments on torture. Plus a key question to answer: does having a religious faith mean you can endure more pain than the faithless?"

Nigel couldn't believe it: the war in the Middle East has obviously stepped up a gear, he thought. Thank God Jerry's missed out on that source of funding. The experiments would have been… torture. And who would have thought it? Ms So-and-So of the Royal Society was now the Miss Whiplash of academe.

He arrived to find Miguel on the edge of the woods. He was sitting with an old man, who'd apparently supplied him with sausage rolls, bacon butties, rock cakes and a bag of crisps.

"Where's the bird?" said Nigel.

Miguel, his mouth full, pointed to a nearby tree.

"I'd best be going mate," said the old man. "I'll see you in Barcelona."

"I hope to be there," said Miguel.

"What was that all about?" said Nigel.

"*Columbofilia, senhor,*" said Miguel. "A meeting of pigeon fanciers."

Nigel, who hadn't eaten, looked at the pile of food and thought there was more to this pigeon business than meets the eye.

Miguel offered him a sausage roll. Then he explained the latest game. Gabriel was circling the woods, exploring the perimeters of the common. Miguel had walked around it twice.

It was now evening, and Nigel was saddened by the thought that Miguel had spent the whole day chasing a pigeon. More saddened when Miguel refused to leave, saying he would find somewhere to sleep in the woods. The bird had settled in a tree, head down; a sign he would sleep there, Miguel said, if he wasn't disturbed. But still he refused to leave him.

Nigel returned to Wembley, alone.

He spent the night in mental torment, torn between the pits of depression and the heights of hilarity, not knowing which to embrace. The idea that tormented him was basically this: his life was now being controlled by the movements of a bloody pigeon!

He woke, still hoping they might catch their flight.

A quick breakfast; words with Mrs O'Sullivan; then a drive to Wimbledon.

He arrived on the common to see a gang of old men standing there, crowding around Miguel. He dismissed the idea that Miguel was being attacked; more likely that he'd finally caught the bird. But no, Miguel was showing them the tracker.

The bird had flown!

Nigel, with difficulty, extricated Miguel from his admirers.

"Let's go to the car," said Nigel, thinking there was still time for Heathrow.

Miguel, looking pained, was in no rush. He was playing with the tracker like a kid playing with a mobile phone.

"Impossible!" said Miguel. "Impossible! He mustn't attempt it!"

"Where is he?" Nigel asked.

"He left just after dawn, *senhor*," he said, pressing buttons. "Look!"

Nigel peered at the tiny screen: it showed a map, with a

green trail marking the bird's path.

"He go south-west," said Miguel, scrolling backwards and forwards. "Can you see?"

Nigel saw the trail, starting from Wimbledon, going through Cobham, Guildford, Aldershot, Farnham, Winchester, Paulsbury – the bird was flying in a straight line, more or less, heading south-west. He looked at his watch: it was 10am. He'd been flying since dawn – about 5am – and he'd done about a hundred and twenty miles. In five hours? It didn't seem very impressive.

"He's stopped," said Miguel, reading his thoughts. "He's resting. See?"

The trail indeed came to a halt, about twenty miles beyond Paulsbury.

"It's very good," said Nigel, admiring the device. "Those times – presumably those are the arrival times, yes?"

"Yes, *senhor*. He arrive… er… 8.30. He fly three hours, now he rests. But look!"

Miguel was almost screaming, his fingers pressing the buttons. The display changed to show the projected flight path, if the bird continued in the same direction.

"He go south-west! He not go south!" said Miguel.

The trail, marked by an orange line, went through Dorset, Devon, Cornwall, Land's End…

"Christ!" said Nigel. "He's heading for the Scilly Isles!"

"*Não, senhor*! Look!"

Miguel pressed a button or two. The screen showed a map of a smaller scale, including the UK and the Atlantic. The orange line, projected, trailed across the ocean and pointed straight to…

"The Azores!" said Nigel. "Christ! He's heading straight for it!"

Miguel looked up, a tear in his eye.

"He wants to go home, *senhor*!" he said, handing Nigel the tracker. "And he won't make it!"

Nigel looked at the screen. The figure, in red: 1,500. Fifteen hundred miles of ocean. With a damaged wing? A bad foot? And what lay beyond the Scilly Isles? Nothing but ocean, till you came to the Azores.

"You said… he knows how to find rocks," said Nigel, looking for the proverbial straw.

"Off the coast of Africa, yes, there are rocks," said Miguel. "But mid-Atlantic? I don't think so."

He shook his head.

Nigel thought of fishing boats, trawlers, oil tankers. A possibility the bird could hitch a ride. A possibility.

"Let's get something to eat," he said, returning the tracker. "You must be starving."

They walked to the car. What next? Nigel was at a loss. Their flight to Lisbon looked extremely unlikely. What was he meant to do? They'd all thought that the bird would head south, cross the Channel, follow the coast through France, Spain, Portugal. But Gabriel was taking the fast route.

Except that he wasn't so fast. In fact, he seemed to be stuck.

Nigel and Miguel sat in the Wimbledon Diner, eating a fried breakfast, the tracker on the table, blinking – but no sign of movement.

They talked about pigeons. Or rather, rock doves – Nigel had realised some time ago that Gabriel was not the sort of bird who stalked Trafalgar Square. He wanted to know, was there a pattern to their long flights? They don't fly continuously, obviously, he said; they must pause and rest. And they don't fly at night.

They stop for a rest, they stop to eat, said Miguel. Sometimes, they have a morning snooze. On a long flight, they may rest for two, three days before taking off again.

A break of journey, said Nigel. Yes, said Miguel.

So Gabriel might be having a break now, Nigel suggested. After all, he's done a hundred and twenty miles already. With a damaged wing.

Miguel agreed; he wasn't worried about him resting, he said; he was worried about him making it over the Atlantic.

We'll just have to hope, said Nigel. Then he remembered Daniel. What was he up to? And when should they depart for Lisbon?

Miguel didn't think Gabriel would make the journey. He didn't want to leave, he said, till Gabriel had left the shore – he refused even to contemplate it.

It meant a waiting game. Again, Nigel's mood bordered on hysteria. They returned to Wembley that night. They watched the news. No sign that the war was ending; the reverse, in fact. There was no chance of flying back; they would have to take the supply ship. And Gabriel was still in Dorset, spending the night there.

He was still there in the morning. And at lunch. And in the afternoon. Now Miguel began to worry for different reasons. He should be away now, he said; he would be away, if he was fit. It was most unlike him. There was no sign of movement; not the slightest movement.

Perhaps he's found a mate, Nigel suggested. It is breeding time, after all.

It was just a suggestion, which he didn't really believe. Because Gabriel was a rock dove, a bird of the sea cliffs, not likely to breed with a wood pigeon or turtle dove. But he didn't want to say what he really thought: namely, that Gabriel may have been shot by an irate farmer, who'd caught him eating his grain.

Miguel shook his head. Gabriel has a mate, he said. They mate for life. That's what makes them good racers, it's what makes them fly home. His wife is at home, waiting for him. And he loves his wife. He likes to be loved, and he loves being at home, with his wife. Love makes him race, to be with his mate.

I think I need to consult Jerry, said Nigel.

The next day, they were driving down to Dorset.

*

While Gabriel had been evading capture on Wimbledon Common, Daniel had been sitting in a pub, thinking about guns. The bird was still on the common, and the only way to catch it, he thought, was to shoot it.

Problems!

For a start, he wasn't a marksman. And then, even if he were, where could he obtain a gun at short notice? Presumably, he thought, if he were a marksman he would know…

Once, as an undergraduate, he'd joined a clay pigeon club. And discovered that shooting wasn't his forte. And even if it was, and assuming he had a gun in his pocket, there'd be Nigel and Miguel to consider…

The alternative was to attract it, he thought. Tempt it with that special *je ne sais quoi*, so irresistible that the bird would fly to your hand. Food, maybe. Or a female bird, on heat. Assuming that a pigeon could be on heat. Which he doubted. Wasn't it something to do with ovulation? The menstrual cycle, yes? Eggs, ready to be fertilised. And pigeons laid eggs, obviously. But did they menstruate? Sadly – for an academic, he thought – his knowledge was surprisingly deficient in such matters.

After the fifth pint, he was struck by the thought that his career was now in ruins. And all because of his madness, his Compulsive Celebrity Disorder. The idea filled him with rage. He staggered to the bar and ordered a sixth. Three old men stood there, supping pints. A large man in a white T-shirt, shaven head, tattooed arms, chatted to the elders. A girl in a short red skirt stood at his side, silent.

"I should watch your mobile if I were you, sir," said the barman, nodding at Daniel's table. "We've had one or two nicked."

The heads at the bar turned in Daniel's direction. Daniel saw the CCTV cameras, suspended from the ceiling.

"Thank you for warning," he said, and staggered to the table, leaving his pint.

The men at the bar had been talking about pigeons on the common. Pigeon fanciers; that was the term. Daniel pocketed the tracker – still no movement – and returned to the bar.

"Excuse me," he said, nudging the large man. "Are you, do you… fancy pigeons?"

"Yer what?" came the reply.

"I need a bird," said Daniel. "A female."

"Huh! I should try the lounge, mate," the man said, and raised his glass.

The girl smiled.

"No, please understand," said Daniel. "I need a pigeon. And you – you fancy pigeons, yes?"

The man placed his glass on the bar, turned to Daniel and said, "Listen mate, we don't want any trouble if you get my meaning. We're just having a private chat, all right? Why don't you sit down and drink your drink?"

Daniel, reaching for his beer, persisted.

"No problem," he said. "But I must ask, please. You must know, if you fancy pigeon. Your fancy pigeon, your female – will she be on heat? Can she be on heat?"

The man stared as Daniel took a swig of his lager. Daniel, replacing the glass with a splutter, realised his mistake.

"Sorry," he said. "Wrong glass."

"Now you really are taking the piss," the man said. Then, taking hold of Daniel's arms, he marched him towards the table.

"We don't mind you coming over here so long as you obey the rules," he said. "And you don't know the rules, do you, frog?"

"Racist bastard," said Daniel.

The man released his grip and took a step back. So did Daniel.

"Who are you calling a racist bastard?"

"You, you big bonehead."

"Right, we'll settle this outside."

"We'll settle it here, bonehead."

261

"Right, come on then."

"Pigeon fucker."

"Right, frog – that's it."

Daniel stepped sideways, avoiding the head charge. Bonehead fell over a table, spilling empty glasses. Hands grabbed Daniel's arms.

"Steady, John," said a voice, but nobody reached out to grab John's arms.

The barman reached for a phone. "Take him outside," he said.

"Come on, bloke," said a voice behind Daniel's head.

"Yeah, take him outside," said John, "before I kill him."

"Pigeon shagger," said Daniel.

"Right, that's it," said John.

This time, Daniel didn't avoid the charge. He landed on the floor, spreadeagled. The barman pressed an alert button, linked to the local police station. They were now being watched.

"John, you're barred!" said the barman, stepping from the hatch.

"He started it," said John.

"Just leave it," said the barman.

"Hold him, Don, for God's sake – he'll kill him," said a voice.

"Hands off, Don," said John, and his arm sent Don flying.

"John, you're barred!" said the barman.

"I've got a job to finish," said John.

"John, don't," said the girl at the bar.

"Just leave it, will you," said the barman, stepping over Daniel's torso.

"Out of the way, Jack."

"Leave it," said Jack, the barman. Then, "Oh shit!" as John swept him aside.

Next – John about to stamp on Daniel when a rugby tackle sends him flying.

Twenty minutes later, the police arrive.

A scene of devastation.

First, the paperwork. Statements from the men at the bar. Fingers pointing at Daniel. A drunken Frenchman out to cause trouble. Telling John his missus was on heat. Wouldn't leave John alone. Calling him names.

Next, a statement from the girl at the bar…

Daniel, cut and bruised, was taken to a police station in Putney. Sat in the back of the car, he wasn't sure whether he was under arrest. He was rather oblivious to what had been said. Wanting him to come to the station and make a statement. Answer a few questions. He heard them muttering in the front of the car. *Did he give you the tape? Yeah, I've got the tape. You'll need to pass it on to Danger Man.* Video evidence, Daniel assumed. Then, something about a charge, drunk and disorderly. It seemed he was being arrested – he didn't care; he wanted to sleep.

On arrival, he was asked to empty his pockets. He didn't want to.

"It's in your interests to cooperate, sir," said the man behind the counter. "It's standard procedure. You'll have everything back when you leave. I make an inventory and give you a copy, so you can check nothing's missing. Is that all right?"

He felt as though he was being stripped of his identity. Embarrassing too. But the most annoying thing was…

"What's this?"

Daniel shrugged. The clerk tutted. Then pressed a buzzer and a plain-clothes man appeared.

"What is it?" said the plain-clothes man.

Daniel shook his head.

"I'll be back in a minute," the plain-clothes man said, and took the item away.

Behind closed doors, he showed it to a second plain-clothes man.

"What do you think?" said the first.

"A map of the world," said the second. "Distances. Flight paths. Speeds. Times. Some kind of… monitoring device, I'd say. And the object it's tracking is flying over the UK... Christ! It's flying over London!"

"Are you thinking what I'm thinking?" said the first.

"Yes, spot on," said the second, putting the device in a drawer. "We'd better tell the Home Sec as a matter of urgency. I'll pass this on to forensics. I'll call them now."

The first nodded and went out, closing the door.

"Do you have any ID?" he said.

*

Paulsbury on a Saturday – market day. The streets were full of shoppers, and the stalls were everywhere. Snailing along the High Street, Nigel was cursing. They'd parked the car in a car park on the east side of town – the only available space. But the shop he was after was on the other side of town. If it was still there. If it wasn't, they'd just have to do without.

This was Jerry's doing, the day before.

"Daniel may well be armed," he said. "I've managed to obtain his medical records, and this man is dangerous. He suffers from a Compulsive Celebrity Disorder, which means he'll stop at nothing to get what he wants. It's best if you're prepared."

"Prepared?" said Nigel. "You mean a bullet-proof vest?"

"A weapon," said Jerry. "Small arms, knife, club, anything. Just get down there ASAP. The bird's probably lying in a field, dead, and Daniel will have a head start."

So Nigel was following a hunch, thanks to a visit to Paulsbury about fifteen years previous. An antique shop, run by a retired Major. Its speciality – old weapons. He could picture the shop window, a large samurai sword in the centre, encircled by ornate daggers. There were guns there too, World War One gear, an old machine gun with a belt of bullets, placed below the samurai sword.

Nigel was hoping for something more manageable.

An ancient shillelagh perhaps.

For that, you didn't need a licence.

Cheaper too.

"Hello Jean!"

Half of Paulsbury seemed to know the woman in front, a short, dumpy woman with greying hair. Ten paces, and there'd be a shout.

Away from the High Street, the crowds thinned out. Most were to-ing and fro-ing between the High Street, the car parks, and the large outdoor market near the centre of town.

Bombasine Lane – he remembered the name.

The shop was still there, with the same samurai sword, dammit, just as he remembered it fifteen years ago. And the machine gun. And the belt of bullets.

Closed!

"He'll be back in half an hour," said an old man, passing by. "He always has his lunch about now."

"Oh, thanks," said Nigel.

He turned to Miguel, who was wiping the sweat off his face.

"Miguel, what are we doing?" he said. "This is madness. A garden tool would be more effective than a rusty old blunderbuss. Cheaper too. A scythe! They're lethal. Shall we wait?"

Miguel looked at the window. And laughed.

"Let's go," said Nigel.

Back to the High Street. Hawkins DIY. Nigel bought a scythe.

"Any news?" he said, as they wandered back to the car park.

"No," said Miguel, tapping at the tracker. "Nothing."

Miguel seemed reconciled to the idea that the bird was dead.

They didn't speak till they got in the car.

"We want the Lydiard road," said Nigel.

Miguel was doing the map-reading.

"Lydiard Forum," said Nigel. "The other side of Magnus

Chase. There…"

"Okay," said Miguel. "I have it."

"Right. First, the ring road."

They'd gone less than a mile on the Lydiard road when they saw the sign: "POLICE – SLOW." Then they saw the police car parked at the side of the road, beacon flashing.

They were flagged down by a policeman in his shirt sleeves, who leant to the window.

"Where are you going, sir?"

"Quinton."

"I'm sorry, sir. The road's blocked with hunt protesters a mile down this way. They'll be there for some time. I advise you to take a different route. Best to turn back and take the Nettleton road."

"Okay, thanks."

Swinging the wheel, "Great!" said Nigel. "We'd better stop and have a look at the map."

They stopped at a lay-by, just outside Paulsbury.

"Nettleton!" said Nigel, looking at the map. "It's the other side of Magnus Chase! This means driving to Stanton Parva and coming out again…"

There were no roads over the chase. They took the policeman's advice and returned to Paulsbury, then looked for the Nettleton road. The road followed the northern edge of the chase. At Nettleton they joined a trunk road and drove south to Stanton Parva, following the western edge of the chase.

Almost a complete circle.

And all because of those hunt protesters, Nigel thought.

Miguel had dozed off.

Stanton Parva – kids hanging about on street corners.

There was very little to Stanton Parva. The main attraction was Binghams, a large hypermarket. Blink, and you could miss the town. As Miguel had done. Too late, Nigel realised they'd missed the Paulsbury road. He gave Miguel a nudge.

"You're meant to be map-reading," he said. "Where's the

next turn to Paulsbury? I can't turn round here, there's too much traffic."

And there was nowhere to stop. Traffic at high speed; they were caught in the stream. They ended up driving to Lydiard Forum, four miles further south.

"Right," said Nigel. "The ring road – we want the Paulsbury road. Pay attention, Miguel."

Then they saw the sign: "POLICE – SLOW." Two police cars parked at the side of the road, beacons flashing. An ambulance. A car in the hedge; another in the middle of the road, the bonnet flattened. Broken glass everywhere.

The ring road was closed. The traffic was being diverted through the centre of town.

"Great!" said Nigel, who felt an impending attack of road rage.

Through the town centre, down a side street, following the signs to Paulsbury. More side streets, till they saw the police cars, and a crowd of people sitting in the road, holding banners saying, "STOP THE WAR!"

"For God's sake!" said Nigel.

They pulled up behind a people carrier. Two policemen were talking to the demonstrators, asking them to move.

"Wait here," said Nigel. "I'll see what's going on."

He spoke to an officer, standing by a police car.

"I'm sorry sir, it's these anti-war protesters. We've moved them on twice already but they just go somewhere else and do it all again. We're extremely stretched today and there's not a lot we can do about it."

"If you need any help, officer…"

"That wouldn't be wise, sir."

"Right," said Nigel, fuming.

He started counting. There were over fifty, sat in the road. And behind them, a cloud of smoke, filling the street from one side to the other. A blue haze billowed forth, drifting over the heads of the protesters.

"You're not using tear gas?" said Nigel, alarmed.

"No sir, that's another lot," said the officer.

"Another lot?" Nigel said.

He didn't wait for a reply. He wandered along the pavement, counting heads. Then he saw the banner: "DEFEND THE RIGHT TO SMOKE!"

Ten people, puffing away at cigars, cigarettes, joints, sat in the road behind the anti-war demonstrators.

"For crying out loud!" said Nigel.

There was a man there in a deerstalker, smoking a pipe, sat on a tartan blanket. The smoke smelt like a hedge on fire.

"What the hell do you think you're doing?" said Nigel, addressing the deerstalker.

"We have every right to protest, my good man," said the deerstalker, in BBC English. "Why don't you join us?"

"I want to go to Paulsbury, and you are blocking the road."

"Civil liberties are being eroded every day, sir, and it's time to stand up and be counted. You can't get to Paulsbury, and I can no longer smoke in the Poachers Arms. We all have rights."

Nigel's face had gone a peculiar shade of red.

"Right," he said, rolling up his sleeves. "Stand up and be counted, is it? I agree absolutely, and you, sir, are Number One."

Nigel grabbed the man by the armpits and tried to yank him upright.

"Here, there's no need for that," said an old chap, sitting next to the deerstalker.

"Yes there is," said Nigel, still yanking.

The man had gone floppy. Obviously well trained for this event, Nigel thought.

The smokers started to jeer and boo.

"Just bloody well stand up," said Nigel, going even redder.

"He'll never make the SAS," said a voice.

Nigel stared at the source – a younger man with long black hair, wearing a Stetson and a T-shirt with *Kings Arms Smokers* emblazoned on it. Nigel didn't like the sneer on his face.

"Right," he said. "Let's try Number Two."

"Take your hands off me!" shouted the Kings Arms Smoker.

This one was lighter, and not well trained. He also stank of beer. Halfway up, he spat in Nigel's face.

The final straw.

Releasing his grip, Nigel hit him on the jaw. There was a crack, and the Kings Arms Smoker fell to the ground.

Five of the smokers were now standing, including the deerstalker.

Success, Nigel thought.

"Now steady on chap," said the deerstalker.

Which inspired Nigel to even greater fury.

"Just clear the bloody road!" he shouted. "All of you!"

Then he was confronted by a spotty-faced youth with a punk haircut, wearing a T-shirt that showed a football made up of Woodbine cigarette packets, *Class War* printed underneath. The youth grabbed Nigel's arm.

"We've every right to be here!" he said. "Leave us alone, granddad!"

"Clear the bloody road, imbecile!" Nigel shouted, and swept the youth aside.

A second youth aimed a punch at Nigel's face. Nigel, ducking, glimpsed that one's T-shirt: *I'm a Militant Smoker!* Suddenly he was surrounded by a ring of them, puffing smoke into his face. And on the pavement, Miguel, about to step in.

What followed was a skirmish, fists flying, Nigel lashing out at militant smokers, Miguel trying to defend him, until…

"I'm sorry, sir. I'll have to ask you to come down to the station."

"They started it!"

"We saw what happened, sir. I'm afraid we may have to arrest you for a breach of the peace. I should warn you that anything you say may be taken down and used as evidence…"

"Ssss… strike a light!"

Miguel in the back of one car, Nigel in the back of another.

And the police station was in Stanton Parva.

"I'll have to ask you to empty your pockets," said the man behind the counter.

Miguel, with great reluctance, did so.

"And what's this?" said the man behind the counter.

"Is a pigeon tracker," said Miguel.

"Is it?" said the man. "Just one moment."

He pressed a buzzer, and a plain-clothes man appeared.

"He says it's a pigeon tracker," said the man behind the counter.

"Does he?" said the plain-clothes man. "I need to check this." And he took the item away.

Behind closed doors, he showed it to a second plain-clothes man.

"What do you think?" said the first. "He says it's a pigeon tracker."

"A pigeon tracker?" said the second. "Let's have a look. It shows a map of the world, with distances... flight paths... speeds... times... Definitely a tracking device, I'd say. And whatever it is, it's flying over the UK... Oh my God! It's flying over Magnus Chase!"

"Are you thinking what I'm thinking?" said the first.

"Indeed, indeed," said the second, putting the device on the desk. "We'd better tell the Home Sec as a matter of urgency. I'll pass this on to forensics. I'll call them now."

The first nodded and went out, closing the door.

"Do you have any ID?" he said.

*

Daniel had never seen a police cell. There was little to see. A dark wooden board, horizontal, fixed to a white wall. A black bucket and a box of hard toilet paper, in strips. A bright tube light with no switches and, next to it, a tiny CCTV camera.

Nothing else.

The board was a bed.

He slept most of the afternoon, waking up and trying to remember the day of the week. It was Wednesday when he came in. Still Wednesday now, he thought. But how would he know? No windows. It felt like evening.

Two men came in, wearing seedy black suits. Seedy black hair, short and gelled. Young guys. One stood by the door with a notebook and pencil. The other stood over Daniel. Questions.

He refused to answer.

"We want to know where you work, who you work for. Okay? You must have an accomplice, a partner at least. How many of you are there? It's in your interests to cooperate."

Silence.

"Listen, sunshine…"

Sunshine! Was this a reference to his olive complexion? Another racist bastard, Daniel thought.

"Listen, sunshine. We have permission from the Home Secretary to hold you here for as long as we like. The sooner you answer, the sooner you can leave. The alternative you won't want to know, so I'll tell you. The alternative is that you could die in this cell. How do you feel about that?"

"Am I under arrest?"

"Ah! He speaks! Are you under arrest? Did you hear that, Ron? Is he under arrest? Ron doesn't know the answer to that, and neither do I. You see, sunshine, the law isn't like that anymore. The question is redundant. Obsolete and extinct, as far as you're concerned. We don't need to arrest you to keep you here, do you understand? We don't need to charge you with anything. We just need suspicion, and you, sunshine, are suspicious. And as long as we suspect, we can keep you here till doomsday. So it's best to answer our questions, do you follow me? You're not helping yourself by playing dumb."

He was held for four days in total. He didn't know that till he came out. Whenever he asked what day it was, they said it was no concern of his. Likewise the time.

"Now why should you need to know the time? Time is for

people who get up and go to work, have a night out and watch the TV, go to bed and shag all night. Not for you, sunshine. You left all that behind when you stepped through this door. Your time belongs to us. For as long as it takes…"

He remembered that when he came out. Stolen time. His time had been stolen. It filled him with rage – stolen time, no lawyers, and medical attention refused. Handed a first-aid box with plasters, and supervised while he stuck them on.

He had answered their questions by inventing a story. Pigeon racing was a hobby, he said. He was here on a short trip, a holiday. With a pigeon. No, there was no organised race. It was a practice run.

His passport had been returned, together with wallet, credit cards, cash. And the tracker. Then there was a packet of polo mints, and various other items sealed in a plastic bag.

There was no apology, no explanation for his release. Presumably, he thought, they'd done the standard security checks and found a zero.

Miraculously, the tracker was still working. Even more miraculous, the bird was still in the UK – and it hadn't moved an inch since Friday.

He couldn't believe this. His time had been stolen; yet time had stood still. Time had frozen, waiting for him to come out. Something has happened to Nigel and Miguel, he thought; something must have happened. And the bird is dead.

It felt as though fate, once again, was dealing kindly with him. The bird was lying in a field somewhere, and he had been summoned to collect – he had been chosen.

The problem was getting there.

It would have been another miracle if the car had still been there, parked in the pub car park. He walked there with hope but no expectations, and was a little disappointed when he saw that it wasn't. Taken by joy riders, he thought. Or by the police, as Nigel would have reported it as stolen.

He travelled by tube to Paddington, asked for travel information. Magnus Chase – nearest stations were

Paulsbury, change at Salisbury; or Stanton Parva and Lydiard Forum, change at Swindon.

Could he hire a car? On a Sunday? He didn't bother asking, he felt like a train ride. It might calm his rage, he thought. Besides, his goal wasn't far from Lydiard Forum; he could walk it.

He chose the faster route, changing at Swindon. The next bit, not so fast; the Lydiard train stopped at every station, it seemed. It was early evening when he got there; the streets were almost deserted.

He found a pub and ordered food, then a drink. The pub was a hotel, packed with tourist information. He asked the barman if they had a local map. They did.

Quinton was a ten-mile walk. Walking fast, it would take him two, three hours. A warm evening too. He memorised the route and bought another drink. It was warm enough to sit outside. He picked up a leaflet about the Lydiard Festival and sat at a table, overlooking the River Chuckle. So refreshing, he thought, listening to the river gurgling over pebbles. After four days of solitary confinement, he deserved another pint.

It was almost dusk when he left the place. He couldn't decide if he'd been foolish. He didn't think so; he felt warm, invigorated. It was good to walk and feel the beer flowing through your veins. And a pleasant summer's evening. A quaint old English market town, with a castle on the hill, and black and white buildings.

Slight problem: getting there before dark.

Two miles out of town, he realised it wasn't possible. He was knackered.

He passed a large house, the drive full of cars. A family gathering. Someone's birthday, perhaps. Cars on the verge too. A Tonto XL5, keys in the ignition. It was an open invitation. So trusting, these country people. Or stupid.

He tried the door. Sat in. Took off.

A quiet engine. It may not be missed for some time, he

thought.

When he saw the artic heading straight for him, horns blazing and with no intention of moving, he realised – just in time – that it was he, Daniel, who was driving on the wrong side of the road.

England!

He swerved at speed, narrowly avoided a hedge, ended up on a farm track chasing a pheasant, tried to brake, and hit a tree with a crunch.

The car was a write-off.

He staggered out, bruised, his back in agony; he headed for the road.

He was on the outskirts of a village. A line of houses. A telephone box ahead. A bus shelter and a little village green.

Then he heard the sirens.

He dived into a hedge, tearing his shirt, found himself in a large garden.

The siren zoomed past, heading towards Lydiard. He saw the beacon flashing. Then a square of light. Voices.

"Is there somebody out there?"

"I can't see. Where's the torch?"

He ran – through hedges, over walls, fences, a shed.

He found himself on the green, by the telephone box. Back on the road.

He ran again, till the village was behind him.

Then he saw the forest, a dark mass in the creeping twilight, stretching up the slope of the chase. A single-track road heading that way, and a signpost to Top Down.

Three hours later, he found the gamekeeper's paths. A strip of blue overhead, still too early for the stars. And off the path, shelters for the pheasants, and a tool shed beyond.

It was a warm night, and the pheasants were roosting elsewhere.

He shifted their food trays, curled up and slept.

2

So here we are in the countryside, Nigel said to Miguel. Let's be positive. The sun is shining, there's no clouds, the car's in the compound, and we've just had an apology from Chief Inspector Perrot. We're free men. No charges.

"Two nights in a prison cell," said Miguel, looking at the gravel.

"It had its educational value, I suppose," said Nigel, looking for the car.

"*Desculpe*?"

"What?"

"I am not understanding."

"Now we know what it's like, being in a prison cell. Being behind bars on a Sunday, when every respectable person is watching the cricket."

"You not face the questions."

"I did so."

Nigel looked at the bruise on Miguel's neck.

"Though not as much as you, obviously," he said. "How many times did he hit you?"

"One."

"Once."

"Sorry?"

"Once, not one. And remember what I told you about talking to women. We don't know who we're going to meet. Come on."

They crossed the car park, blinking in the light.

"Saturday night, you say," said Nigel, musing. "It's their busiest night of the week. Lots of drunken farmers, having fights. He was probably a bit excited about something."

They stood by the car. On the roof, a layer of dust, warming in the sun.

"I am not English," said Miguel.

"No," said Nigel. "So that makes you suspicious. You could be a terrorist. More so now, with that bruise. In fact, Miguel, you remind me of Che Guevara."

Nigel on one side of the car, Miguel on the other, swapping looks over the roof. Miguel smiled, then jumped and reached for his pocket. A flock of pigeons passed overhead.

"Don't tell me he's flown! We've just got here!"

"No. Nothing."

"Right, let's go and find him."

Stanton Parva on a Monday morning. Road works and a queue of lorries.

"Six, seven miles," said Nigel as they joined the queue. "And we have hold-up number one already. What can happen between here and Quinton?"

After a wait, they turned onto the Paulsbury road and flew along, most of the traffic going the other way. It was a winding, narrow road, with little space for overtaking. A forest on one side, fields of stubble on the other, littered with bags of silage. Three miles later, the forest came to an end, and the fields rose to the downs. And nothing happened, apart from a tractor queue, and a near collision with Bad Boy Bill, only avoided by another one with a hedgerow.

Bad Boy Bill, shaven head, rings in his nose, was in a rush.

And the hawthorn was just as fast, squealing as it scratched the glass, scraped the side panels, scattering debris through the open window.

"Jesus!" said Nigel. "He's obviously late for work. Why don't they leave earlier? This road's like a Formula One circuit. I wonder what happened to Sean and Tracy."

"*Desculpe?*"

"Oh, those stickers on the windscreen. They used to say Sean and Tracy a few years back. Now it's Bad Boy Bill. Miguel, we're here! We'd better find somewhere to park."

A crossroads, with Quinton Monkton on the left, Quinton

Rushton on the right. No-through roads, and both barely wide enough for traffic. A few yards further, a pub called the Moon. They turned into the pub's car park.

"We'd better ask the landlord if he minds," said Nigel.

He tried a side door first; the way in from the car park, with a porch and two doors. No one answered. He tried a door at the front, looked through the windows. A spider ran across his gaze.

"No sign of life," said Nigel. "Let's go."

A steep hill, almost enclosed by arching trees. At the top, a gate in the hedge. Greenslade Cottage – they were looking down on it.

"Here," said Miguel.

"How precise is your tracker?" said Nigel.

"Is very good, the – how do you say, scale? – I can change it, see?"

Nigel looked at the display. It meant nothing. It seemed to show field boundaries, but there were no names, no indication as to where they were. The bleep though, when Miguel pressed a button, was alarming. Rapid tones. He was reminded of that childhood game, Hide and Seek, warmer and colder. They were getting warmer; the cottage was a hot spot.

"We'd better see if there's anyone about," he said. "You'd best wait here."

Through the gate, down a path, past another gate, and there was a door. Front or back, it wasn't clear. He knocked.

"Hello!" he said.

No response.

He walked round the house, passing old sheds, looking at the birds. There were pigeons, yes, but no Gabriel. Nigel was surprised by his memory: he had an image of the bird, eyes and plumage, his mannerisms – which none of these birds matched.

Then he saw the front of the house, and gasped.

The garden… But could you call this a garden? More of a

jungle, he thought. The grass was waist high in places; it was like a meadow, waiting to be cut for silage. There were beds of nettles where butterflies flittered and chased. There were beds of thistles, going to seed, where a flock of goldfinch were feeding and twittering. Fruit trees, wild and abandoned, where blackbirds were singing. Flower beds running amok with herb Robert, forget-me-nots, and tall thistle-like plants with yellow flowers. Bird tables and seed hangers, hanging from trees. Nesting boxes, food balls, and birds everywhere – tits whistling, finches twittering, a wren singing. House martins under the eaves, sparrows chirruping, swallows swooping into a greenhouse on the far side of the meadow.

Nigel felt as if he was walking on sacred ground. Like being on a private nature reserve, without permission. He knocked on the front door, and saw that it was ajar.

"Hello!" he said.

No response. He tried a few times – likewise. He continued walking round the house, and ended up at the back door. Another knock, another blank. He walked up the path to the gate.

"There doesn't appear to be anyone at home," he said. "The windows are open upstairs. They can't be very far. There's no car here, is there? There's no garage either, come to that. We'll just have to wait. Let's sit in the… let's sit down here, there's a bench."

Rounding the house, Nigel heard Miguel's gasp.

"Yes," he said. "That's what I thought. Rather wild, isn't it? Whoever lives here, they're not the keenest of gardeners. An elderly couple, I'd say. So where are they? The front door's open."

"Out walking," Miguel suggested.

"Or hard of hearing," said Nigel. "I'll try again."

This time, he pushed the door open and shouted.

"Hello!"

He walked round to the back door and tried the handle – that too was unlocked. He opened it and shouted.

"Somebody could be dead in there," he said to Miguel. "Sorry, I didn't mean Gabriel, I meant the occupants. What does your machine say?"

"She say – the bird is inside."

"Inside?"

"In the house."

"Oh!"

They swapped frowns.

"Let's give it half an hour," said Nigel.

He had an odd feeling of dread, which he couldn't explain. Haunted by the movies again. A House of Horrors. An elderly couple, seemingly respectable, who ate pigeons for breakfast, slaughtered their guests and stored them in the freezer. Psycho – a demented youth with the body of his mother in a rocking chair, stealing glances at the strangers outside. He looked up and shuddered.

"This is ridiculous," he said. "Let's take a peek inside."

The room was dark, dust motes flying by the window. Again, that feeling of death or decay; Nigel wasn't sure which. It took a while to get used to the gloom. The house nestled in a slim gorge, and the window faced a row of trees and a slope of grass and chalk. The sun was somewhere else.

"Is here," said Miguel, pointing to a door.

Nigel opened it and found a light switch. It was a utility room, with a large freezer, a washing machine, a worktop laden with bird food and several pairs of binoculars. There were shelves of knick-knacks, drills, hammers, screws, walking gear hanging on pegs, some on a shelf, neatly folded. A range of overtrousers, cagoules, boots, socks, wellingtons…

"Here," said Miguel.

The tag was lying on a shelf.

Miguel picked it up, turned it over, stared at it.

"So where's Gabriel?" said Nigel.

He was looking for a decapitated bird, pigeons hanging on skewers, a tub of pigeon stew. He opened the lid of the freezer. Stacked with food, but no pigeon. He turned to Miguel, and saw the gloom in his eyes.

"We'll just have to wait, Miguel," he said. "Someone's got a story to tell. You'd better hang on to that. You never know, we may still find him. Let's go outside. This place is giving me the creeps, and I don't think we should go upstairs."

He picked up a pair of binoculars and handed them to Miguel, who slipped the tag into a pocket.

"We might as well amuse ourselves while we're waiting," Nigel said, picking up a second pair of binoculars.

They returned to the bench.

Time passed, and no one showed. The birds came and went, sang and ate. And down below, the occasional sound of a car, lorry, tractor, driving along the main road.

"I'm going for a walk," said Nigel. "Just to the end of the garden there. You'd best wait here, in case anybody shows."

He walked across the yard and followed a path through the wilderness. It led to a gate, two old apple trees on either side, a mass of fruits taking shape. He raised the binoculars and looked towards the downs.

He dropped them straightaway.

"My God!" he said, out loud.

He looked again, just to check, then raced back to the bench.

"Miguel!" he said. "There's a man up there who's got no clothes on. Totally starkers. Stripped bollock naked, as my granddad used to say. We'd better help him. He seems to be heading this way. He must have been robbed. Go and have a look – at the gate there."

He stood there, waiting for the verification. At the gate, Miguel stared and laughed.

Nigel rushed inside, into the utility room. He grabbed a pair of overtrousers, a cagoule. And on reflection, a pair of wellies.

"It's no laughing matter, Miguel," he said. "That poor bloke has been mugged, stripped of everything. And we think we've got problems! You wait here – I'll go up there and meet him – I shouldn't be long."

And Nigel raced off – up the path, through the gate, along the lane.

What a terrible thing to happen, he thought. What would you do, stripped of all your clothes? Forced to walk naked, till a kind soul passes your way…

Quinton Monkton flashed by – a handful of houses, and no sign of life. Apart from one house, high up on the slope, where a little old lady sat in a chair, on a verandah, waving. He waved back. God forbid that she should be a witness to that, he thought.

The lane came to an end. He climbed a stile; there was only one route. The path was muddy, winding between trees and tree roots, following the bank of a stream. It was a struggle, tripping over roots; he wasn't used to walking so fast.

He saw a pool of light, a green field beyond. And then he saw the naked man, striding into the light. Not totally naked, he noticed – the man had walking boots, and a maple leaf covering his privates, tied about his waist with a length of vine.

Nigel was speechless. Not only a maple leaf, but the leaf was wagging like a dog's tail – the man was nursing a massive erection!

Too late, Nigel saw the root. He tripped, slid, tumbled, rolled down the bank and grabbed a branch, just missing the stream.

"Greetings, fellow traveller!"

"What? Hey, look! I've brought you some clothes!"

"Clothes are a burden, friend. The apparel of a sick society, weighed down by regulations, rules, laws and bureaucracy."

"What? I don't believe this…"

"Clothes are an invention of the devil, my friend. Man's punishment, for eating the fruit of knowledge. Do you know the story? Eve was tempted by Satan to eat the apple of knowledge, and having eaten, she became aware of her nakedness and felt ashamed."

Nigel stood to his feet.

"Paradise lost," he said.

"Absolutely," said the naked man. "And I reject the idea. Paradise is a state of mind, available to all who have the will to seek and find. Milton's myth is a cracking story, but why should we abide by it? Why should we be punished for seeking knowledge? Punished for being curious – it's in our nature to be curious. Would you like a hand, my friend?"

"No, no, I'm quite all right, thank you."

Nigel was rather distracted by the man's appearance. He had black hair, a beard, a hairy chest, and a mass of pubic hair, which seemed to be brushed. Yet on top, his hair was going thin.

Alarmingly, the maple leaf still wagged as the nudist continued.

"People don't understand my motives, which is very sad I find. You see, we live in a society that stifles creativity, that wants to turn artists into robots, that stifles thought of any description. Where are the philosophers? The intellectuals? You won't find them in the universities, my friend. They've been turned into degree factories, churning out a workforce of Yes people, people who aren't curious. It's a sad state of affairs, don't you think? And those who criticise are castigated. That's the reason for my walk – I am walking as a protest. A one-man protest it may be, but I think it's our duty to protest when human rights are being trampled every day of the week. I can tell you're an intelligent man. Do you not agree with me?"

"Yes but, going around naked... Wait, don't go, I've brought you these clothes!"

"Your need is greater than mine, my friend. May I bid you good day, and thank you for your concern. It's refreshing to know that the cup of human kindness is not yet empty."

And with those words, the walker turned and strode off through the trees, his backside caught in a sunbeam, the maple leaf still wagging.

Nigel scrambled up the bank. The man was right. He was

covered in mud, from top to toe. He slid on the overtrousers. Then he remembered the little old lady…

Too late! He heard a high-pitched yell, somewhere between a gasp and a full-bodied scream. Then all was silent. And where, he wondered, was the naked man bound? Surely not along the main road?

"Oh God!" he said, out loud. "What a world! We live in strange times…"

He pulled on the cagoule. He looked at his shoes, mud spattered. He sat on a stile, took them off, put on the wellies.

And then he thought, I'm going potty. Why have I done this? I've only got to walk back a few yards, then I'm on tarmac.

He blamed the nudist. The nudist had suggested he put them on, and Nigel had done so. Such was his persuasion, the seduction of his argument. Or the distraction of a maple leaf and a massive stiffy.

So here I am, he thought, dressed for walking. I might as well walk to the top.

He climbed the stile, crossed the field, saw the track, winding upwards. A little while later, he was standing on the downs, admiring the view. There was no one about, no one at all. Surely, he thought, the naked man isn't the occupant of Greenslade Cottage? It seemed to fit – a garden that's a wilderness, full of birds and wild things; doors and windows left open; saying No to the idea of clothes… And I've let him walk past, and he's going to stun Miguel with his maple leaf…

He looked through the binoculars. There was no sign of Miguel, and no sign of the naked man. No sign of Gabriel either, which was, he recalled, the whole purpose of their being there.

He sat down. The grass was warm and dry. The chalk was so bright, dazzling in the sun. He lay back. The ground was hard, but not as hard as a wooden board. He'd hardly slept the last two nights. And he must have dozed off, because the cry of a buzzard pulled him upright with a jolt.

He looked through the binoculars. Now he could see a

stranger down there, walking across the yard. He stood up. The stranger was a tall lady with a bob of brown hair. Stopping, turning, looking around as if she were searching for somebody. Or some thing. Where was Miguel?

He lowered the binoculars. There was a man sat on the slope now, opposite the house, on the slope that curved steeply down to the stream. Through the glasses, he could see that it was Daniel.

Daniel! He'd forgotten about Daniel. Daniel was carrying a metal rod; it looked like a crowbar. And Daniel looked as if he'd just crawled out of a cement mixer. He must have walked over the fields, Nigel thought – there were no roads or paths on that side. And to get to the house, he would have to drop over a cliff face.

Nigel shifted his gaze to the house below. The stranger was now standing by the gate at the edge of the wilderness, back turned towards him. And suddenly she turned, as if she knew she was being spied on, and raised something to her eyes. Oh my God! Scanning the trees and seeking out *him*! She was leaning against the gate, staring at him through a pair of binoculars!

He was stunned, electrified. And the stranger must have felt the same and sooner: the glasses dropped, she seemed petrified; then she raised them once more to stare.

From her position in the garden, she couldn't see Daniel on the slope; he was hidden by the trees.

Nigel pocketed the binoculars and raced off, down the track and into the gorge, checking first that he was indeed… fully clothed.

*

Sat on the bench in the shade, Miguel was feeling sleepy. Yet he mustn't doze off, he thought. When he heard the yell, he decided to investigate. He walked up the path to the gate of the cottage, and saw a naked man walking down the lane.

Not totally naked – he had a small backpack, socks and walking boots, and a maple leaf covering his rude bits, which wagged up and down as he walked. The man was blessed with a big stiffy!

"Greetings fellow traveller!"

"Nigel?"

"I am generally known as Doug, and a host of other names besides. You may call me Nigel if you wish."

"My friend – he give you clothes…"

"Ah! Your friend is very kind, but I had to disappoint him."

Stood by the gate, the nudist pointed to the maple leaf and said, "You see, friend, these are my clothes. Normally I am totally naked, I prefer it that way. Unfortunately, Her Majesty's forces don't prefer it that way. So now I wear a leaf when there's a chance of meeting strangers. It's a compromise, I know, but I've upset a lot of people on my travels, *tu comprends*? Are you French?"

"Portuguese."

"Oh, Portuguese! My greetings to you! I'm afraid your friend had a little accident. He slipped and fell, but he's quite all right, nothing broken. I'm off to the local hostelry for refreshments, if they'll be so kind as to serve me. You wouldn't believe the hassle I have to put up with. There are a lot of sad people about. Would you care to join me?"

"No thank you – I wait for someone."

"Good man! May I bid you good day, my friend."

And with those words, the walker turned and strode down the hill, the maple leaf bobbing.

Miguel shook his head and walked back to the bench. The urge to sleep was overwhelming. He'd hardly slept the last two nights. A wooden board and constant wakings; the same questions. They didn't believe him. Even though they'd taken his *columbofilia* card, they didn't believe him. They didn't want to believe. The nudist was a breath of fresh air…

In his dreams, he was lying on the grass, naked, his favourite cousin by his side, also naked, and his mother, father, brothers and sisters picking fruit, all of them naked…

A noise woke him. It sounded like a stone falling.

Sleep was so refreshing, he thought. Seeing the nudist was strangely refreshing. And now he felt the urge for a bowel movement. Where could he go? There was a toilet, he recalled, by the side of the utility room.

He went inside, opened the door and sat. It took several minutes.

The sound of the flush had just faded; he was drying his hands when he heard a voice, a lady's voice; a plaintive voice, calling: "Where are you, piggy?"

Now what? He was inside; she was outside. He couldn't step out; it would frighten her.

He saw a shape pass the frosted glass. And seconds later, that call: "Where are you piggy?"

Then he remembered the binoculars – they were outside, underneath the bench.

He waited, then edged towards the front door. The lady was walking through the long grass, alone. He stepped outside, crept to the bench. She hadn't noticed. He crept inside, into the utility room, replaced the binoculars. And outside again – the lady was staring at the greenhouse, and seemed to be in a trance.

Should he call her? No, he thought, she'd be terrified. Calling from the house, as though he'd just stepped out of it. Which he had. He would enter anew, and give her the impression he had just arrived.

He crept round the house, up the path to the gate, thinking of the lady.

A very sad lady, walking through the long grass, looking for a pig.

Then he remembered the scythe. It was in the boot of the car. He could offer to cut the grass for her. A gardener, offering his services.

He walked swiftly down the lane, turned the corner, raced along the road and into the car park. It was lunchtime now;

there were more cars. And roars of laughter coming from the pub – the nudist!

He tried the boot. Locked, of course! And Nigel hadn't left him the keys.

Back along the road, up the hill to Greenslade Cottage.

He opened the gate, walked down the path, and knocked on the back door.

"Excuse me," he said.

*

When Nigel reached Greenslade Cottage, he glanced at the kitchen window and saw the unexpected.

On the left, Daniel, encrusted in mud and blood, wielding a crowbar and threatening to use it. On the right, Miguel, seemingly quite relaxed, yet muscles poised for action. And centre stage, that woman in her long summer skirt, reaching for the door handle behind her, a look of terror on her face.

What happened next was one of those moments that Nigel would never forget.

The woman glanced at the window and saw his face, glanced at the label on his cagoule, smiled swiftly and sweetly as if she recognised him, and fell to the floor as if her dying wish had just been granted.

During which, two more glances were thrown at the window, Miguel the first to respond. Head lowered, covered by his hands and arms, he reminded Nigel of a matador as he charged at Daniel and butted him in the stomach. Daniel fell to the floor, dropping the crowbar; Miguel pounced; and Nigel could see no more.

He entered to find Miguel astride Daniel, the woman lying on the floor, unconscious.

"Bloody hell!" he said.

"Gone out," said Miguel, feeling Daniel's wrist.

"What? He's not dead?" said Nigel.

"No," said Miguel. "The door – he hit, bang!"

287

"I think we'd better ring Chief Inspector Perrot," said Nigel.

He raised the woman's head and shoulders, pulled her into the living room, lifted her onto a chair. The dust flew in all directions.

"Bloody hhh…!" he said, sneezing.

He looked for the phone and dialled.

"Yes please, there's been an accident," he said. "Quinton Monkton. Greenslade Cottage. We've caught a burglar. No, we're not, we happened to be passing by. He, er, fell over. Okay, okay, thank you."

Walking into the kitchen, "Worse than ringing for a taxi," he said.

He sprinkled the woman's face with water, felt her cold wrist. He was still doing this when the police arrived – two cars and an ambulance. And a familiar face.

"It's you two again, is it," said the officer. "Now what brings you here? I thought we'd seen the last of you this morning."

"We're looking for a racing pigeon, as I explained," said Nigel. "We identified its location as… Well, here, more or less. We were about to make enquiries when we chanced to meet that man in there, attempting a burglary."

"We've been looking for him," said the officer. "He's wanted in connection with a stolen car. And there were several attempted burglaries reported last night, the same night the car was stolen. Now I'm not jumping to conclusions but let me put it this way – I can do my sums."

"I'm glad to hear it," Nigel said, and turned to the medical chap. "Is she all right?"

"She's fine," said the medical chap, unplugging his stethoscope.

The woman sat up, holding her head.

"Suffering from shock, nothing serious. There's no need to take her in. I'll ask Rachel to sit with her for a while," said the medical chap, and he went out.

"I thought I'd given her a heart attack," said Nigel.

"You?" said the officer.

"I mean all of us, generally. You know, the incident. The event."

"Perhaps you'd like to explain exactly what happened," said the officer. "We'll need a statement."

"Right," said Nigel.

In the kitchen, Miguel was making his statement. Nigel listened.

"Er, you'd like that now, would you?" said Nigel.

"Yes please."

"Well…"

"It's quite all right officer," said a woman's voice.

George had opened her eyes and was staring at Nigel.

"This is Richard, my husband," she said. "He went out for a walk. And now he's come back. He saved my life."

"I think you're… suffering from shock," said Nigel.

"Yes," said George. "Yes, I am. You've been gone such a long time. It feels like… years."

"Excuse me one moment," said Nigel. And to the officer: "Can we have a private word, please?"

The officer looked bemused. "Certainly," he said.

Nigel nodded at the kitchen. They went out, passing Rachel, who sat and spoke to George: "How are you feeling, George?"

"It's the clothes," said Nigel, in a heated whisper. "I must be wearing her husband's clothes."

"Is that so? And would you like to tell me how it is you happen to be wearing her husband's clothes?"

"Well, you'll never believe this. You see, there was this naked man…"

*

The police were there for two hours and more. It seemed an age. Daniel was taken away in the ambulance, but Rachel was reluctant to leave George alone with the two men.

George, walking in a trance, went to the kitchen to fetch a glass of water. She saw the bags of shopping, still unpacked. It stirred her into action.

"Look at this!" she said, peering into a bag. "This lot needs to go in the freezer. They'll be ruined!"

She went through the motions of unloading, trying to piece together what had happened.

"Honestly, I'll be all right," she said to Rachel. "I'd be grateful if you could leave me to get on with my chores. Thank you, thank you, but I must talk to Richard in private."

Nigel, meanwhile, had taken off the cagoule, the overtrousers, the wellies, and put them all back in the utility room. Their story had been cobbled together; the statements had been signed. The police would return, they said, to collect one from George. Tomorrow morning, they said.

George didn't look at the new Nigel; she carried on with her tasks, coaxing the police to leave. Miguel, meanwhile, was swapping glances with the young and perky Rachel, whose long, dark hair was tied in plaits and twisted in an intricate fashion around the top of her head. Nigel thought Rachel had another reason for hanging about.

George started giving instructions.

"Please, do you mind going now?" she said to the police, holding the sides of her head. And to Miguel: "And would you mind sitting outside, please? I want to ask you some questions but I really must sort out my shopping, I should have done this ages ago. No, no. Thank you, but no; I'd rather do it myself. Just let me get on with it, and I'll be with you in a few minutes."

And so the police went. The two men returned to the bench, outside.

They didn't speak. Both were flagging, dying for sleep.

Time passed, a lazy stupor. Then, a voice:

"Would you like a cup of tea?"

"Hmm? I'd love a cup of tea," said Nigel.

Miguel was quietly snoring. Nigel poked him in the ribs.

"Tea?"

"Tea? Yes, tea. Thank you, please. Tea, yes. Black please. Three sugars."

"Milk and no sugar for me please," said Nigel.

George carried a cane chair from a corner of the yard. She placed it by the bench.

"I'm so dry," she said, sipping her tea. "My schedule's been thrown out." Then, looking at Nigel, "I'm sorry," she said. "I realise you're not my husband. But you do look very much like him. And those clothes…"

"I'm sorry about the clothes."

"Can you explain, please?"

"We're, er, looking for a pigeon…"

"The pigeon! I'd forgotten about the pigeon. He's probably upstairs, in bed. I'll go and have a look now."

She placed her cup on the stone flags and went inside.

Nigel and Miguel swapped glances.

"In bed," said Nigel, thinking of sleep.

Miguel laughed. "He is looked after," he said.

When George saw the dust on the quilt, she remembered that it was still Monday, and that she had been shopping that morning, leaving the pigeon on a telephone pole. And she knew for certain that Nigel wasn't Richard; she'd guessed so when she walked into the utility room, and saw *Squiggles* hanging on its peg again.

She went outside.

"I'm sorry," she said. "He's gone. He was here this morning. I looked for him when I got back, but he wasn't around."

"Gone!" said Miguel, thinking of the lost pig. Not a pig after all, but a pigeon. A pig with wings. Gabriel. She had been looking for Gabriel, calling him Piggy. Why Piggy?

"He's a racing pigeon, I take it," said George.

"Yes, racer," said Miguel. "He go home." And he pulled out the tracker.

"Has he got far to go?" said George.

"Yes," said Miguel. "Far, far."

Nigel was staring into a timeless void of futile pursuits, each one taking longer than the previous, and each one doomed to fail.

"I think," said George, "I'm going to have something to eat. I know it's almost teatime, but I haven't had lunch yet. Would you like anything? Can I get you a cheese sandwich?"

"A cheese sandwich! That would be most welcome," said Nigel.

"Right," said George.

She went inside. They sat in silence for a while.

"So," said Nigel at last, standing up and stretching his legs. "Gabriel has flown."

"Yes, flown," said Miguel.

"There's not a lot we can do about it," said Nigel. "The tracker's useless now. We'll just have to wait and see."

"Wait and see," said Miguel. "And hope."

"Yes, have faith," said Nigel. "And here comes charity."

"What?" said George, carrying a tray.

"We're very grateful to you for looking after the pigeon," said Nigel.

"He had bad foot," said Miguel. "And bruised wing."

"I thought so," said George, returning to her seat. "There was something else about him…"

"He had an electronic tag on his wing," said Nigel. "That's how we tracked it here. We found the tag on a shelf. I'm sorry we intruded, but the doors were open, and we didn't know where you were, or how long you'd be away. We were looking for the pigeon."

"He was carrying something," said George.

"Yes?" said Nigel.

"On his leg," said George. "He had a locket. There was a tooth inside it."

"You found the tooth?"

"I found a tooth, and it was disgusting."

"It is the tooth of King Arthur!" said Miguel.

"King Arthur?" said George.

"Yes, er, we're archaeologists," said Nigel. "Tell me…"

"You've found King Arthur's tomb?" said George. "I thought it was a myth."

"It hasn't been confirmed yet," said Nigel. "The tooth will be important evidence. But please tell me, what happened to it?"

"I planted it," said George.

"You planted it?"

"Yes."

"Why?"

"I don't know, but it reminds me of that story about the serpent's teeth, from Greek mythology. Was it something to do with the founding of Thebes? I can't remember. Anyway, Cadmus sows the serpent's teeth, and armed men spring out of the ground. Jason did the same, with the teeth that were left over. You must have heard of Jason and the Argonauts?"

"I've seen the film," said Nigel.

"Well, the same thing happened there. He sowed the teeth, and armed men sprang out of the ground."

"A dangerous thing to do then," said Nigel.

"Yes, I suppose it was, because it turned out to be true, didn't it? I planted the tooth, and armed men turn up at the house. And they end up fighting each other, just like in the stories."

Nigel reached for a sandwich.

"And where did you plant it?" he said.

"I… I can't remember," said George.

"Miguel, have a sandwich," said Nigel. "We've got some digging to do." And to George: "Have you got a shovel?"

"Yes, there's a tool shed…"

"We have a scythe," said Miguel. "We cut the grass, if you want."

Nigel looked at Miguel. George looked at Nigel.

"That would be… terrific," she said. "If it's no trouble."

"No problem," said Miguel.

"Well, er, it's no trouble," said Nigel. "But…"

"You couldn't finish it today, obviously," said George. "But you're welcome to stay. I have plenty of room. I just need to sort out the bedding. If you want to stay, you're welcome. You both look very tired. Have you travelled far? I'm sorry, I don't even know where you're from! And I don't even know your names!"

"Nigel," said Nigel. "And this is Miguel."

"And I'm George," said George. "It's short for Georgina, but I'm generally known as George. And have you travelled far?"

"We came from London today," said Nigel. "No, actually we came from London on Saturday, but we got held up. It's a long story."

"So you've been staying… in a hotel?"

"We spent two nights in a prison cell," said Nigel.

"Oh, gosh!" said George. "What did you do?"

"What did we do, Miguel? We, er, got into a disagreement with some road protesters. Not road protesters, I mean people who were sat in the road, they were protesting about something else…"

"The right to smoke!" said Miguel, and he made puffing noises.

"Yes, that was it," said Nigel.

"In Lydiard Forum?" said George.

"Yes, that was it," said Nigel.

"I see," said George. "And please tell me, why were you wearing my husband's clothes?"

"Well, you'll never believe this. You see, there was this naked man…"

"The Naked Rambler!" said George. "Damn! I missed him."

*

The Moon on a Monday night – two men and Eric Finch, the landlord, discussing the nudist who had turned up at lunch.

When Nigel and Miguel walked down to the pub that evening, they didn't know quite what to expect. And they didn't particularly care. It was warm and pleasant, the blackbirds were singing, it was nice to be out. Nice, too, to feel that hunting instinct, Nigel thought – they were out, seeking food.

This was Nigel's suggestion. George was very sweet, very kind, he thought, but food was such a palaver for her. She'd offered to cook, then apologised for her deliberations. She rarely had visitors, she said. Normally she shopped for one, every week, and she couldn't get to the shops again till next Monday; there was only one bus a week. She wasn't sure what she had in store, she said, but she would find something, don't worry.

"No, no, no," said Nigel. "We don't want to put you out. We can go to the pub. Do they do food?"

"Oh yes," she said. "They do food. Very good food. And Eric – that's the landlord – brews his own beer."

"Right, we'll give it a try then," said Nigel.

George declined his offer to buy her a meal; she would sort out the bedding, she said, while they were out. Besides, Eric did such large portions…

Good, thought Nigel, who was starving: another reason for eating out. He hated the idea of dainty eating. And having to be so polite about it, when really you were feeling ravenous and could have eaten the same again, three or four times over.

So off they went.

The bar was empty. The men were standing in the lounge, propping up the bar on that side. The silence was punctuated by the squeak of Eric's shoes.

"Gentlemen, good evening! And what can I get you?" he said.

"I'm looking for the meaning of life," said Nigel; a favourite retort.

"Would that be a pint or a half, sir?" said Eric.

"What?" said Nigel.

"The Meaning of Life – it's my latest brew. I've got it on draught, no bottles yet; I'll be doing those tomorrow."

Stunned by Eric's response, Nigel laughed. A first time for everything, he thought: a lifetime's quest is at an end.

"I'm speechless," he said. "A pub that serves the meaning of life – you'd better make that a pint. And one for my friend here. Yes? Yes. And do you do food?"

"Yes, there's a menu in the lounge, sir, if you'd like to come through."

So they wandered through. Good evening, good evening. Two locals; they looked like farm workers, one big and one small. Steak and chips, twice, with all the trimmings. We'll sit in the bar, said Nigel.

They sat and drank, sat and ate, listening to the conversation in the other room.

"It wasn't a maple leaf, it was a sycamore," said one, a booming voice.

"Ah, a sycamore is a maple," said the second, softer tones.

"Oh, is it now? I didn't know that. My God though, it didn't cover much did it? Horse chestnut would have been better."

"A fig leaf," said Eric.

"No, Eric, you see, a fig leaf isn't as big as horse chestnut. They don't come any bigger than horse chestnut."

"You've tried them, have you, Roger?"

Roars of laughter.

"Adam and Eve had fig leaves, didn't they? You know, in the Bible?"

"A fig leaf! You couldn't cover much with a fig leaf. Horse chestnut is your best bet."

"I dunno though Rodge. I'd say it depends on the size of your conkers."

More roars.

"The size of his dongle!" said Eric. "I had customers, the Paulsbury Anglers Club were in for lunch, and he walks in! I've never seen anything like it. I don't know about leaves, he'd need a bloody hedge to hide that thing."

More roars.

"You fancy a bit of hedge laying, Roger?"

Another round of roars; Roger's laugh was booming. Then:

"I see the police were up at Greenslade Cottage this afternoon."

"Yes," said Eric. "I don't know what was going on. Two police cars and an ambulance. It's all been happening today."

"He probably gave Mrs Tindall a heart attack."

"He nearly gave me an art attack!" said Eric.

In the bar, Nigel was thinking of the car, and parking. The food devoured, he said to Miguel, "We'd better join the locals. I need to talk to the landlord."

They wandered through. Good evening, good evening. Did you enjoy your meal, gents? Yes, thank you, just the job. Can I get you anything else? We'll have, er, two more pints of the Meaning of Life, thank you very much. Fresh glasses? No, these will… You haven't quite finished. Oh yes, er, fresh glasses then please.

"Gives him something to do," said the smaller man, smiling.

"And where are you staying, gents?" said Eric, pouring the pints.

"Actually," said Nigel, "we're, er, staying at Greenslade Cottage."

"Are you?" said Eric. "Hang on a minute."

The pints poured, he gave Nigel a studious look. And then, as if the mental candle had been lit, he snapped his fingers and said, "I knew you reminded me of someone! You must be Richard's brother."

"No, we're not related," said Nigel.

He was searching for an explanation that would satisfy local curiosity. Failing, desperately.

"We're helping her with the garden, actually," he said. "We're just, er… old friends."

"Ohhh, the garden," said Eric. "Yes, it certainly needs doing…"

The big man laughed. The small man chuckled and said,

"You've got a job there. How long are you staying?"

"I don't know," said Nigel. "We'll see."

"Were you there this afternoon?" said Eric.

"Yes, just in time," said Nigel. "We rumbled a burglar."

"Ohhh," said Eric. "Only I saw the police cars and wondered what was going on, you know. And when I saw the ambulance, I thought someone had been taken ill…"

"We had a bit of a set-to," said Nigel. "With the burglar. He fell over…"

"Is George all right?" said Eric.

"Yes, she's fine."

"She'll be glad of your company, I expect," said Eric. "She hasn't had visitors for years."

"Hmm," said Nigel. "I wanted to ask whether you'd mind if we left our car in your car park. We can't find anywhere to park it up the lane."

"No problem," said Eric. "It's a devil driving up there, I don't know about parking."

"Thanks," said Nigel.

"My charges are very reasonable," said Eric.

Another round of laughs. Only joking, he added.

Nigel sipped the beer and wished he'd ordered a half. One pint of the Meaning of Life and he was feeling rather tipsy. It wouldn't do, he thought, to turn up at the house in a drunken stupor. And Miguel was beginning to sway.

"It's, er, strong stuff, this beer of yours," said Nigel.

"I like to keep my customers happy," said Eric.

Nigel's cerebellum was beginning to throb a little. Not only with the beer, but with the thought that he now had a pint to get through, and that he must chat – because it was unavoidable – with the local rustics.

Silence, while he searched for a suitable topic. And from the rustics, obvious glances at Miguel, the stranger who looked foreign, and who hadn't spoken a word.

Then Eric asked about the burglar, and the ice was broken.

They talked about crime and punishment, about burglars,

and whether it was right to use force against them. They talked about the right to defend your own property, about a farmer who'd been jailed for shooting a burglar. And then, the conversation returned to the nudist. Nigel said he'd seen him; they'd both seen him, he said. He was sorely tempted to tell them the story of Richard's clothes; it was the beer, making the words flow. But he refused another pint, saying they had to get back before dark; they didn't want to annoy George.

Even so, they staggered up the hill.

George was sitting outside, on her cane chair. Let me show you where you're sleeping, she said, leaping up. I'll be going to bed soon, when it gets dark. Did you have a good meal? Oh, good. Miguel, I thought you could sleep downstairs, in here. There's bedding but I haven't dusted, she said.

She showed them the lounge, a bed settee made up. And Nigel, she said, I thought you could have the room above. Come on up, both of you, and I can show you the bathroom...

Up the stairs, they both followed.

It's a double bed, she said, will you be all right? The bathroom's at the end of the corridor, I'll show you. Please don't pull the chain after dusk, it disturbs the sparrows, they're nesting in the eaves, you see. The house martins won't mind, but the sparrows tend to worry. You can always use the toilet downstairs if you need to pull the chain, that won't upset them. There's a wash basin in there as well...

Halfway along the corridor, she stopped.

In fact, she said, perhaps you'd better use that after dusk, and not the bathroom. I sleep down this end, you see, and I'd rather you weren't wandering about in the middle of the night. It's not that I don't trust you, but I'm not used to visitors you know, and it might frighten the life out of me if I wake up and find strangers...

She ushered them downstairs, missing out the bathroom.

They didn't mind – in the end, they went to bed before she did.

Under the quilt, Nigel turned off the bedside lamp, closed

his eyes, and listened to the owls, whooping and screaming. Then he thought, Why is it so bright? He looked at the open skylight and saw the moon, half full, rising over a hill. And on a chair, a pile of Richard's clothes, neatly folded.

*

George thought she'd planted the tooth in the cabbage patch, she said. But Nigel had been digging and trowelling for an hour now, and hadn't found anything like a tooth. Hadn't found any cabbage either, come to that. It seemed to be rhubarb, not cabbage, that had grown here once. He was finding the tubers, thick red things, tough as concrete. And underneath, a layer of chalk.

Meanwhile, Miguel was attacking the grass with a scythe, and George was feeding the birds.

He'd rung Jerry that morning, told him of the latest developments.

In summary, because the line was bad.

Bird has flown, Daniel in custody, treasure buried in a garden, we're there now, it's a long story. You'd better get digging then, said Jerry. You told me there wouldn't be any digging, said Nigel. It wasn't planned that way, said Jerry. How come it got buried? Don't ask; it'll take a book to explain. Nigel, get Miguel on the case; he's used to that sort of thing. Can't, he's cutting the grass. Cutting the...?

They were cut off.

Which was a relief, Nigel thought; they'd have been on the phone for hours, else. And the irony of it all! No digging, and here he was – digging.

He'd looked at the ground the day before; Miguel had looked at the grass. Tomorrow they said, and agreed that the pub was the better option. Now he was having second thoughts – the evening would have been cooler. But then, yesterday they were starving and totally knackered.

The sun was blazing. It was hard work. He wasn't used to

it; he was an academic, for God's sake. Time to take a breather.

The smell of one's own sweat! You can't beat it, he thought, sniffing his armpit. There's nothing quite like it – inhale, deep breath, it's wonderful!

He looked at Miguel, then at George.

And yet, he thought, another's sweat is so off-putting. Strange. Why should it be? Even when you're intimate with someone, with their smells, there's something about the smell of their sweat which is definitely off-putting.

He couldn't explain it.

Maybe, he thought, it's genetic. An automatic response, out of our control. We have been programmed in such a way that one's own smell triggers good, the other's triggers bad.

But that wouldn't make sense, he thought. One's own smell may be encoded – but how could millions of others be lodged there? It isn't possible. It would have to function in a negative sense, so that any smell that isn't one's own is rejected as obnoxious and possibly dangerous.

Which didn't make sense either, because some smells were obviously delicious. So it was something to do with the body. A filtering mechanism, that rejected all bodily odours unless they matched one's own. Which they would never do, because one's own smells were unique. Possibly encoded in your DNA. And possibly in a tooth.

He returned to the digging.

*

George was worried about the birds. They weren't used to seeing strangers in the garden. The finches were hanging back, sitting on a wire, observing. They wouldn't come down while Miguel was there, hacking away. The swallows didn't mind; they were swooping into the summerhouse as usual. The house martins were flying high, beyond her range of vision. And the sparrows were on the other side of the house, chirruping. But the blackbirds were suspicious. As were the tits, churring in a hedge, annoyed because they couldn't get to the peanut cake.

It was the nesters she worried about. The wrens, the robins, the blackbirds – they were all on their second or third broods, and wanting food for the nestlings.

Still, the work needs doing, she thought. The birds will have to wait. And there's plenty of food about, for the nesters.

Midway through feeding, she remembered where she'd planted the tooth. Not in the cabbage patch. And she'd got that wrong; it wasn't even a cabbage patch. But she didn't say anything to Nigel. He was doing so well, she thought, removing the rhubarb tubers with great care, placing them in a bucket. He was a born gardener.

And he was an archaeologist, after all. He was used to working with the soil. She had done it herself a few times. Volunteering as a student, many years ago, working on digs in York and thereabouts. The volunteers shifted the soil. Sat on your knees, scraping away with a trowel, removing any finds, bits of old pot. It was all old pot. That and clay pipes. Nothing very interesting. She'd found a metal buckle once; that was quite a find. But on the whole it was back-breaking work. The worst was wheeling a wheelbarrow, full to the brim with heavy soil and stone, over a labyrinth of planks with deep pits on either side. Tricky.

Nigel's job was a lot easier.

But when should she tell him about the tooth? If she left it too late, he might be rather cross, justifiably so. Miguel was more relaxed about the work. He'd taken off his shirt now, he was very brown underneath.

Mid-morning, and already three cars had driven up the lane and driven down shortly after. The locals were so nosy. It hadn't taken long for the news to get round, obviously – George had two strange men staying with her, doing the garden, so Eric had said. Now they were taking a peek. Checking up on her. She would be a topic for local gossip, and the news would spread over Magnus Chase.

And now there was a fourth car, stopping by the house. People getting out to spy. It was all a bit too much. Too much like being a celebrity. Imagine! She hated the idea.

She heard a shout: "George! Are you there?"

It wasn't snoopers after all. It was the police – Rachel and another woman, wanting her to make that statement.

She turned to the workers and called: "Are you ready for a cup of tea?"

"Yes please!" Nigel shouted.

The house was cool, even at the height of summer. You felt like putting on a cardigan when you stepped inside. Except for the upstairs lounge, where the picture window drew the sun, and the temperature soared to greenhouse proportions.

"I'm just making a pot of tea," she said. "Do come in."

They sat in the kitchen. Rachel's blouse was the purest white. The other woman had her jacket on, and that funny hat that only policewomen wear.

George didn't have much to say, couldn't add much to what she'd told them already. Her memory was fine, she said. But things had happened so fast; it was all a bit of a blur. The burglar might have been in the house, before she arrived. She wasn't sure. She was talking to Miguel when he burst in. Then he threatened her with a crowbar; threatened Miguel too. And then Richard – Nigel – arrived, just in time. He had saved her life.

Nigel and Miguel sat outside, drinking tea. Miguel, listening to the women's voices, kept leaping from the bench whenever there were hints of their departing. When the volume increased, Nigel too stood to his feet and walked to the corner of the house, where Miguel was staring up at the lane.

He could understand why. The lovely Rachel had the top buttons of her blouse unbuttoned; you could see a white bra, the shape of her breasts…

"Hi!" she said, waving.

"Hi!" said Miguel, raising his cup.

The other woman, a senior, tugged Rachel's arm and whisked her away.

Miguel sighed, staring at the empty space. A glimpse of Rachel was food to his eyes.

"Right!" said Nigel. "Back to work."

He returned to the trowel, amusing himself with a conundrum: why does a pure white blouse make a woman look so sexy?

George, meanwhile, sat upstairs by the picture window, feeling vexed. Now that she had signed a statement, she was doubting the truth of what she had signed. Events had happened in the way she had described, but there were things that she didn't understand. The man had threatened them, yes, but he was looking for something. He wanted the pigeon. Who had said he was a burglar? Nigel. It was Nigel's story. And she had gone along with it, believing at the time that he was Richard, and not to be doubted.

The man had wanted the pigeon. Why was he so desperate? Probably, she thought, for the same reason that Nigel was now trawling the soil with such care. It wasn't the pigeon he was after; the pigeon was only the messenger. He was after the message – the tooth, carried in a locket.

King Arthur's tooth.

She didn't think so. She knew too much about history to believe that the elusive tomb had been discovered. And not only his tomb, but his remains too!

Why a tooth? And why choose a pigeon to carry it? Where was he flying? Portugal, apparently. It was all very strange. Nobody would go to such lengths to recover a tooth, unless the tooth was very special. Which she doubted.

On the other hand, what was the alternative explanation? Was the tooth really an artificial construction, containing a secret weapon, a deadly poison, anthrax or that raisin thing? Were they terrorists?

She didn't think so. Basically, they were quite harmless; she wouldn't have invited them to stay if she'd thought otherwise.

Miguel, in particular, was as innocent as a lamb; she could tell. Nigel was more furtive, slippery. He was hiding something; that was obvious.

So.

She could be slippery too. If he was that desperate, he would dig up the whole garden in his search. Why tell him the location, when he was such a deceiver?

She could string him along, lead him up the garden path – literally!

And if he grew suspicious, she would challenge him.

Tell me the truth, and I'll show you where I planted the tooth.

*

Nigel and Miguel walked to the pub again that evening, famished. For lunch, a cheese sandwich, thanks to George's generosity. Miguel's progress had been quicker than Nigel's: a quarter of the field, roughly, had been cut. Nigel, meanwhile, had gone through the rhubarb patch, formerly known as the cabbage patch, plus the cabbage patch proper, plus a potato patch, without finding a tooth of any description, animal or human. Sweet wrappers, cigarette butts, a rusting can, an old shoe, the remains of a dead mole – all these and more, but no teeth.

The most exciting item was a lollipop wrapper, whose letters he could just make out – *Stingray*. He remembered the lolly quite clearly, shaped like the TV spaceship, multi-coloured fins. Circa… when? Late 50s, early 60s? Too much effort to recall, but he remembered sucking it when his peers had moved on to the hard stuff – fags behind the bike shed.

"We may be here for a few days," he said to Miguel, wearily. "I think we should buy some food tomorrow. We can't rely on George's generosity. It's very hard on her, for one thing – she can only get to the shops once a week."

"Okay," said Miguel. "No problem."

"Also, I need to go to a bank and get some cash," said Nigel. "God, I'm thirsty. I can understand how brickies drink several pints a night. It's thirsty work, do you not think?"

"I drink water, lots of water," said Miguel. "Is good to drink water. And siesta. No work in hot sun. Work evening is better."

"Yes," said Nigel. "Or mornings. I'll try and wake up earlier tomorrow."

They walked into the bar. There was a family in there, playing pool.

"Gentlemen, what can I get you?" said Eric.

"The Meaning of Life," said Nigel. "Two pints please. And we'll order some food."

A similar arrangement: they ate in the bar, at a table; then joined the locals in the lounge, standing at the counter. The same two men were there, big and small. Plus two others, an elder and a younger; possibly father and son.

"Hello there, how are you getting on?" said the smaller man.

"We've made progress," said Nigel. "It's hard work, mind. It was very hot today."

The cue for a conversation. Working in the heat. Ways of coping. The difficulties of wearing wellies. Socks that slid down to your toes. Feet that were dripping with sweat. It was all very physical. And Nigel wallowed in it. So refreshing, he thought. The trouble with academics is that they have no inkling of real life, the real world. The world of physicality – these people are up to their necks in it, every day.

But all this time, he was aware of the father and son, standing at the end of the bar. The elder in particular, who kept staring at him intently.

After a while, there was a pause in the conversation, and the elder man said to Nigel, "I'm sure I know you from somewhere."

Nigel looked. The man did look vaguely familiar.

"I can't think where," said Nigel.

"Me neither," said the man. "But I know I've seen you

before. Have you been on the tele?"

"Me? No," said Nigel.

"I'm damned sure I've seen you before," said the man.

"I thought that," said Eric. "Richard Tindall, George's husband. He's the spitting image. I thought he was Richard's brother."

"No," said the man. "I never knew Richard Tindall. I don't know his wife either. But I know I've seen you before. It'll come back to me, don't you worry. Anyway, we'll be off now, Eric, I'll be seeing you. Cheerio Rodge, cheerio Paul."

After they'd left, Eric shook his head and said, "Stephen Grove! He's never been the same since he came back from the Azores."

Nigel felt a chill of recognition ripple down his spine. Miguel opened his mouth and looked pretty much like a man about to exclaim. Nigel turned to him with a severe frown, and Miguel took a sip of the Meaning of Life.

The conversation around them had moved on.

There was talk about the costs of dairy farming, and the farmers who had sold up and emigrated. Then it was back to Stephen Grove and his trip to the Azores. They talked about his campaign for public ownership – of everything, it seemed. They talked about his defence of Robert Mugabe, and how Mrs Chilcott had fainted...

Nigel heard but no longer listened. He was thinking of genetic implants, and the farmers who had turned up on Torre de Columba, hoping for a cure for their depression.

They drank up swiftly and left.

*

George couldn't face a therapy session this week. Early on the Wednesday morning, she rang Carol McGregor and left a message on her answering machine: George can't make it due to unforeseen circumstances. It would cost her – Carol wanted forty-eight hours' notice for a cancellation; otherwise she charged the full whack. But George couldn't face it. She would rather pay the fee and not attend. Besides, she had her guests to see to. And a niggling question. She couldn't get to sleep last night, thinking about it. Today, she thought, she must have an answer.

"Were you warm enough last night?" she said to Miguel, who was eating a piece of toast.

Nigel had yet to appear. She could hear him in the toilet, downstairs. She closed the living-room door to block out the noise.

"Warm?"

"In bed. I thought it went a bit cooler last night. I had to close my window. Did you have enough bedding?"

"Ah, warm! Yes, thank you, madame. I was hot."

"Oh, good. I'm sorry I missed you. I was very tired. I heard you come in."

"We are noisy?"

"No, no. It's just that it's very quiet here. So the slightest sound can be quite noisy. Unusual sounds, you know."

"Ah! Yes."

She poured a cup of tea.

"Miguel..."

"Yes?"

"Where was the bird flying to? Did he have far to go? I think you said Portugal, am I right?"

"No, no, I from Portugal, my family in Portugal. Gabriel, he live in Açores. Azores. I live there also."

"Gabriel?"

"The bird."

"Ah!"

The Azores! A strange coincidence, she thought. Stephen Grove went there for a paid holiday, taking part in a secret experiment, a trial of a new antidepressant, he'd said. She couldn't see a connection. But the Azores! What happened on the Azores? Nothing at all; it was never on the news. She knew nothing about the place, except that there was an American airbase there, which they used for refuelling, US jets zapping east and west.

There's no point asking Miguel, she thought. He's been fed a story too. They're using him, exploiting him, using him for his knowledge of racing pigeons. Probably knows as much as me. King Arthur's tooth!

She turned on the radio.

"Don't mind me," she said. "I usually listen to the morning news. Help yourself to toast."

War news. More bombing raids in the Middle East. The Azores must be a busy place, she thought.

Nigel walked in.

"Good morning! We thought we'd do some shopping today. We've been here two nights now, and we must be making a hole in your larder. It's not on."

"Oh! It's no problem, really…"

"Yes it is. You've been very kind and generous, and we don't want to abuse your hospitality. It's only right that we contribute. And… Well, I'm not sure how long… I mean, do you mind us staying here? We could always check in to a hotel, and pop in during the day."

"No, no, don't do that. You're very welcome to stay for as long as… Well, you're doing the garden for me, aren't you, and I'm pleased to have you here. After all… you saved my life."

"Please don't say that. It was just good timing, that's all."

"Well, anyway, I owe you… Would you like a cup of tea?"

The news droned on in the background, George straining to hear. An item about that freak wave in South-East Asia: the number believed to be dead had increased, by several thousands. She'd missed that now; they'd moved on to the next item. A shooting in America. At least ten schoolkids dead. Teenager storms into class, firing at random, then shoots himself. No apparent motive…

George felt the threat of the suicide virus, closing in.

"I think it must be genetic," she said. "Don't you?"

"What?"

Nigel looked startled. He hadn't combed his hair this morning. It looked like a hedge. George almost laughed.

"The urge to kill," she said, pointing to the radio. "It goes on all the time in America, doesn't it? Killing people at random, and then killing yourself. Teenagers, young people – why do they do it? There's no rational explanation. I think it must be in their genes."

"Sorry," said Nigel. "I was daydreaming."

"Another school shooting in America," said George. "Do you think there's such a thing as an American gene? They've got no control, have they? Something's gone wrong over there. If they're not bombing other people, they're killing themselves for no apparent reason."

"It happens over here," said Nigel. "Shootings. Gun crime."

"Yes, but most of it is related to gangs and drug dealing," said George. "Over there, you have these random shootings, and then the killer kills himself. I think it's awful. Anyway, that's enough of that."

She turned off the radio and returned to the grill.

"Where's the best place to shop?" said Nigel. "We thought we'd do it this afternoon, and then work in the evening, before it gets dark."

"Oh," said George.

"Is that not a good idea?"

"I'd rather you didn't work in the evening, if you don't mind. Well, late evening would be all right. It's just that the birds can't get to the feed while you're out working, and it's a busy time for them, two hours before dusk. They like to feed up before they go to bed."

"Supper time!" said Miguel.

"Yes, supper time, and breakfast isn't a good time either. But that's all right, because they've finished their breakfast by the time we're up and about."

"Oh," said Nigel. "Perhaps we could go shopping this morning then, and work in the afternoon, till supper time."

310

"Fine," said George. "Do you think you could do the carrot patch next? It's next to the potato patch. I'll show you later."

"The carrot patch," said Nigel. "Er, yes, I suppose... Do you think you might have buried it there?"

"It's possible, I really don't know. I know it was somewhere near... somewhere in the vegetable garden. It's just that you're making such a good job of it, it seems a shame not to round it off."

"Yes, yes, of course. I might as well finish the job."

"I'd be very grateful. Are you ready for toast?"

"Yes, thank you."

The kitchen table could only seat two. Unless she pulled out the extra flap, which she didn't want to do. It would mean moving everything, and putting it all back. So she stood by the cooker, watching the toast, waiting for the right moment.

"Have you eaten?" said Nigel.

"Yes, I've had mine," she said. "I woke up early. Did you sleep all right? Were you warm enough?"

"Yes, but I closed the window, I hope that was all right."

"No, no, that's fine. I had to close mine last night."

Nigel sipped his tea, buttered a piece of toast.

"Nigel, there's something I must ask," she said. "About that man who turned up here, with a crowbar..."

"The burglar," he said.

"He wasn't a burglar. He was after the bird, Gabriel. That's why he threatened me."

"Oh!" said Nigel, his mouth full of toast.

"You said he was a burglar, didn't you? To me, and to the police."

"I did? Yes, I did... I thought he was a burglar."

"But he knew you, he knew Miguel at least, he used his name. He wasn't a burglar. Who was he? A friend of yours?"

Silence, while Nigel sipped his tea.

"A colleague," he said. "He was out for personal gain."

"And why did he want the bird? This tooth of yours? King Arthur's tooth?"

"Well..." said Nigel. "I suppose it would fetch a lot of money if he sold it on the black market. Stolen treasure changes hands every day, these collectors are fanatics..."

"Nigel, I studied history at university. I used to be a history teacher. I think, if someone had discovered King Arthur's tomb, the public would have heard about it."

Bitch!

No, she wasn't a bitch.

Nigel placed the toast on his plate, thinking of last night's episode. A tiny hamlet in the middle of nowhere, a pub with two or three customers, and then a farmer turns up who recognises him. The world was smaller than he thought.

He'd thought about this in bed last night, trying to decide whether it fitted the laws of probability. Was it a freakish coincidence, or a likely event? The farmers had come from all over; they'd been chosen that way. And there were several, all told. And then, rural areas were sparsely populated; neighbours lived miles apart, and they travelled. The entire stretch of Magnus Chase was like a village in itself, where everybody knew each other. All in all, he concluded, it was highly likely he would come into contact with someone who had taken part in the experiment, or knew someone who had been involved. Highly likely. The middle of nowhere turns out to be the centre of the universe, and he had stepped right into it.

And now this.

"You're right," he said at last. "I'm very sorry. The problem is that it's a long story, and the details are a closely guarded secret. A secret from the general public, I mean."

"A secret? I see. So this tooth is a secret. Perhaps it's not surprising that I can't remember where I buried it then, is it? It means nothing to me. Perhaps, if I knew why it was so valuable, it might help me to remember."

Bitch!

No, she wasn't a bitch.

Here they were, total strangers, and she had invited them

to stay. She had trusted them. Fed them. She deserved an explanation.

Silence, while Nigel pondered.

Where to begin?

What should he say?

Should he tell her the complete story, beginning with Professor Pipi?

3

On the Azores, Liz Kendal was testing a piece of software called Dialectical Materialism. Designed by Boris Vladimov, following Jerry Mendoza's specification, which was based on a program written in California. Which was, in turn, based on Liz's PhD thesis. Now she couldn't decide whether the results were of any use.

"This is just data," she said, "which we already have. The software that was written at the Business School produces the same results."

"Good," said Jerry. "That's precisely what we want. We're testing it, and it's working."

"Yes, but two points," said Liz, raising a finger. "One is that it produces facts and figures, according to a given formula. There's no prose that explains the results. I can't see how a volume of *Capital* is going to come out of this. We've yet to produce a replica of Volume One, remember – I had to stop working on that to do this. And two, my program does exactly the same thing. I thought this one was meant to be producing an explanation. Instead it's giving us data that we already know."

"I take your points," said Jerry, "but you have to remember we're in a serious financial crisis. You don't know who's backing the project. They're wanting results fast. Boris's program has a predictor indicator, which is an added bonus. Our backers want to know how long the system's got to survive if they follow certain strategies. I'm talking about counter-tendencies that'll offset the tendency for the rate of profit to fall. Like increasing credit and so on."

Liz had a feeling of déjà vu – the funders calling the shots.

"I thought the US government was the major backer.

They're getting worried then, I take it," she said.

"They used to be our major backer, but no longer. The war effort's become a big drain on resources and it's taking away funds from R and D. Not just for the US, I should say. The UK government's stopped funding us, for one. Our major backers are now private sponsors. Individual financiers, company chairmen. One of whom you know – Humphrey Dillinger. He's put more money into this project than the US government. He's basically the chairman of the board, so to speak. And it's Dillinger who's pulling the strings."

"Oh great! So what does this mean for the writing of a new *Capital*? What are the implications?"

"He sees it as a second priority," said Jerry, dismissing the idea with a shrug. Then, the passion popping out of his eyes, he said: "I'm cheesed off as much as you are, Liz, but what can you do? I've been stalling as it is. Nicolai's working on the text software and the biocomputer's waiting for a new stock of chemicals. Then we have to analyse the DNA samples, when they arrive. It's a slow job, as you know, but we're getting there. The problem is that Dillinger has no great interest in producing a book. What he wants is facts and figures so that he can make snap decisions."

Jerry scratched his chin and looked away.

Then he said: "I'm afraid I've got some bad news. I haven't told anyone else, and the news isn't public yet. I'd like you to keep it between ourselves. And Bob, I guess."

"So what's the bad news? You've run out of cash? We're bankrupt?"

"Not yet, and it may not be a problem if we produce the results. The bad news is about Humphrey Dillinger. He's been appointed head of the World Bank."

"Oh great! So he's really pulling the purse strings?"

"I'm afraid so. Our future lies in his wallet."

*

Liz didn't waste time telling Bob the news. Bob guessed she was out of sorts by the clanking in the kitchen. She came out carrying a bowl. I've had a bad day at the Business School, she said. There you are – carrot soup. Good for the eyes, and it'll keep you alive.

Bob was in bed, reading from a frame, expecting another interrogation about Dr Lee. Liz might have seen her; the gap was only ten minutes. Yet it was quite harmless. A Chinese massage, using the wisdom of the ancients. So he was told. True or not, it felt good, and she was no ancient. Her hands were young, disciplined and rigorous. He was thinking of taking acupuncture.

Liz had other things on her mind.

She told him about Humphrey Dillinger.

"Weren't you doing some research on him?" she said.

"I was, I am. I mean, I will be, when my back's recovered. It turned out to be a big job. There are ten thousand references to Humphrey Dillinger on the Web. It can't all be the same one. There's a Humphrey Dillinger who owns a chain of poodle parlours, another who sells second-hand kayaks. I'm trying to sort out who's who."

"Maybe he comes from a large family. So what did you find out? Anything interesting?"

"Yes. This New Development Corporation – you remember, I found that receipt. Couldn't find any info on what they do, but I found out who sits on the board. The board has about twelve members, including our friend Humphrey. And they all have something in common. I've traced their company interests; they're on other boards too. It's all biotech. Several of these companies are doing research on cloning. That's the link. And the first ones are due out soon."

"The first? What do you mean, the first?"

"Clones. You know about Dolly the Sheep. Now it's cats. There's a company in California who are offering to clone your pet cat. Tiddles reincarnated, lots of wealthy widows are going for it. They've paid loadza bucks, but nobody's seen a cloned cat yet. I think Dillinger's chain of poodle parlours may be implicated. If cats, why not your pet poodle? They're making loadza dollars out of people's grief and gullibility, and nobody's seen a result."

"So what does this mean? Humphrey's investing all this money because he wants to…"

"Clone Marx. That's why these DNA samples are so crucial, that's why Jerry's so keen on getting hold of them – that's what I think."

"Dillinger wants to clone Marx? No, that doesn't make sense. He wants facts and figures. He's got no interest in producing a book, why should he want to clone Marx?"

"I've got no idea. I guess it's only a step away from a simulated brain. Why not do the whole poodle?"

"I don't think you take this project very seriously."

Bob nearly spilled the soup.

"I do! That's why I started doing this research. I want to know what I've got involved in."

"I'm beginning to wonder."

"So why don't you ask Jerry?"

"Ask him what?"

"What we're involved in. Tell him there's a rumour that he's into cloning. Ask him if it's true. Are we cloning Marx?"

"Maybe I will. How's the job hunting going?"

"Give me a break."

"So how was your day at the office, dear? Did she give you a good hand job?"

"Absolutely! She's fantastic. Her hands are as soft as lotus petals."

Liz blew a raspberry and returned to the kitchen.

*

Déjà vu, twice in one day. Liz had a vision of her student days, lying in bed with Phil, talking about the role of the revolutionary party, stoned out of her box, yackety-yak. Now

317

she was lying in bed with Bob, talking about the structure of *Capital*, both of them naked under a cotton sheet. Too hot to sleep, no inclination for sex, and the sound of the jets shaking the stillness of the night – a night of yackety-yak.

Liz was explaining the computer program called Dialectical Materialism and its relationship to *Capital*.

"The key to understanding the software is the axioms," she said. "The axioms give rise to the structure. Such as value. What is value? A large chunk of Volume One is devoted to defining value. And then we have profit. Where does profit come from? Another large chunk. Now, the definitions give rise to categories, which the software uses to make sense of the data. And to calculate the rate of profit. Are you following me?"

"I, er – I think you might have lost me. Give me a concrete example."

"Okay. Let's take Britain. The government says Britain is prosperous, wealth is increasing, the economy's on a sound footing, there's low unemployment, etcetera. And that's the appearance. But if you analyse the figures, you get a different picture. For a start, about three-quarters of the population are home owners. The cost of housing has rocketed. Home owners are more wealthy because their property's increased in value. But homes don't produce anything. A home isn't a factory. Its increase in value means you can sell it at a greater price than what it cost you to buy it. Apparently you've made a profit, in inverted commas. So what do you do with your profit? Do you plough it back into the business, buy more property? There are limits. Most people aren't in the property business, their so-called profit is just a credit balance, a gain as opposed to a loss. The companies who buy the land, build houses and sell them are making a profit, in the Marxist sense of the term. The rest is just illusion. Are you listening to me?"

"Yeah, yeah, I'm listening. So what are you saying? That Britain isn't really wealthy?"

"What I'm saying is that the wealth is only apparent. Home

ownership gives people the illusion of wealth. Britain's prosperity is based on credit and inflated property values. The whole system is propped up on credit. The government borrows, consumers borrow, students borrow. Higher education has been transformed, so that's now dependent on credit. Free education is a thing of the past. It's a symptom of the underlying malaise. On the surface, the appearance of wealth. Underneath, an economic time bomb waiting to explode. Crisis? What crisis? We've been here before."

"Hmm. Boom and bust. So Britain's on the road to going bust. The property bubble's going to burst."

"No, it's got nothing to do with boom and bust! What you've got are economic cycles, which are a feature of the system, and over which you have limited control. You can't understand the system by looking at property values..."

"Please – will you do me the honour?"

Bob had turned his back on her. He pointed to a spot below his neck and said, "Just there. I've a terrible itch. Will you, please?"

Liz scratched and said, "Where was I?"

"Property values."

"Oh yes. I was going to say that homes are commodities, which are bought and sold like any other commodity. They have an exchange value, and they also have a use value, because people want to live in them. What's happened is that their exchange value has become more significant than their use value, because people buy in order to sell, they buy to invest, etcetera. But the rise and fall in the price of commodities tells us nothing about profit, this is my point. To understand the economy, you have to analyse the whole picture, the companies who are producing commodities. Now, if you look at manufacturing, you get a different picture... Is that better?"

Her nails had left a red blotch.

"Yeah, thanks," he said.

"I think you should have a shower," she said. "I think you

need one."

"I know I need one, but not now," he said. "Come on Liz, give me the whole picture."

"Okay. So, manufacturing. In the UK, it's been on the decline for years. To maintain profits, companies are shifting operations overseas, where the cost of labour is cheaper, the cost of materials is cheaper. That goes for services too. To increase profit, you reduce costs. So you import labour, you employ people from overseas who are willing to work for peanuts, or you shift your operation overseas with the same result. Or you increase the length of the working day, so that people work longer for the same wage. These are strategies that are intended to maintain profits, but the overall tendency remains – which is the tendency for the rate of profit to fall. Ultimately, war is the only solution…"

That's when Liz had her vision – she was back in her student days, lying in bed with Phil.

"Oh God!" she said, sitting up. "Nothing's changed! Here I am, carrying on as I used to do about thirty years ago. Nothing has changed!"

"The world has changed," Bob said.

"Yeah, the world has changed," she said, lying down. "The world's descending into war and barbarism, just as Marx predicted, and people in the West have been conned into believing they're wealthy. It's a total mess."

Bob sniggered.

"I'm not sure I totally agree," he said. "I think we are wealthier. Speaking personally, that's a fact. In any case, there's little you or I can do to prevent wars."

"It's worse than that," she said. "Now it turns out that we're providing the head of the World Bank with the info he requires to prop up a failing system. It's worse than working at the Business School. I don't see any chance of producing a new version of *Capital*."

"Maybe you should write it yourself. Have you thought about that?"

"Yes. Yes, I have. But I couldn't do it on this project. I'd have to resign."

Another snigger from Bob.

"So we'll both resign," he said.

"I'll think about it," she said.

"Yeah, sleep on it," he said.

"It's far too hot and far too noisy," she said, and reached for his genitals.

*

Where to begin? With Cecil Redmayne perhaps – it was Cecil who had introduced Nigel to the subject of Professor Pipi. Nigel had known Cecil as an undergraduate at Cambridge. They had shared a house, together with two others, and had become close friends; they'd followed one another's progress ever since.

When Nigel told Cecil that he might be leaving the country to take up a lucrative post on an ambitious research project, location unknown, Cecil had invited Nigel to stay for a weekend. Cecil still lived in Cambridge. He was now a professor of bioethics, and a member of a worldwide committee that proposed laws on such matters. They also monitored their operation and, in some cases, investigated possible transgressions.

Nigel had heard of Salvador Pipi. It was impossible not to; the man was front page news in the national dailies – one of the crazies, who had declared openly that their intention was to clone a human. To be the first.

Sat in the kitchen at Greenslade Cottage, staring at a piece of toast, he remembered the scene vividly. Polished wood, leather armchairs, walls lined with books. Cecil's study, where he raised the subject over a glass of Scotch.

"Nigel, this seems the appropriate time to make a confession. I invited you here for a purpose."

That was the beginning, and Cecil wasn't smiling. He

wiped his thin grey moustache, lowered his glass, and gave Nigel a grave look.

"You've heard of Salvador Pipi, no doubt," he said. "Yes, who hasn't? It won't surprise you then if I tell you we've been keeping a close watch on his research for some years. Until recently, that is. The fact is, he's disappeared, and no one knows where he is. Not only Pipi, but members of his research team – vanished, off the face of the earth. We believe he's found a sympathetic government somewhere, and a secret location where he can carry out his research without interference. He may have done it by deception, we don't know, and we don't know where he is. However, we do have a few clues. Until his disappearance, he was in regular email contact with Jerry Mendoza, the man you mentioned over the phone. It raised the alarm bells, I can tell you, particularly when you told me what the project was about…"

"But this project isn't concerned with cloning," Nigel said. "It's a simulation, using current technologies, which include biocomputing. I don't see the connection."

"Nigel, you know of that celebrity professor down in Reading, the chap who walks round with a microchip stuck in his arm and presents himself as the first cyborg? Right, so the technologies are out there, this is my point, for good or for bad. Microchips to help the disabled, victims of strokes who may be paralysed, devices that enable them to become more mobile – all well and good. But can you imagine the fusion of microchips, cloning techniques and DNA computing? What might emerge out of that?"

"I can't imagine," said Nigel.

"No, you were never very good with the imagination, were you, Nigel? So let me explain. Professor Pipi wants to be the first to clone a human. This Mendoza wants to recreate the brain of Marx. Put the two together, and the mind boggles. Teams of Marxist robots, spreading the doctrine of communism, infiltrating key establishments, turning people's thoughts to world revolution, just when we believed the whole thing was dead and buried…"

"But this is science fiction! This is just… too fantastic!"

"Isn't it? But we have every reason to be suspicious. We were intercepting Pipi's emails. Mendoza was a regular correspondent. He wanted to know about Pipi's progress; he was asking for details about his methods, giving him encouragement, wishing him luck. They swopped information about automation techniques for multiplying DNA fragments. And we know that Mendoza has a longstanding interest in cloning. In short, there must be some reason for Mendoza's interest – that's all I'm saying, those are the facts. Beyond that is speculation."

"So you invited me here to warn me?"

"Speaking as an old friend, I thought it wise. And speaking as a member of a bioethics committee, I'd like you to help us. We'd like you to be a watchdog, Nigel."

Cecil paused for a sip of whisky. Nigel took a swig of his own.

"Let me put it this way," Cecil continued. "Mendoza and Pipi are in regular contact, and then Pipi disappears. We think Mendoza may be hiding him. He may have offered him sanctuary. This secret location you mentioned – it may be Pipi's hiding place…"

"I've got no idea of the location," said Nigel. "The location wasn't disclosed. I know it's on an island, many miles offshore. It may be Hawaii for all I know. I won't know where it is until I fly to California. It could be the Isle of Wight, though I doubt it."

"We do know something about the location," said Cecil. "More than I can tell you, I'm afraid. Our intelligence is generally reliable and we've added Mendoza to our intercept list, so we're keeping a note of his emails…"

"This is all very MI5," said Nigel.

"There is no such thing as a private email," said Cecil. "Electronic communication is logged, recorded and monitored by somebody – if not your boss, then by your ISP at least..."

"So you know where I'm going, even if I don't. Do you?"

"We've got a pretty good idea where you'll be located, but I'd rather wait for your confirmation. I'm sorry, Nigel, but you could be stepping into muddy water. Please let me finish what I was about to say."

"Sorry, do go on."

"Right, on our suspicions. The point I wanted to make concerns Mendoza's emails. He's made no attempt to contact Pipi since his disappearance, and we think there must have been face-to-face contact, an arrangement of some sort. The coincidence is too striking. It's possible that Mendoza is helping Pipi financially, we don't know. These are our suspicions, but we have no evidence."

Cecil took a sip of whisky. He looked more relaxed now, as though the serious stuff had been said.

"Nigel," he continued, "what we're asking is very simple. We'd like you to keep your eyes and ears open, that's all. Especially for any evidence that Mendoza is in contact with Pipi. We'd like to know what Pipi's up to. Obviously we can't recommend a prosecution unless we have solid evidence. We need to catch him in the act. If our suspicions are correct, you'd be the ideal person to gather the evidence. When do you fly out to California?"

"In a couple of weeks. I've yet to agree terms and conditions. As far as I understand it, I shall be asked to sign a contract when we next meet, in San Diego. The whole team is meant to be meeting there. Do you think I should pull out?"

"No, that's the last thing I'd want. Do the job, carry out your duties as normal. Just be careful. Be attentive. Give me a call when you know the details and the location. Think of yourself as a honorary member of our committee. You can be our inside man, which is just what we need."

"Our man in... wherever."

"Yes, quite... wherever."

Cecil leant forwards, looking for the bottle of Talisker.

"Now," he said, "will you join me in another glass? By the way, I've got a new Mozart you might like to listen to…"

*

Staring at the toast, Nigel remembered the scene vividly. Polished wood, leather armchairs, walls lined with books. Cecil's study, red and brown and golden – he could see it in the toast. And the warning about Professor Pipi; the request to be a watchdog – it all came flooding back.

The sound of the tap shattered the flow of his thoughts. Here he was, sat in the kitchen at Greenslade Cottage, George standing by the sink, waiting for an answer – the value of the tooth.

"I think," he said finally, "you deserve an explanation, and I'd like to explain, I will explain, but, as I said… the problem…"

He fumbled with the toast.

"The problem is that it's a long and complicated story. It would take an evening to relate. What do you say if we offered to cook a meal tonight? I could explain it all then, if you're agreeable. It would give me time to gather my thoughts."

"Oh," she said.

She tried to recall the last time a visitor had used her kitchen.

"Cook a meal," she said, musing.

And these were strangers, more or less. She knew little about them. One, a Portuguese pigeon fancier; the other, an archaeologist. Or so he said.

"All right then," she said. "I'm agreeable."

"Fine," said Nigel.

They finished their breakfast, Nigel talking about the weather. George washed the dishes, half listening. Then – I must go out to feed the birds, she said. They left her to it.

They drove into Lydiard Forum, shopped in Templetons, parked in the car park, no problem; there and back in less than ninety minutes. An early lunch, bread and cheese, moving swiftly to the shovel, the trowel and the scythe.

And the toilet. Nigel was struggling with the Meaning of Life.

Back to the trowel. Time to ponder.

He hadn't told anyone about his diplomatic mission. His role was known only to Cecil, and to members of the ethics committee. So far, there had been little to report. There were no signs that Jerry was in contact with Salvador Pipi, and no sign of Pipi's presence on Torre de Columba. The chemical plant in Sebo was a bit of a mystery, it was true. The lab workers seemed to be Chinese, and most of it was out of bounds, even to members of the research team. Jerry cited as the reason the need for a dust-free, spotlessly clean environment, the DNA molecules being prone to contamination. So there were labs that no one had seen, not even Bob Rheingold.

And then, there was the farmer who had disappeared, and strange sights by the old whaling post. People had been spotted at night up there, wandering about like ghosts. But what did it amount to? Hints of oddities, strangers by the whaling post – nothing that was tangible. Most of it was hearsay, native rumour – the ghost of Christopher Columbus, the ghosts of shipwrecked sailors and ancient whalers. Nigel had taken a walk up there and seen nothing, apart from the crater. He had sat on the edge, thinking of a Bond movie. *Thunderball* – the lid of the crater slides open, to reveal a set of missiles, aimed at strategic targets. Or was it *Goldfinger*? No, he was pretty sure it was *Thunderball*.

So, was Salvador Pipi and his team embedded in the volcano, cloning the first human, using as a backup the spare parts of the vanished farmer, coming out only fleetingly for a breath of air at midnight?

It was too incredible, Nigel thought.

But then, why was Jerry so keen to have the DNA samples? Was it just that they contained the key to the brain's inspiration, or was his motive more sinister? And, Nigel wondered, will I ever find out?

The carrot patch was full of old carrots.

He was relying on Miguel's expertise for cooking the meal. Nigel hadn't cooked for weeks. Back on the island, the recent pressure had seen him living on Chinese takeaways. And he wasn't renowned for his cuisine at the best of times. He would have to disguise his ineptitude. Having offered to cook, he could hardly present her with a boiled egg. He had wandered the aisles in Templetons, unable to find anything, and not knowing what he was looking for. Apart from the obvious, like tea, coffee, sugar. Fortunately, Miguel had risen to the occasion, offering to cook a fish dish, Portuguese style. The result was a division of labour – Nigel in search of the obvious, Miguel seeking the ingredients. Tonight, Nigel would be the chef's assistant.

Then there was the question of what to do with Miguel. Nigel wanted to talk to George, but he didn't want Miguel to hear the whole story. He had dropped a hint in the car. Tonight, he said, I'd like to talk to George. About science, he said. Miguel had raised an eyebrow and a smile, as if there was a flirtation in the air. Would you like me to go for a walk, he said. Well, Nigel began. Then Miguel cut him short, saying he needed an early night, no problem. So hopefully he'd be out of the way. And fast asleep.

Having cooked a meal for them all.

It wasn't cricket, Nigel thought, but what was the alternative? The chef was expected to disappear…

And then, what was he going to say to George? How much should he reveal? And how was he going to approach the subject? George was rather like a character in a Walt Disney movie: she seemed to talk to the birds, constantly, when she thought Nigel was out of earshot. And strangely, the birds seemed to respond. It was very Walt Disney, he thought. And why did she feed them every day, at the height of summer?

He would ask her. Perhaps he would talk about science. Perhaps that was the way of approaching the subject. After all, people like George lived in a fairy-tale world, where animals were well behaved and innocent, deserving of our sympathy and affection. Cows and sheep were seen as pets; all animals were seen as pets, and given human characteristics. It was a fallacy, of course. These people had no concept of science.

Still, she wasn't a vegetarian; he had seen the fridge, stacked with bacon and sausages.

Science...

He would talk about science. The nature of the scientific endeavour, and people who were devoted to the cause. People who had lost the way, becoming obsessed, not with science, but with their own personal agendas, their own successes and achievements, with not a care for moral questions, or for the consequences of their actions.

He would talk about science.

The carrot patch was almost complete. Still no teeth.

*

Where to eat? George was in a quandary. Her guests had been having breakfast in the kitchen, lunch outside. She usually ate in the kitchen, whatever the meal, occasionally outside if the weather was fine.

Usually – until the trauma, two days ago.

Now she was wary of sitting in the kitchen on her own. She had a fear that an intruder would appear, brandishing a crowbar. She felt safer upstairs. Breakfast and lunch were okay, because Nigel and Miguel were there, eating too. She was grateful for the company. But the last two nights had been scary. She'd sat at the table, looking over her shoulder; her guests had gone to the Moon. Every little creak made her jump. And the constant urge to look over her shoulder! There were too many doors. So she'd sorted out the food and taken it upstairs, sitting by the picture window to eat.

They could eat in the kitchen, she thought. It would mean clearing the table, and lifting up the extra flap to seat three.

Or they could eat upstairs, in the lounge with the picture window. That would mean a lot more work. The table was loaded with books and papers, with an empty corner big enough for one plate. It would need a big tidy. Unless they had trays, and ate on their laps.

But the real problem was that the room was very much her private space. No one else had sat in it for years. The last time would have been her brother's visit, four years ago. Or was it five? The years flew by; she really couldn't remember. Anyway, it was more conducive to intimacy up there.

Intimacy! What was she thinking of! She wasn't looking for intimacy; she only wanted to hear Nigel's story; the kitchen would suffice for that.

But then, he might be more relaxed upstairs; it was a lounge, and lounges were intended for lounging – it was a large space, where he might not feel so intimidated.

Then again, some people were intimidated by a large space; they felt dwarfed, shrunken, insignificant. And it was a very personal space. Her guests hadn't set foot in it. Perhaps the kitchen would be best. It was more familiar to them.

She couldn't decide.

They were outside now, working. The food had been put away. She had the afternoon to do a bit of tidying.

She would tidy the lounge, just in case. And then, she thought, she would sort out the kitchen table. She could offer them the option: upstairs, or the kitchen. But then, if she invited them upstairs, one or both might take it the wrong way, and think she was planning a seduction. It would be better to eat downstairs, and then retire upstairs later for drinks. But even that could be taken the wrong way…

They could retire to the living room, which is what normal people would probably do. People who were accustomed to having dinner parties, that is.

But that was out of the question. She couldn't face the dust. It would need a vacuum the size of a JCB to suck it all out. Besides, it was dark and dingy in there. Upstairs was better;

they would have the view. They would see the sun set, and the moon rise; she rarely closed the curtains in the summer. The room was designed for a romantic evening.

Romance! She wasn't looking for romance! She wanted to hear Nigel's story. He would be totally put off the telling if he thought she'd planned a romantic evening. She must check out the room, and remove any items that might give him ideas.

But that would depend on where he was sitting, where his eyes might wander. She would sit in each chair, and see what he might see. But then, he might decide to move the chair, so what was the point?

She ought to decide on a plan of action; they'll be wanting a cup of tea soon.

She will tidy the lounge, first.

*

They'll be missing you at the pub, said George, hovering in the doorway. Nigel was slicing an onion. He looked up and said, Do you think so? Well, said George, two nights on the trot – they don't see many new faces, apart from passing tourists. Your absence will be noted, I'm sure. Anyway, I'll get out of your way.

It was quite a pleasant change to have two men in the kitchen, cooking a meal, she thought. A first, and very pleasant. She could sit outside, and listen to the sound of the chopping board, the sound of their voices. They were cooking a fish dish, and it smelt delicious.

The kitchen table had been cleared for eating; she had tidied the lounge for sitting. She had shown them what pans to use, what knives, what boards, what plates. Occasionally they called her if they couldn't remember. She sat outside within calling distance, drinking a glass of wine, yet wanting to do something.

She found a broom and swept the yard.

Then Nigel shouted, "Ready!"

They sat down to eat with a smatter of small talk. Portuguese food; their fondness for sardines; different ways of cooking fish; Portuguese wine. Miguel had chosen the wine, a red one from Estremadura. Smooth, full-bodied, richly coloured, with a hint of oak, vanilla and cinnamon – George read this on the label.

Is that where you're from? she asked. Is near, Miguel said. His home is in the south of Portugal. He was brought up in the countryside, not far from Lisbon; his family still live there. Now he lives on the Azores, has been for some years, he said, working on a farm and breeding pigeons.

George has been to France, Italy, Spain, and the north of Portugal; they didn't venture to the south, she said. And that was years ago, when Richard was alive. Now she doesn't go anywhere, she said, apart from Lydiard Forum, and that's mostly for shopping.

There was a pause as they savoured the food. The sound of teeth and gums. Nigel was going to ask her if she felt lonely, but he declined. The question was too personal, he thought; it might embarrass her. George, listening to herself chomping, suddenly felt self-conscious. It's very good, she said. It's very tasty, thank you very much, this really is a pleasant change.

More wine, said Nigel. Yes please, she said, I like this wine. I normally drink white, I find red rather bitter, but this isn't bitter at all, this is very smooth. And full-bodied. With a hint of oak.

She asked Miguel about his pigeons. A good racer fetches a lot of money, he said. People come from Taiwan to buy them, they spend thousands of pounds. He's sold one or two, but he doesn't do it for the money, he said, and it's a problem parting with the birds after training them from a young age; he's very attached to his birds.

Another pause.

Then George turned to Nigel with a twinkle in her eye and said, How long have you been working in archaeology, Nigel?

It was time to confess. A little, at least. I'm actually a

neuroscientist, he said, dropping his fork. I'm what's known as a cognitive neuroscientist. I deal with matters of the brain, I was based at Imperial in London, till I started work on this project. Now I'm working on the Azores.

She didn't ask him about the project. She didn't say anything at all. She knew he wasn't an archaeologist, but neuroscience? What was that all about? He didn't seem the type to be walking round with a scalpel and what have you; he seemed much too gentle. But then, you couldn't tell these days. Look at that Shipman character. He looked fairly innocuous, yet there he was, killing off old ladies because it gave him a thrill, the semblance of being God.

Do you carry out vivisection and that sort of thing, she asked.

Nigel had an inkling as to where this might be leading. George is probably an animal rights activist, he thought. If I say the wrong thing, she might lean over the table and stick a fork up my nose.

No, he said. My work involves studying the brain at work, the human brain. We use scanners and computers. I spend most of my time looking at computer screens, video images. I've never been involved in that sort of work, he said.

Oh, she said. And it's just the brain you work with. Yes, he said, just the brain.

So why am I looking for a tooth, he thought.

And George thought, so why is he looking for a tooth?

That was delicious, she said, clearing the plate. I enjoyed that very much, thank you.

For afters, we thought yoghurt and fruit, said Nigel. More wine? There's plenty more. It was on special offer – three for the price of two. So we bought six – for the price of four.

George was beginning to feel a bit tipsy. She'd forgotten what it was like to feel tipsy; normally she didn't drink. But this was a special occasion. Yes, she said, and moved her glass.

Outside, the owls were starting to mew. A sure sign of dusk approaching.

What is that noise? Nigel asked. I heard it last night, it woke me up. Little owls, said George. There's a family, two young ones, they've just started to fly. Once they get going, they make a hell of a racket. Yes, I've heard, said Nigel.

Miguel served the dessert. Now Nigel too was beginning to feel tipsy. He tried to recall that opening line, his way of explaining their presence here. Science; it involved science.

I thought we could sit upstairs, said George. She didn't look at Nigel. She spooned the yoghurt and said, You haven't seen the upstairs lounge, have you? There's a very good view from the window. Yes, I've noticed the window from the outside, said Nigel. It looks very spectacular.

I will be going to bed soon, said Miguel. If you excuse me please, madame.

Yes, yes of course, said George. This has been arranged, she thought, and said, Thank you for your cooking, Miguel, I enjoyed it very much.

Pleasure, he said.

Miguel's yawn was genuine. He offered to wash up. I'd rather you didn't, actually, said George. Thank you for offering, but I prefer to do it myself. It's just that I know where everything goes, and I have a particular method of washing up, so leave them if you don't mind, and I'll see to it later. Thank you anyway.

Pleasure, he said.

Nigel was very pleased that he'd spoken to Miguel about meeting women. Of course, it all came out sounding rather quaint, but women seemed to like that sort of thing. Especially from a young, handsome, swarthy athletic type.

Miguel excused himself and went to the toilet.

This was the awkward time, for both of them. Sat in the kitchen, alone – George, hoping that Nigel wouldn't think she was hoping for a seduction; Nigel, thinking that George wasn't a fool and would know that Miguel's absence had been arranged. They sat facing each other across the table, looking for something to look at other than themselves, and neither knowing quite what to say.

The toilet was flushed. Then they heard the sound of the tap.

"I'll take the wine upstairs," said George. "Will you carry the glasses?"

She knew that she was blushing, yet she couldn't help it. And her heart was racing as she walked up the stairs, as if she really was leading a lover to her private sanctum.

Nigel followed her into the lounge. The view was a spectacle. He stood by the doorway and marvelled. Magnus Chase spread east and west – from the east, a line of small hills, the silver thread of a river, a forest, a village, a glimpse of a church spire, the valley down below – and further to the west, Lydiard Forum and the castle on the hill, golden in the sun's last rays. And above it all, a vast expanse of sky, still a light blue, and a procession of clouds, blowing from the west.

"Wonderful," he said. "What a wonderful view. It's a wonderful room. A room for contemplation. I could sit all day in a room like this."

"I do, sometimes," she said, smiling. "Take a seat, I've tried to clear a space. I'm afraid it's very cluttered. I don't have many visitors."

"Here?" he said. There were three possibilities; the other chairs were piled high with books and newspapers.

She put the wine on the table; two bottles and a corkscrew.

"Yes," she said, "or that one, I don't mind. I usually sit on that one, but I'll sit over here for a change."

So they sat facing each other, Nigel on the east side, looking west towards Lydiard Forum, and George on the west side, looking at the valley of the River Chuckle. The table was between them, and the empty chair; George's usual seat.

"Cheers," she said.

"Yes, er, good health," he said.

"So," she said. "I suppose Miguel doesn't know much about… your project."

"No," he said, sighing. "I, er, don't know where to begin."

"From the beginning?" she said.

"Yes," he said. "The beginning... Er, can I ask you something?"

"Yes, go on," she said.

"Why do you feed the birds in the summer? I would have thought there was plenty for them to eat."

"It's a habit," she said. "But it's a good one, I think. They know that there's always food here, whatever happens elsewhere. It's not so pressing as it is in winter or spring, but it's best to be constant. Nature's unpredictable, and you can't rely on farmers to provide food. They see birds as pests because they eat seeds and grain and fruit. And the farmers tear out the hedgerows to make it easier to plough, so you have these big prairie fields that you see round here, which means a shortage of plant life and nesting places. They do so many things that affect the food supply. They use chemical sprays that kill off the insects, and they don't care where they spray it, because it's generally contractors who do it. It all has a knock-on effect."

"Modern farming," said Nigel. "It's all about increasing productivity."

"Yes, modern farming," said George. "It's not about wildlife."

"No," said Nigel. "I was interested in your motivation, actually. I can see the ecological reasons. You're ecologically minded, then?"

"No, not particularly. Well, yes, I suppose I am. But that's not the reason why I feed the birds. My motivation, you say?"

She stared at the world outside. The dusk had darkened. Eastwards, it was almost night; westwards, the sky was a dark blue, going lighter as she raised her eyes to the heavens. Then she turned and said, "Basically, I think it's quite simple. It comes down to curiosity."

"Curiosity?"

"Yes. I like observing animals. I like seeing how they interact with one another, how they breed, how they handle

335

stress, how they communicate, that sort of thing. Curiosity. I think they're fascinating, and we can learn from them."

"Oh!" said Nigel.

He was thrown now. This wasn't Walt Disney. This was... science?

"Don't you?" she said. "Aren't you a scientist?"

He laughed, thrown even more now. She was reading his thoughts, it seemed. And turning things on their head.

"Well, yes," he said. "It's funny you should mention curiosity. It was one of the points that naked rambler made, when I was stuck in the ditch. And it's true. Generally, people aren't curious anymore. I'm thinking of young people in particular – the calibre of students these days. They seem content to be mere robots. Science is on the decline because people aren't curious. The seekers after knowledge are few and far between."

"That's because the whole education system is on the decline."

The conversation wasn't moving in the direction that Nigel had planned. But it made his task easier, not harder. They found themselves in agreement over the current state of education – George had worked as a teacher, she knew of the latest developments, she was well informed.

They finished a bottle of wine, started on another. Nigel felt more relaxed now. He had no qualms about telling her the story of Professor Pipi. George would understand, he thought. Curiosity...

"Of course, going back to curiosity, curiosity can be a dangerous thing," he said. "You've heard of Salvador Pipi?"

"Yes," she said. "The man who wants to clone a human?"

"Yes," he said. "Him. Well, some years ago, I was about to take up a new post..."

And he told her the story, beginning with his old college friend, Cecil Redmayne. He told her how he'd lost interest in the project, how he was carrying on only because it suited the ethics committee. He told her how he'd gained Jerry's confidence, secured his trust, played the part of a buffoon to throw off any suspicions that he had a double role.

"That's the worst aspect of it," he said. "I don't think I'm a very good actor."

George stood up and turned on a lamp. Low wattage: it threw a cone of orange into a corner of the room.

"Oh, I don't know," she said, finding her seat. "You had me fooled, for a while. Twice, in fact. First, I thought you were my husband. And then, you had me thinking you were an archaeologist."

"I'm sorry," he said. "But I wasn't very good, was I? King Arthur's tooth – I can't remember where that came from. Miguel is so trusting."

"You still haven't told me about the tooth," she said. "Is it connected with this Brain of Marx Project?"

"Yes," he said. "You may not believe this, but…"

George was horrified. And the relevance of the tooth was still unclear.

"DNA," he said. "It's a solid DNA sample, and it contains valuable data, which Jerry thinks is crucial to the project. Me, I'm not so sure. But I have to go along with it. If there's a possibility of human cloning, I have to be there with the evidence…"

"You mean, he's planning to clone Marx?"

George was even more horrified.

"Possibly, I don't know," he said. "I won't know till I return with the teeth. That's why they're essential. The teeth could be the preliminary stage to a cloned Marx. In which case, I need to catch Jerry in the act."

"This is a fantastic story," she said. "I'm bound to believe you, because nobody could possibly invent such a tale."

"Well, yes," he said. "It is a fantastic story. More wine?"

"Yes please," she said. "You know, you do remind me of Richard."

"I take it as a compliment," he said, reaching for the bottle. "Look, the stars are out!"

"Jupiter," she said. "It's very bright tonight. Thanks. Thish is going down like water."

"Yes, it's... very pleasant," he said.

They sat in silence for a while, watching the stars appear.

Then the owls started a round of whooping.

"I think," said Nigel, "I ought to go to bed."

"Yesh," said George. "I think – me too."

They stood up, turned to the window.

"Do you ever close the curtains?" Nigel said.

"Not in the summer. In winter I do, to keep out the draughts. And the nights are so long."

"There's no one to look in, is there?"

"No," she said.

She had a vision of Stephen Grove, on the other side of the wide valley, looking out through a pair of binoculars. She had an inexplicable urge to throw her arms around Nigel, just in case there was someone watching. Would she regret it in the morning? Maybe; it might lead to other things, she thought. And she wasn't prepared for that.

They edged to the door. They were inches apart. She felt for his arm.

"Shorry," she said. "I'm falling over. I'm feeling very wobbly."

"Let me escort you to the door," he said.

"Can you turn off the light?" she said.

She clung to his arm and followed him as he walked across the room, turned off the lamp, walked back in the half-light.

"It's just next door," she said.

They walked the short distance. She kissed him on the forehead, patted his shoulder, and said, "Goodnight Richard."

"Goodnight George," he said, and watched her stagger through the door.

He heard a bump as she fell on the bed. Then all was silent.

He walked along the corridor, turned off that light.

Into the bedroom. The room was in darkness; there was no moon.

He fumbled for the light switch and looked around.

There was a photograph on top of a wardrobe; he hadn't given it more than a glance before. Now he picked it up and held it to the light. George and Richard. In their younger days, judging from the clothes. But George hadn't changed much at all. And it was a remarkable likeness. Almost like looking into a mirror.

*

Are you still awake? Yes, Bob said, and wondered at the number of times he had heard that question. It was such a stupid thing to ask, he thought. Because, if you weren't, the very act of asking it would wake you up. So why not be straight and say, Wake up, I wanna talk? The protocol of the bedroom! As old as he was, he still couldn't fathom it. Straight talking was forbidden, it seemed.

"Why?" he said, turning.

"I've been thinking," said Liz.

"You don't say," he said.

She poked him in the ribs. She couldn't sleep. The sound of the jets was relentless, and it was too hot to close the window – she wanted that breeze, and the smell of the seaweed.

"About writing *Capital*," she said. "Are you ready for this?"

"Go on. What's the time?"

"I've no idea. Just listen to me and pay attention. I've been thinking about the writing of it – me myself I mean, not the artificial Marx – and I can see what the problem is."

"Your motivation is slack."

"No, my motivation is first-rate. You see, Jerry thinks the problem is one of inspiration. If you have all the material, all you need is that vital spark which… which…"

"Will ignite the world with the fire of communism."

"Just be serious for a minute. The vital spark will enable you to see the structure of the whole, okay? But I don't see

339

that as the problem. I don't think it would take that much inspiration to produce an updated version, taking as your subject matter the developments of the last century. The age of imperialism – World War One, World War Two. The problem, I think, is the latest developments, post-war, the current period."

"What's the problem?"

"I'm coming to it. You have to remember that Marx was writing when there was still a great deal of optimism about science and what it might deliver for the emancipation of us humans. And the idea that we humans are basically rational creatures – that was influential. So, when it came to ideas about how the system would be overturned and an alternative put in its place, you had various scenarios, like people working in the trade union movement, the labour movement, fighting for workers' rights, campaigning for a decent wage, shorter working hours, and so on. All of which was very reasonable, but not compatible with the needs of capitalism and the needs of the bosses, who wanted to increase profits etcetera. So – this is a caricature – the working class would eventually realise that capitalism offers them no escape from drudgery, and that the future lies with organising society on a different basis. It was all seen as a rational process, in terms of consciousness – awareness of the situation, or class consciousness, growing into a greater awareness of the need for change, or revolutionary consciousness. All very rational."

"Yeah – so what's the problem? Now we're all bonkers?"

Liz barked a laugh.

Then suddenly she sat up and said: "Yes, in a way that's it. We've all gone bonkers. I was thinking of the global terror movements being irrational, but yes, we've all been conned."

"Being conned isn't the same as being bonkers. You'll have to explain and it's getting late."

"Okay, so let's get back to Marxism. It was seen by many as a science, personally I still think it is. As a social science, which gives you a framework for understanding society at any given moment in its development. And going back to rationality, the opponents of capitalism were seen as rational creatures – they *were* rational creatures, who realised that society had to be organised in a different way to fulfil its true potential. All that went with the disappearance of communism, so that now, generally speaking, nobody can see any alternative to capitalism. Any rational alternative, that is. Look at Britain – there's no class conflict anymore, there's no class consciousness, so how can there be any revolutionary consciousness? The majority think of themselves as middle class, and they identify with the state when the state declares a war on terror. Whereas before, in the old days, the good old days, we'd be cheering on the Viet Cong in their war against the US."

Bob laughed.

"The good old days," he said. "Things have changed."

"There are no comparable national liberation struggles," she said. "These days, what we have are these terror movements, who strike willy-nilly against anything Western, and declare war in the name of Islam. It's a throwback to the Middle Ages and the Crusades. We're descending into barbarism, with high-tech catapults. And the fightback is totally irrational. What can be more irrational than a suicide bomber, for God's sake? There's no political movement out there with a coherent platform. These people are motivated by anger – against Western imperialism – and they're united by their religious fervour. That's the frightening thing. It means there's no scope for discussion."

"I agree, but I can't see what this has to do with the writing of *Capital*."

"The problem is basically this. We could write a scientific thesis, based on economic analysis, and make certain predictions, based on current tendencies, but… How account for these new developments? That's my question. What place science and rationality in the face of religious fervour?"

Bob noted the "we" but didn't speak. He was beginning to

feel very tired. And he was suffering from another itch; this time, his big toe. At least Liz was lying down again. It was a good sign...

"Marx got it wrong in any case," she continued. "He believed Britain would be the first country in Europe to go through a revolution, partly because of the strength of the labour movement. And also because Britain was, is, the oldest capitalist power, therefore the first to go into terminal decline. Again, it was too rational, you see. He didn't foresee what happened in Russia. And that, when you think about it, was motivated by the irrational. No, I don't mean that. It was motivated by hunger. That's what I'm talking about. Basic human needs, like eating. If society can't provide, it's a good motivator. People will rebel. And the same thing's happening now, in the Middle East. People are angry because they lack basic facilities; they see the West as having everything yet wanting to expand further, to plunder their own country for its riches, minerals, materials, etcetera..."

Bob was beginning to doze off.

He loved the sound of Liz's voice. So sexy, he thought.

"The West wants everything, in their eyes. So what's the result? They fight back, against the West. And there's no politics – what we have is blind anger, because of hunger, and blind destruction, because the West is seen as the enemy. And blind faith, because they're united by Islam, and they see Osama what's-his-name as the only voice who will speak up for them. That's where the irrational enters, because you can't argue with religious fervour. It's a question of faith, not reason. Marx could never have foreseen this. Except that he did, in a way. Barbarism or socialism. We've moved on from the age of imperialism to the age of barbarism. What he couldn't foresee was the form that barbarism would take. What are you doing?"

"Scratching my toe. I hope I haven't got fleas."

"Why should you have fleas? What's Dr Lee been doing to you? On second thoughts, don't answer that, I don't want to know. Now you've got me started…"

An itch, at the back of her knee.

She scratched and said, "Anyway, I think, to give proper consideration to these developments, we would have to delve into Darwin and his analysis of animal behaviour – will you stop scratching? – because what we're really faced with are people who are angry because of hunger, and that forces them to behave in a way that's not dissimilar to animals…"

"Those hijackers weren't hungry."

"What?"

"They were all Arabs from wealthy homes. Fighting for a cause."

"Yes, religious fanatics…"

"Maybe."

"You have other ideas?"

"Not at this hour. Try me in the morning."

"Oh, all right. It is rather late, I suppose. My God! It's nearly five!"

"Three hours of sleep! Liz, what are you doing to me?"

"I'm sorry. I'll shut up."

A jet passed, slicing the silence with its roar.

She couldn't resist: it was becoming automatic. As soon as she stopped talking, her hand was reaching…

"It doesn't seem worth going to sleep now, does it?" she said.

"It'll be worth every minute," he said, and held her hand.

They kissed and slept. And scratched.

*

Liz sat at a terminal, feeling drained. And in no mood for running the software called Dialectical Materialism. Three hours of sleep! Yet her mind was still racing. It was her body that was flagging. Sleep deprivation can send you mad, she thought. There was no risk of that, but she was aware that she was feeling irritable, and that it showed.

When Jerry stood there, looking over her shoulder for the second time that morning, she felt like packing up. Results, results! He was so impatient.

"I don't want to be doing this," she said, staring at the screen.

"What do you mean?"

"This program," she said. "These statistics. This project, in fact. I feel like I've been doing this all my life. This project was meant to be breaking new ground. And what do we end up doing? We're supplying data for the benefit of the World Bank, so they can make informed decisions about monetary policy. We shouldn't be doing this, Jerry. We're meant to be writing a new volume of *Capital*."

"I know exactly how you feel," he said. "I feel the same as you, believe me. I don't want to be doing this either, but there's no alternative. We're lumbered with the funding situation, so what can we do? If we don't produce results, we'll have Dillinger telling us he's terminating the project."

She swivelled her chair and tried to read his eyes.

"Is it really as bad as that?" she said.

"Yes, it's as bad as that. I told you so yesterday."

"I'm not sure you're giving me the full picture," she said.

"I don't know what you mean," he said. "You know more than anyone else. I guess you've told Bob..."

"The full picture includes Humphrey Dillinger's interest in cloning. It includes the use of DNA samples for clandestine purposes."

Jerry was going pink. This was a rare event.

"You'll have to explain," he said, lowering his voice. "The DNA samples are intended for the biocomputer. I thought that was understood – by everybody working on the project."

"Yes, and the purpose of the biocomputer is to produce a new volume of *Capital*, right?"

"Right – so what are you driving at? I can't see the point of this discussion."

"Resolving contradictions, Jerry; that's the point. You said yesterday that Dillinger has other priorities, which don't include producing a book, right? Isn't that what you said?"

"His priority is statistics, that's what I said."

"So why should he fund the biocomputer? Why this urgent need for DNA samples?"

"Because that's my priority, Liz. That's the project's priority. We have a conflict of interests, between the funder's priorities and ours. Surely you can see that?"

"Yes I can, but…"

"But what? Look, I know how you feel, but we all have to do shit work on occasions. If you're not up to working today, why not take the day off, for God's sake. You don't look so good, if you don't mind my saying so…"

"I'd like to have a look at the plant in Sebo. A guided tour."

"Oh! Sure! Why?"

"I think you're hiding things, and it's not good for trust. Nobody's ever seen the inside of those labs, have they?"

"Yes, and there's not a lot to see – Karen Sparks has seen them, Titus Cranfield has seen them – that's where they're based."

"And their interests are in cloning."

"So? Do you have any moral objections to cloning?"

"It's not my field. And it's not what the project is about, is it?"

Jerry looked away. Liz could hear him thinking.

"It wasn't, as originally envisaged," he said.

"And now?"

"There may be possibilities," he said, looking around the room. "The situation is evolving."

"What the hell is that supposed to mean? You're planning on cloning Marx?"

He turned and said, "Liz, we can't have a serious discussion when you're in this sort of mood, and I refuse to be interrogated. I know I've put you under a lot of pressure lately and I'm sorry, you're obviously feeling the strain. I suggest you have the day off. Go home and get some sleep – you look worse than me."

She'd gone too far now; there could be no turning back.

"Jerry, I'd like an honest answer to my question. Is it your intention to attempt to clone Marx? To bring him back from the dead?"

"It may not be possible," he said.

"You're still not answering the question."

"Liz, let me ask you a question. Let's suppose we had the technology to carry out such an act. Karl Marx, one of the world's greatest thinkers – imagine if we could transport him to the here and now. Would that be such a bad thing, do you think?"

"We're not talking about time travel, Jerry. We're talking about cloning."

"Whatever. We're talking about technology, science, scientific research. I'm asking you to use your imagination, Liz. You'd like to see a new volume of *Capital*, right? Okay, and so would I. So imagine – if you could talk to the man who created the original. Wouldn't you want to do that, if it was possible? Wouldn't you?"

"Yes, but…"

"So move a step backwards. Imagine that you could develop the technology that would enable you to do that. Wouldn't you want to develop the technology?"

"I don't know."

"Liz, science has only developed because of people with a mission, whatever that mission might be. They have an idea – call it an obsession – and they pursue it for the rest of their lives, at the expense of everything else. The rest of the world calls them mad – but out of their sweat comes inventions, discoveries, ideas, which no one else has ever thought of…"

"So you're planning to clone Marx? You're developing the technology?"

"We have a lab that's exploring possibilities."

"And Humphrey Dillinger's funding this! I don't understand. He has no interest in producing a book, so why

346

does he want to clone Marx?"

"He doesn't – I do."

"Right! So the secret's out! And Dillinger knows about this? Look, I ought to tell you we've been doing research into this guy, and we know he has an interest in cloning. A big interest – I mean, financially – like, big bucks interest. So I still don't understand."

"We?"

"Bob and me."

"Oh, okay. So now you're digging for dirt."

"No! We just want to know what we're involved in – is that such a bad thing? This is not good for trust, Jerry."

"No, you're right."

"So what's Dillinger's interest? He's into cloning, right. He's investing millions into bio-research. What's he expecting to get out of it? Who does he want to clone?"

"Himself."

"What?"

"He wants to clone himself."

"Oh."

She felt as if her head had been deflated. Someone had pulled out the cork, and now she felt exhausted. She wanted to go home, to bed, to sleep.

Hundreds of Humphrey Dillingers, exporting democracy around the world, taking up posts in Africa, the Middle East, the Far East, anywhere that smelt of a potential market – she could see it all now.

"So," said Jerry. "Now you know. We have another conflict of interests. Humphrey Dillinger wants to clone himself, I want to clone Marx. And so far, no one's been able to clone a human of any description."

"You're working on it, I take it."

"We have a lab."

"Jerry, I think I need a lie down."

"So go and have a lie down."

"Right."

"Before you go, something to think about."

"Haven't you given me enough?"

"It's related."

"Okay, fire away."

"You're not a vegetarian, are you?"

"No. This is related?"

"Yes, I'm talking about science. Let me put it like this. I'd like to see a new volume of *Capital* – so would you. I'd like to talk to the man who wrote the original – so would you. I'd like to develop the technology that would enable me to do this – and here you dither, saying you don't know. And you're meant to be a scientist! I tell you what it's like. It's like wanting to eat meat, yet not supporting the building of abattoirs. People enjoy eating meat, yet the majority wouldn't want to see animals being slaughtered. Fair enough, I'm squeamish too. I don't want to see the inside of an abattoir, but I enjoy eating meat, and I'm not going to argue against the building of abattoirs. The same with technology. People enjoy the fruits of technology, but the majority aren't involved in research and design, and there's no reason why they should be. The designers get on with it, and the people out there enjoy the fruits. So do we stop our research, simply because the majority don't want to see the inside of the abattoir? I think not. Are you following me?"

"Yes, I agree with what you're saying, but cloning…"

"It's a new technology, it's in its infancy. It's always the case that people are squeamish about new technologies. They don't know how it's going to affect them, what the consequences are going to be. This research is going on, independent of you and I. So isn't it better to be involved, and develop it for our own purposes? Think about it. You're a scientist."

"I'm very tired."

He placed a hand on her shoulder.

"Liz," he said. "I know your heart is in this project, and I appreciate the work you've put in. Our goals are the same, believe me. One more thing."

She placed a hand on top of his.

"What's that?" she said

"You've never had children, have you?"

"No."

"Have you ever wanted children?"

"No, not really. My work has always come first."

"As I thought. True dedication. There may be a way of combining the two."

Without being aware of it, Liz had been playing with Jerry's fingers. Now she stopped, thinking, Is he wanting to have sex with me?

"Now what are you thinking of?" she said

"The most difficult stage of the process, assuming we get that far, is the, er, surrogate problem."

"The surrogate problem?"

"Yes. Finding a suitable mother. A surrogate mother, who would play the host, as it were. Or the hostess, I should say. A mother who would incubate the embryo, assuming that we had an embryo to implant. Obviously, it would be best if she were someone who was dedicated to the aims of the project..."

Liz removed her hand. Jerry followed suit.

"Hang on a minute!" she said. "What are you suggesting?"

"I'm asking you, Liz, whether you'd be willing to be a surrogate mother. A mother to the new Marx, if the cloning process is successful. I'm thinking ahead."

"Right! That's it! I'm logging off!"

She was standing now.

"Just think about it," he said. "That's all I'm asking. This is still in the planning stages. Karen Sparks has expressed an interest. She was quite taken by the idea."

"Was she? She's younger than me, Jerry. Less chance of a miscarriage."

"Liz, don't be offended. Think of what it could mean for posterity."

"Yes, of course. And for science. Where's my bag?"

Jerry stood there dumbfounded. Liz was pissed off with the statistics, she was eager to produce the new *Capital*. What better way to be involved in its production than to be the mother to the man who was best suited to write it? If no one was forthcoming, they would have to use an incubator. Very unreliable, he thought.

"I'm off," she said. "See you later."

"Think about it," he shouted.

No reply – she stormed out.

4

The man was a nutter. On that point, they were both in agreement. But what should they do about it? Liz, sat on a chair, confronted the supine Bob.

"Do you think he planned this from the start?" she said.

"There was no indication," said Bob. "When I started working on it, the project was one of economic forecasting, pure and simple. The World Economy and Enterprise Project – you remember, creep?"

"WEEP! How could I forget?" she said.

She wanted to resign – today.

"He was so straight-faced about it," she said. "He was asking me because he thought he was doing me a favour. I told him to stick with Karen Sparks. This is serious, Bob. I can't work with him anymore."

Bob told her to hold her fire.

"We should wait till Nigel gets back," he said. "We need to talk to Nigel. He's not gonna support this. If we all walk out, the project will collapse."

"I'm not so sure it will," she said. "And I don't think everybody'll want to walk out. Karen Sparks, for instance. There are people who were invited here because of their interest in cloning – they're not going to walk out. The project has changed, Bob, you said so yourself. Aren't there laws on this sort of thing?"

"There are national laws," he said. "They vary from country to country."

"And what's the law in the US? If they can clone cats and dogs, what's to stop them cloning humans?"

"We're not in the US, Liz. We're on Portuguese territory. I don't know what their law says about it, but I can't imagine a country of devout Catholics is gonna condone human cloning. Problem is they know little about the project; they think it's military research."

"Are there no international laws?"

"No. Who makes international law? There's no such thing. There are treaties, conventions, resolutions, but there ain't no body that makes international law. For that, you need an international government, and there ain't none. Okay, the UN makes international law, but they're laws only on paper. There's no enforcement, is there? Let's face it, the UN's a joke. And the laws in the US vary from state to state. In some states, reproductive cloning is banned, in others it's not. Jerry could set himself up in California, no problem."

"The point is, what are we going to do about it? I want to resign. Now."

"Let's wait till Nigel gets back. Nothing's going to happen before then. Nothing may happen at all. His plan will take years to implement, and I don't think it'll happen. Too pie in the sky, the whole thing's a nonsense."

"I'm not so sure. His mind is fixed, he's got people working on it, and we don't know how long they've been working on it. That chemical plant was here when you arrived. How do you know when it became operational? I think we ought to stop him now, before he gets too far down the line."

"Liz, it's not my immediate concern right now. Take a look at this."

Bob lowered the sheet, to reveal a chest covered in red blotches.

"My God," she said, "you've got measles. Have you called a doctor?"

"I spoke to Dr Lee. She should be here shortly. It's not measles, Liz. They showed up after I took a shower this morning."

"They may be bed sores. You've been lying in bed for too long, Mr Rheingold. Let's have a look. My God, your back's covered in them. They look like insect bites."

"They feel like insect bites, and they itch like crazy. I think I've got fleas."

"I can't see any. Fleas are pretty big. Can you feel them jumping?"

"There's no jumping, just a terrible itch. They must be bites, I'm sure."

"If you've got fleas, it means I've probably got them too. Don't start scratching! You'll make it worse!"

There was a knock on the door. Bob pulled up the sheet.

"This'll be Dr Lee," he said. Then he shouted, "Hello?"

"Lee," said a woman's voice.

Liz walked to the door. Dr Lee won't be expecting to see me here, she thought. As she opened the door, she felt a rush of triumph. Which evaporated when she saw the face on the other side.

It was covered in red blotches.

*

George was late. Even the swallows had failed to stir her. As she walked down the stairs, her head bounced and throbbed with each step. She'd forgotten what it was like to have a hangover.

There was no one in the kitchen. She went into the utility room to sort out the bird food. Then she heard a shout, outside.

She stood at the front door. Miguel was crouching in the grass, the scythe in one hand, covering his head with the other. Nigel was kneeling in the strawberry patch, both hands over his head. And the swallows – the invaders – were making a racket, diving at the two and bombing them with droppings.

They'd started on their second brood, it seemed.

"Hello!" she called. "You'd better come in for a minute. I'm just about to make a pot of tea."

They ran for cover.

"Damn things!" said Nigel, wiping his sleeve.

"They're nesting," said George. "And those two pairs are

pests. They've dived at me before now. I thought they'd moved on, but obviously not."

"And you feed them!" said Nigel.

"I don't feed the swallows," said George. "They look after themselves. They live on a diet of flies. Have you had anything to eat?"

"We thought we'd wait for you," said Nigel.

"Oh," she said. "Well, you could have helped yourselves. Have you been up long?"

"About an hour," said Nigel.

They sat in the kitchen.

"I'm glad you're carrying on," she said. "With the garden, I mean."

"No problem," said Miguel.

"We intend to finish the job," said Nigel.

"I'm very grateful," she said.

"It's a pity the birds aren't," said Nigel, inspecting his shirt.

"I'll go and talk to them," she said. "Can you see to the tea?"

She went out.

Nigel looked at Miguel. Miguel smiled. Nigel, shaking his head, noticed for the first time that Miguel was missing at least three teeth. He looked away and listened. George was delivering a lecture.

Why can't you behave? You're a disgrace. This is no way to behave. I won't let you nest here if you carry on like this. Look at that other family – they don't carry on like you. Why can't you be like them? You should be ashamed. Just stop it, will you. I've had enough of this. Are you listening to me? I won't tell you again. Just stop it…

"Classroom management," Nigel muttered, and rose to pour the tea.

"So have they understood?" he said, when George walked in.

"Probably not," she said. "This lot aren't very bright."

"The voice of reason," said Nigel. "Even humans have

354

difficulty with that. I can't imagine birds doing any better. I don't mean to be insulting, but I can't imagine them understanding a word of what you said, let alone taking notice."

"How would you know?" she said.

It was her hangover speaking. She felt very irritable.

"Well," he said, and faltered.

"You don't think birds have any reasoning powers? You don't think that they listen?"

"They may listen, but do they understand?"

"Probably not, but I think one has to try," said George. "To communicate, I mean."

Nigel was struck by a vision. He was sitting on a plane, talking to Liz Kendal. They'd only just met. They were on a flight from Moscow, and he was talking about animal intelligence. Specifically about parrots, and their ability to learn human language. Not simply to repeat words that they'd heard, but to use them in other contexts. To communicate. The words had a meaning for them. They had an understanding.

George lowered her voice.

"Sorry, I didn't mean to be so ratty," she said. "It's just that I've been observing them for a long time. It was some years before I realised that they might be talking to me, as well as themselves. The swallows, especially. Their language is quite sophisticated. They have different kinds of warning calls for different kinds of threats. They're very organised, especially when it comes to nesting. One of them acts as a messenger, keeps watch and warns the others. They tell other birds too. And they tell me, if it's urgent. I scare off the predators. They come and nest here every year, you see. I've been learning their language. They have one kind of call if the threat is on the ground, and another kind if the threat is in the air. And then there's the intensity of the call, plus its duration and repetition, which tells you how serious the threat is, and also how close, though I haven't quite worked it all out yet. It's

355

like a kind of Morse code. I'm sure if you knew how it worked, you could tell how far away the threat is. You might even be able to identify the threat. I know if there's a sparrow hawk about, because they circle round it, up in the air. Other threats they might dive-bomb…"

"Yes, so we discovered," said Nigel. "I'm sorry too, I didn't mean to sound so, so…"

"Human-centred," said George. "I don't think humans are the only creatures on this planet who use reason. Animals use reason, though it may not appear to us as reason."

"I don't know. It may be that they're more reasonable than us," said Nigel, thinking of Jerry Mendoza. "It's a bone of contention with scientists as to whether animals think…"

"I'm sure they do," said George. "On the basis of my observations, at any rate."

"Perhaps we could talk about this later," said Nigel. "But while we're on the subject of bones…"

"Ah yes, bones. I didn't say anything silly last night, did I?" said George.

"Silly? No. Why?"

"I was a bit tipsy."

"I wasn't completely sober myself."

"I didn't misbehave?"

"Misbehave! No, not at all. It's them outside I'm worried about."

"I'll just see what they're doing," George said, and went out.

Nigel turned on the grill.

"They've quietened down now," said George, returning. "I think it may have been a squirrel. They get very excited, those two. They're not the usual ones who nest here. They think they own the place. I'm sorry about that."

"Bones, George," said Nigel. "You still haven't told me…"

"No I haven't, have I? Let's see to the toast, and then I'll show you. I'm glad you're doing the strawberry patch, by the way. It needed doing."

356

"I think it all needs doing," said Nigel.

"Yes, but some parts I'd like to keep wild. There's a nettle bed and a thistle bed, for a start. They're good for insects and caterpillars and butterflies."

"Right," said Nigel. "In that case, you'll have to direct me."

An hour later, George was showing Nigel the mound. The mound rose at the bottom of the garden, in a corner by the stream. Nigel hadn't walked down this end.

"I planted it here," she said, waving a hand. "Next to the mound."

"What is it?" he said. "It looks like a heap of rubble."

"It is," said George, staring at it. And then she said, "This is the mound," as if that explained everything.

"Right," said Nigel. "The mound."

The mound was indeed a mound – made up of broken house bricks, bits of old paving, flagstones, slates, bits of guttering – all of which could be spotted through the tufts of grass, the piles of soil.

"It's a rubbish heap, is it?" said Nigel.

George hesitated.

"Yes," she said, finally. "Though it's not our rubbish. It was here when we moved. There was a building here at one time. You see, the people who lived here before us used to breed dogs."

Nigel looked at the heap.

"Dogs?" he said, frowning.

"Yes, they used to breed boxers. They had kennels here, apparently. And this bit," she said, waving a hand at the side of the mound, "was where they buried them."

Nigel looked at her.

"It's an animal cemetery," she said. "Well, a dog cemetery actually. I suppose they had to bury them somewhere, the ones they didn't sell. They don't live forever, do they? What do you do with a dead dog? I don't think there's many down there."

"Right," said Nigel, raising the shovel. "An animal

357

cemetery. And this is where you buried the tooth?"

"Yes," she said.

He lowered the shovel, put his foot on it. A few inches down, it struck the rubble. He levered the soil away. Underneath, strewn among the rubble, was a pile of bones. And a pile of teeth.

"I'm sorry," she said. "You'll have your work cut out, won't you?"

Nigel had gone a milky shade of white.

"I think," he said, "I could do with another cup of tea. I feel rather faint."

*

Lunch – Nigel was starving. He couldn't face another cheese sandwich. He offered to organise a fry-up. They'd bought sausages, bacon, eggs, beans – from Templetons. George didn't want any; she'd have a cheese sandwich, she said. She hovered in the doorway. Nigel gathered the ingredients. Then the pans, following George's directions.

"I don't suppose you'd recognise it, would you?" he said.

"No," she said. "Not among that lot. I did think it was a dog's tooth, I wasn't sure. It seemed the natural place for it. Wouldn't you recognise it?"

"I have the other one as a guide. They're both canines, which is unfortunate. But hopefully they should match."

Miguel was still outside, cutting the grass. He'd passed the halfway stage now. And by the bench outside, Nigel had placed a carrier bag, laden with teeth.

"I wonder how I'd get it through customs," he said, cracking an egg. "How would I explain a bag full of teeth?"

"I've no idea," said George. "You're intending to take the whole bag?"

"I'll have to, if I can't find the one we want."

"It all seems rather futile," she said. "The whole plan."

"I agree," he said. "But I'm working for someone who

doesn't. He's on a different wavelength altogether. A different planet."

"When do you think," she said, "you might be wanting to go?"

"Don't worry," he said. "We'll finish the garden first. Anyway, as things stand, we can only fly as far as Lisbon. Then we go by boat. Unless the restrictions have been lifted. It'll take ages, and I'm not looking forward to it."

"I'll put the news on," she said, and turned on the radio.

The war had little coverage. The US have stepped up their bombing raids, said the newsreader. And that was about it. No news of targets, no news of casualties. The war wasn't news, it seemed. And George thought: the banality of bombing.

Next item – a snippet. Observers have noted that the fatal tidal wave in South-East Asia, which killed several thousand people, has made no impact on the area's wildlife. No bodies of animals, no dead birds have been found. Commentators suggest that animals have an intuitive warning system which alerted them to the threat.

And now the weather…

She turned it off.

"So," she said. "Did you hear that?"

"Yes," he said. "It sounds like we'll be catching the boat."

"Oh," she said. "I didn't mean that. I meant… never mind. I'll call Miguel."

They sat and ate and talked about the next meal. Miguel was keen to cook again. Nigel said they'd have to go shopping. Miguel said there were leftovers from the night before. George said she'd have to go easy on the wine. Her hangover was lingering.

Nigel was eager to inspect the teeth.

But he'd promised, so after lunch he returned to the strawberry patch.

He was becoming more attracted to the idea of gardening. You had tangible results. Instant too. It was quite satisfying, he thought. You felt as though you'd actually done a job.

A job. A proper job!

Unlike academe, he thought, where results may take years to materialise. And then, were they ever that tangible? If you were inventing something, designing something, producing an artefact, then yes. But in his field, it was experiments and findings, to be written up in research papers, monographs, conference proceedings.

Slow progress, unless you were privileged with a revolutionary new theory. And then you might be ostracised for criticising the orthodox.

He wasn't far off retirement age.

And then what?

*

Sat upstairs by the picture window, George couldn't see much of the garden; only the bottom bit, including the mound. She sat with a cup of rosemary tea, watching two blackbirds, one chasing the other. They were both male. The one in pursuit was very playful.

She was struck by that news item. It confirmed what she'd been thinking for some time. How do you define intelligence? She had often pondered the question. Because generally, she thought, humans were self-obsessed creatures, who saw themselves as the most intelligent species on the planet. The superior being.

There were these evolutionary people who said that our superiority came at the starting gate – the moment when we decided to stop swinging from the trees and stand on two feet. Standing on two feet made us superior, they said. Fair enough, she thought, but birds have two feet. And they can fly. It took thousands of years before we took to the air, and then, only with the aid of machines.

Ah, yes, but machines! Who else makes machines? We are the supreme tool producer, so the argument goes, and it all began with flints – using our hands to make tools.

But then, she wondered, are we the only creature who makes tools? And what if we are? Does that make us more intelligent? Intelligent when it comes to making tools, maybe, but our tools are now so enmeshed into our lives that we've become dependent on them. Could we do without them? Without tools that help us to move, tools that help us to work? It was inconceivable. So what happens when a tool breaks down? Chaos. Panic. We're lost, helpless, no better than a newborn babe. Who else is so dependent on tools? And is dependency a sign of intelligence? Surely not, she thought.

And then, there was the language argument. Our language is the most sophisticated, so the argument goes. It was the use of language that made our brains expand and evolve – as if the size of the brain was an indicator of intelligence. And as for language, it had taken scientists an age to find out that other creatures had communication systems which were just as complex as ours, and they still had much to learn. She too was still learning.

The arguments were so human-centred, she thought. Our superiority was taken for granted. Discussions about it focused on the evolutionary question: how did we become this superior being? Nobody questioned the nature of our intelligence.

But then, intelligence was generally the province of psychologists. Being scientists, they liked to measure things. Was intelligence something you could measure? This she doubted.

But for scientists, she thought, it had to be measurable; otherwise, there was no science. So you had IQ tests and the like, designed by psychologists such as Eysenck. You were given a score, an intelligence rating.

A cow, though, wouldn't know how to complete such a test, or even start it. Their hooves weren't suitable for holding pens, and they'd yet to pass a basic literacy test. A cow would stare at you blankly if you showed her the form. She would chew the cud and stare, and question the nature of your intelligence in asking her to do such a ridiculous thing.

So when it came to animal intelligence, scientists had to think of something else.

They designed experiments, intended to show how clever or how stupid a creature was. All of which seemed to be based on food. The question: could an animal develop a new method or learn how to use a tool for finding food? Generally they could, so scientists were forced to agree that animals possessed this thing called intelligence, though some were more intelligent than others. Animals, that is.

But scientists, being human-centred, seemed to resent the finding. Intelligence and thought were assumed to be human characteristics, features of our superiority. So they designed experiments that were increasingly more difficult for the creatures.

A monkey, presented with a Rubik's cube. If he solves the puzzle, he's given a plate of chips. If he can't solve it, he's not so intelligent after all. That sort of thing.

Preposterous, George thought. Perhaps he decides it's not worth the effort; perhaps he doesn't like chips; perhaps he's concerned about his weight. And perhaps he's more intelligent than us. Now there's a thought!

And then there was the question of emotions. On the news recently, it was reported that scientists had made the earth-shattering discovery that animals could express a range of emotions. Didn't we know this already? Hadn't Darwin alluded to the fact, over a hundred years ago? Talk about reinventing the wheel!

George found it all rather depressing. Scientists spent large amounts of public money proving things that were intuitively obvious to anyone who took the time to look and listen.

The philosophers fared a little better, in her opinion. Being philosophers, they were less concerned with measurement, so they might give you a broader definition of intelligence, which may or may not be measurable. There was no agreement on how to measure intelligence, or even how to define it, but at least they talked about such matters.

She remembered a discussion on the radio, two weeks ago. A philosopher had argued that you couldn't compare one species with another as far as intelligence was concerned, because there was no uniform measure that you could apply to all species. You could only compare bird with bird, human with human. And you could only conclude that some birds were more intelligent than other birds. The same with animals; the same with humans.

Which sounded very reasonable, she thought.

But then, when it came to the question of superiority, people did make the comparison, and argued that we humans are the superior being.

Ultimately, she thought, it was founded on the struggle to survive argument, which came from Darwin. We are superior because we are the survivors, who have multiplied and expanded, so that now we can be found in all corners of the globe.

True in a way, she thought, but what about the future?

Thanatos, for a start. The suicidal urge. The urge to bomb.

And then, the struggle for resources, the ecological problems.

Interdependency, that was the thing. If every other species died out, it was logically impossible for humans to survive.

And then, that tidal wave. Who died, and who survived?

If only, if only…

Look and listen. And take note. Other creatures do it. We humans used to, but now we've wrapped ourselves up in our mobile multimedia machines, she thought.

Intelligence – the ability to survive without doing any damage.

If comparisons must be made, she decided, and on that criteria, then humans as a species come pretty low on the scale.

And now she felt certain that it was he who always made such a fuss at dusk. A flapper, for sure, and George had discovered his secret. There on the wall, he'd come out of the

363

hedge-closet. The blackbird was gay. What did Darwin say about that sort of thing?

*

Nigel couldn't handle the bag of teeth. He'd do it later, he said. Or tomorrow. That would be better. In the morning; he would get up early.

"I've forgotten what day it is," he said. "You'll have to remind me."

"Thursday," said George. "What are you planning on cooking?"

They were standing in the kitchen. Food time was approaching.

"It's a variation on last night's dish," said Nigel. "Miguel's organising it, I'm the assistant."

"He's very good, isn't he?"

"Yes, he's very talented."

"He's worked wonders with that scythe. About three-quarters done, would you say?"

"Yes, I should say. By this time tomorrow, you should have a lawn."

"A lawn! It'll make a change from having a field. It hasn't been done for years. Richard was the gardener, not me."

"You'll have a pile of silage for the farmers if that lot could be bagged up. In fact, we have a slight problem with the grass cuttings. Miguel's been piling them up on the other side of the stream, as you suggested, but it's rather a mountain I'm afraid. It's threatening to topple over."

"Oh dear. And the compost bins are all full, I suppose."

"Yes. There's a spare corner behind the shed at the far end. The tool shed. We could pile some there."

"Right. Well, do that then, and I'll have to sort it out. I feel I should be paying you for this."

"Don't be silly. We thought we should be paying you for the accommodation, so perhaps we can agree to call it quits."

"That's fine by me."

"Good. You were right about local curiosity, by the way. We've had more stares today from people stopping in the lane. Three minutes later, they're driving down again. They're incredibly nosy, aren't they?"

"I warned you. They're checking up on you. God knows what stories are doing the rounds. If you weren't outside, they'd suspect we were up to hanky panky. Me with two men! That's how their minds work."

She laughed at the idea, as if the scenario was totally implausible.

Then, thinking of blackbirds, she said, "Mind you, I suppose I'd be the same. One can't help but speculate."

Staring at the window, she looked very serious.

"It's only natural," said Nigel. "I guess not a lot happens around here. People like to fill in the gaps."

"You wouldn't believe the gossip! Nobody talks about what's happening in the world, unless it affects them. It's all about what Mrs Whatsit said to Mrs So-and-So."

"It's probably more interesting than what's happening in the world, I should imagine. Real people with real problems."

"Well, yes, it can be interesting. I didn't mean to sound snobbish. You surprise me though. I thought, being an academic…"

Another glance at the window.

"Yes? Being an academic, what?"

George was blushing. She wished she hadn't said that now. She couldn't think of a reply that wouldn't sound rude. She was saved further embarrassment by Miguel's entrance.

Miguel looked swiftly at them both.

"I am sorry madame, I am intertruding," he said.

"No, no, do come in," she said. "We were just talking about the meal."

"You are not hungry?"

"Yes, I am. I was just telling Nigel which pans to use."

"Ah, yes! Pans!"

George left them to it. Sweeping the yard, she felt she had achieved very little that day. She wondered – not for the first time – why it was that doing very little was actually very tiring. For some reason, Carol McGregor sprang to mind. What would they talk about when they next meet? Strangely, it gave her a thrill to think about it. Their next meeting seemed a long way off.

They sat down to eat in the kitchen.

George was curious about the scythe. Why were they carrying a scythe in the car?

"Were you expecting to do some gardening?" she said.

"I bought it in the heat of the moment," said Nigel. "We were anticipating an encounter with the man who showed up here. I was advised to bring a weapon, just in case."

"Oh!" she said. "A weapon!"

"Yes, though God knows what I would have done with it. In fact, I'd forgotten we had it until Miguel mentioned it."

"I can't imagine you using it," said George. "As a weapon, I mean. How ghastly! Were you planning on slicing his head off?"

Nigel choked.

"I hadn't really thought about it," he said, laughing. "It was more of a deterrent."

He asked George whether she fancied going to the pub tonight.

"I don't think so," she said. "I go there very rarely. I've no objections to the pub, it's just that it can be a bit awkward. You never know who's going to be in there. You have to be prepared to chat, you see. It's not a place you can hide away in a corner. I'm not sure if I can handle it tonight. Maybe tomorrow. You'll still be here, won't you?"

"Er, yes," said Nigel. "You'll have to tell us if we're outstaying our welcome."

"Oh, not at all!" she said. "Don't mention it!"

A pause; then she said, "We can sit upstairs again, if you like."

"Fine," said Nigel.

"And Miguel," she said. "If he wants to."

"Hmm?"

Miguel's mouth was full.

"The lady's inviting us upstairs, Miguel," said Nigel.

"Pleasure," said Miguel. "But I am very tired, I am sorry…"

"You'll manage a glass of wine with us, Miguel," said Nigel.

Miguel was confused. Was his company required or not? Last night, no. Tonight, what?

Nigel had to spell it out for him.

"Come upstairs for a bit," he said. "Before you go to bed. You must see the view, it's wonderful."

So they all trooped upstairs.

Miguel was stunned by the panorama. George placed him in the middle, in her usual seat. He swept a hand over the view. He had been to England before, he said, for pigeon racing, but he hadn't seen anything like this. The countryside was beautiful here, he said.

George was now on her second glass of wine. She was taking it easy, she said. Nigel was on his third, as was Miguel.

She'd wanted to ask Nigel for his opinion as to whether animals think, but now they were all sat up there, reclining, she didn't have the inclination.

Sometimes, she thought, it was nice just to sit and not talk about weighty matters. It was nice just to sit and not talk at all, in fact, but simply to look at the view and watch the day's ending.

Intelligence – knowing when to speak.

She'd just thought of that definition. It could only apply to humans, of course. But no – it applied also to birds, and to animals. Sparrows were generally chattering all the time, for instance, and they weren't so high in the Bird IQ table. Was there a correlation?

"Is that your phone?" said Nigel.

"Oh yes, so it is," said George. "I'm glad you've heard it, I don't know what I was thinking of."

She rushed downstairs.

It was the first time that Nigel had heard the phone ring. He found it hard not to believe that George was a rather lonely person.

Miguel was dozing off.

Downstairs, George's voice. Too muffled to hear the words. It sounded like "oh," repeated. Or was it "no"?

Miguel was snoring. Nigel gave him a nudge.

"Oh… oh… quite all right…"

Nigel caught the odd phrase; then he heard George's footsteps, coming up the stairs.

"That was a surprise," she said. "That was Mary Holloway, a friend of mine, asking me if I was all right. She'd heard about the burglar and the police turning up. I suppose the whole of Magnus Chase has heard about it by now. She was asking about you two. People must think you're holding me captive. Oh well! It's nice to know that people are thinking of you."

Miguel excused himself; he couldn't stay awake.

As the sound of his feet reached the bottom of the stairs, Nigel said, "He's very in tune with nature. Up at dawn and bed at dusk. Or thereabouts."

"I'm a bit like that," said George. "In spring and summer at least. Not in winter though; you'd spend most of your time in bed."

"Can I ask you a personal question?" said Nigel.

"Oh! Go on then," said George. "Nobody asks me personal questions."

Nigel was slightly alarmed by George's smile. He hoped he wasn't about to open a can of worms.

"I was curious about your husband," he said. "Has he been dead long? If it's too painful to talk about it, don't worry, we can talk about something else. We can talk about birds."

"No, I don't mind," she said. "He died ten years ago, almost to the day."

"Oh!" said Nigel. "As long ago as that."

He wished he hadn't said that. It sounded rather callous,

as though George was too fond of Richard's memory. The trace of her smile was overcast now.

"I'm sorry," he said. "That was brutish of me. It must have been a big upset. Still is, I should imagine. Was it... sudden?"

"Yes. We'd only been here just over a year. A year and three months, to be precise. We'd both taken early retirement, we were both teachers. It was very traumatic. He was run over. It was a hit and run accident. We were crossing the road, just by the pub. I still have nightmares about it."

"I am sorry. I didn't mean to pry."

"No, no, it's good to talk about it. The worst thing..."

She looked into her lap at her clasped hands. Her fingers were constantly moving.

"The worst thing," she said, looking at Nigel, "was that it could have been avoided. Richard stopped to pick up a worm. He was bending down in the middle of the road. He didn't hear the car till it was too late. Neither did I. I'd already crossed, you see. I saw him trying to pick it up. You know what worms are like. They curl up, and he was struggling to grab hold of it, it was so slippery I suppose. I didn't wait, I went striding ahead. Then I heard the car and a bump, and I turned and... Oh God!"

She held her face. She was shaking.

"I'm sorry," he said.

He waited, not sure whether to go over and comfort her. The moment soon passed.

"I'm sorry," she said, releasing her face. "It still upsets me when I think about it. Can we talk about something else now, please?"

"Of course, of course," he said.

"Why don't we talk about you?" she said.

"Me?" he said.

"Yes, you," she said. "Have you ever been married, Nigel?"

And Nigel thought: truly, a can of worms.

*

369

The next morning, Nigel, kneeling among the weeds, wondered what he was getting involved in. No, he'd never been married. He'd been informally engaged once, he said, in a previous life as a student. That was in Cambridge, and their career paths had taken them to different locations. They saw each other at weekends, for two years, until Denise made that announcement. There was someone else; they were getting married.

There had been episodes since, he said. Brief encounters, which didn't result in anything long-term. His career was half the problem. The people he met were also career-minded, and there was little space for relationships on either side – he and a potential partner were never in the same place long enough to become more than friends, he said. And for the last ten years, he'd spent much of his time on planes, flitting here, there and everywhere. Never a dull moment, he said, but no, I've never been married.

And now he asked himself, why did I tell her all this?

Because, he recalled, he'd asked her a personal question which had given her grief. Feeling that he owed her something. His turn to confess.

It was all getting a little complicated, he thought. He had a vague memory that he'd intended to check the bag of teeth this morning. But talking to George, he'd forgotten about it.

Strange, the ground they were covering. This morning – the question of animal intelligence. George had raised the subject: she was very perky this morning. They'd ended up talking about parrots and their ability to learn human language. Yes, that topic! Which George had prompted, talking about feeding the parrots. What parrots, he asked. I'm talking about the greenfinch, she said, I think of them as my little parrots, they're very parrot-like, they're very happy crunching seeds all day. And do you talk to them, he asked. Yes, of course, she said, but our conversations are private. Fair enough, he said. Not as private as she believed though; he'd heard her calling, "Finchy, finchy! Seeds are out!" God knows what the parrots made of it. Finches, rather. Anyway, that was the cue for a discussion about parrots and language, and the whole question of animal intelligence.

He couldn't imagine talking to a greenfinch. But his imagination was spartan, as Cecil Redmayne had said. He couldn't imagine talking to a parrot, yet people did. George said she knew someone who had a pet canary that talked. Or was it a budgie? Whatever, George said he ought to try talking to a greenfinch. Let's both do it, she said. We could organise language lessons.

God! The idea was mad! His field was the human brain, he wouldn't know where to start. Was there a textbook on the subject? A primer, like Janet and John? Beaky and Twitters go looking for seeds...

He didn't know much about animal intelligence. George seemed to know far more than he did. He didn't know much about nature, or gardening come to that. Yet he wasn't looking forward to leaving. And leave they must.

He would take the whole bag, and tell Jerry to sort it out.

All this fuss for a second tooth. And what a palaver, if he lost the first. Then what? The brain of Marx would be inspired by a dead dog.

Or not, as the case may be.

Damn it all! Tonight they would all go out, and search for the meaning of life. At the pub.

*

Lunch was tense. Nigel and Miguel were sat at the kitchen table, dunking bread into bowls of leek and potato soup. George was putting pans in cupboards. Nigel said they ought to do some shopping for the weekend. But how long is a weekend? That calculation wasn't on his mental agenda, and his suggestion raised the question of their departure.

"Do you want to come along?" he said to George.

"No, I don't think so," she said. "I always do my shopping on a Monday."

"We have the car," said Nigel. "It would save you the bus trip. You could stock up."

"Thanks, but no," she said. "I quite enjoy the bus trip actually. It's a social occasion. I meet all the regulars."

"Hmm," said Nigel. "I hadn't thought of that. But you could still catch the bus on Monday and do the shopping today."

"I could," she said, "but I have a routine. It's quite involved. I'd rather go on Monday."

"Okay," he said. "So we'll just get some things for the weekend. Tonight, tomorrow, and... Sunday. And then... Well, I think we ought to be heading back on Sunday."

"Yes, I thought you might," she said. "I was going to ask, but I didn't want you to think I was trying to get rid of you."

"No, no," he said, "it's a fair question. I hadn't really thought about it, to be honest. I suppose I should."

He chewed a chunk of bread.

Then he said, "We, er, haven't started on the hedges."

"That's all right," she said. "I wasn't expecting you to. The birds are still nesting. The end of September, beginning of October is a better time. When the swallows have gone. Another time."

Nigel wondered. Was she dropping a hint?

She closed a cupboard door and turned to them both.

"I, er, I'll be sorry to see you go," she said. "It's been good having you here. Good for me anyway. I rarely have people coming to stay."

Nigel looked at her.

Her wan smile. The sadness in her eyes.

"Good for us too," he said. "We've enjoyed it. Perhaps we can come again. And, er, carry on with the garden."

"Yes, do," she said. "That would be great."

She looked brighter now, as if a hurdle had been leapt.

"Right, well, let's not get maudlin," said Nigel. "Tonight,

George, we're taking you out. You're going to join us on our quest. We're looking for the meaning of life."

*

George didn't know what to wear. It's a Friday night, she said. People dress up on Friday nights. Typical woman, Nigel said to himself, the words rising unbidden from the depths. Always fretting about their appearance, he thought. And to George he said, You look quite acceptable as you are.

Typical man, George said to herself, the words rising unbidden from the depths. Any old rags will suffice as long as they're served at the bar, she thought. And to Nigel, she said, Do you think so? I'll just have a look upstairs.

Nigel washed the plates. George had supplied him with instructions. Miguel was having a nap.

Fish and chips weren't very wise, Nigel thought. He felt bloated. A good idea at the time though; it saved cooking. And the fish was surprisingly very good. He'd driven into Lydiard, shopped at Templetons – which was open all hours – gone to the fish and chip shop that George had recommended, and brought them back to eat at the house.

The tension at lunch was forgotten now. They were all in a celebratory mood, prompted by the transformation of the meadow. It was almost complete, thanks to Miguel, with a little help from Nigel in shifting the cuttings. The remaining portions were tidying-up jobs, trimming borders and corners and awkward bits by trees and bushes; Miguel had said he'd finish them in the morning. He'd worked hard today in an attempt to finish the job, so Nigel had done the shopping on his own.

Which was quite an achievement too, he thought. He hated shopping. And Friday wasn't a good day; the aisles were packed. His second visit, and he still didn't know where to find things. The signs weren't much use. Why was Marmite stuck on a shelf labelled desserts? Was Marmite a dessert?

This was news to him; he often had it for breakfast, spread on a piece of toast. The stackers were untrained imbeciles, he thought; they needed lessons in basic Aristotle.

Upstairs, George rummaged through a wardrobe. She chose a dress she hadn't worn for years, not since Richard's time. The thing with fashion, she thought, is that it cycles round. Keep an item long enough, and you'll be dressed à la mode. This one she'd bought from Stags and Hinds, the country clothing shop in Stanton Parva which had lasted less than a year. Richard had bought a jacket and a pair of trousers. It was part of their attempt to fit in with their new surroundings. Was it in fashion? It was very Laura Ashley. The ladies at the Lavender Club wore similar designs. This one – flowers and vines in reds and browns and golds – looked a little autumnal. But she liked it. She put it on.

Nigel gulped when she entered the kitchen. George was wearing a curtain, he thought. It reminded him of the drapes that used to hang up at his Aunt Mabel and Uncle Bill's house, about fifty years previous. Passed on now, bless them.

"Oh, very charming," he said.

"I thought I'd try something different," she said, reddening. "I rarely go out. I just need to find a cardigan."

Nigel was a bit stuck for clothes. So was Miguel. They didn't know they'd be away this long. Now everything needed washing; more than once probably.

George came in again, wearing a brown cardigan.

"George, your washing machine…" said Nigel.

"You want to use it?" she said. "Of course, why didn't you say? Did you want to use it now?"

"We haven't really got the time now. In the morning perhaps."

"Certainly," she said, glancing at the stains under his armpits. "If you're stuck for clothes, perhaps I could find…"

"No, thanks, I don't think so," said Nigel, remembering Monday's events. "I don't want to give you another shock. We'll be all right for tonight. I'll just have a quick wash."

"Well, use the bathroom upstairs," she said. "I've put out extra towels."

It was almost nine o'clock when they walked down the lane. Still daylight but cool, and rapidly turning to dusk. George was glad of her cardigan. Nigel was carrying a brolly, in case of rain later. Miguel had produced a red scarf, which he wore in the style of a cravat. The hedgerows were busy with blackbirds, pinking before bedtime. George pointed out the sites of various nests.

The pub was crowded. The windows of the bar were steaming up. They could hear a jukebox, the sound of pool cues, the hubbub of many voices. They looked through a window to see the bar full of youths, their faces daubed with paint.

"Red Indians," said Nigel. "What's going on?"

"Oh, I didn't warn you, did I?" said George. "There's an outdoor adventure place three miles down the road. They run courses for city kids – you know, the underprivileged. They quite often come up here, so I'm told."

"The underprivileged?" said Nigel, peering through the steam. "They all look sozzled. Aren't they a bit young to be drinking?"

"They're not the kids, they're the instructors," said George. "We'd best go round the back."

The lounge was less crowded. The last diners were just leaving. Stood at one corner of the bar were the two farm workers who seemed to be regulars: Roger the boomer and the smaller man. Two men stood at the other corner, by the door that led into the bar; embroiled in a heated discussion, it seemed. Three men stood in the nook of a large stone fireplace. Another group were sitting in an alcove at the edge of the dining area; George was relieved to see women among them.

The chatter had ceased when they walked through the door. All eyes stared.

"George!" said Eric, stood behind the bar. "This is a

surprise! And gentlemen – what can I get for you?"

"Two pints of the Meaning of Life, please," said Nigel. "What are you having, George?"

"Oh, what am I having?" said George.

"Do you drink beer?" said Nigel. "I recommend you sample a Meaning."

"Okay," said George. "I'll try a half. Half a Meaning."

"And the lady will have half a Meaning," Nigel said to Eric.

"Evening, gents," said the small chap in the corner.

"Hello both," said Roger. "Hello, George. I haven't seen you for a while. Have you been hiding?"

"No, just… doing this and that," she said.

Roger looked like he'd had a few. His face was red and streaming with sweat. And as he stood there, eyeing the newcomers, he swayed precariously, as though his body had turned to jelly.

"Two and a half Meanings," said Eric.

"Very ambiguous," said Nigel.

"What?" said Eric.

"Only joking," said Nigel.

"I thought you'd left us," said Eric. "I saw your car had gone this evening, you know…"

"Ah! A shopping trip," said Nigel, remembering Eric's joke about overnight parking. Was he dropping a hint? Was he expecting a tip? No, he thought; being nosy more likely.

The chatter, which had resumed, was suddenly brought to a halt by Roger's booming voice.

"Hey! You! Amigo!" he shouted, staring at Miguel.

Miguel stood there looking petrified. Roger was a big man, twice the size of Miguel. Roger slapped his glass on the bar, the beer spilling over his thick hand, and staggered three steps in Miguel's direction. Everybody watched. Nigel didn't know what to do. It was like a scene from a Western, he thought. And George began to sweat, expecting a kafuffle.

"I've got one thing to say to you!" Roger boomed.

David Bowie, singing *Golden Years* on the jukebox,

struggled to compete with the drama. Even the Red Indians had gone quiet.

Then Roger held out his hand and shouted, "You've done a bloody good job with that scythe, man!"

He grabbed Miguel's hand and shook it profusely. The whole pub burst into a round of laughs.

"My God! I was going to offer you a mower, but then I sees this afternoon you'd done the whole bloody lot!" And turning to his friend, the small chap, Roger said, "It takes some doing, that, hey Paul? Remember when we used to do Ben Weaver's with those rusty old cutters? It took me back, it did, seeing him with that scythe."

Eric leant over the bar and said to George, "Roger's been working at Quinton Farm, bagging the silage."

"Ah!" said George. It explained everything. Quinton Farm stood on a rise on the other side of the main road, opposite Greenslade Cottage. Roger would have seen the gardeners at work.

Then she noticed the two men in the other corner. One was looking at her intently. It was Stephen Grove. She smiled in recognition. He nodded briefly, as if he didn't remember her, and turned to stare at Nigel.

Nigel caught his glance and blushed.

"Shall we sit down, George?" he said.

"Yes, if you like," she said. "There's room in the corner."

They moved away from the bar, into the alcove at the edge of the dining area. They sat on the edge of the crowd, who had moved chairs and a table to form a large circle. They were sitting next to a group of hot air balloon enthusiasts, it seemed.

"I thought you said not a lot happens here," said Nigel, swigging his beer.

"I spoke out of ignorance, obviously. There's probably all sorts of things going on, but I don't get to hear about them."

"Perhaps you should get out a bit more. I suppose it's difficult, being a single woman."

"There's clubs and what have you, I have started going out

more. Do you know that man over there? He keeps looking at you."

Stephen Grove was staring at Nigel again, and Nigel was blushing.

"He, er, he looks familiar, but I can't think where…"

Stephen Grove was walking over to them now. He looked very serious. It was Nigel's turn to sweat.

"I do know you," Stephen said. "You're one of those science boffins. We've met before."

He lowered his voice, turning his back on the hot air balloonists.

"I won't say where," he said, winking. "But let me tell you something."

Now he leant forwards, so that only the three of them could hear.

"I'm a new man, thanks to you."

And then he grabbed Nigel's hand, shaking it profusely.

"Yes," he said, almost whispering, "I'm a new man. I've never felt better in my whole life. Never felt better since I had those drugs you lot gave me. I hope we can have a private chat some time. I know one or two people who'd be interested, given the chance."

He winked at Nigel, nodded at George, nodded at Miguel, and walked back to the bar.

George looked at Nigel with a quizzical expression.

Nigel turned with a flushed face.

"It's, er, a long story," he said.

"Another one?" she said.

"I haven't finished this one," he said, taking a big swig.

"I was talking abut your long stories," she said.

"Ah, yes. It's sort of… related," he said. "George, whatever you're thinking, I am not a drug dealer. I'm far too old for that sort of thing."

"Oh, I don't know," she said, her eyes twinkling. "Some of them are quite old. With yachts, and their own islands in the Bahamas. Where did you say you worked?"

"I'm going to the bar," he said. "Who's for a Meaning?"

But the bar was going through a crisis. The Meaning of Life had been devoured by a crowd of Red Indians. Eric marched outside to change the barrel. His new brew, he said – Magnus Opus.

*

Nigel thought the effort had to be made, just in case he'd missed it: the Pearl of Wisdom. He hadn't spoken to Jerry about returning. He would ring him before they left. Now he sat on the bench, a polythene bag by his side.

Inside the bag was another bag. And in that one, a tooth. And by his feet, a carrier bag from Templetons, full of teeth. He picked them out, one by one, and compared them to the other. In the background, the rumble of the washing machine, the whoosh of the scythe. And alarmingly, George seemed to be singing.

She'd said, Forget about the rest of the garden. You've done enough. Take it easy. You're leaving tomorrow. I'd like you to go for a walk with me. Not very far, a couple of miles across the valley, same distance back. We'll be two hours roughly, walking slowly. Would you like to do that?

Miguel was out of the picture; he was determined to finish the tidying up, and wouldn't be persuaded otherwise.

So Nigel had said, I'm not really a walker, I have to say, but yes, that sounds manageable.

Okay, good, said George, we'll go when you've finished your dental work.

And now she seemed to be singing.

It was the song that had been playing on the jukebox the night before – *Golden Years*, by David Bowie.

Strange, Nigel thought. The song had been playing in his head too. It must have had a subliminal effect, he thought: going through your ears as the entire pub held its breath, anticipating a disaster.

She wasn't exactly singing; it was more of a hum. Alarming though; she hadn't done this before. Was it because they were leaving? Or because he'd promised to go for a walk? Either way, she seemed to be happy, and her happiness seemed to be connected to him. That was the alarming thing. After all, he thought, I haven't really done anything to make her happy, apart from weeding the garden. It made him feel... sort of powerful. Yes, as if he had a mysterious power – to make someone happy. Which was even more alarming. The discovery was so unexpected. Yet it was rather pleasing; his ego felt inflated by it. And it may be my ego that's making the connection, he thought. She's simply happy and it's nothing to do with me. In fact, she may be elated because we're going tomorrow.

When they left the house and walked down the lane, her mood had changed. Sombre it seemed, and not in the mood for talking. The road was busy. It was Saturday afternoon. On an impulse, Nigel grabbed her arm and they raced across the road. They walked down the lane through Quinton Rushton, another line of detached houses and cottages.

"It's very affluent here," said Nigel, scanning the drives. "Where do the peasants live?"

George laughed.

"Not here," she said. "When we moved here, it was before the celebrities started moving in. Now they're everywhere. They say it bumps up the house prices, so it's good for business. Did you find what you were looking for? The matching pair?"

"You asked me that a few minutes ago," he said. "I think I've found it. I'm not sure."

"Did I ask you that?" she said. "I'm going daft, I'm sorry."

Triplecheek St Mary...

They had walked there once, following the stream across the fields.

"We go through this gate," she said, "and follow the stream. The Quinton Brook."

A field of stubble. George led the way.

It was hot and sticky. Low cloud and mist. There were no birds singing, no birds to be seen. There was thunder in the air.

They were both wearing cagoules, Nigel wearing one of Richard's. Not *Squiggles,* but a shapeless green thing that was several sizes too big for him. George said it was meant to go over a backpack.

At the end of the field, they climbed over a stile.

The next field was a field of maize. A maize jungle.

The path followed the edge. The stream trickled on one side; and on the other, the maize towered above them. Squeezed by the jungle and the bank of the stream, they continued to walk single file.

"Two miles?" said Nigel.

"Two or three," said George. "It's not all like this. Are you struggling?"

"No, I'm, er, okay," he said.

"Look, a badger sett," she said, pointing to the opposite bank. "Those small holes are vole holes."

She didn't pause for long; she strode onwards, through the jungle. Finally, they reached the end of the maize. They climbed over a stile. The next field had been ploughed. Now they were squeezed between the bank of the stream and deep furrows.

Nigel wasn't impressed by the route. He liked mountains and views, but he wasn't a walker. This was a trudge.

The next field was a strip of pasture.

"At last, grass!" said Nigel.

"We cross the river down here," said George. "This is the River Chuckle."

A line of trees, tracing the river. A wooden bridge, made of old railway sleepers. A gurgling stream. Another strip of pasture. Then a field of stubble.

"Is this… a favourite walk of yours?" said Nigel.

"No, I haven't come this way for years," she said. "We're

nearly there. See – the church tower. That's Triplecheek St Mary."

Two more fields of stubble; then they reached a track, which led to a farm. The farm was on the edge of the village. Now they were on tarmac.

Triplecheek St Mary…

A gypsy caravan, red and golden; a white parrot in a cage, hanging from the wall of a house; and the rooks above the Scots pines, feeding the squawking rooklings…

Nigel looked at George, her head turning here, there and everywhere.

"Were you looking for something?" he said.

"I was looking to see if there were any rooks about," she said. "It's the wrong time of year. In the spring, they nest in those trees. A great big flock."

They turned a corner. They heard the squawks, and there it was.

"A parrot!" said Nigel.

"Yes!" she said, grinning.

The gypsy caravan was there too, red and golden.

"Still in the same place," she said.

She looked delighted.

"It's like a scene from a DH Lawrence," said Nigel.

"Yes, that's just what we thought when we saw it," she said.

Thatched cottages, picture gardens, a little old lady cutting the lawn with shears, the church behind the trees, the trill of a wren, echoed by another.

"There's not much to see," she said. "Just this, basically."

"It's worth seeing, even so," said Nigel. "It's very Dorset. Tucked away, and no tourists. It's a gem of a village."

"Isn't it?"

"Is there a pub?"

She laughed.

"No, there's no pub," she said. "And if there was, it wouldn't be open now. The nearest pub is the Moon. Are you thirsty? I've got some water."

She dug into a pocket and handed him a bottle.

"Right," she said. "We'll walk back now then."

Nigel had the impression that her curiosity had been satisfied. They didn't speak much on the way back, but her mood was more buoyant. When they reached the end of the maize jungle, she offered him an explanation.

"I've only walked this way once," she said. "The second time we didn't make it. We got as far as the road, and then, you know. I haven't been able to face it since. Thanks."

Nigel, taken aback, said, "You're very welcome."

He took her arm when they reached the road. This time, he did it with ostentation, and she smiled.

And she really did feel relieved. Relieved that things could still look exactly the same after ten years. There was something else too. Now she knew that if she never saw Nigel again, it really didn't matter. It would be no great loss, she thought; she would survive. Richard was irreplaceable.

*

Miguel was still working when they got back. He was trying to stabilise the grass mountains, piled by the side of the stream. The corners of the field, the awkward bits, had all been trimmed.

"He's a professional," said George, looking over the hedge. "I do feel guilty, I feel I ought to give him something. I can't think what, apart from money."

"He wouldn't accept that," said Nigel.

"In that case, I'll have to see if I can find a memento or something," she said.

They walked down the path. It was food time. This time, Nigel organised it – leftovers from past meals, gathered together in a vegetable curry.

"This is one thing I can cook," he said. "I've been spying on your spices, George."

George went upstairs, looking for a suitable memento.

What? Nothing sprang to mind. In desperation, she opened a box of unwanted bric-a-brac. There she found a brown owl, made of porcelain. It was an ugly-looking thing, she thought, but was there anything else? There were no pigeons. The owl may remind him of their nightly racket, she thought, which hadn't ceased since they'd been there. She would offer him the owl.

As it turned out, Miguel was thrilled. His family were keen collectors of bric-a-brac, he said. He grinned, showing the gaps in his teeth, and kissed George on the cheek. He would find a good place for it, he said.

A success! It just goes to show, she thought, that one man's junk is another man's treasure. She put it down to his Catholic upbringing. Every Irish guest house they'd been to was full of the stuff. Quite strange, she thought. You would have thought they would look on such objects as idols. But then, she knew little about their religion. Or anyone else's, come to that.

They sat outside after the meal, with a bottle of wine. The heavy clouds had all gone. Now there were fluffy white ones, sauntering across a blue sky.

George was overjoyed at the sight of the lawn, the smell of the grass. Two, three, four rabbits were scampering here and there, as though they were lost.

"They'll have to find a new home," she said. "I hope they settle down. Oh well! I haven't been able to do this for years. It's wonderful."

"The birds like it too," said Nigel. "Look at the blackbirds! They're looking for worms."

"They're listening," said George. "Their hearing is incredible. They can hear them moving about underground."

Secretly, she knew that scientists didn't believe this. Scientists believed they were just looking for worms, not listening. But she had her own beliefs, based on observation, and she wanted to provoke Nigel into responding.

But Nigel sat there musing, as if he hadn't heard a word.

Or wouldn't be provoked.

And secretly, she was hoping they wouldn't find any. There were two of them, hopping over the grass, cocking their heads now and then, listening. Joined by a third, a female; then by a robin. The swallows were there too, catching flies. And then a pair of wood pigeons hopped to the ground.

"I wonder where Gabriel is," said George.

"Who knows," said Nigel.

"Flying home," said Miguel.

They stayed out till dusk. Then Miguel excused himself. He hoped to see her in the morning, he said. She stood and shook his hand, kissed him on the cheeks and said, "Thanks, Miguel."

Nigel said he'd have to retire soon too; he felt exhausted. George hadn't pressed him on his connection with Stephen Grove, and Nigel hadn't expanded. She didn't seem troubled by it. In fact, returning from the pub last night, she'd found it highly amusing. Soon there'd be rumours, she said, that she'd been fraternising with a drug dealer.

"George, I'm not really a morning person, so I'll say cheerio now," he said.

"Oh!" she said. "Okay. I'll see you in the morning though, won't I?"

She was sitting on her cane chair; Nigel was sitting on the bench. Now she stood, and Nigel followed her lead.

"I hope so," he said. "It's just that I'm a grumpy old sod in the mornings."

"Oh!" she said. "You'd better say cheerio now then, you grumpy old sod."

They both smiled, both aware it was one of those delicate moments. He took her hand; they kissed cheeks; they stood apart. Then, fumbling like a gawky teenager, he kissed her on the lips, and she laughed.

"I'll see you again," he said, tasting the wine.

"I hope so," she said.

They went inside.

The morning was brief and frantic, gathering belongings, making sure they hadn't left anything. They wouldn't stop for breakfast, Nigel said; they wanted to be away; there was loads to do. They were hoping to be on a flight by the evening, he said, and he must return the car, which meant driving to London.

More handshakes, kissed cheeks, then waves as they walked down the lane.

George sat on the bench, looked at the lawn, saw the rabbits, and didn't know whether to cry. Then she saw the scythe, propped against the tool shed, with a note attached. She walked over. The note said: "Our gift to you – much love from Nigel and Miguel."

She smiled, then remembered that today was Sunday, and tomorrow was Monday.

Monday!

The shopping list...

*

Sat upstairs, looking through the picture window, she doubted now whether that blackbird was in fact gay. Chasing another male and being playful about it didn't make him gay. They could be brothers, she thought; young ones. Though they didn't look young; they both had full black coats. Young at heart maybe.

So why, she wondered, did I think he was gay?

She had to dig deep.

She'd heard that gays were obsessed with cleanliness. Everything had to be scrupulously clean, domestically speaking. They were very fussy about that sort of thing, so it was said. It was because they were anally retentive, or whatever the expression was. That's what the psychologists said, anyway.

And out there was a very fussy blackbird, hypersensitive to sights and sounds of all kinds.

Now she thought he was psychic. This was the bird who could see through net curtains. Not only that, but he could see through walls. She'd heard his alarm call three times today, just before she'd stepped out of the door.

It was dusk now, and they were all at it.

And now the owls had started, mewing and screaming.

She looked at the chairs – to her left, to her right.

The room seemed very empty.

*

Liz had decided. She'd discussed the future with Bob. He wanted to return to the States. He wanted Liz to go with him. She'd already thought about this. There were more opportunities over there; that was a fact. Academics were leaving the UK in droves. She wanted to sit down and write the new volume of *Capital*. She would do it in the States.

She couldn't wait till Nigel's return. She would hand in her notice now; she was legally bound to give six months in any case. A lot could happen in six months. Like a plague, for a start.

She too was suffering with red blotches and a terrible itch. At first, she'd thought Bob and Dr Lee were more than just acquainted. There was nearly a thunderstorm. She'd gone out for a walk. Then she bumped into Boris Vladimov, and he was suffering too.

While Bob's blotches were declining, hers were blooming. And everyone, it seemed, had been affected. The doctors were stumped. The symptoms were consistent with insect bites, they said. They were carrying out tests. In the meantime, they were recommending the use of an antiseptic cream.

Liz walked into Jerry's office and told him of her intentions.

"Jerry, I want to resign," she said. "I'm giving you six months' notice, as I'm legally bound to do."

Jerry leapt from his swivel chair, which spun around and nearly toppled.

"You want to resign?" he said. "You can't resign. Why do you want to resign?"

"You know my reasons more or less," she said. "The project isn't turning out as planned. I'm being asked to produce statistics for the World Bank, and you're pursuing an obsession with cloning, which, quite frankly Jerry, I think is totally bonkers and a waste of resources. I don't see any chance of producing a new version of *Capital*, so I'm leaving. And there you have it."

He looked horrified.

"You don't understand," he said, scratching his neck. "You can't resign. Not now."

"What do you mean?"

"You, you're essential," he said. He pointed in the direction of the computer room. "This is all we have," he said. "The biocomputer's contaminated. God knows how, I've only been told this morning."

Liz was feeling ruthless.

"I thought you were waiting for a new stock of chemicals," she said. "What's the problem?"

"Something's got into the baths," he said. "They think it's a micro-organism. The whole set-up is contaminated. New chemicals aren't going to help. We need to disinfect everything and start again."

Now he seemed on the verge of tears. He was almost shouting.

"Liz, we don't have the resources," he said. "We're gonna have to shelve it till we get more funds. And the funds are dependent on Humphrey Dillinger. He wants the stats, and you're the one to provide them. You can't resign!"

"You've got six months," she said, scratching her back.

"Six months," he said, scratching his ear. "Liz, it could take us a year to recover. A micro-organism is a total disaster. They don't know what it is yet, they're carrying out tests. We'll be starting again from scratch, and that's if we get the funding. The supercomputer is all we've got. You can't resign now, we're dependent on you."

"I'm sorry, Jerry," she said, and walked out.

The sound of the jets was driving her mad.

In six months' time, she thought, the war would be over, and the no-fly zone would be a thing of the past. They could take a plane at last.

George stood at the bus stop, skimming the fields with her gaze, looking for swallows. In vain. It was now the middle of September, and the nesting season was over. They'll be up on the downs today, she thought, family with family, feasting before the big departure. Two weeks of fun and sport. Then the big take-off.

The winds had turned now. No more westerlies. Cooler winds from the north-east, bringing the smell of autumn. The smell of wet leaves, fallen by the verge. Smoke from a peat fire, drifting down the gorge from Quinton Monkton.

A car zoomed past: the bus shelter rattled. She withdrew into the shelter and counted her change.

The bus was late. Time to glimpse the letter.

An address in Holland Park.

She wondered if he was staying with friends.

And nearly missed the bus.

The operator had changed. The bus was a different colour. Different drivers; they barely knew the route.

"Return to Lydiard, please," said George.

"Hello George," Jean shouted.

"Hello Jean," said George.

Jean Mortimer, sat in a corner on the back seat. Maurice Warnock, sat in the opposite corner. Mr and Mrs Bartlett, sat halfway down the bus. No one else, yet still she looked for a seat behind Mary Holloway. Then remembered that Mary Holloway wouldn't be on today. She was going to Mrs Foss's funeral.

Maurice Warnock gave her a wink and a leer.

"Hello," she said to him, bluntly.

She chose a seat in the centre, opposite Mr and Mrs Bartlett.

"Good morning," she said.

"Morning," said Mrs Bartlett. "How are you, George?"

"Fine," said George. "And how are you?"

"Oh, surviving," Mrs Bartlett said, and chuckled.

George wished she'd sat somewhere else now. How could she read the letter without Mrs Bartlett asking awkward questions? She didn't really want to chat. All she wanted was to be seen sitting next to Mr and Mrs Bartlett. She wasn't expecting to talk to them.

Oh well, she thought, the letter will have to wait.

She looked through the glass. Two months had passed since her guests had departed. And Maurice Warnock had been on the bus every week, giving her a leer. It was disgusting, she thought. What was he thinking of? He was a married man. Now he'd got the idea that George was a bit of a strumpet.

Not only Maurice Warnock, it seemed.

Mary Holloway had been cool towards her all through the summer holidays. George had a job on her hands, explaining these long-lost friends who had turned up out of the blue. She'd never mentioned them before. The world of Magnus Chase believed that George didn't have any friends.

But then, Mary Holloway had her grandchildren with her through the holidays, so she was rather preoccupied…

"Turn right here, driver!" Jean shouted.

The narrow road to Top Down.

Even so, George wondered if there was a little jealousy there. More likely though, Mary – who's a wise old owl and never misses a thing, she thought – doubted my version of the story. And suspicion is the seed of mistrust.

Then there was Kate Wimbourne, who had been prompted to reveal aspects of her teenage love life. Sneaking a glance at *Lady Chatterley's Lover* when the lights were meant to be out. We had candles, she said, and gave George a lascivious look, which George found quite unnerving…

There she was, standing by the bus shelter in Top Down, talking to Barbara Smiles. Arthur Blagdon stood a few yards away, looking lost. No Tina Weymouth today. There was a rumour she was working in Templetons.

Arthur Blagdon's smell was particularly rich this morning. It wafted in through the door, competing with the smell of Kate Wimbourne's perfume. George preferred Arthur's smell. It blended in with the smell of the leaves. He must have been shovelling chicken dung again, she thought. The smell of Autumn, incarnate. Kate's smell made her cough. A bit like roses, but no rose that George had ever sniffed. Splashed too liberally, and so strong that it hit the back of your throat.

While Kate made the usual fuss, George was tempted to sneak a look at her letter. She'd read it once before leaving, but read it in a rush; she was on her way out when the post arrived.

"So that means you want another 20p then," said Kate, fumbling in her purse. "Just a minute..."

"Hello Kate," Jean shouted.

"Good morning ladies," said Kate.

Kate's head bobbed here and there as she checked the seats for unfamiliar faces, only to find that there weren't any, as usual.

Mrs Bartlett turned and said, "Have you heard from your friends, George?"

And George thought: Damn! I can't even check the date stamp. Her eyes are everywhere.

"I had a postcard from Portugal," she said. "About, er, six weeks ago."

"Oh, well done," said Mrs Bartlett. "Our son's gone to Portugal for a surfing holiday..."

"Portugal?" said Kate, taking a seat in front of the Bartletts. "Are you going to Portugal, George?"

Mr Bartlett coughed into a handkerchief.

"No," said George.

"We were talking about our son," said Mrs Bartlett. "He's gone to Portugal for a surfing holiday."

Barbara Smiles sat in front of George.

"Our son's coming over from Australia this week," said Barbara.

"Oh, that'll be nice for you," said Mrs Bartlett.

Kate turned to wrinkle her nose and shake her head as Arthur Blagdon took the seat in front. George felt like laughing. If truth be told, she thought, Arthur was being a gentleman in not turning round and giving Kate a wrinkle.

Mr Bartlett chuckled. George wondered if he was thinking the same.

Mrs Bartlett said, "When's the next meeting of the Lavender Club, Barbara? Is it this week or next week?"

Kate turned, looked about and said, "Where's Mary?"

"She was going to Mrs Foss's funeral," said Barbara.

"Was it today?" said Kate.

"It's at twelve o'clock at Charlton Minster," said Barbara.

"Oh," said Kate. "I didn't know it was today. I would have gone, but it's getting there. She never recovered from that fall, did she?"

"She never came out of hospital," said Mrs Bartlett.

"How awful," said Kate.

George reached into a bag and dug out last week's paper. The Lydiard Advertiser, opened and folded on that item about Stephen Grove.

Stephen Grove was about to launch the Land Reform Party, the item said. He was preparing for the next election; there were rumours it would be held in the spring, next year. Now he was refusing to debate with Ebenezer Hackett, president of the Brutal Party. The Brutal Party, should it be elected, was offering a free axe to everyone over the age of 50. "In these dangerous times, with the threat of muggers, armed burglars, armed drug dealers, drunken yobs and antisocial behaviour, old people are frightened," said Ebenezer. "We believe we're entitled to carry an axe when we walk down the street. Why shouldn't we defend our property? People over the age of 50 have every right to be brutal. An eye for an eye, as the good book says."

Stephen Grove said they were fascists. He didn't debate with fascists, he said. Ebenezer said the Land Reform Party represented a threat to every property owner. They were funded by Robert Mugabe, he said. And not only by him, he said, but also by the Argentine government, who were taking land away from decent hard-working families. Stephen said, while he fully supported the land reforms instigated by the Argentine government, the idea that he was receiving funds from them was complete and utter nonsense. He was working on a manifesto, which would clarify…

A click of the tongue from Kate.

"Hilda!" she said, turning to Barbara Smiles.

The outskirts of Middleton Magna. Hilda Faber on her hair day. No Cynthia Butterwick. The bus slowed down and stopped.

"Return to Lydiard, thank you, driver," Hilda barked.

"Hello Hilda," Jean shouted.

Hilda was deaf today. She took the seat in front of Arthur Blagdon.

"Hello Arthur," she barked.

Staring at Hilda's bare legs, Kate Wimbourne shook her head.

George was trying to slide her letter into a fold of the newspaper. Then she might be able to read it unnoticed…

"It's not very good news about the bus, is it?" said Mrs Bartlett.

"Sorry?" said George. "What's the news about the bus?"

"It's in this week's paper," said Mrs Bartlett. "They're talking of stopping it next year."

"Oh!" said George. "That is bad news. I haven't heard, this is last week's paper."

Mr Bartlett chuckled.

"You're a week behind, George," he said.

"Yes, I am," said George. "I don't have it delivered, you see. I buy it when I go into town, so it's always a few days late."

"Oh," said Mrs Bartlett. "You won't have heard about the bus then."

"So what's happening?" George said.

"They're reviewing the services," said Mrs Bartlett. "They say most of the local buses don't pay. They've got to make big savings next year, you know how it is, they say that every year. Now they're talking of cutting some of the routes, and this is one they want to cut."

"Oh," said George. "They've only just changed the operator."

"I know," said Mrs Bartlett. "Stupid, isn't it? I don't know what we'll do if they get rid of the bus, I'm sure."

"It's a lifeline!" said George, thinking of the weekly shop.

"Yes, of course it is," said Mrs Bartlett.

"Mind you, you can see their argument," said Mr Bartlett. "There's not many on today, is there? It's very thin on the ground. It used to be full at one time."

"They've all got cars now," said Mrs Bartlett. "The young ones don't want to travel by bus. And they're not very good for old people, this seat's very uncomfortable, don't you find George?"

"There's not a lot of leg room," said George.

Dear George, she read. *Yes, I'm back in the UK!*

"There's somebody waiting here, driver!" Jean shouted.

Middleton Magna. Susan Chard, no daughters today. That girl whose name George could never remember, with a pushchair and two tots. No Mrs Webb. No Mrs Norton either.

"I suppose some people have gone to Mrs Foss's funeral," George said to Mrs Bartlett.

"Yes, we were thinking of going, weren't we?" said Mrs Bartlett. "But it's getting there and getting back. We could have caught this bus to get there, but then it would have meant standing around for two hours, and we didn't fancy that, did we? They speak of rain later."

"Turn right here, driver!"

George looked through the glass. The clouds were

gathering now. The winds had turned again, blowing rain from the west. She wished she'd brought a cagoule.

The hamlet of Puddleton St Margaret: no more than two houses and a farm. The bus turned a corner, and there was Mrs Drake, standing by the door of her house, clutching a stick as usual.

The project is a total mess, she read.

"Morning everybody," said Mrs Drake.

Looks like it's going to fold very soon.

Bowldish Farm – the huge puddle. No Sally Weymouth today.

I arrived to find the place in chaos. Thought the staff had got measles...

The golf course – Mrs Snape and her ancient shopping trolley, and that green plastic mack as usual.

The bus joined the ring road and headed for the town.

George slipped the letter into a pocket.

Kate Wimbourne stretched her neck to check for new developments.

George remembered that strange news item, which had appeared in the Stanford Chronicle a few weeks back. It was on the World News page.

"Italian Professor Found on a Boat," said the caption. "Salvador Pipi, an Italian professor, who absconded without warning from his university post some years ago, was being held by police and medical experts in Portugal today, having been found on a sailing boat off the coast of the Azores. The boat was reported to be drifting aimlessly across the Atlantic. Professor Pipi was found covered in red sores. He said he had been sightseeing when he and his crew members had been attacked and savagely bitten by a swarm of mosquitoes. He was heading for the island of Corvo, he said, when he was picked up by coastguards. He refused any further comment. Professor Pipi gained notoriety some years ago for his plans to clone a human. He is reputed to be still drawing a salary from the University of Altamura, though his whereabouts have been a complete mystery to the authorities."

There had been no further news about him since. Till this letter.

At the foot of the hill, the bus stopped to let Hilda Faber off. Jean Mortimer rushed down the aisle, and Susan Chard got off too.

"Have you been in Templetons yet?" said Mrs Bartlett.

"Yes, I have," said George. "I prefer Samways though."

"So do we," said Mrs Bartlett.

"It's an eyesore, that building," said Mr Bartlett. "Spoils the character of the town."

"Oh, I agree," said George.

The top of the hill now; the bus had stopped.

They all piled out.

Mrs Snape marched away, pushing her shopping trolley as if it were a tank. Mrs Drake strolled to the nearest shop window. Barbara Smiles joined the stream of passers-by. Kate Wimbourne helped the girl with the pushchair. Mr and Mrs Bartlett stopped to talk to Maurice Warnock. Arthur Blagdon stood there looking dazed, as if he'd just landed from the planet Hedge.

George had a few words with Kate. Then she saw Maurice Warnock leering at her. The urge to throttle him was particularly strong this morning. Time to go, she decided; she agreed to meet Kate in the Forum Rooms as usual.

First: into Pomeroys, looking for bargains.

Two for the price of one: jars of strawberry jam, this week only. Plus: tins of red salmon, special offer – when it's gone it's gone.

Next: Popes the newsagents for the Lydiard Advertiser and the Stanford Chronicle.

She didn't look at the cafeteria beyond; she avoided glancing till she was outside. No Mary; she was at Mrs Foss's funeral. And no Kate either. Mrs Snape, the only familiar face, sat in the corner with her trolley.

She went back inside.

The usual waitress. Tall and surly, wearing torn jeans and a crumpled T-shirt, turning to George with a frown.

"And what do you want?"

"A cup of tea, please."

"Milk?"

"Please."

"60p – the sugar's on the table."

"Thank you, you're so kind."

You little trollop.

She found an empty table. She took out the Lydiard Advertiser, then the letter, which she placed inside the newspaper.

I arrived to find the place in chaos. Thought the staff had got measles. Covered in red sores, and everyone scratching…

Damn! Mrs Drake had entered now.

Nobody could tell me what the problem was. They were all waiting for tests. & they didn't know if it was contagious. Wished I hadn't stepped off the boat…

"Do you mind if I join you, dear?" said Mrs Drake.

"No, take a seat," said George.

"Oooh, I need a sit down," said Mrs Drake. "It tires me out walking through town. I'm expecting to meet my brother, he'll be giving me a lift back. You won't mind, will you, if I sit here a minute?"

"No, of course not," said George.

And now, Kate Wimbourne had entered.

Spent a couple of weeks in solitary confinement more or less, till the problem was sorted…

She folded the newspaper. Kate rushed over from the counter, spilling her tea.

"Have you heard the news?" she said.

"What news?" said George.

"Samways is going to close," said Kate.

"Oh no!" said George.

"Oh, that is bad news," said Mrs Drake.

"I've just come from there now," said Kate. "They say

they're closing in two weeks."

"Why?" said George.

"It's Pomeroys, isn't it," said Kate. "You know they own Samways?"

"Yes," said George.

"Well, they're, what's the word? It was on the news, you must have heard. Streamlining, that was it. Or was it downsizing? Anyway, they're closing twenty or thirty stores, nationwide. They say they don't pay."

"That's what they're saying about the buses," said George.

"Oh, it's always cutting this and cutting that," said Mrs Drake. "We won't have anything left."

"And where do our taxes go, that's what I'd like to know," said Kate.

"The war," George said, and wished she hadn't.

"Hmph!" said Kate. "And that's a fine mess, isn't it?"

"I think," said George, "I'd better do my shopping, while there's still something left to buy."

"I'll see you in the Forum Rooms," said Kate.

"Yes, I'll see you later," said George. "Cheerio, Mrs Drake."

"Goodbye dear."

It was all very depressing, she thought. And she wasn't prepared to believe it yet. She wanted confirmation. If it were true, it would signal the end of an era, she thought.

Samways, where you could easily get caught up in a discussion about the rising cost of a loaf of bread, or the relative merits of Samways mature cheddar. Shopping in Samways was a social event, as well as a shopping event.

When it's gone it's gone...

Meanwhile, the post office; then the cashpoint machine.

Next, meat. Or should she leave it till later? No, she thought, best to do it now. Rearrange the itinerary, so there's no walking three or four times along the High Street. Go to the Forum Rooms early, before Kate arrives...

Millers the butchers: eggs, bacon, sausages.

She stood on the pavement, studying her list, mentally

rearranging the sequence. Youngs the chemists next, for the personal items. Wheeler's Wholefoods for the toothpaste. Bread from Helliers. Samways. The market.

But then there was the fruit and veg, from Thatchers...

And now, Jean Mortimer.

A diversion.

Jean had just taken a bag of old clothes to the Cats Protection League. Jean was still very upset about her cat. She'd had it put down recently; his kidneys had gone. It was the best thing, the vet said. She missed her cat. She still had Florence. But poor old Florence was getting on...

Mrs Snape was marching along the pavement. They were forced to move aside. George excused herself; she was in a rush today, she said.

Youngs the chemists. Wheeler's Wholefoods.

Then into Thatchers for the fruit and veg. The usual banter.

She consulted the list.

Pickards the DIY store: no time for that now; it was on the other side of town. No time for Homer's Books either. Samways next; then Helliers for the bread.

She walked into Samways and bumped into Hilda Faber. Hilda was almost in tears.

"Oh, I'm so upset, George," she said. "They're closing! I feel like crying, I really do. I've been coming here for years, I can't believe it's happening. They're ruining this town, take it from me, it'll never be the same if they close this place. And what am I going to do if this place closes? Where can I go, with my arthritis? I can't carry bags of shopping from Templetons, all the way up that bloody hill. And I don't like Pomeroys, they're so rude. They never help you, I had to tell them to get stuffed, they were so rude. Do you find that?"

"Yes, they're not very helpful at all," said George.

"Oh, I'm glad you've said that, I was beginning to wonder if it was me," said Hilda. "It's not just me then?"

"No," said George. "Several people have said the same."

"I'm so glad you've said that," said Hilda. "That's why I

always shop here. They're always eager to help you, always have been. Oh, I'm so upset I could cry. It's terrible George, it's the worst news I've heard for donkey's years."

And Hilda reached into her handbag, pulled out a tissue, and blew her nose.

George looked at the tills.

Today, it was Cinderella. Or was it Snow White and the Seven Dwarfs? Whatever: grandiose costumes, massive bustles, powder puffs and mountainous wigs. Despite the news, the show must go on. Or possibly, George thought, because of the news. Collecting for charity regardless, they were cocking a snook at the owners.

Hilda was on her way out.

George studied her list.

The basics. First: tea, coffee, sugar…

The show must go on.

Diversion: Mrs Snape blocking the aisle with her shopping trolley.

Next: lamb chops from Mr Pike the butcher, who had his own shop in Samways. And where would Mr Pike go, should Samways close?

"We don't know," said the man in the white coat. "We're looking around. It's early days yet."

"I'm very sorry," said George. "You'll be missed."

"Thanks," said the man in the white coat.

Next: a selection of cheeses. Washing-up liquid, bleach and washing powder. Another chat with Jean Mortimer. The price of lamb chops. Things you could get in Paulsbury that you couldn't get in Lydiard Forum. Paulsbury market on Saturdays. Cereals – don't forget the cereals…

"We don't know," said Madame Pompadour, sat at the till. "We only found out this morning."

Then it was George's turn.

"So it's true," she said. "You're closing?"

"Two weeks," said Madame Pompadour, scanning the items.

"I'm very sorry to hear it," said George. "We'll all miss you."

"Thank you," said Madame, and George put a note in the collection box.

The end of an era, she thought. Shopping would be more tiresome than ever. Either the rude girls at Pomeroys, or miles of aimless wandering at Templetons, followed by a trek up the hill. What a choice!

And Helliers had sold out of bread, which meant another visit to Samways. So much for the revised sequence, she thought; should have gone there first.

Finally, she emerged from Samways with a Hovis.

Next: a quick walk around the market.

Bird food from the pet stall; cheese from the cheese stall; tomatoes; nuts…

And there was Maurice Warnock at the hot dog stall, leering at her.

She pretended not to notice. Then she saw Hilda Faber's stately waddle. A suitable diversion.

"Your hair looks nice, Hilda," she said.

"Thank you, George," Hilda barked. "I'm still upset, I really am. I don't know what I'm going to do. And you know they're talking of stopping the bus? How do they expect people to get about? I can't bloomin walk into town. And my son doesn't drive, you know that, don't you? We sometimes get a taxi, but it's so bloody expensive. Do you know, we caught a taxi into town on Saturday to go shopping, and it cost us nearly twenty quid return. Twenty quid! How can I afford that on my pension?"

"It's an awful lot," said George.

"You're telling me," said Hilda. "And I have to come into town to collect my pension and pay my council tax…"

Maurice Warnock had gone now. George listened to Hilda, and thought about her own situation. What would she do, she wondered, if there were no bus? It was one of those things you didn't like to think about. She couldn't imagine there not

402

being a bus. But then, she couldn't imagine there not being a Samways. It was part of the landscape.

Hilda went off to get a cup of tea; she was going to the hot dog stall. George went into the Forum Rooms. She didn't have much time; about ten minutes before Kate arrived.

Susan Chard was there with her daughter. George found an empty table. She took out this week's Lydiard Advertiser, and slipped the letter inside it.

Dear George, she read. *Yes, I'm back in the UK! The project is a total mess. Looks like it's going to fold very soon. I arrived to find the place in chaos. Thought the staff had got measles. Covered in red sores, and everyone scratching. Nobody could tell me what the problem was. They were all waiting for tests. & they didn't know if it was contagious. Wished I hadn't stepped off the boat. Spent a couple of weeks in solitary confinement more or less, till the problem was sorted. & the problem – well, one doesn't know whether to laugh or cry. Nature fights back, as you know. The problem was a microscopic midge, Diodorus Siculus. A swarm of them, flying over the Atlantic, blown off-course by westerly gales. Flying from the Amazon to the West Indies, I believe, but it might have been the other way round. Anyway, they make the trip once a year to breed, and then make the return flight home. Would have carried on flying apparently, had it not been for the jet traffic across the Atlantic. Caught in the slipstream, blown east, west, east, west, east, west – it would cheese anyone off, wouldn't it? So they decide to come to earth. No prizes for guessing where. I'm told that they don't bite unless they're angry. For a good reason – they've only got one bite, one bite and they die. And this lot were angry. Took it out on my colleagues. A suicide bomber of the insect world…*

Kate Wimbourne!

George pocketed the letter.

"You're early," said Kate.

"Yes, I did it in record time this morning," said George.

"Oh, I don't like to rush," said Kate. "It wears me out walking up them stairs. The lift's not working again."

"I don't like lifts," said George. "I'm frightened of getting stuck."

403

"Have you been in Samways?" said Kate.

"Yes, it's not good news, is it?"

"I think this town's going downhill," said Kate. "We all said this would happen."

"That's where we'll be going, I suppose," said George.

"What?" said Kate.

"Downhill, to Templetons," said George.

"You won't catch me shopping in there," said Kate. "I think that's why Samways is closing. They can't compete, can they? We all said it'd be the death of the shops in the town, and we were right. Oh, there's Sue over there…"

George slipped the newspaper into a bag.

"Have you heard anything from your friends?" said Kate.

"I had a postcard from Portugal," said George. "That was about six weeks ago. I think I told you."

"Did you? I can't remember. George, I'd like your advice. I want to send a birthday present to my nephew…"

Without Mary Holloway to watch the time, they nearly missed the bus.

Kate was a hopeless timekeeper, always dependent on others for the time, even though she wore a watch. And Susan Chard wasn't going back on the bus, which confused Kate. George kept an eye on the clock, but forgot that the lift wasn't working, which meant Kate must walk down the stairs, and she wasn't very fast.

The bus was parked outside the Forum Rooms, waiting for them.

"Oh, I am sorry," said Kate, to the driver. "Blame me, I didn't realise what the time was." Then she turned to the passengers and said, "The lift wasn't working. We had to walk down the stairs."

Kate found a seat at the front, opposite Hilda Faber. George sat behind her, opposite Arthur Blagdon.

"Is that it now?" said the driver.

"Where's Mr Warnock?" said Mrs Bartlett.

"He wasn't coming back," said Kate. "He was going to the

hospital to see his father. And that lady who gets on in Puddleton, what's her name?"

"Mrs Drake," said George.

"She wasn't coming back. She's got a lift with her brother," said Kate.

"What about that girl with the pushchair?" said George.

"She bought a single," said the driver.

"We're all on then," said Kate, and the bus drove off.

Arthur Blagdon sat there looking dazed, clutching a metal bar. It looked like the element from an electric heater.

George turned to Barbara Smiles, sat on the seat behind her. She wanted to know about the progress of her bees. Barbara reminded George of the next meeting of the Lavender Club, this week. We've got an arts and crafts evening, she said. Do come. Mrs Whitmarsh will give you a lift, if you want to go.

George said she'd think about it. She had a few jobs to do about the house, she said.

Which was a feeble excuse, she thought, but she didn't want to sound rude. Arts and crafts wasn't really her cup of tea. And a lift with the Whitmarshes wasn't the greatest inducement.

On the other hand, she thought, there's no Carol McGregor this week.

George had decided to cut down on the therapy. She was seeing Carol every month. It didn't feel so essential these days. She felt with each session that she was paying for the privilege of talking. A costly exercise, she thought, when there were cheaper outlets. But she didn't want to cut her out altogether.

The golf course – Mrs Snape was first off, together with the ancient trolley.

Then the winding lanes through Puddleton St Margaret. There was no Sally Weymouth to drop off. No Mrs Drake either.

"Turn left here, driver!" Jean shouted.

Back to the main road and into Middleton Magna. No Susan Chard, and no Girl With Pushchair And Two Tots. Next stop

– Hilda.

"Thank you driver," she barked. "I don't think I'll be sitting outside this afternoon. Look at them bloomin clouds! They say we're going to have a wet week." Then she turned and said, "Cheerio Arthur," before stepping from the bus in her stately fashion.

Kate shook her head, turned to George and said, in a voice that was almost a whisper, Hilda was a miserable so-and-so.

George reminded her that Hilda was very upset about Samways. The news was enough to make anyone feel miserable, she said.

"Left here, driver!"

Kate agreed. Then she said that she didn't get much from there now; she did most of her shopping in Binghams, in Stanton Parva. She caught the community bus, Skylarks. The driver was very good, she said. Took you right to your door, helped you with your bags...

A lurch forwards as a milk tanker turned a corner and the bus was forced to brake.

The single-track road to Top Down.

"They go much too fast down this road," said Kate. Then, gathering her bags, "Right, back to the city centre," she said.

"Just here, please driver," said Barbara Smiles.

But she was so soft-spoken that the driver didn't hear. The bus flew past Orchard Cottage and stopped at the bus shelter by the church. Barbara muttered a lament.

"Bye everybody, see you next week, all being well," said Kate. "Oh, I'll be seeing you on Wednesday, won't I George, at the Lavender Club. Are you going?"

"I'm not sure yet," said George.

"She's thinking about it," said Barbara.

Kate clicked her tongue, tilted her head and said, "You can think too much you know, George. Bye!"

Barbara followed, chuckling. Then Arthur Blagdon, clutching his metal rod, said, "Hokey cokey! Bye everybody!"

The bus turned, drove back along the valley to the main

road. And remembered to turn left, without a shout.

George gathered her shopping – two bags in one hand, three in the other – and walked down the aisle, saying goodbye to Jean Mortimer, Mr and Mrs Bartlett, the driver. There was no one else on the bus.

It stopped at the bottom of the lane

George stepped off, Jean waving as usual.

Up the hill to Greenslade Cottage.

She was panting when she reached the gate. A pause. Then, down the path to the yard, in through the back door, which she'd forgotten to lock in her morning's haste, and straight to the kettle, dumping the bags on the stone floor.

A cup of tea, before the ordeal of unloading. The best part of Monday, taken up with shopping. The major event of the week, and soon it would be over.

But not yet.

She sat at the wooden table, took a sip of her tea, and looked for the letter.

Damn! She'd left it on the bus!

It wasn't inside the newspaper. She shook it, and nothing fell out. And it wasn't in the bag. It must have fallen out, she thought. But no, she hadn't slipped it inside the newspaper. It was in a pocket. Still there, thank God!

She sat down and read.

Then the unloading.

Two hours later, she went upstairs, a cup of tea in one hand, the letter in the other. She sat by the picture window, and read it again from the beginning.

Dear George

Yes, I'm back in the UK! The project is a total mess. Looks like it's going to fold very soon. I arrived to find the place in chaos. Thought the staff had got measles. Covered in red sores, and everyone scratching. Nobody could tell me what the problem was. They were all waiting for tests. & they didn't know if it was contagious. Wished I hadn't stepped off the boat. Spent a couple of weeks in solitary confinement more or less, till the problem was sorted. & the problem – well, one doesn't know whether to laugh or cry. Nature fights back, as you know. The problem was a microscopic midge, Diodorus Siculus. A swarm of them, flying over the Atlantic, blown off-course by westerly gales. Flying from the Amazon to the West Indies, I believe, but it might have been the other way round. Anyway, they make the trip once a year to breed, and then make the return flight home. Would have carried on flying apparently, had it not been for the jet traffic across the Atlantic. Caught in the slipstream, blown east, west, east, west, east, west – it would cheese anyone off, wouldn't it? So they decide to come to earth. No prizes for guessing where. I'm told that they don't bite unless they're angry. For a good reason – they've only got one bite, one bite and they die. And this lot were angry. Took it out on my colleagues. A suicide bomber of the insect world.

Flushed out a few skeletons though. Don't know if it made the news, so you may not have heard. Professor You-Know-Who was found on a boat, apparently trying to escape the ravages of this suicidal beast. I've been informed since that some people are allergic to its bites. Can even be fatal. More on this later; he's now in the hands of medical experts and it's strictly hush-hush.

Anyway, Diodorus Siculus somehow crept into the bio-process and contaminated the whole works. Could take months to recover, we were told. & that's dependent on finances, which are precarious to say the least. Years of work, scuppered by a midge! Meanwhile, half the staff have handed in notice, inc yours truly. The others are hanging on; some are hoping for a redundancy package. No chance of that – there's money owing to suppliers and the financial situation is looking increasingly hopeless. Despite it all, the director is still optimistic – he wants to start afresh, in California, and I'm sure he'll attract a few supporters. As for me, I'm owed several weeks holiday and I intend to take it. In fact, I was thinking about Greenslade Cottage. Yes, the garden! Isn't it time for a spot of hedge pruning? I'm ready and willing, if you're agreeable. Thought I ought to make contact this time, rather than land on you! Sorry, my sense of humour is a bit warped at times.

Miguel's fit and well, by the way. He was overjoyed the last time I saw him. Told me he'd been praying & his prayers had been answered by a miracle. He was woken up one morning by a noisy chorus of coos, he said. Looked out of the window to see Gabriel with his mate. God knows how the bird did it, but there you are – 1,500 miles of ocean, and it took him six, seven weeks, I believe. A miracle? That or love, plus a heavy dose of animal intelligence, I'd say. You see, Miguel told me once they mate for life. Love makes them good racers, he says; they race home to be back with their mate. I guess Gabriel must have a pretty good home life. I'll give you a call in a week or so. Perhaps you could get out the scythe and give it an airing.

Bye for now, kind regards & best wishes from Nigel.

George stared at the window. This year's swallow droppings will have to be cleaned soon, she thought.

She turned to the door, still wedged open. When the winds blew from the north, you knew about it. A cold draught would blast from the skylight, even though it was closed, and blow straight into the lounge. The skylight needed fixing. And it wasn't warm enough now to keep the door propped open.

She took out the wedge and stood by the skylight, letting the door swing to behind her. She remembered that funny old pigeon who had landed there in July.

In her mind's eye, she could see his face, his twinkling eyes, his beak opening and closing. Far away now, yet what better news than the fact of his homecoming, she thought. Far away, but she could see his face, those eyes, that beak, opening and closing. And a smile. Yes, his smile! Wrinkles and crinkles and twinkling eyes. Just like the smile of an old granny, she thought. And somewhere in the Atlantic, on an island far away, there he was, back home with his mate, smiling.

She really must do some tidying.

ACKNOWLEDGEMENTS

Innovations in computer systems, including the use of materials other than silicon, were first brought to my attention by Roger Knott at Loughborough University way back in 1989. Thanks are due to Roger for sowing a few seeds. The research for this book made much use of the Internet where there is a mine of information on Josephson Junctions, superconductors, SQUIDs, bio- / DNA / molecular computing, and their applications. This includes the 'Ask the Experts' pages of the *Scientific American* website; 'SQUIDs: A Popular Account' by Rich Dawe; 'DNA Computing' by Teddy Byrd, Ben Elgin, Dan Moran and Jascha Swisher; 'Digital Soup: DNA as a computational device' by Mark Fischetti; and the polemical 'Neuro-Internetics' by John & Byron Barksdale. I am indebted to these authors and their publishers for making science accessible: this mine of information helped me to design the technical aspects of the Brain of Marx Project. In addition, I consulted the *Times Higher Educational Supplement* for news of the latest developments in DNA research, including the use of DNA techniques in archaeology and evolutionary biology. Likewise, a debt of gratitude here; in particular to Chris Bunting, Jerome Burne, Karen Gold, Claire Sanders, Linda Vergnani, Rebecca Warden, Geoff Watts and Jonathan Weiner. For information on text analysis software, I am grateful to Professor Valery Belyanin at Moscow State Linguistic University. The news of Lenin's brain was released by the Itar-Tass news agency and reported in various forms in the Western media.
Finally, a reminder that this book is a work of fiction. Names, characters, places and incidents are either imaginary or are used fictitiously, and any slights of persons, places, nationalities or institutions are unintentional.

ABOUT THE AUTHOR

Anthony Bloor grew up in Wales and the West Midlands. He has worked as a computer programmer, as a researcher in higher education, as an editor in book publishing, and in various capacities in film and television. He is the author of a study of fiction writing, first published in New York, 2003. His novel *The Big Wheel* was published by Simon Siabod in 2010 and was followed by *Larry's Lessons*, a second novel, in 2012.

Also available by the same author

LARRY'S LESSONS

A satirical take on the misery memoir, *Larry's Lessons* is a fictional autobiography which tells the story of Larry Tonks, a former mathematician, who loses his virginity at the age of 50, and earns a fortune by ghost writing for the celebs.

Larry's mathematical career is ended prematurely when his subject is axed from the educational agenda. And after twenty years of searching for a new role, he discovers the reason for his failing: he's too ugly!

Help is just around the corner, however, thanks to a government scheme to assist the radically non-glamorous. And in a rambling mansion, somewhere in Wales, Larry embarks on a course in storytelling. The menu is voluptuous: there's food for thought, sexual capers, a love affair or two, and the start of a new career.

Featuring the total absence of algebra, *Larry's Lessons* is a literary exploration of the art of storytelling, and a romantic comedy with a difference. Or two.

For further information, visit www.simonsiabod.com

Also available by the same author

THE BIG WHEEL

It's 1999. Prophecies are rampant, and one of them is about to be fulfilled. But which? That's not the only problem Tom Jones must solve as he finds himself re-enacting a John Buchan adventure. He's in a race against time – and the candy bars are running out…

"A Hitchcockian shocker with a satirical edge for the virtual age; a twisted, knowing version of *The Thirty-Nine Steps*, relocated to Wales on the eve of millennium madness; and a conspiracy thriller which puts the world we think we live in into the blender. What emerges is a vision that's dementedly, entertainingly all too plausible" Michael Eaton, screenwriter

"Thoroughly enjoyable" Peter Guttridge, novelist
"High-quality fiction" Hazel Cushion, Accent Press
"Fluent and intelligent writing" Jon Thurley, literary agent
"Most entertaining" Alan Mahar, Tindal Street Press

For further information, visit www.simonsiabod.com

For the latest news on our publications, visit
www.simonsiabod.com